THE
Boyfriend
Project

FARRAH ROCHON

HEADLINE
ETERNAL

Published by arrangement with Forever
An imprint of Grand Central Publishing

First published in Great Britain in 2020
by HEADLINE ETERNAL
An imprint of HEADLINE PUBLISHING GROUP

2

Cataloguing in Publication Data is available from the British Library

ISBN 978 1 4722 7380 2

Offset in 11.69/15.43 pt Garamond 3 LT Std by Jouve (UK), Milton Keynes

Printed and bound in Great Britain by Clays Ltd, Elcograf S.p.A.

FSC
www.fsc.org

MIX
Paper from
responsible sources
FSC® C104740

Headline's policy is to use papers that are natural, renewable and recyclable
products and made from wood grown in well-managed forests and other
controlled sources. The logging and manufacturing processes are expected
to conform to the environmental regulations of the country of origin.

HEADLINE PUBLISHING GROUP
An Hachette UK Company
Carmelite House
50 Victoria Embankment
London EC4Y 0DZ

www.headlineeternal.com
www.headline.co.uk
www.hachette.co.uk

USA Toda... .... hails from a
small town .... rnered much
acclaim for her ...., ..., Bayou Dreams
and Moments in Maplesville series. When she is not writing in her
favorite coffee shop, Farrah spends most of her time reading, cooking,
traveling the world, visiting Walt Disney World, and catching her
favorite Broadway shows. An admitted sports fanatic, Farrah
feeds her addiction to football by watching New Orleans
Saints games on Sunday afternoons.

For more information, visit her website: farrahrochon.com,
and find her on Facebook: /farrahrochonauthor,
Twitter and Instagram: @FarrahRochon.

Raves for *The Boyfriend Project*:

'Farrah Rochon writes intensely real characters with flaws and
gifts in equal measure. *The Boyfriend Project* is a multilayered story
about friendship, love, and following your dreams – all of it
told with heart and emotion' Nalini Singh

'Farrah Rochon deftly explores what it means to go viral, the
unique joys of strong female friendships, and the particular
struggles of Black women in the workplace, all within a
great love story' Jasmine Guillory

'Farrah Rochon writes delectable love stories with characters
so warm that I want to hang out with them in real life. Samiah's
hopes and dreams and fears are relatable and real . . . I smiled
the whole time I was reading *The Boyfriend Project*'
Andie J. Christopher

'A masterpiece of modern-day Jane Austen with effortless,
razor-sharp social commentary, romance, and humor. Farrah
Rochon is one of the absolute best romance writers
today. Period' Kristan Higgins

'Swoon-worthy romance, the power of true friendship, and a grand
gesture that makes your heart sigh with pure satisfaction.
Absolutely a must-read summer romance!' Priscilla Oliveras

'Rochon is a romance master who adeptly writes interesting and
dynamic characters . . . A richly layered conflict adds depth and
complexity to this charming workplace romance' *Kirkus*

For my Destin Divas. Thank you for the sisterhood, the support, and the laughs.

CHAPTER ONE

"Alexa, play Drake."

Releasing an intentionally loud, dramatic sigh, Samiah Brooks lolled her head toward the opened bathroom door and called out, "Don't just tell it to play a certain artist, Denise. Tell it what song you want it to play."

Muffled footfalls shuffled across the bedroom's alder hardwood floors. A moment later her sister appeared in the doorway.

"I don't know any Drake songs. That's why I asked the damn Alexa thingy." Denise lumbered into the bathroom, plopped onto the toilet's closed lid, and palmed her substantial belly. The opening bars of Drake's "Best I Ever Had" began streaming through the HD speakers discreetly positioned throughout the condo. Denise pointed upward. "Is that him? Is that Drake?"

"Yes." Samiah sighed again. She capped her Fenty Beauty 410 foundation and traded it for the liquid eyeliner. Tugging her lower lid downward, she muttered as she swiped the thin brush along the rim of her eye. "You know you can't fake this kind of thing, right? Your students will see right through it."

"Shows how much you know. I've been faking it for years. No one's caught on yet."

Samiah glanced over her shoulder and grinned. "Make sure you don't say that around your husband."

"Oh please." Denise batted the air as she adjusted her position on the toilet seat cover. "He knows I sometimes have to fake it with him too."

"Dammit!" Samiah nearly poked herself in the eye with the eyeliner brush. She swung around and glared at her sister. "You said that shit on purpose."

"What?" Denise asked with wide, guileless eyes. Her knowing smirk nullified her weak attempt at innocence.

"If I gouge myself in the eye with this thing, I'm telling Mama it was your fault."

"She'd never believe you." Her sister gestured to the array of palettes scattered across the leathered granite vanity. "Why didn't you get all dolled up before you went out with me? You wait until we get back to pull out the heavy artillery?"

"Jealous?"

"As if. I can barely remember to pack lip balm in my purse."

Samiah tsked as she used the smudger brush to blend the shadow into the crease of her eye. "Master the smoky eye and you can conquer the world."

"Is that your new motto?" Denise said with a snort.

She cocked one perfect brow as she peered at her sister in the mirror. "As someone who hasn't worn a fully made-up face since cassette tapes were still a thing, you can't grasp just how difficult it is to achieve this look." She turned, closed her eyes, and pointed at her eyelids. "Girl, do you see this blending? I honestly just want to stare at myself in the mirror all night."

Samiah dodged the incoming bath puff, pitched with precision by her National College Softball Championship–winning older sister.

"Hey, help me pick out something else to wear. I'm not feeling the silver dress anymore. It's too dressy for the club Craig and I are going to tonight." She pushed down on Denise's shoulders when her sister tried to rise. "You stay here. I'll bring the outfits to you."

Samiah made her way to the bedroom's huge walk-in closet and slid the knotted pine barn door—the deciding factor in buying this condo—to the side. She stepped in and thumbed through her dresses.

"What about that blue one you wore to your classmate's wedding a few months ago?" Denise called. "What was her name? Tabatha?"

"Tamyra." Samiah grimaced, recalling that night. She'd spent much of the wedding reception getting hit on by Tamyra's sexagenarian uncle, whose fake silk shirt seemed to lose more buttons as the night dragged on. She'd spent the next morning scrubbing a stain from the bustline after he'd sloshed her with his Jack and Coke while pressing her to dance to an Isley Brothers tune from the midseventies. Samiah doubted she'd ever wear that dress again.

"Not that one," she said. In fact, if Denise wanted it, she could have it.

She settled on dark blue skinny jeans and a red cowl-neck sweater, which seemed more appropriate for this evening's amended plans and the unseasonable nip in the air on this early-August night. Austin usually felt like a sauna until at least late September.

Originally, she and Craig were supposed to start their

evening with dinner, but he'd texted just as she was leaving work to tell her that he'd gotten caught up at the office and wouldn't be able to make it downtown until late. He'd offered to call and cancel, which was the least he could do since she had been the one who'd spent a half hour on the phone securing the dinner reservation.

Samiah would be lying if she said she wasn't annoyed. She'd been looking forward to returning to the Asian fusion spot where they'd had their first date. The restaurant continued to generate an insane amount of buzz around town and reservations weren't easy to come by.

But she wouldn't bitch about it. At least not too much. Joining Denise for beef patties from the Jamaican food truck down the street, along with Amy's Ice Cream, had soothed the sting of missing out on good sushi. And the night was still young. She and Craig would enjoy a little late-night noshing and gritty blues music at the new club that had recently opened on Sixth Street, the epicenter of Austin's nightlife.

She unhooked a faux suede cropped jacket from the hanger and held it up just under her chin.

Come to think of it, each of her four dates with Craig had been at a club or bar on Dirty Sixth, as some locals called it. Granted, she was the one who'd suggested they go to this new blues club, but only because it was the first thing that came to mind on such short notice, and Craig never seemed to have any suggestions. Next time she would propose something with a different flair, like exploring the caverns in Georgetown or hiking in Bastrop State Park.

"Let's see what you'd say to that," Samiah murmured as she returned the jacket to the hanger.

A couple of the guys she'd dated in the past had been surprised to learn that, despite her sharp business attire, perfectly styled hair, and always on-point makeup, she was an outdoors girl. Hell, it had surprised her too. Samiah had grown up in Houston's Third Ward. The closest she'd ever gotten to the outdoors was eating a sandwich on a bench in Moses LeRoy Park, with the traffic from I-45 whizzing overhead. But in the years since she'd moved to Austin, she'd acquired a taste for the unique adrenaline rush one received at the completion of a hike to the summit of Mount Bonnell or a bike ride through Zilker Park.

She tried to picture Craig trotting up the rocky terrain of the Texas Hill Country in his loafers. The image refused to even take shape in her mind.

Maybe they could compromise and go to one of those indoor rock-climbing places. At least there would be air-conditioning. Craig would insist on air-conditioning. And no bugs.

Are you sure about this guy?

Samiah quashed her pesky inner voice that had started making an appearance more frequently than usual. Craig wasn't perfect. No one was perfect. But at least he was employed, had manners, and could sorta tell a decent joke when the occasion arose.

Okay, fine. So his sense of humor left something to be desired. Was that a good reason to write someone off? If she wanted a laugh, Netflix provided a vast selection of comedy specials to choose from. Having a sense of humor had fallen several notches on her list when it came to attributes she required in a significant other.

A lot had fallen off that list. These days, a full set of teeth and a playlist that consisted of something other than the Isley Brothers would earn you at least a wink.

Craig might not be her ideal Mr. Right, but he was right enough.

The sound of her sister's distinct laugh drew Samiah's attention. "What are you cackling about in there?"

"Just something on Twitter. This poor woman is on the absolute date from hell."

"And she's tweeting about it?"

"Yes. In real time. It's like watching a train wreck." She heard Denise's footsteps padding toward her. Her sister's extremely pregnant belly appeared before she did. "Apparently, the guy she's with thinks he's the answer to every woman's dream. The lines he's trying on her are sooo tired."

Been there. Done that. Got the ticket stub, T-shirt, and bad memories to show for it.

"Listen to this," Denise said. "So, this fool told her he works in clean energy and is all about the environment, yet he's driving a Mercedes SUV. Not a hybrid, but a gas-guzzling SUV."

Samiah frowned. A tiny knot formed in her stomach, but then she reminded herself loads of people drove Mercedes SUVs.

"Oh, and get this. His Benz? It's a rental."

"How does she know it's a rental?"

"Hold on, let me scroll up." Her sister paused for a moment. "Okay, here it is. She said she knew it wasn't his the moment she got in because she'd rented that exact Mercedes from a luxury car dealership in Round Rock to impress people during South by Southwest last year. She got a discount because it has a cigarette burn on the passenger seat. The exact cigarette burn his has."

Samiah's hand halted on the faux camel leather jacket she was about to pull from the hanger. "Did she mention a color?"

"No. I've been refreshing my feed like a crazy person, but she hasn't updated her timeline in the last minute." Denise looked up from the phone, a wide grin on her face. "This is why I love Twitter."

"To read about bad dates between two people you don't even know?"

"Yes." Her sister's unapologetic response would have elicited a laugh from Samiah if she wasn't so busy trying to quell the manic butterflies whirling in her belly.

Stop being ridiculous. Plenty of people who work in clean energy probably drive a Mercedes SUV with a cigarette burn on the passenger seat.

"Did I mention the tweet about his apartment?" her sister asked. "He told her he lives in those fancy apartments up near the Domain, but this girl happens to know the property manager there. She had her friend run his name and, of course, the fool was lying about that too." Denise laughed again. "He messed with the wrong one."

The unease that had settled in the pit of Samiah's belly began to blossom.

"Oh, she tweeted again!" Another laugh. "Now he's trying to woo her with his favorite dish."

"The volcano sushi roll," Samiah said, barely able to get the words past her clenched jaw.

Her sister's head popped up. "How'd you know? You're not even on Twitter."

Samiah jerked the jacket loose and flung the hanger on the floor.

"Oh, shit," Denise said. "Don't tell me..."

But Samiah didn't have to tell her anything. She could tell by her sister's horrified expression that she'd figured it out.

She pulled on her jacket and stuffed her feet into her favorite quarter-strapped heeled boots. She'd be damned if she walked in there looking like an enraged, spurned woman. Or worse, some wounded animal. She would burst through those doors showcasing her fabulousness. Let that bastard see what he would be missing out on for the rest of his sorry-ass life.

"Where are you going?" A thread of panic lined the edges of Denise's voice.

"They're at the new restaurant a couple of blocks away," Samiah answered. "The same place we were supposed to go tonight." She stopped short. "He used the reservation I made. Son of a bitch. I was on the phone for a half hour trying to get that reservation."

"You mean he had the nerve to bring another woman to a restaurant in *your* neighborhood? He must have balls of steel."

"I wouldn't know." And thank God for that.

She'd actually considered Craig a gentleman because he hadn't tried to get her into bed on the first date. Of course, he'd tried on each subsequent date, but Samiah had made a promise to herself long ago not to give up her goodies until she was good and ready. The fact that it had never felt right should have been her clue that something was wrong. Apparently, her vajayjay had sensed he was a rat long before she had.

"And just what do you plan to do when you get there?" Denise asked as she followed her back into the bathroom. "Beat him up in the middle of the restaurant?"

"I won't lay a hand on him. I just want to see his face when I walk in."

Her sister looked down at the phone and gasped. "You've got to be kidding me!"

"What?" Samiah ran to her side.

"Another girl just tagged herself on the Twitter thread. She's been dating this Craig guy too."

Samiah didn't just see red; she saw a burst of fiery crimson.

"This is like that TV show. You know, the one where the people meet online but you don't know if they're telling the truth about who they really are? What do they call it?"

"Catfishing," Samiah hissed.

She'd been catfished. Or, at the very least, scammed into believing Craig was something he definitely was not.

A combination of mortification and rage congealed in her blood. Every single time she heard one of those stories, she'd felt sympathy for the poor, unsuspecting fool who got caught up in it. But that sympathy always came with a heavy dose of judgment. She couldn't understand how anyone could be so gullible. Never could she imagine that she would become the victim of some slick-tongued, rental car–driving asshole's scam.

"I'm not sure going to that restaurant is a good idea," her sister said. "Maybe you should take some time to cool off."

"Nope." Samiah unwound the silk headscarf from around her head and used a wide-toothed comb to release her flat-ironed hair from the wrapped style. She parted it on one side and let the soft locks fall to just under her chin in a sensible yet sexy bob. Because, yes, she was determined to look like a queen when she cursed Craig's lying, three-timing ass out.

She left the bathroom and, with one last look in the

full-length cheval mirror she'd inherited from her grand-mother, grabbed her clutch from the dresser and stalked out of her bedroom.

"What time is Bradley coming to pick you up?" she asked her sister.

"In another half hour."

"This shouldn't take long, but if I'm not back by then, use your key to lock up."

"Don't get yourself arrested," Denise called from the condo's front door. "And text me as soon as you get back."

Samiah stuck a hand in the air and waved in answer as she marched down the hallway and into the elevator. She concentrated on taking deep, calming, cleansing breaths as she traveled from the twenty-first floor to the lobby without interruption.

She exited her building and started down Nueces Street, arriving at the restaurant in minutes. She spotted Craig's clean-shaven head at a table in clear view of the entrance. Couldn't the bastard at least *try* to be discreet? This place was steps from her home. She could have strolled by at any time.

Samiah told the hostess she was meeting friends. The young girl didn't even question her as she invited her in. She made a beeline for Craig's table, sidling up to him with a bright smile.

She infused as much cheer into her voice as she could muster and said, "Well, I guess your work meeting got canceled, huh? Lucky you!"

He jumped at the sound of her voice and looked up at her over his shoulder, his eyes wide with an *oh shit, I'm caught* look.

She hit him with a supersweet grin.

That's right, bitch. You're caught.

Samiah looked to the woman sitting across from him. The red globe over the light fixture that hung above the table cast a rosy glow across her light brown skin. Her reddish-brown hair was done up in thick box braids and she had cheekbones Samiah would sell her soul for.

"Hi." She extended her hand with a genuine smile. "I'm Samiah."

"Taylor," the woman answered with matching politeness. "I thought for a minute that you were London."

Samiah nodded toward the phone sitting next to a half-eaten plate of sushi. "Is London the other woman on Twitter?"

Taylor nodded. Amusement glittered in her light brown eyes.

"Twitter?" Craig asked, his sweat-slicked forehead scrunching up in confusion. "What's going on here?"

"Your lies are catching up to you," Samiah answered. She nodded at Taylor, who'd propped her elbow on the table and now perched her chin on her closed fist. "Let me take a stab at this. He invited you to go out to a club after dinner, but just gave you a lame-ass excuse for why he needs to cut the night short."

"His mom is sick," Taylor said, biting her lip to contain the smile turning up the corners of her mouth.

"Ah, yes, I've heard about his sick mama. Actually, *I'm* his sick mama. He's supposed to meet me in another half hour." She tilted her head to the side. "I wonder who played the sick mother when he fed me that line on our first date."

"That would be me."

The three of them turned as a statuesque woman with rich

brown skin, a head full of enviable coily, natural hair, and shoes to die for approached the table.

"At least I think it was me. Hello all, I'm London." She plunked her hands on her hips, her wry smile directed at Craig. "The Internet is amazing, isn't it? One of my fellow *Walking Dead* tweeps retweeted this hilarious first date from hell into my timeline. Imagine my surprise when it turns out to be the exact first date I had, down to the volcano sushi roll."

"You have to admit that sushi roll is amazing," Samiah said.

"Incredible," London agreed.

Taylor pushed her plate toward them. "It's the best. Dig in, ladies."

They'd started to garner attention from the other tables. A number of people were openly staring, and the hum of whispers filtered in from various corners of the restaurant.

"I haven't had dinner yet," London said. "Should we order another?"

"Okay, now, wait a minute." Craig put both hands up. "Let me—"

"Shut up." Samiah cut him off. "You don't get to speak here."

"Come on, Sammy."

"Shut. Up." If he knew how close she was to elbowing him in the throat, he would walk out of here without saying a word. The grip she had on her rage was tenuous at best. "And don't call me that stupid nickname. My name is Samiah."

"That's a beautiful name," London said around a mouthful of sushi.

"Yes, it is. So is that jacket," Taylor added. "I love the way it cinches a bit at the waist instead of being all boxy."

"That's the reason I bought it," Samiah answered, looking down at her jacket. "Hey, are you ladies up to listening to some blues music? My 'date,'" she said with an eye roll, "was supposed to take me to that new club on Sixth. I'd hate for this makeup to go to waste."

"Oh, I don't blame you," London said. "That smoky eye deserves to be seen. I end up looking like a raccoon whenever I try for that look."

"I can give you some tips," Samiah offered. "It's all in the primer you use."

"All right, enough of this." Craig pushed his chair away from the table and stood. "I can explain—"

Samiah whirled on him. "Read the room, Craig. Read the fucking room," she snarled, unable to pull off the blasé pretense a second longer. She was hurt and upset and ready to lay into this asshole. "You're caught, you lying piece of dog shit. Your stupid little game is over."

The other patrons weren't even bothering to hide their interest now. Even the waitstaff had stopped what they were doing. All eyes were on them, but Samiah was too incensed to care about the scene they were causing.

"I don't know how many other women fell for it, but it's over." She jabbed her finger against his chest. "Lose my number. If you try to contact me again, I'm calling the police."

"Same goes for me," London said as she pulled Craig's chair to the side of the table to get closer to Taylor's sushi roll. Taylor passed her a new pair of chopsticks from the container in the center of the table and slid the soy sauce closer.

"The number I gave you was a fake, so I don't have to worry about hearing from you again," Taylor said. She tossed her napkin on the table and joined Samiah. Folding her arms across her chest, she said, "Make sure you fill up your Benz before you return it to the car rental place. They charge an arm and a leg if you bring it back on empty."

His eyes widened. "How'd you know?"

Samiah had to refrain from punching him in the gut. "You're pathetic," she spat.

"Can I get a to-go box?" London called. "Also, add another volcano roll to the order. He'll pay for it. His cheap ass still owes me from our last date."

"Oh, let me guess," Samiah said. "He forgot his wallet at work?"

"And the Apple Pay on his phone was acting up," London said with a nod. "He isn't very creative, is he?"

Two women at a nearby table laughed out loud. One of them held up a phone to snap a picture.

Great.

Samiah turned back to Craig. "You are a horrible person, and your jokes are corny. I wish nothing but the worst for you."

A waiter arrived with a black paper bag and handed it to London. She stood and motioned for Samiah and Taylor to walk ahead of her.

"Don't I get a chance to explain?" Craig called.

"No!" the three women said in unison as they marched out of the restaurant without a backward glance.

CHAPTER TWO

Samiah squinted against the sunlight slicing across her face through her living room's floor-to-ceiling windows. Grimacing, she expended a supreme amount of effort to open her left eye. She quickly shut it. A dull thud repeatedly beat against the back of her skull, reverberating around her brain like a Ping-Pong ball in slow motion.

"Is there coffee?" a strange voice croaked. "Please tell me there's coffee."

Samiah bolted upright and twisted around on the sofa. London Kelley stood next to the eight-foot soapstone island that separated her kitchen from the living room. Make that *Doctor* London Kelley, as Samiah had discovered last night.

"I'll take kombucha if you have any," came a muffled voice from somewhere underneath the mound of pillows on the living room floor. Taylor Powell moaned before leveling herself up on her elbows. "You see this headache right here? This is why I don't drink alcohol." She straightened. "I gotta pee," she said before scrambling up from the floor and racing toward the bathroom.

Exhausted and hungover, Samiah still had the presence of mind to acknowledge that she should be concerned about waking up to find two strangers in her home. Strangers who were now familiar enough with her home to utilize the kitchen and bathroom without her help or permission.

Yet in the few short hours since she'd met them, Taylor and London no longer felt like strangers. Being conned by the same lowlife accelerated the sisterhood-development process.

Samiah placed her bare feet on the cool hardwood floors and rested her elbows on her thighs, covering her face with her hands. She still wore her jeans from last night, but at some point had changed into her favorite blue-and-gray Rice University T-shirt.

"Hey, chica? Coffee?" London called again.

"There are coffee pods in the cabinet above the Keurig." She turned to Taylor, who had just resumed her spot on the floor. "Sorry, no kombucha. I've seen it, but I'm too chicken to try it."

"Chicken? After the way you went after Craig last night? Woman, there is nothing chicken about you. You are badass."

Samiah grimaced. She didn't want to hear the name Craig ever again. She'd cloaked herself in fury and indignation last night, but in the light of day his treacherous deception cut through her like a switchblade. How could she have been foolish enough to trust him? Why hadn't she seen through his lies?

"Did he try calling either of you last night?" London asked.

Samiah reached for her phone and checked the screen. Other than a couple of missed calls from her sister and an exorbitant number of Facebook notifications, her phone was clear. She would call Denise later. She didn't know when she would look at Facebook.

"I guess he heeded my warning," Samiah said. "He didn't try to contact me at all."

"I wasn't lying when I said I didn't give him my number," Taylor remarked, wrapping her arms around her bended knees. "It was a burner phone. A friend suggested I use one after this guy she met on a dating site started stalking her."

"Shit, that's scary," London said. She plopped onto the sofa next to Samiah, her fingers wrapped around a steaming cup of coffee. Her crinkly curls were mashed on one side. "This place is gorgeous, by the way. I didn't get a chance to tell you that last night."

"We were all too busy bitching about that asshole," Samiah replied. "But thanks."

A foggy veil obscured her recollection of the past twelve hours, but she remembered inviting London and Taylor back to her place after deciding she wasn't up to going to the blues club. She'd probably never step foot in there now that it was linked to Craig and his lying ways.

Samiah glanced to the right and noticed the empty vodka bottle, stray lime wedges, and copper tumblers on the glass end table, remnants of the Moscow Mules she'd made last night.

"Is anyone up for breakfast?" she asked. "I can order something."

London lifted her cup. "This is my normal breakfast."

"Aren't you a doctor?" Taylor tsked. "You should know better. You need protein to get your day off on the right foot."

London replied with a grunt before sipping her coffee.

"What is it you do for a living again?" Samiah asked Taylor. "Sorry if you mentioned it last night. Everything is a bit fuzzy."

"Personal trainer and nutrition expert," Taylor answered. She was way too bubbly now that she was fully awake. Samiah would have found it endearing if her head wasn't pounding so much. "Which means that I should know better than to pollute my body with the half liter of vodka I consumed last night."

"It was warranted." London settled back on the sofa, crossing one long, slim leg over the other. "If you can't get drunk after finding out your boyfriend has been cheating on you with who knows how many other women, when can you get drunk?" She turned to Samiah. "By the way, I figured out this morning that you were the first to date him, at least among the three of us. You went out with him on the Friday of the Fourth of July holiday weekend, and my first date with him was that Sunday night."

"He told me he had to go to Dallas that weekend. Things were just *sooo* busy at his job that he couldn't take the holiday off." Samiah snorted out a humorless laugh. "I swear I thought I was smarter than this."

"Hey, I'm no dummy, and he fooled the hell out of me too." London shrugged. "He ran a good game. I'm just happy I never slept with him."

"I didn't either!" Samiah said. "It's as if our instincts knew better."

They high-fived each other.

Taylor pouted. "I'm kinda bummed I found out he was a dog before I got the chance to sleep with him."

"What?" Samiah and London's simultaneous screeches echoed off the condo's high ceilings.

"What?" she asked with an incredulous shrug. "It's been a minute, okay? I swear I saw cobwebs the last time I looked down there."

Samiah burst out laughing then regretted it. The hammering that had all but subsided returned to her skull with a vengeance. She drew her feet up on the sofa and tucked them underneath her.

"You can do better than Craig Walters's lying ass," she told Taylor.

"I thought his name was Craig Johnson?" London said.

"He told me his name was Craig Milton," Taylor said. "And if I could do better, I would have been out with better last night. I don't know about you, but this dating shit has been brutal for me since I moved to Austin."

Samiah was still reeling from the revelation that Craig's cheating behind had given them all different last names. She'd looked him up on social media. Everything had seemed legit. She wondered if he'd set up profiles for all his different names. How much time and energy had that leech put into this little scheme of his?

"I hear you on the dating front," Samiah said. "Craig was the first guy in six months who'd made it past a second date."

"Look, I'm from this area and it's been brutal for me too," London added. "I guess that's how he was able to dupe the three of us. There's slim pickings out there." She drained her coffee mug and set it on the sofa table. "And now I have to find someone else to take to my damn class reunion. Shit."

The three of them released commiserating groans.

"My ten-year reunion was a nightmare," Samiah said.

"I used my move to Austin as an excuse to skip mine," Taylor said.

"Well, this makes fifteen years for me, and there is no skipping it. That's what I get for being class president."

"When is the reunion?" Samiah asked.

"Thankfully, it's still a few months away." London shoved her hands in her hair and fluffed out her mangled curls. "I hate this shit. The only reason I started dating Craig is because I didn't want to show up alone. I did that for both the five- and ten-year reunions." She choked out an incredulous laugh. "You'd think this whole pediatric surgeon thing I have going on would make up for being single, but not with that crew."

Samiah knew that song all too well. Whenever she went back home to Houston, the talk quickly shifted from her career to her relationship status. It was nauseating. And infuriating.

"You know you can rent a date, right?" Taylor asked as she gathered her braids in one hand and wrapped a purple scrunchie around them. "And not just from Craigslist." She gasped, her eyes widening. "I'll never be able to go on that website again after last night."

"Taylor's right," Samiah said. "Why don't you just go with one of those escort services?"

"I kind of wanted it to be real, you know? A fake relationship with a Rent-A-Date guy sounds like something from a supersweet Hallmark movie."

"That's only if you two end up married with two-point-five kids and a basset hound named Molly."

Samiah grinned at Taylor's quip. Her sense of humor beat the hell out of Craig's.

"If I took an escort to my class reunion, I'd spend the entire night worrying about whether or not we'd get found out. I'd rather go alone than deal with that kind of anxiety." Her resigned sigh struck a familiar chord. "What's a little judgment from people you only see once every five years, right?"

"I get what you're saying, but to be honest, why do you even care?" Samiah asked. She looked from one woman to the other as her question began to resonate in her head. "Why do any of us care? So what if I'm not dating the perfect guy? Who says everything on my checklist needs to get checked off?"

"You have a checklist?" One of London's perfectly shaped eyebrows arched. "Do tell."

"Everyone has a checklist. And mine is almost complete." She ticked items off on her fingers. "I've got the fancy downtown condo I always wanted. I have a fabulous job in my field. I still expect at least a few promotions in the near future, but to say I've only been with my company for three years, I've done pretty well for myself."

"Is that the extent of the list?"

"No. I also drive the car of my dreams."

Taylor perked up. "Oooh, what kind?"

"Mustang GTE."

"Full package?"

"Full package."

"Oh, you are definitely a boss bitch. Why did you think you needed someone like Craig in the first place?"

"Because even with this nice condo and her incredible job and her boss-bitch car—whatever that is—people will still question why she doesn't have a man," London said.

"Bingo." Samiah sighed, her shoulders wilting in defeat. No matter how successful she became, there were some who would still think her life was lacking because she didn't have a significant other.

But why should she care what those people thought? What anyone thought? Why in the hell was she putting herself through this kind of trauma for the sake of attaining some impractical, ideal life that would never be enough for those people?

Samiah sat up straight, planting her feet back on the floor.

"You know what? Fuck that," she said. "Fuck. That."

"Fuck what?" London asked.

"This. Craig. All of it. And fuck anyone who says what I've accomplished isn't enough. Do you know how much time and effort I've put into finding someone? The hours I've wasted filling out dating profiles alone makes me wish I'd gone ahead and punched Craig in the stomach."

"You're right," Taylor whispered, her voice tinged with awe. "You are absolutely right. Want to know how I ended up on that date with Craig? Because one of my friends signed me up on a dating site because *she's* tired of imagining that I'm lonely." She pointed to her chest. "I'm not lonely. I'm too busy to feel lonely. Hell, when I wasn't livetweeting our date last night, I was invoicing clients. My time would have been better spent at home working on my marketing plan."

Taylor directed her attention at Samiah. "Maybe it's time you rethink that checklist. If a con man like Craig is all there is out there, you're better off using that time to do something that will actually make you happy."

Her words collided with the beliefs Samiah had held since her freshman year of college. She had not gone into any of this lightly. She'd taken stock of her life, examined every crevice, and devised a list of goals that she firmly believed were crucial to living the kind of life she wanted to live.

Happiness had not been part of the equation when she'd made her plans. The concept was too vague for her to fully grasp it. She felt safer, more in control, when dealing in absolutes. True happiness—whatever that meant—would follow once she finally achieved these concrete items she'd set out to attain.

But she *could* define happiness for herself if she tried hard enough. She thought about the boxes of sketch pads and reams of notes in her closet and knew one thing that would make her happy.

No. You been over this already. You don't have time for that.

Samiah cradled her head in her palms. This was too much for her hungover brain to think about right now. "Why are you making so much sense?"

"Right?" Taylor asked, as if she'd surprised herself. "But it *does* make sense, doesn't it? Imagine if we'd all devoted the time we wasted with Craig to doing something worthwhile. Isn't there something you've always wanted to do that you haven't done yet? Stick that on your checklist instead of looking for some man who doesn't deserve you."

"Of course you wouldn't have discovered the volcano sushi roll if not for Craig," London said. "But I get your point."

"Her point," Samiah stressed, "is that we're three beautiful, successful women who swallowed the bullshit society tries to feed us. Every single one of us is much too good for Craig Walters. Or whatever his name is. The point is—"

Their heads turned at the sound of two sharp knocks on her front door, followed by the distinct click of the lock disengaging. A second later, the door opened and her sister and brother-in-law, Bradley, walked in with wide eyes and big smiles.

"Oh, wow," Denise said as she took in the sight before her. "I didn't think I'd find all three of you here."

"It's a good thing we went with the half-dozen bagels

instead of just three," Bradley said, following his wife to the sofa.

"Carbs," Taylor said with a dreamy sigh, making grabby hands toward the bag Bradley carried.

He held up a finger. "Just a sec." He pivoted toward the kitchen.

"So, how are you, ladies?" Denise asked as she rested on the arm of the sofa next to London. "It would seem you all had quite a night."

"Yes, we did," Taylor said with a cheeriness Samiah couldn't comprehend after the night they'd had. Her disposition was as bright as the sun streaming through the tall windows.

Samiah made the introductions. "Ladies, this is my sister, Denise, and her husband, Bradley. Guys, this is—"

"Oh, we know who you both are," Denise said, her cagey smile setting off an alarm in Samiah's head.

"I'm pretty sure the entire world knows who they are by now," Bradley said. He set a platter of bagels with flavored cream cheeses on the glass sofa table, then rested his hands on Denise's shoulders and started massaging her neck with his thumbs. "Well, maybe not the people in Australia."

"Yet," Denise added.

Dread slithered down Samiah's spine. "What are you two talking about?"

"I figured you hadn't seen it yet, based on how calm you all are." Denise pulled out her phone, swiped across the screen, and held it up. "It was at five hundred thousand views last I checked."

"What!" Samiah, London, and Taylor all yelped at the same time.

Samiah grabbed the phone. London and Taylor gathered

around her. Someone at the restaurant had captured their argument with Craig and posted it online. Her stomach dropped.

"Bossip picked it up. So has BuzzFeed. No TMZ, though," Denise said around a mouthful of the cinnamon raisin bagel she'd just bitten into.

"Only a matter of time," Bradley chipped in.

Samiah increased the volume on the phone, although now that the fogginess of the alcohol had worn off, she recalled what was said last night with stunning clarity.

Lying piece of dog shit?

Yikes. She hadn't remembered that.

"There's another video that was shot from the opposite angle. That's the one I saw first," Denise said. "I was so afraid you'd punched that Craig guy, but then I saw you'd only poked him."

"You should have punched him," Bradley said. "I would have punched him if I was there." His ginger-colored brows curved inward with his frown.

Samiah looked up at him and wasn't sure if she wanted to laugh or cry. Craig wasn't linebacker-big, but he probably had a good seventy pounds on her perpetually thin brother-in-law. What Bradley lacked in heft, he made up for in heart. She handed the phone back to Denise, then stood and walked over to him, wrapping him up in a hug.

"Thank you, honey." Samiah sniffed. "But I don't think any of us have to worry about Craig anymore."

"I'm just hoping his other women have seen the video and know not to trust him either," Taylor said.

"You think there were others?" Bradley asked.

"Yes," the four women in the room answered.

Her sister and brother-in-law left them with breakfast and
a promise to check up on Samiah later in the week. Once
they finished off the bagels, she, Taylor, and London sat in her
living room, encountering the first awkward silence between
them since their eventful meeting. The horror of knowing
the most painfully embarrassing moment of their lives was
now fodder for memes around the world muzzled all other
thoughts.

London was the first to break the silence. After crossing
her legs, she rested her clasped hands on her knee and said,
"I'm happy I changed out of my scrubs before going to the
restaurant last night. If I'm going to get caught on camera, I
want to get caught in something that shows the world I have
a nice ass."

"You have a great ass," Taylor said.

"So do you," Samiah told her.

There was another beat of silence before the three of them
burst out laughing. Now that the dam had broken, Samiah
couldn't hold it in. She rolled over on the sofa, cackling until
she caught a stitch in her side.

"Oh, my God." She took another moment to catch her
breath. "I needed that."

"We all needed that," Taylor said, wiping tears of mirth
from her eyes. Silence fell over them again, then Taylor added,
"Well, I should probably get going. I've got a bunch of meal
plans to put together for my clients." She reached for her
ankle-high boots and slipped them on.

London slapped her hands on her knee and stood. "I should
go too. It's been forever since I drank like this. I need to
sleep off the rest of those Moscow Mules before my shift
tomorrow." She braced her hands against her lower back and

stretched. "Thank God I pushed those hernia surgeries to the middle of the week."

Samiah looked from one woman to the other as something akin to panic stole over her.

"So is this it?" she asked. "*This* is how this ends?"

London hunched her shoulders in a cautious shrug. "Are we supposed to hug or something?"

"Yeah. No." Samiah shook her head. "I mean...maybe?"

She didn't know what she meant, but she knew it didn't feel right to just walk away from one another after everything they'd been through over the past twelve hours.

"This just feels...I don't know...anticlimactic. We should share phone numbers. Or, at the very least, connect on social media."

"I guess you're right," Taylor said. She reached into her black clutch and drew out a couple of business cards. "I like you two. You get to have my real number," she said with a wink. "Give me a call sometime and let me know how you're both doing."

"I'll go you one better," London said, slipping the business card in her back pocket. "Why don't we meet for drinks next week? Just to check in on each other. I have a feeling things will get a little crazy following this viral video." She shot Taylor a good-natured grin. "I'll even bring the kombucha."

"I prefer the ones with ginger, thank you very much."

Relief flooded Samiah's veins. She would explore just why it was so important not to lose touch with these two later. For now, she was just happy they were going to connect again.

"It's a date," she said. "Shoot me a text with whatever time works best for the two of you and I'll come up with a place to meet."

"Aww, now I *do* want a hug," Taylor said. She stretched her arms wide and gathered London and Samiah in an embrace.

Samiah saw both women to the door with a promise to contact them later in the week. Then she went to her bedroom and fell face-first onto the bed. She grabbed her phone, pulled up the YouTube video, and groaned. Another twenty thousand views since she'd last watched it less than a half hour ago. This was such a freaking disaster.

She set the phone beside her on the mattress and twisted around, staring up at the stark white ceiling. She wondered if she should add another item to her list.

Item 58: Have half a million people witness the most humiliating moment of your life.

At least it would be an easy one to check off.

CHAPTER THREE

Samiah had always viewed her condo's proximity to the high-rise that housed Trendsetters IT Solutions as a bonus.

Today, she regretted the hell out of her short commute to work. The compulsion to retreat grew stronger with each loathsome step she took toward the building.

She'd considered calling in sick, but quickly recognized the futility in that. Her coworkers' scrutiny would be waiting for her whenever she returned to the office. It was better for her to face their judgmental reaction to Saturday night's disaster now and get it over with.

As she pushed through the building's revolving doors, trepidation slithered along her spine like a serpent, poised to bite her in the ass at any moment. The lobby teemed with employees of the various tech companies occupying the building. As usual, Samiah felt overdressed in her Anne Klein jacket and pencil skirt, surrounded by all these people who had never grasped the concept of Casual Fridays. Every day in the Austin tech world was Casual Friday. Maybe *she* should have opted for jeans today. Maybe then she wouldn't stand out so much.

Hyperaware of the gazes that followed her as she walked

through the brightly lit lobby, Samiah focused on the bank of elevators straight ahead. The swirling hum of the floor buffing machine drowned out any chatter before it hit her ears, but she caught several people pointing out of the corner of her eye. One woman even gave her a thumbs-up. Samiah acknowledged her support with a brief nod and smile before slipping onto a nearly full elevator.

Familiar faces surrounded her, but she didn't know a single name. This building had over thirty tenants. Everyone treated one another with reserved politeness and congenial respect, but other than the smokers who congregated in a corner of the concrete patio on the south end of the property, no one took the time to get to know anyone who was not a coworker.

Unless someone was hunting for a new job, of course. That's when Samiah usually found herself engaged in a casual conversation with a fellow building-mate. It would start out innocent enough, but would eventually meander into a discussion about possible job openings with the company that occupied the building's top two floors. Trendsetters' forest-green-and-white badges were the envy of the building.

She was blessed to have joined the firm just before its newest iteration of WiMax integration software hit big, making them the industry leader in providing Wi-Fi hotspot payment systems in developing countries. Numerous hotels, fast-food chains, and coffeehouses around the globe utilized Trendsetters' products to pay for the "free" Wi-Fi they offered their customers. And their client list continued to grow. Everyone wanted to work here. Samiah wouldn't give up her position for anything or anyone.

But that didn't mean she couldn't use a day off every once in a while. Like today. She'd have loved to play hooky today.

With stops on nearly every floor, it took a full eight minutes to finally arrive at the twenty-second. The elevator doors opened directly into Trendsetters' very trendy lobby. Its focal point, the Water Wall, took up the entire space behind the receptionist's semicircular desk. It featured a waterfall that changed colors throughout the day and cascaded down a steel wall speckled with embossed quotes from tech giants. Her favorite was the one from Steve Jobs: *I want to put a ding in the universe.* She'd made it her motto the moment she first read it.

On either side of the Water Wall stood twin glass-and-chrome curving staircases that led to the twenty-third floor, where Engineering and Security were housed. Even more eye-catching than the water feature was the row of brick-red benches on either side of the lobby. Each seat was held up by a strong, transparent acrylic rod that extended from the wall, making it appear as though the benches were suspended in midair.

"Good morning." Jamie Claiborne, Trendsetters' receptionist, greeted her with a bright smile.

Samiah braced herself for the onslaught of questions she knew awaited her. "Good morning," she replied.

She waited.

And waited.

When Jamie returned her attention to her computer monitor without mentioning what happened Saturday night, Samiah breathed her first easy breath of the morning. Maybe today wouldn't be awkward after all.

But the moment she stepped behind the Water Wall and into the main work area, an eruption of applause broke out. Heat suffused her face; her ears felt as if they were on fire.

She was all for being applauded at work, but not for something like this.

Get it together. Be cool. Be charming. Don't let them see you sweat.

Holding her hands up, she summoned a smile from some part of her being that hadn't shriveled up and died over the weekend and addressed the office as a whole.

"I know everyone is dying to hear whether or not I beat Craig up after the video ended. I did not. See." She flipped her hands back and forth, showing them her unblemished knuckles. "No scars."

Laughter and more cheers rumbled throughout the office. Samiah hoped that was enough to satisfy them.

She should have known better.

She couldn't take two steps without being stopped by a coworker wanting to know how it felt to be YouTube famous or asking if she really didn't know that Craig had been conning her. Because *of course* she would knowingly date a guy who was conning her. Managing to not roll her eyes every ten seconds would likely be her greatest feat of the day.

It took a full twenty minutes to make it to the sanctuary of her private office, although it wasn't all that private. Ninety percent of Trendsetters' office space was transparent—literally. The walls and doors of most offices and conference rooms were made of tempered glass.

Before she could stow her purse in her desk drawer, Aparna from Research and Development and Christy from Engineering came into her office wanting to know the scoop, followed by Rashad and Ali from the Marketing Department. Samiah didn't know which she wanted to do more, bang her head against her desk or scream at the top of her lungs. Neither was acceptable, so she pasted on a fake grin and entertained the teasing jibes.

She wouldn't have to feign an illness if she wanted an excuse to leave work early. Pretending this was all some hilarious joke and not her fucking life they were laughing about had sparked a headache the size of the old Houston Astrodome.

An announcement that there were donuts and hot chocolate in the communal kitchen granted her a reprieve from the constant stream of nosy coworkers dropping in. Grateful for the first moment of quiet she'd experienced all morning, she used the opportunity to read over her notes for the presentation she and the members of her Implementation team were scheduled to give this afternoon. As she edited one of the slides, a message popped up, informing the entire team that their two o'clock meeting had been moved to noon.

"Shit."

It was bad enough she'd lost half the morning to coworkers pestering her about that viral video. Now Grant Meecham was stealing another two hours of prep time from her.

She shouldn't have been surprised. Grant, Trendsetters' director of Global Sales, had called the meeting, and whenever Grant set up a meeting he did everything he could to schedule it over lunch so that he could eat on the company's dime. Cheap bastard.

"Hey there, Miss Celebrity," came an irritatingly sweet voice from somewhere over her shoulder.

Samiah's eyes fell shut at the nauseating sound. She dialed up another fake smile before turning her chair around.

"Good morning, Keighleigh. Can I help you?"

Her coworker moved from where she'd stood just outside the door, sauntering up to Samiah's desk. "I just wanted to know how you were doing. Sounds as if you had yourself an...um...interesting weekend."

Samiah fought the urge to roll her eyes.

There was one in every company. For Samiah, Keighleigh Miller was *the* one. The one who clawed at her nerves on a daily basis, the way Denise's pesky cat Boomer used to claw at Samiah's bedroom door whenever her sister wasn't home. The one who constantly kissed up to management. The one who, on more than one occasion, had tried to take credit for Samiah's work.

She was willing to play along with the *rah-rah, we're all in this together, there's no "I" in "team"* bullshit Trendsetters pushed onto their employees, but only to a certain point. If the side-eye she'd caught several members of their team throwing Keighleigh's way at last week's meeting was any indication, Samiah wasn't the only one who'd grown tired of her coworker's shenanigans.

"Yes, it was an eventful weekend," Samiah said, dropping her smile. She was tired and overwrought and unwilling to engage in any further pretense. She sat back in her chair and asked again, "Can I help you with something?"

"No." The purple tips of Keighleigh's white-blond hair swished along her leather jacket's upturned collar. "Like I said, just checking on you."

Keighleigh tried way too hard to be the rebel who thumbed her nose at society's rules, but Samiah knew better. She'd happened upon her Facebook page while killing time one lazy Friday evening and encountered several pictures her coworker had been tagged in from high school. Keighleigh had been your average, run-of-the-mill cheerleader type. This edgy persona was all an act. Samiah wouldn't be surprised if her nose ring was a fake.

Stop it.

She despised cattiness among women in the workplace. Things were rough enough for their gender, especially in the male-dominated tech world.

But Keighleigh Miller had started this shit. From the moment she'd joined the Implementation team, she'd shown her willingness to double-cross whomever she deemed a threat or impediment to her rise to the top. Another of their coworkers, Amy Dodd, had learned that the hard way after Keighleigh innocently let it slip that Amy had confided in her that she was struggling with a project she'd been assigned. Their supervisor, Justin Vail, had placed Keighleigh on the project and she'd taken over—after Amy had already completed most of it.

Samiah refused to fall victim to Keighleigh's backstabbing.

"Thanks for checking on me, but honestly, I'm fine," Samiah continued. "Now, I really need to get back to work."

"Oh!" Keighleigh's green eyes—probably contacts—lit up. "Are you working on the proposal for Swiss Burger?"

"I am," Samiah answered, her Spidey senses on red alert.

"I wondered what you were thinking when it came to that conundrum their CTO mentioned. I mean, I can understand them wanting to reduce connection speed after someone has been online for more than thirty minutes, but I don't know how they do that without coming off as, well, cheapskates."

"Well, that conundrum is what today's meeting is about."

Keighleigh leaned in closer, her lips turning up in a wily smile, as if she and Samiah were in a partnership and she had a secret to share. In a conspiratorial whisper, she asked, "So what are you planning to present to Grant?"

Was she serious? Samiah wanted to tell her that she was

born on a Tuesday, not *to*day. Instead, she said, "A few ideas I've come up with."

She matched Keighleigh's smile with one of her own as she picked up her coffee mug and pushed back from the desk. "You know what? I just realized I haven't had any coffee yet. No wonder I'm feeling all ragey." She started for the door, but turned when she sensed Keighleigh wasn't following her. Samiah arched a brow at her coworker.

"Oh, I guess that's my cue to get back to work," Keighleigh said.

Samiah nodded. As if she would leave her to snoop around in her office. "I know you want to wow Grant with all those awesome ideas you've come up with." Samiah sent her another saccharine smile. "Meet you in the conference room."

CHAPTER FOUR

W e call this a semi–open concept work environment. Studies show that team members work better when they're able to bounce ideas off one another without the obstruction of walls, but too much of an open environment impedes productivity. I think we've found a healthy balance here at Trendsetters," the HR director said, his bald head gleaming under the panel of LED lights high above.

Daniel Collins nodded and smiled. A response wasn't expected. Having experienced more than a dozen episodes such as this one over these past two years, he'd learned the subtle nuances of navigating the first day on the job. He knew based on the inflection in Owen Caldwell's voice when a polite, interested nod would work and when the man expected him to make an actual comment. So far, he'd gotten by with a few hums of approval.

As they continued the tour, Daniel compared the layout of the software company's vast office space to the mental map in his head. He'd meticulously studied the floor plan weeks ago, but things changed. Desks were moved, partitions were erected. Being cognizant of the space around him was imperative to the success of his new job.

"And here we are at your home away from home." Owen's cheerful voice was a bit grating, but the man was trying to make a good first impression. Interesting how that went. It should have been the other way around, but Daniel's résumé had spoken for itself. Trendsetters was lucky to have him and they knew it. He'd made sure of it.

They approached a polished, six-by-three-foot desk made of thick light oak. It was identical to the two dozen that were arrayed in neat rows in this section of the office, each with two large monitors that angled toward each other. There were a few people milling about, but for the most part, everyone seemed focused on their computers, earbuds and earphones shutting them out from the rest of the world. They could all be in cubicles for this.

"Jamie set you up with the basics, but if you need additional supplies, they can be found in the supply closet I pointed out earlier. Except for external hard drives," Owen added. "If you need an extra one, you'll need to see Laurie in Operations and sign for it." The HR director clapped his hands together. "Did I miss anything?"

Daniel shook his head. "I think you've covered it all. I'm ready to dive in."

"That's what I like to hear. And remember, we take ourselves seriously, but not *too* seriously. Work should be fun."

Owen clamped a hand on his shoulder, and Daniel fought the urge to knock it off. As the head of Human Resources, Mr. Caldwell here should know better than to put his hands on an employee without their express permission.

He let the incident pass. He wasn't here to start shit. At least not with some straight-out-of-central-casting HR director. He had a job to do, and it required him to lie low and not make waves.

Daniel rolled the ergonomic office chair back from his desk and sat, nearly groaning at the way it cradled him. Trendsetters didn't skimp when it came to office furniture, that's for damn sure. He could live in this chair.

He powered on the twenty-four-inch iMacs and jerked back as a barrage of welcome messages populated the screen.

Owen's cheerfulness should have forewarned him that Trendsetters was one of *those* work environments. He'd hoped for at least a day or two before he would be expected to actually interact with people. That was always the hardest part.

He'd been stoked when his new supervisor, Justin Vail, explained that the Research and Development Department was trying to get away from emails and migrate to a messaging system. Nothing chapped his ass more than a bunch of Reply All emails. And that one guy who always replied with *Ditto* to every email? That asshole could go jump in the river. He wouldn't be surprised if Owen Caldwell was Trendsetters' Ditto Guy. He fit the part.

But Daniel wasn't sure this messaging software was any better than email. Was he expected to reply to each individual message?

Relief rushed through him when he hovered his mouse over the first one and a thought bubble filled with a half-dozen emojis popped up. He quickly clicked the thumbs-up on each message, then took a few minutes to familiarize himself with the company's software, opening his orientation folder to the page with his login information and setting up new passwords.

Five minutes in, he got an uneasy feeling. It prickled the

back of his neck. He glanced to his right and discovered the source. The pretty brunette with the Catwoman glasses was staring at him.

Morgan Broomfield. Twenty-five. Graduated top of her class at Texas State. Considered a genius for her work with data structures and algorithms. Was arrested for staging a Black Lives Matter march on campus her senior year.

No one he had to worry about.

She smiled. He smiled back.

Daniel returned his attention to his computer. He counted to four before looking up to find her standing at his desk.

"Hi. I'm Morgan," she said, sticking her hand out. "Welcome to Trendsetters."

"Nice to meet you, Morgan." He shook her hand, his eyes following her movements as she settled a hip against his desk.

"You'll be introduced to the entire team at the Morning Crush—that's what they call the daily department meeting where everyone gives a brief update about what they're working on for the day—but I wanted to introduce myself ahead of time."

She had a pretty smile. And those light gray eyes were stunning. Daniel knew exactly what she was saying with those eyes, which is why he kept his expression intentionally neutral.

It happened every time he started a new job, usually within a matter of hours. He could count on at least one or two new coworkers—male or female—to engage in some kind of behavior that broadcasted their interest. A flirtatious smile. Overly aggressive eye contact. Some were brazen as hell, but others, like Morgan here, were refreshingly subtle.

Planting her backside and thigh on his desk was a bold move, but it could also be seen as just an open, friendly gesture from a coworker who wanted him to feel welcome. It was the eyes that gave her away. They were assessing, with just a hint of eagerness. Daniel could sense her trying to gauge his reaction, wondering if he would reciprocate.

He would not.

A workplace romance wasn't on his agenda. That didn't mean he would immediately rebuff her advances if any were forthcoming. He needed to discern whether his extremely friendly new coworker could be a possible asset before he threw any *I don't do office hookups* vibes her way.

He would have to revisit his notes before he decided what to do about Morgan. Just because she didn't automatically stand out to him didn't mean she wasn't useful. Maybe he'd missed something.

"Thanks for the warm welcome," Daniel told her. "It's been a while since I went through this whole first-day-on-the-job thing," he lied. "It means a lot."

"It wasn't that long ago since I was the new kid on the block," she said.

She'd been here a year already.

"You'd think I'd be used to it," he said. "Military kid."

He knew Morgan would jump on that. He remembered from her dossier that she'd spent much of her formative years traveling from one Army base to another.

"Same here." Her teeth sparkled like freshly polished

pearls, and that flirtatious glint in her eyes moved her closer to the aggressive category.

Rule number 50 in the handbook. Make them believe you share something in common. It encourages people to let their guards down.

"We Army brats have to stick together," Daniel said.

Shit. She hadn't revealed that her family was Army.

His heart began to hammer within his chest as he waited for her to call him on his mistake. His entire body wilted with relief when she continued smiling the kind of smile that told Daniel she was mentally staging the Instagram selfie that would announce their new relationship.

Damn. He'd caught a lucky break with that one. He would have to be more careful.

Her ringing cell phone saved him from having to endure any more of this conversation. She looked down at the screen and said, "I have to take this. Enjoy your first day on the job. And if you need anything, I'm right over there."

She pointed toward her desk, and Daniel caught sight of another of his new coworkers—*Jessica Lui, UCLA grad, owner of a budding homemade soap-making business*—giving him serious eye action.

Unlike Morgan, Jessica already had a spot on his potential asset list. Not only did they have the connection of their Asian heritage, but she'd also been a member of the development team that launched Trendsetters' WiMax software. It had been over a year since she'd been a part of the team, but it was still worth building an alliance with her.

Maybe an office romance wasn't off the table. Whatever it took to get the job done.

* * *

"Are you ignoring me?"

"I'm not ignoring you. I'm working." Samiah glanced up at the camera on her computer screen and shot her sister an exaggerated smile. "See. I'm still here."

"Stop smiling like that. You look like a deranged serial killer. Have you checked the view count today?"

"If you keep bringing up that stupid video, you're going to turn me into a deranged serial killer."

"Just look at the view count!" her sister shrieked. The giddiness in her tone was so uncalled for, but then Denise thought the response to the video of her fight with Craig was something Samiah should be excited about.

"Again, I'm working," she said. "I don't have time to look at YouTube every five minutes, and to be honest, I don't care how many views it has."

Lie.

"Over eight hundred thousand," Denise said, not catching Samiah's not-so-subtle hint to drop the subject. "I wouldn't be surprised if it hits a million by the end of the night," her sister prattled on. "Oh, and I heard that sushi place is getting inundated with reservations. The three of you should be given your own special table there. You've put that place on the map."

"It was on the map even before that video went viral."

"Well it's not just *on* the map now, it *is* the map. Maybe they'll name a sushi roll after you! Hey, don't roll your eyes," Denise said. "It could happen."

The doorbell chimed and her sister's face froze on the screen. A moment later, she reappeared, sporting a huge smile. "Sorry, my phone automatically switches to the doorbell app whenever it rings. Guess what's being delivered?"

"Lunch?"

"The baby's crib!" The unmitigated joy on her face triggered the first genuine pleasure Samiah had felt since Saturday. "I need to let the delivery guys in. I'll talk to you later."

"Wait!" Samiah stopped her before she could hang up their FaceTime call. "I had to listen to you go on and on about that stupid video for the past twenty minutes, and *now* you want to disconnect? No! I want to see the crib too."

"Not until the nursery reveal," Denise said. "Besides, it's still in a box. The delivery guys have to assemble it."

"Fine. But text me a selfie of you standing in front of your microwave with the time showing once they leave. I want to make sure they don't murder you."

Her sister rolled her eyes. "No more *Forensic Files* for you. And I know it's my fault," she added before Samiah could speak. "But maybe you should take a break from it." Denise was the one who'd forced her to sit through an all-day marathon of the true-crime show. Now she was hooked.

"Love you, honey," her sister said.

"Love you too," Samiah returned before ending the call.

She tried to focus on the presentation she was set to deliver at lunch, but thoughts of the escalating view count on that damn video continued to grab at her attention. A couple more minutes ticked by before she gave up the fight. Minimizing the window with her presentation, she opened the browser and went to YouTube.

She did a double take. Had the video made the home page?

"No way."

It was in her browser history. That's why it was the first thing she saw. Had to be.

Yet, even as she begged her brain to believe the lie, Samiah knew better. She peeked over at the Trending tab and saw the still image of her mouth wide open, preparing to light into Craig's lying ass. Denise was right, the video would definitely hit a million views before the end of the day.

She tipped her head back, releasing an aggrieved huff toward the ceiling. She wanted to take a nap and wake up to find all this humiliation behind her.

Samiah pushed away from her desk before she gave in to the urge to throw the monitor against the wall. For one thing, she'd probably hurt herself. Second, she doubted her boss would appreciate the destruction of company property.

She grabbed the WORLD'S GREATEST AUNTIE mug Denise and Bradley had given her—their way of announcing that, after four years of trying, they'd finally gotten pregnant—and went in search of a caffeine boost. She'd blown past her two-cup limit an hour ago, but it was either caffeine or alcohol, and Saturday night had put her way over her limit. Her boss probably wouldn't approve of alcohol consumption on the job either.

The moment she walked out of her office, the redhead from Quality Assurance, with bad acne and a penchant for wearing plaid flannel shirts like her grandfather used to wear, approached her. He held his phone up to her face.

"Snapping a pic for my roommate. He didn't believe me when I told him I work with you," he said, his thumbs flying across his phone screen.

Stunned, Samiah just stood there, watching him walk

away. Was this how it would be from now on? Being accosted by coworkers whose names she didn't even remember?

No. She wouldn't allow it. She just had to make it through today. The fervor over her encounter with Craig would die down and things would get back to normal. *Just make it through the damn day.*

She inhaled and exhaled, allowing the deep, calming breath to flow through her.

There. That's better.

She rounded the wall that separated Trendsetters' kitchen from the rest of the office and sent up a silent prayer of thanks when she found it relatively empty. It wouldn't be that way for long. This was more than just a place to heat up leftovers for lunch; it was the epicenter of the entire office.

A half-dozen octagonal alcoves were cut into the walls, housing individual booths that were designed more for impromptu breakout sessions than eating. That was normally reserved for the twelve-foot-long frosted-glass bar, with a dozen stools on either side. The kitchen area's left wall housed two stainless-steel microwaves, an industrial refrigerator, and a beverage cooler stocked with juices, sodas, and most recently, kombucha. Taylor would be proud.

To the right was the coffee bar, which rivaled anything you'd find in a coffee shop. At the press of a button one could enjoy a cappuccino, macchiato, latte, or any number of beverages. An array of coffee and tea accompaniments resided next to the space-age coffee machine, from flavored syrups to individually wrapped chocolate-covered spoons.

As usual, Samiah opted for straight black coffee. On occasion she'd add a couple pumps of toffee syrup when she was feeling fancy. Today wasn't a fancy kind of day. The lingering effects of those Moscow Mules from Saturday night demanded nothing less than the strongest coffee she could find.

"Hey, hey, hey! It's our own Real Housewife!"

Samiah cringed at the sound of Peter Stawell's voice. She turned and immediately wanted to slap the jovial grin from his face. Why did everyone think this was some kind of joke? This was her *life* that had been plastered across the Internet for everybody and their mamas to judge.

Peter nudged her arm. "I have to say, I'm disappointed a catfight didn't break out between you and that girl with the braids. She looks like she can throw down."

"Oh, do you want me to contact her for you?" Samiah asked with exaggerated enthusiasm. "I'm sure she'd be willing to demonstrate by kicking your ass."

Peter's smile disappeared. "I was just kidding around. Sheesh, Samiah, don't take things so seriously."

Yep. She should have taken the day off.

A week ago, she would have apologized to Peter for being a bitch. After what happened Saturday night—and the public's reaction to it, how people now felt as if her private life was a free-for-all—she felt justified in her bitchiness. She had no intention of apologizing ever again.

She grabbed her coffee mug from underneath the espresso spout and started for her office. She dipped her head down to blow the hot coffee and nearly crashed into a firm chest covered with an oatmeal-colored vest.

"Whoa." Two strong hands gripped her upper arms, steadying her.

Samiah looked up and had to remind herself to take a breath. Who'd ordered this midmorning snack in khakis and loafers?

"You okay?" he asked.

His eyes were the prettiest shade of brown. Almost like honey. Or was that considered hazel?

Stop staring.

"Yes, yes. I'm fine," Samiah said with a shake of her head. "Sorry about that."

"No apology necessary. I ran into you too." He held a hand out. "I'm Daniel, by the way. I started in R&D today."

Ah. She remembered hearing something about a new hire. "Welcome to the team." She shook his hand. "I'm Samiah."

His eyes widened for the barest second, but it was long enough for her to catch it.

She narrowed her gaze, then with irritation said, "You heard about the video."

He hunched his shoulders apologetically. "Pretty hard not to. It's kind of the talk of the office."

Dammit! Could she have one fucking moment when that stupid video wasn't at the center of everything?

"I haven't seen it," Daniel quickly added. "But I hear you put on quite a show."

Great. So this is what she would be forever known for. Not for single-handedly debugging Trendsetters' signature utilities software just months after she started, or launching their annual Thanksgiving donation drive last year, but for cursing Craig Walters out in a sushi bar. Her grad school advisor would be so proud.

Samiah put a hand up before he could ask an intrusive, asinine question. "Please don't say anything else. I don't want to talk about that video."

"That's fair," he said. "But I was only going to ask if you were okay. Are you?"

She blinked several times, unsure if she'd heard him correctly. "I'm sorry?"

"I asked if you were okay." His shoulder lifted again in a slight hunch. "I've never had anything like that happen to me, but I can imagine it sucks to be put on display for everyone to see."

Oh, God. It sucked *so* much. How did he know?

"It does," she said with a vigorous nod, her hand tightening on the mug. She was so overwhelmed by what appeared to be genuine concern in his eyes that she nearly wept.

He was the first person to ask about her well-being. Her other coworkers hadn't given a damn about how she was doing. They were all too caught up in the glamour and hype of knowing someone at the center of a viral video.

"Having the entire world witness the most humiliating moment of your life and judge you for it sucks like you wouldn't believe. And it makes me question my judgment about pretty much everything."

"Don't." He made a move, as if he were about to reach for her. But then he backed off, slipping his hands into the pockets of his pressed khakis. "Don't blame yourself for what happened. It sounds like that guy was a pro. It says nothing about you."

She nodded, the sudden emotion welling in her throat making it hard to speak.

"Thank you for that," she finally managed to get out. "It means a lot to hear it put that way." Samiah swallowed, then continued. "I'm just hoping it will eventually all blow over. Hopefully someone will record their cat playing Beethoven on the piano and that video with Craig will become a distant memory."

Daniel snapped his fingers in a gosh-darn kind of way. "I knew I should have gotten a cat. I'm more of a dog person, but those videos don't catch on as well as the cat ones."

He smiled and, for a moment, Samiah forgot that she'd said just yesterday that she was putting men on the back burner.

It's just a smile. Calm the hell down.

It was a nice smile, but still just a smile.

"Samiah?" she heard her name a second before John Kim, a member of her Implementation team, walked up to them. "Oh, sorry," John said. "I didn't mean to interrupt, but I was hoping we could go over the presentation before today's meeting."

"I'm sorry?" She frowned. It took her a moment to remember she was at work. "I mean of course," Samiah said with a breathy laugh. *What the hell?* She never got flustered.

She turned to John. "Yes, of course. Grab Katie and meet me in my office. I'll be there in a sec."

John nodded to Daniel and held out his hand. "You're the new hire in R&D, right?"

"Daniel Collins," he answered.

"I'm John. I'll be the one bugging you when it's time to work on the regression testing for the new CRM software."

"I look forward to it," Daniel said with a smile.

Good Lord, the man had dimples. He had outrageously gorgeous cheekbones and freaking dimples. So not fair.

John left them standing at the coffee bar. An awkward silence stretched between them.

No! No! No! No!

Why did this feel so awkward? There should be no awkwardness here. He was just her coworker.

Samiah cleared her throat and held up her coffee mug. It was probably cold now, but she wouldn't dare stick around to brew another cup. "I should finish this in my office. I have a presentation to give at noon."

"I heard," he said, pitching his chin toward where John had just left. He stepped aside, giving her ample room to pass. She slid past him, ignoring the quiver in her stomach.

"Hey, Samiah?" Daniel called after she'd taken a couple of steps.

She coaxed herself into showing a bit of restraint by turning slowly. "Yes?"

"Don't sweat all the attention that video is getting. You did what you had to do."

Her heart lifted with a rush of gratitude that nearly brought tears to her eyes.

"Thank you," she said. "I really needed to hear that." Then she raced for the sanctuary of her office.

CHAPTER FIVE

She couldn't hear it, but she felt it. The methodic ticktock of her internal clock as the seconds quickly ticked away. It was getting closer. Closer.

Samiah reached for her phone and extended the time on the alarm before it had the chance to blare with the annoying sound that was the bane of her existence. She'd set the alarm to go off at seven thirty, determined to leave the office, whether her work was done or not.

Yeah, that wasn't happening.

She'd moved the goalpost three times already. The first was a promise not to stay past dusk. When the sun started to dip below the pinkish horizon, she changed it to leaving before seven. After gauging the amount of work she still had to complete before she uploaded a draft report of Monday's presentation for her team's review, she knew she wasn't making it out of here before eight o'clock. And that was if she was lucky.

It's a good thing she'd emptied her DVR a couple of weekends ago, after Craig canceled their date at a club near the University of Texas that she hadn't wanted to go to anyway. She couldn't remember the excuse he'd given her. No doubt it had been a lie.

"Asshole."

The urge to pick up the phone and curse him out gnawed at her, but she resisted. Allowing that sack of wasted skin to consume any more of her energy would serve no purpose. It was time to move past the Craig Walters episode of *The Life and Times of Samiah Brooks*.

Of course, doing so would be a lot easier if interest in that inane viral video decreased, but any hope of that happening dwindled with every hour that passed. It continued to rack up views in the tens of thousands per hour.

She just didn't get it. The video wasn't *that* entertaining. Men were called out for being lying, cheating jerks all the time. Yet, between the thousands of comments on YouTube, the memes on Twitter, and people constantly tagging her on Facebook, it was obvious that the public remained obsessed with the thing.

Samiah hadn't realized just how obsessed people still were until she had received a call from a local news station earlier today, seeking to interview her for a story. After emphatically stating that she had nothing more to say about the incident with Craig, she'd texted both Taylor and London. Sure enough, they both had been contacted.

Just as she reached for her phone to reply to their group text, it dinged with the arrival of a text message. It was from Taylor. She'd sent a meme about an actual catfish that had been catfished by a shark, accompanied by Taylor's commentary, At least we're in good company.

She replied with three laughing-crying emojis before setting the phone back on her desk and returning to her computer. She stared at her report for a solid three minutes before pushing her chair away. She couldn't concentrate on work right now, not with the tug-of-war taking place inside her head.

She couldn't deny that having Taylor and London with her as she faced this Craig mess had made the experience easier than having to deal with it on her own. But the swiftness with which this friendship had developed unnerved her. She didn't have room for new friends right now. Friends required time and effort. FaceTiming and group texts. Meeting up for drinks and dinner and shopping. Having to reply with an actual response to Facebook posts instead of getting away with a simple Like or smiley face. The overall plan for this particular stage of her life left very little room for cultivating relationships.

Establish a career.

Buy a home.

Find a man.

That was the plan. Sure, she'd backed away from that final item in the heat of the moment on Sunday, but after thinking it over, Samiah had started having second thoughts. Why should she allow one scheming con man to derail her from accomplishing those goals she'd set for herself years ago?

And even if she *did* have time for new friends, she wasn't sure inviting London and Taylor into her life was the best move. The two were irrevocably intertwined with this Craig debacle, and Samiah wanted to distance herself from that entire episode.

It was a task she was beginning to think would be impossible. Case in point: She'd dipped into the cute shop across the street that sold gourmet olive oils and vinegars to pick up a gift for her high school librarian who she still sent a birthday gift to every year. When another shopper recognized her from the video, Samiah had nearly dropped the bottle of white grape balsamic she'd been holding.

If a random stranger could identify her in her work attire, how much more of a spectacle would she, London, and Taylor be out together on a Friday night?

She'd contemplated ghosting them more than once in the five days since they'd met. It would be easy enough to do. She could make up an excuse for skipping their get-together this coming Friday, and simply start ignoring their texts. They were both smart women. They would take the hint once she started to pull away.

Yet every time she considered it, a surprising realization stopped her. She wasn't ready to give them up.

The intuition she tenaciously relied on warned her that she didn't have space for Taylor and London in her life, but something equally powerful told her that she needed them. She didn't have any close female friends. She didn't have any close friends. Period. Her existence consisted of her work with a few hours dedicated each week to checking off the final item on her current checklist. If not for Denise and Bradley, she wouldn't have meaningful contact with anyone outside of her office.

But her sister and brother-in-law were about to be swept up in the trappings of new parenthood. Samiah had shied away from thinking about the adverse changes that would result from the blessing of her future niece's arrival.

She would be alone.

Having friends she could turn to, vent to, friends to just be there for her because they understood what she was going through—was that something she wanted to just toss away? No one else could relate to the week she'd had the way those two could.

More than that, she *liked* them. She adored Taylor's quirky sense of humor and London's wry wit. It had been so long since she'd had true girlfriends—not since high school—that she'd forgotten just how cathartic it could be. Although the thought of veering away from her well-laid plans gave her heart palpitations, maybe she could try to be at least a *little* flexible.

Maybe it was time she revisit her master plan, toss aside those items that seemed hell-bent on giving her angina, and replace them with something that would make her the talk of the Internet for a different reason.

Like my app.

"Give it a rest," Samiah told herself with an exasperated sigh.

Ever since Taylor had put the question to her on Sunday, asking whether there was something she'd always wanted to do that she hadn't done yet, thoughts of the app she began developing soon after she moved to Austin niggled at her conscience like an annoying, persistent gnat. It wasn't the first time the idea had tried to worm its way onto her checklist, but Samiah was determined to keep it on the back burner until she checked off the items on her initial plan.

Except now she wasn't so sure she wanted to stick with that plan. There was something about having her most humiliating experience broadcasted for the world to see that made her want to rethink everything.

What if she'd devoted some of the time she'd wasted swiping through profiles of guys who never seemed to live up to their online personas to working on her app? Where would things stand right now? Would people be using her app at this very moment, making connections with other like-minded people in cities all around the country? Around the globe?

How much of her own potential had she sabotaged by sticking so doggedly to her master plan? She was halfway through her checklist; what did she have to show for it? Sitting at her desk in a deserted office building, eating a granola bar for dinner as she worked on a project that listed her as one on a team of six?

Becoming one of those workaholics who threw everything into her job while the best years of her life flew by had *never* been a part of the plan. So why was she here?

Samiah shut down her computer, locked her desk, and left the office. An hour later, she was showered and dressed in dark blue jeans, an off-the-shoulder mohair sweater, and boots. A half hour after that, she was sitting at a small round table, listening to the first set of the blues band that was playing at the club where she and Craig were supposed to have their date this past weekend.

Maybe it was time she accepted that plans changed. And sometimes they changed for the better.

CHAPTER SIX

Claude Sanderson. Forty-eight. Divorced. Father of three. Still pissed over leaving his former business partner just before the software they created together hit big. Was a member of the initial WiMax rollout team.

Mia Palmer. Twenty-four. Mensa member. Top of her class at MIT. Clinically on the autism spectrum but does an excellent job of utilizing social tools. Played a key role in setting up Trendsetters' security system. Definitely knows all the ways to bypass it. Doesn't seem to have a sinister bone in her body.

Jake Gorge. Thirty. Cheated his way through college. A classic bullshitter who pretends to work. Probably scared as hell that he'll one day get found out. Would likely sell out his own grandmother to get ahead if the opportunity arose. Definitely someone to keep an eye on.

As he stood against the glass-paneled wall, Daniel mentally cataloged the people around him. They had all been called to the Collaboration Room. Unlike a normal conference room, there was no long table surrounded by a dozen rolling desk chairs. Instead, the room was interspersed with numerous beanbags and gaming rockers that sat low to the floor. A cluster of rolling standing desks occupied one side and three state-of-the-art treadmill desks dominated the other. On his initial tour of the office, Owen explained that the setup fostered an atmosphere of synergy and engagement, but Daniel wasn't sold on that yet.

The room was filled to capacity for the multidepartment meeting. It was only his fourth day on the job, and he still wasn't sure why he'd been asked to attend or what was expected of him. But it did give him the opportunity to be a fly on the wall and observe several of his new coworkers.

From the corner of his eye he caught sight of luminous brown skin and shiny, chin-length hair approaching the room.

Samiah Brooks. Thirty. Undergraduate studies at Rice University. University of Texas for grad school. Made a name for herself when she found a bug in a new software program, saving the company's reputation. Had rocketed up Trendsetters' ladder of success in the three years since she was hired.

The very definition of gorgeous.

Prior to Monday, Daniel hadn't paid much attention to the dossier on Samiah Brooks. He'd noted that she'd amassed an impressive reputation for getting the job done, but she was considered an ancillary subject to his current project. The only significant detail regarding her was that, at one time, two years ago, she'd worked in Trendsetters' Cybersecurity Department. But her tenure had ended well before the suspicious activity surrounding Hughes Hospitality had surfaced.

Yet for the past three nights he'd spent more time researching her than anyone else on the company's roster. He'd watched the video that had been the talk of the office more times than he would ever admit. But not for the spectacle of it. He didn't give two shits about that Craig guy. Every time he watched, he focused entirely on Samiah.

He'd never witnessed anything so outstanding in all his life. Seeing the way she handed that guy his ass? It was breathtaking. And badass. The combination enthralled him.

She opted to stand at one of the pub tables, opposite and just to the right of where Daniel stood. He could watch her out of the corner of his eye without cluing her in to the fact that he couldn't go longer than a few seconds without staring at her when she was near. He would need to work on that.

His new best friend, Owen, entered with his signature so-bright-it-bordered-on-creepy grin. He flipped a switch and the conference room's transparent walls immediately changed to frosted glass.

Daniel soon learned that this particular strategy meeting had nothing to do with the WEP encryption project he'd been assigned to work on. Owen introduced him to the room at large.

"Daniel is here as an observer today. Let him see what happens when all these great minds merge."

This was yet another part of the immersion-style employment strategy Trendsetters utilized. Instead of a typical employee handbook, they plopped new hires directly into situations that allowed them to experience different aspects of how the company operated in real time. He was told to expect several such instances over the next month or so, until they felt he was settled into the job. But if all went as planned, he would be in and out of Trendsetters in a couple of weeks.

Owen started talking about a potential new client, and Daniel let his eyes travel around the room. Not surprisingly, they landed on Samiah. Extremely surprisingly, she was staring right back at him. She quickly looked away, but then returned her gaze to his and smiled the subtle, embarrassed smile of someone who had been caught.

An answering grin drew across his lips.

Dude, what the hell?

He knew better than to engage. His normal modus operandi was to come into a job, lie low, complete his assignment, and get out. Landing on anyone's radar wasn't just foolish; it was potentially hazardous to his career. People talked. If he stood out at any particular company, word could spread and he wouldn't be able to operate as he had for the past year.

But as he searched for a reason to tear his gaze away from the magnificent dark brown eyes staring back at him, Daniel couldn't seem to come up with one. As long as he didn't get distracted from the *real* reason he'd come to work for Trendsetters IT Solutions, what harm was there in being friendly to one of his fellow coworkers? And just because she wasn't on the list of people he'd been tasked with keeping an eye on, did that mean he should ignore her?

Hell, he couldn't ignore her if he tried. He was aware of her every breath whenever he was near her.

He'd spent the past couple of days pretending that he just so happened to want coffee whenever she did, but Daniel had no doubt that by this morning she'd caught on. He was a good actor—he had to be in his line of work—but he wasn't *that* good.

The fact that she hadn't called him on it gave him way more to think about than was healthy. Had she written it off as mere coincidence? He couldn't buy that. She seemed too smart not to have noticed what was blatantly in front of her. The other possibility—the thought that she might enjoy their "chance" encounters—accelerated his heart rate.

The meeting ended and everyone started to file out of the room. Daniel lingered. What point was there in pretending that he wasn't waiting for her?

"I'll bet you're happy this meeting's over," she started. "This must have been torture for you."

He cocked his head to the side. "Why would you say that?"

"I know your type. Programmers want to program. Having to sit through meetings like this one is like being forced to listen to fingers down a chalkboard on repeat."

He dramatically shivered. "Too graphic."

Her smile brightened and the meager resolve he'd built up to keep his distance from her all but dissipated.

"It wasn't all bad," Daniel answered. "There were a few bright spots to being here."

The crests of her deep brown cheeks darkened as she blushed.

That was it. Game over. As far as his power to resist was concerned, he would just stop trying. Figuring out how to best navigate this attraction would be a far more effective use of his mental energy when it came to Samiah Brooks.

Mercifully, an all-day meeting that kept her behind the closed doors of Trendsetters' largest conference room saved him from further encounters. He could use some time away from her while he determined how he would pilot his way through these feelings.

Instead of hitting the gym after work, Daniel changed into a pair of basketball shorts before leaving the office, then parked along the banks of the Colorado River that meandered through downtown Austin. His feet pounded the pavement in time to the rhythmic beats of the eighties Run DMC track that had just come up on his "Short Runs" playlist. He accelerated his pace after recognizing that he'd adjusted to match the song's slower tempo. Concentrating on his breathing pattern, he inhaled for every three steps, exhaled for every two. The sweet burn flowing through his quads and hamstrings signaled that he'd finally hit his stride.

He took to the grass to bypass a woman pushing a double stroller on the concrete path that wound along the riverbank. Families who'd come out to enjoy the relief the early cool front had brought packed the greenbelt lining both sides. They reclined on blankets strewn across the ground, their barking dogs leaping about. College students from UT or one of the other half-dozen colleges and universities nearby tossed Frisbees, Rollerbladed, or studied on the freshly trimmed grass.

Daniel mentally smacked down the complaints his brain conjured regarding the crowds. He could have easily gone to the gym to exercise, or picked one of the running paths near the apartment he'd been issued. He was the one who had chosen to come here.

He slowed to a stop and bent over, pulling the earbuds from his ears. He flattened his palms against his thighs, drawing shallow breaths.

This shit was getting out of hand.

He straightened and peered out into the distance, survey-ing the buildings of downtown Austin. His eyes focused on the upper floors of one glass-and-steel high-rise in particular that sat a few blocks from the river.

God, what was he doing?

He'd already decided that he could no longer pretend their coffee station encounters were by chance, but relegating them to a harmless morning ritual made him seem quirky, not creepy. Did he think Samiah would find it harmless if she spotted him jogging in her neighborhood?

"She's going to think you're a fucking lunatic stalker," he huffed out underneath his labored breaths.

Mentally recoiling at the chance he'd taken by coming here, Daniel fitted the earbuds back into his ears and retraced the route he'd taken. Once back at the generic sedan he hated driving—what he wouldn't give to slide behind the wheel of his 4x4—he called in an order to Franklin Barbecue, picking it up on the way to the square box he'd called home for the past two weeks. The two-bedroom apartment in the area of Austin known as the Triangle was one of many sprinkled throughout the country that was leased by the government under various guises. Even though his supervisor had regis-tered him for a four-month stay, Daniel had all but convinced himself that he would be out of there within a matter of weeks. A month at the most.

Talk about a misread. If the first four days at Trendsetters had shown him anything, it was that this job would be much harder than he first thought. That's what he got for being cocky.

Shoving the key in the apartment door's dead bolt, Daniel shook his head at his own naïveté. He could hear his Marine

Corps drill instructor back at basic. So young, dumb, and full of—

"You here already? Thought you were going for a run," Quentin Romero called from the living room sofa, cutting off Daniel's train of thought. Sheaves of paper covered the area that wasn't occupied by the federal agent's stocky build. A bottle of Powerade looked perilously close to falling off the edge of the cheap Ikea coffee table.

"I cut it short," Daniel said, rubbing at the goose bumps that had already formed on his arms. Quentin always turned this place into an icebox. "I've got two reports I need to file with HQ before the end of the day."

Filing reports was always a good excuse. It was a requirement of everyone in the field, no matter which government agency you called home. And everyone hated it.

"A call just came in. I need to head down to San Antonio for a couple of days."

Daniel paused before setting his running shoes in the closet, then turned. "Anything I should be worried about?"

Quentin waved him off. "It's not related to the Trendsetters case. It's an old investigation that's been a pain in my ass." He huffed out a laugh. "Probably since you were still in high school."

Daniel had gotten used to the jibes about his age. It didn't help that his part-Korean/part–African American heritage made him look younger than his twenty-eight years. It was also why the people he encountered in law enforcement were skeptical when they learned he already had a couple of years under his belt. Their assumptions that he was barely out of college often led to even more incredulousness when they discovered he'd put in four years with the Marine

Corps before earning his degree from Stanford and joining the Treasury Department's Office of Terrorism and Financial Intelligence.

"I'm going to grab a shower." He went over to the galley kitchen and set the bag from Franklin's on the counter. "I brought back barbecue for dinner tonight. It's a lot, so help yourself."

"I was told if I do not show up to dinner tonight that I shouldn't bother showing up at all," Quentin said as he closed his laptop and slipped it into a leather messenger bag. "Which means I'm having dinner with my wife. But thanks for the offer." He gathered the papers that were scattered around the sofa, stuffed them in with the computer, and stood. "I'll see you on Wednesday at the earliest. Good luck getting into that database at Trendsetters."

Daniel nodded toward him. "You too. Whatever's going down in San Antonio, be sure to watch your back."

"I always do." Quentin gave him a casual salute, hoisting the bag strap onto his shoulder as he left the apartment. He had his own key, even though he used the space here only sparingly as he worked on the Department of Homeland Security's aspect of the case.

Daniel stepped into the apartment's compact bathroom for a quick shower. He pulled on a pair of gray sweatpants and a Phillies T-shirt, then twisted open a bottled water and took it into the second bedroom—Quentin's room, if, on the off-chance, anyone asked. Unlikely, since the only people who'd ever stepped foot inside this apartment were himself, Quentin, and a Grubhub driver who had gone the extra mile by delivering the Thai he'd ordered a few nights ago to the little two-person table shoved against the wall in the living room.

The second bedroom served as command central. They'd managed to squeeze two L-shaped desks into the eight-by-ten-foot space, along with a separate folding table, a filing cabinet, and a portable air-conditioning unit that ran twenty-four/seven to cool the computer equipment. Four twenty-seven-inch monitors rimmed the rear periphery of the desks. A fifth stood off to the side, its connection perpetually linked with a monitor fifteen hundred miles away, in a large room in a nondescript building in Vienna, Virginia.

Daniel sat and rolled his chair to the third monitor. He logged into his encrypted email—the one he wasn't allowed to check on his cell phone, even though that was encrypted too. Some things were too sensitive to take chances with.

When it came to the US government's handling of nefarious activity, people typically thought of the FBI and CIA. Few knew the US Treasury Department was the only government agency with its own in-house intelligence division. The extremely capable men and women out of Quantico and Langley were damn good at what they did, but when it came to financial crimes—especially those related to terrorist activity—there was no farming it out.

Daniel had just completed his second full year with the Office of Terrorism and Financial Intelligence's Financial Crimes Enforcement Network—FinCEN to those who worked there. With a vote of confidence he'd damn well earned from his superior, Lowell Dwyer, he'd been assigned to work on a joint task force with DHS in Austin.

Agents within FinCEN's Intelligence and Enforcement divisions had detected activity that led them to believe a hotel chain based out of San Antonio, with properties across the Caribbean and Central America, was using software developed by Trendsetters IT Solutions to launder money. After further digging and bringing in Homeland Security, the two agencies determined that Hughes Hospitality wouldn't be able to execute that level of concealment on their own. There had to be someone inside Trendsetters helping them out. Daniel was tasked with uncovering the connection between his new tech employer and the hotel conglomerate.

He'd thought the hardest part would be getting hired on by the firm. Their turnover and attrition rates were practically nil due to the attractive salaries and outrageous perks Trendsetters offered their employees. Once he'd jumped over that hurdle, Daniel had assumed the complexity of the assignment would be on par with the others he'd completed since joining FinCEN.

It wasn't.

The tech company had a security outfit unlike any he'd seen, and in this first week he hadn't gotten close to infiltrating it. He'd barely figured out where the damn security team was located, let alone gained access to their system.

"But I will," Daniel murmured as he read over the emails that had come to his inbox since he last checked it. He made several notes and shot off a half-dozen replies. There seemed to be more activity than usual for this late in the day, but then again, there was no such thing as a normal nine-to-five at FinCEN. When he left Trendsetters in the afternoon, he gave himself a couple of hours to exercise and have dinner. But by eight p.m. he was in front of this wall of computers, hard at work. He'd take a day off once this case was solved and the proper people were behind bars.

Making sure he found the culprits should have been sufficient motivation to put Samiah Brooks out of his head.

His sole focus had to be on figuring out who at Trendsetters had given Hughes Hospitality the means to clean their dirty money.

Daniel closed out his secured email and rolled the chair back to the main computer. He logged into another secured site and downloaded from FinCEN's cloud server the report he'd started working on last night. Hours of analysis lay in front of him. He settled his headphones over his ears, fired up his "East Coast Hip Hop" playlist, and got to work.

CHAPTER SEVEN

Samiah slipped off her sunglasses and tucked them in her purse as she hustled toward the peach-and-turquoise door of the Tex-Mex restaurant in Austin's Market District. She was the one who'd suggested this place for tapas and margaritas, yet she was the one running late.

After giving a brief description of Taylor and London to the hostess, she was led to the bar area. She spotted London's bouncy coils first, then saw Taylor, who'd taken out her braids and now wore her hair in a sleek bob, the tips a dark magenta.

"Sorry I'm late," Samiah said, climbing onto one of two unoccupied stools at the pub table. She nodded her thanks to the hostess and accepted a menu. "I rarely lose track of time, but today has been one of those days. I can use this drink." She looked up at the hostess. "A watermelon margarita, please."

"I'll let your waiter know," she said before taking off in the direction of the entrance.

"Forgive us for starting without you." London gestured to the frothy concoction in front of her. "I was ready for my celebratory drink the moment I got here."

"You forgot to mention what we're celebrating," Taylor

said, holding up her cup of water with lemon for a toast. Samiah picked up the glass of water that had been waiting for her on the table and raised it.

"I performed a successful Meckel diverticulum resection today," London said, clinking her margarita glass to their water glasses. "And the baby boy's very grateful grandmother has promised me homemade banana bread for the rest of my life. Shower me with applause and I may send you both a slice every now and then."

Samiah tapped the side of her water glass with her fork. "Congratulations on your Meckel . . . thing. And I'm not saying that only because I want banana bread, which I do."

"I want banana bread too, but you still deserve props," Taylor said. She clinked London's glass again. "That's for saving a life today. You are one of the good ones, Doctor Kelley."

Samiah nodded her agreement as she dunked a chip into a bowl of salsa that had been placed in the center of the table. How had she considered giving this up? Meeting these two was the only positive thing to come out of last weekend's debacle.

"It's good to hear this mess with Craig wasn't able to suck all the joy out of this week," she said to London. "Other than the successful surgery, how'd the rest of your week go?"

London relayed how her coworkers, like Samiah's, had been all over the viral video, but that things had slowly started to die down later in the week.

"Of course, all it will take is some fool with five million Twitter followers retweeting it and it'll go viral again." London shrugged her slim shoulders. "That's just how these things work."

"Okay," Taylor said, a pensive look on her face. "I know what went down last weekend was supposed to be a bad thing, but this week has been sick!" She turned to London. "Sick in the other way, not in an 'I need a doctor' way."

"I know what the other sick means," London said. She looked over at Samiah and mouthed, *I don't know what she means*.

Samiah swallowed her chuckle. "What made this week so sick?" she asked Taylor.

"Okay, so ever since that video went viral, I've had so many people contact me that I can't keep up with them. There's no way I can take them all on as clients, which is crazy, because I *need* clients. But most of the people who have contacted me aren't interested in having a full-time nutrition and exercise coach."

"You ever thought about offering classes?" Samiah asked.

She shrugged. "I posted the YouTube videos for that. If all people are looking for is a fitness class, they can just watch one of my videos."

"It isn't the same as being part of a live class," Samiah pointed out.

"Teach the classes," London stated in that direct way Samiah was coming to learn was just London. "It's a no-brainer. Not everyone can afford a personal trainer, and not everyone wants to belong to a gym or work out at home alone. You can provide an alternative."

The waiter arrived with Samiah's drink and took their order of three sharable appetizers. When he left, Samiah placed her forearms on the table and said, "So, other than the news station, have either of you been contacted by anyone else in the media?"

London shook her head.

"No, but I did find a couple of bullshit hot takes," Taylor said, picking up her phone and swiping her fingers across it. She held it face out. "This one believes the three of us can benefit from a life coach who can help us build up our self-esteem, because the only way a woman would allow herself to be taken in by a guy like Craig is if she secretly hates herself."

"*The fuck?*" London said, grabbing the phone from Taylor. "Who in the hell is Andrea Krammer, and who in the hell asked her opinion?"

"She's not the only 'lifestyle blogger' with an opinion about us," Taylor said.

"That pisses me off so much." Samiah pitched the tortilla chip she'd just grabbed back into the bowl. "Everyone has a platform to spew nonsense these days. They make assumptions based on what they *think* they know about a certain situation without knowing jack shit about what's really going on. And you know the worst part? People believe them! Just because this Andrea person has made a name for herself online, she's considered an expert by random people who will now judge all three of us."

"Forget her," London spat. "Why should we care what this Andrea person or anyone else has to say?"

Samiah nodded her agreement. She shouldn't care. She *knew* this.

She'd come up against this crap ever since she told her high school guidance counselor that she wanted to study computer engineering. It didn't matter that she'd had the grades to back it up, or that she once took apart and then reassembled an entire circuit board in science class. People made assumptions about her based on what they *thought* she was—a black girl from inside the Loop in Houston who couldn't possibly have the capacity to understand how microprocessors and custom integrated semiconductors worked.

She hadn't allowed Mr. Sharp to attach his own labels to her back in high school and she'd be damned if she would allow some Internet blogger to do it right now. This situation with Craig would *not* define her.

She authored her own narrative. No one else had the power to write it for her. It was time she take back control of her life story. If she was going to be known for something, let it be a kick-ass idea that helped to create some good in the world.

Like her app.

Thoughts of it had bugged her all week long, lurking around the edges of her brain. She'd become a pro at talking herself out of giving that long-held dream a passing thought. The fear of devoting precious resources to her app without a guarantee that it would be a success had stymied her for years.

Not this time. This time, that nagging voice wouldn't be silenced. This time she would take her normal excuses—she was too busy at work, she didn't have enough seed money, it wasn't part of her master plan—and poke a hole through each one.

Because there were no more excuses. If she was serious about ever seeing her idea come to fruition, it was time she make it happen.

Samiah had to breathe through the tightness suddenly gripping her chest. Was she ready to take that leap? Was she really prepared to veer so far off course from the plans she'd set in place?

"What about Craig?"

Samiah jerked her head back, knocked out of her preoccupied musings by London's question. "What about him?"

"Did he contact either of you since we last talked? Did any other creeps contact you?"

"Just some guy named Timothy," Taylor said.

Samiah and London both nodded and simultaneously answered, "Me too."

"After the fourth DM from Timothy I forwarded his name to the feds," London said. "That shit is harassment."

"Other than Timothy it's just been your run-of-the-mill, ashy dick pics," Taylor said with a shrug. "But that's nothing new." She added a heaping of nachos to her plate. "I have to be honest, ladies. I'm kinda bummed I didn't talk to that news reporter. I would probably have had even more weirdos flooding my inbox, but can you imagine the new clients that exposure would have brought?"

"You know, Taylor, it's okay if you call the news station back," Samiah said. "You're in an entirely different position than either me or London. Neither of us would fault you for using this situation to plug your business."

"Absolutely," London said.

Taylor waved them off. "I'm still not sure I'm ready for that. But I do have to admit that this disaster hasn't been all bad for me." She gestured to both of them. "I met you two." She shook her head and huffed out a laugh. "It's ridiculous that it took something like this to finally make new friends. Shit, there has to be an easier way, right?"

Samiah had just bitten into a mini empanada. She stopped chewing, barely registering the taste of the food. She had to think back to the conversations they'd shared this week to figure out whether she'd mentioned the idea for her app to either of them. But she knew she hadn't. She'd never told anyone.

She'd encountered the same difficulties Taylor mentioned when it came to meeting new people when she'd first moved to Austin. After downloading every dating app known to man, the dearth of options available to help make platonic connections—other than broad social media sites like Facebook and Twitter—had stood out in stark relief. She'd come up with the idea for an app-based way for those moving to a new city to meet people who shared their same interests. There were several apps on the market with a similar concept, but her idea went a step further.

Not only would her app pair newcomers with like-minded people; it would also give businesses a way to create one-of-a-kind experiences for all these new friends to share. A wine bar could put together a special wine-tasting event specifically for lovers of wine from a particular region of France. Or a fitness guru, like Taylor, could create classes explicitly for single mothers who wanted to get healthy.

None of the social apps that constantly appeared in her phone's App Store had the added element of allowing businesses to create the kind of in-person experiences she had in mind. It seemed like such a no-brainer, Samiah was still floored that another developer hadn't put forth the idea.

It's only a matter of time until they do.

Taylor slapped her palms on the table. "I cannot believe I forgot to tell you both this. The friend who sent me out on that date with Craig? She tried setting me up with another rando for this weekend!"

"And you didn't punch her in the throat? How civil of you," London said.

"I told her no more blind dates. Actually, no more dates. Period. At least for the foreseeable future. I have a business I'm trying to get off the ground. The video going viral gave me a boost, but the likelihood that any of those people will become long-term clients is slim. Once the 'celebrity' wears off," she said, making air quotes, "I'll be back to the client hunt."

"Or they *will* become long-term and you'll have so many clients you won't know how to manage them all."

"I like your version better." Taylor made pistol fingers at Samiah. "Either way, I need to focus on work."

"And I'm the opposite," London said. "I've spent too much time focused on my career and not enough on me. And when I say me, I mean *me*." She pointed at her chest. "It's not that I'm anti getting-a-man, but I'm tired of taking what little extra time I have and putting it into someone who turns out not to be worth the effort."

"I hear you," Samiah said.

"You know." London tipped her head to the side. "I took one of those silly online quizzes and when it came to the question about hobbies, I had no idea how to answer. I have no hobbies. I have nothing but the hospital."

"Get yourself a hobby, girl," Taylor said.

"That's just it, I don't know where to even start. Medicine has been my life since my freshman year of college." Her hands flailed haplessly. "Where does one even find a hobby?"

"You look," Samiah suggested. "You try different things and see what makes you happy. Take a painting class." She looked pointedly at Taylor. "Sign up for one of the fitness classes that *someone* will soon add to her business's repertoire."

"Fine." Taylor rolled her eyes. "But she's right. You need to find something you like to do outside of work." She picked up her phone and started typing. "Okay, I'll make the list. We each need to figure out what we're going to do with all this new time on our hands." She tapped on the screen with her thumbs. "Oh, wait! First we need a name!"

"Do we really?"

Samiah chuckled at London's pained drawl.

"Yes, a name," Taylor reiterated. "Something fun."

"The Margaritas," Samiah offered, saluting them both with her watermelon-flavored drink.

Taylor shook her head. "That sounds like a bunch of alcoholics. We need something that will make people jealous when they hear about us. Something that will make them want to *be* one of us."

"Squad Goals," London said. They both just stared at her. "What?" she asked with a dubious frown. "That's what you call it, right? When you see a group of people who hang together and you wish you were a part of it. You say that they're squad goals."

"I freaking love that!" Taylor screeched. "Hashtag Squad Goals! That's what the hell I'm talking 'bout!" She typed on her phone. "So, now that we have a name, we need to make a list of what we're going to focus on now that we're not wasting time on dating."

"Wait. Is this no dating ever?" Samiah asked. She was already thinking about ways to both work on her app and tackle that last item on her original checklist. Thirty years old was too young to give up on finding a significant other.

Taylor rolled her eyes again. "Of course not. Let's give ourselves six months. I bet we can conquer the world in that time. And once we've each taken time to work on ourselves, we can commit to jumping back into the dating scene."

"So, the objective of this little project is to make ourselves better so that we can eventually find boyfriends?" Samiah asked.

"Hell no. It's to make ourselves better because we deserve to be our best selves. The boyfriend is just a bonus."

"Does the six-month hiatus we're taking for this little boyfriend project include no maintenance dates?" London asked.

Samiah's brow shot up. "You have a maintenance man?"

"No, but I was thinking about getting one." She drank down the rest of her margarita and set the glass on the table with a pronounced thump. "You know what? Forget about the maintenance man. I just bought one of those megapacks of batteries at Costco. I'm good for the next six months."

"And your goal?" Taylor asked.

"Easy. To find myself a hobby."

"Samiah, what about you?"

"I have—" Samiah started, but then stopped. She couldn't tell them about her app. If she actually spoke it out loud she would *have* to work on it. No more excuses.

If you commit to it, you wouldn't need any excuses.

She mentally pointed her middle finger at the voice in her head.

"I'm in the same boat as London," she said instead. "My job keeps me so busy that I never take time to relax and do something that's just for me. I'm going to find myself a hobby too. One that will help me detach from the job."

"All right," Taylor said, typing again. She set the phone on the table and smiled. "We got this, ladies. We are going to rock this." She motioned to the array of dishes. "So, are we making this a weekly thing, or what?"

"Tapas and margaritas?" London asked.

"Or dim sum, or hot wings, or whatever." She shrugged. "Not that either of you should get a big head or anything, but I've actually been looking forward to this all week."

"Aww." London reached over and pinched her cheek. "I like you too."

Taylor scrunched her face and stuck her tongue out at London. These two reminded Samiah so much of herself and Denise. It was amazing to think they'd all met just last week.

"So Hashtag Squad Goals will have a standing date every Friday?" Taylor asked.

"Yes. And these are to be our *only* dates for the next six months," London said. "We're working on ourselves."

"I'm in," Samiah said. "We get together once a week and update each other on how things are going. Sounds like a plan."

Sorta. She still wasn't 100 percent sure about this no-dating thing.

They finished off their tapas and margaritas, then parted ways with reminders already set in their phones to meet at the Mediterranean place across the street at the same time next week.

As she made her way to her car, Samiah couldn't shake the uneasy feeling that had settled in her stomach since Taylor started making that list. She should have told them about her app. Saying it out loud, having others to hold her accountable—it was the kind of motivation she needed to finally see her dream through.

She slid behind the wheel of her Mustang and gripped the steering wheel.

"What are you so afraid of?" she whispered.

What else but fear was stopping her from pursuing the dream that had once been so important to her? If she weren't serious about developing her app she would have tossed out all those notebooks when packing up her apartment earlier this year. She would have put that box out with the trash instead of stashing it in the back of her hall closet once she moved into her condo. Seriously, what was stopping her?

You know what's stopping you.

It took a lot more than just an amazing idea to bring an app to market. It took money to develop it and man-hours to work on it. Her handsome salary was enough to allow her to live credit card debt–free and save well for retirement, but it wasn't enough to launch an app.

Maybe she should just do as she'd said she would and find herself a hobby. Hobbies were more realistic. If a hobby didn't work out, she wouldn't feel as if she'd wasted all her time and money. She wouldn't feel as if she'd failed.

"Okay, so that's a lie," Samiah said. She'd always been notoriously hard on herself, regardless of what she was trying to accomplish. But she had a feeling that failing at this particular thing would affect her differently than if it was some random hobby she'd decided to take up.

She caught every red light on her drive home. On the way in, she stopped at the alcove of chrome-plated mailboxes just left of the elevator bank. She opened her mailbox and slid out a bundle of letters and magazines. Standing next to the recycling bin, she threw away the flyers and junk mail. When she got to one of the half-dozen tech magazines she subscribed to, Samiah stopped short.

On its back cover was an advertisement for the Future

in Innovation Tech Conference. One of the hallmarks of the FITC was the opportunity for start-ups in the tech world to showcase their products and secure venture capital.

The conference would be held in Austin next spring.

"Seriously, universe?" Samiah grumbled.

On the way up to her floor, she leafed through the magazine until she found the two-page spread listing the highlights of the upcoming conference. Once in her condo, she dropped her purse on the kitchen island, grabbed a can of soda from the fridge, and went into the living room. Samiah kicked her heels off, plopped onto the sofa, and spread the magazine open on her lap.

Her grandmother used to say that God always sent you signs. And for the really stubborn ones, he knocked you in the head.

God had used a sledgehammer on her.

"Okay," Samiah whispered as she looked over the magazine. "I guess I'm doing this."

She squelched the panic that bubbled up in her chest. Would it be a risk? Maybe. But what good was she if she wasn't ready to risk it all for something she believed in?

She could do this. She *would* do this.

She was going to make the Just Friends app happen.

CHAPTER EIGHT

Daniel sat hunched over his keyboard, a Philadelphia 76ers hoodie covering his head, Wu-Tang Clan blasting through the headphones covering his ears. He was dimly aware of the activity going on around him, but his brain's focus remained locked on the continual string of white letters and numbers flying across the black screen. The feeling that came over him when writing code like this was a natural high.

Writing code was part of what he would be doing if he'd gone into the private sector. But that wasn't the path he'd chosen and he was okay with that.

He didn't regret his decision to join FinCEN after graduation, despite it costing him his ex-girlfriend. Joelle had assumed his four years with the Marines would be the extent of his commitment to embracing his family's long history of serving the country. She left after he turned down a lucrative offer from a tech firm in Boulder, Colorado, claiming she didn't sign up to be with someone who wanted to live as a pauper in some government job.

Yeah, his bank account would look better if he'd gone with any of the offers he'd received after finishing at Stanford, but Daniel knew he would never feel fulfilled in those jobs. The obligation to serve had been ingrained in him since birth.

Not to say he didn't enjoy plunging into some ColdFusion or Python or any of the other programming languages Trendsetters allowed code heads like him to indulge in. And when one of his new coworkers clued him in to a new programming language being developed by some hotshots on GitHub, Daniel realized just how out of the loop he was. He wondered what other cool things he'd missed while spending the past couple of years on assignment at FinCEN.

He straightened in his chair, stretching his neck from side to side to regain his focus.

Learning about new innovations in coding wasn't the reason he was here. He was here to catch a criminal.

At this very moment, someone in this building was using Trendsetters as a front to launder money. If only he could find a way to breach their airtight security so he could uncover the intricacies of how they were doing it and bring in the bastards running the thing.

His colleagues back at FinCEN had learned as much about Trendsetters as they possibly could before Daniel even applied for the job. The plan had always been for him to get hired without having to tip anyone in management off to what the government was doing, because it was unknown whether anyone in management was in on the laundering scheme. Getting hired had been the first obstacle. His impressive résumé was complete fiction, but if anyone at Trendsetters called the people at his previous places of employment, they would get glowing stories of how much of an asset Daniel had been while on their payroll.

He hadn't realized getting hired would be the *easy* part.

Breaching Trendsetters' security so that he could gain access to the particular database he needed made getting hired seem like a cakewalk.

He'd come up with the plan to go into the Security Department by mistake, using the excuse of being the new guy who didn't know his way around as his cover. He'd calculated that it would take between seven and ten minutes to copy the portion of the database he needed onto a flash drive.

But just before he'd started, Trendsetters had undergone a massive overhaul of their security system after highly publicized security breaches at several big companies across the country. Now there were only a handful of people with access to the closed-off room that housed the cybersecurity personnel. Those few had separate keycards that allowed them to enter the room, and he wasn't one of those people. His assignment had gone from difficult to downright impossible. Two weeks since he'd started and he was no closer to infiltrating the database than he'd been on day one.

An alarm bell sounded and a voice rang out. "Two minutes until a flash! It's R&D versus R&D. Implementation and Software Development, you're up!"

The first time he'd heard that bell, Daniel had bolted out of his seat, his body instinctively switching to rescue mode. He'd hardly registered that no one else seemed alarmed. He soon learned that the bell had nothing to do with an actual crisis. It was the signal for the contests Trendsetters held between employees.

Each department had been broken up into several teams, and even some subteams for the larger departments like Research and Development, where he worked. The teams were pitted against each other to "promote healthy competition."

The contests ran anywhere from twenty minutes to about an hour, with parameters set by each team leader, based on the project the teams were currently working on. Whichever team got closer to accomplishing its goal won whatever prize was up for grabs.

Last week his team had missed out on all the caramel corn and cotton candy they could eat from a local food truck. He'd been pissed. He loved cotton candy.

A message popped up on his screen with instructions from his team leader about the guidelines for today's competition. Daniel switched screens and logged into the editor for the new paywall software currently in development. He pulled up a new playlist and readied himself for the start of the competition.

Trendsetters CEO Barrington Jacobs, who looked like the guy funneling beer in every frat party movie scene, stood in the center of the main walkway with a bullhorn.

"Are our teams ready?" he asked. And before anyone could respond, he started counting. "Five. Four. Three. Two. Go!"

Daniel's fingers flew across the keyboard. He wasn't thinking about Hughes Hospitality, the guys back at FinCEN, or anyone else. He was in the zone. He had no idea how much time had passed when the alarm bell sounded again. All he knew was that his fingers hurt like hell. But it was a good hurt, especially after learning that he and his teammates were the victors.

"To the main conference room, Software," Barrington called through the bullhorn.

Daniel lagged behind the fourteen members of his team as they filed into the larger, more traditional conference room. He wanted to give Morgan Broomfield a wide berth. She hadn't heeded any of the cues he'd given. If she made another reference to the two of them having drinks after work, he would just have to come right out and tell her he wasn't interested.

The conference room's glass walls had been set to frosted mode, so Daniel had no idea what he would encounter as they were ushered inside. The space had been turned into an oasis. A half-dozen upright massage chairs lined the back wall. Just as many lounging chairs occupied the opposite side, with massage therapists standing at the ready. In the center of the conference table sat a fruit and cheese platter and shot glasses filled with what looked like fruit smoothies. A soft, clean scent filled the space. Something citrusy and minty.

It was easy to see why jobs at Trendsetters were so coveted. The perks alone were worth more than the salaries some of the tech companies out there offered.

Daniel climbed onto one of the cushioned massage chairs and placed his head on the donut. The massage therapist began her ministrations on his neck and shoulders and a deep moan escaped his lips.

Goodness, that felt good! Maybe he should try to get his supervisor at FinCEN to implement weekly massages back at headquarters. Lowell Dwyer would put him out on his ass, but it was worth a shot.

Once done, Daniel walked over to a lounge chair and sat while another massage therapist gave him a full hand massage. Why had he never treated himself to a hand massage before? This shit was amazing.

As he sipped a strawberry and kiwi smoothie, he couldn't help but wonder why anyone employed here would mess it up by getting involved with a bunch of criminals. He knew the answer, of course. Money and greed were powerful catalysts for all kinds of bad behavior. He'd never get used to witnessing what people did for those two things. Sell out their own families. Trade their own children.

After another ten minutes of eating enough grapes and Brie to make up for the breakfast he'd skipped this morning, Daniel returned to his desk amid good-natured boos from many of his coworkers. It was all in good fun. Eventually, they would win some awesome prize that would make him envious.

He grabbed his coffee mug and made his way to the kitchen. Samiah was waiting for him at the coffee station, her arms crossed over her chest. She'd had meetings out of the office both yesterday and this morning. The outright euphoria rushing through his veins just at the sight of her after missing her for two days was his first clue that he was barreling headfirst into a crapload of trouble.

"I am so disappointed," she said. Daniel's head snapped back in surprise. "I totally misjudged you."

His heart pounded erratically against his rib cage. Had he been made? He was almost afraid to ask, but he couldn't just stand there like a tree stump.

"Uh...what did I do?"

"After the rough couple of weeks I've had, I just *knew* you would offer to switch places with me after you won that competition. Do you know how much I could have used that massage?"

Relief made his knees weak. He perched his backside on the counter, hoping the casual pose would mask the fact that he couldn't stand without the extra support.

"I didn't realize that was an option," Daniel finally said after ensuring that his voice wouldn't expose the last dregs of apprehension still creeping along his nerve endings.

Her lips twitched, and the pout she wore curved upward. "I'm just messing with you. Well, kinda. I really could have used that massage."

"Sorry," Daniel said. "It was a good one too." He flexed his right hand. "Just what these digits needed after all that coding."

He chuckled at her outraged gasp.

"You're going to rub it in?" Samiah shook her head, her eyes wide with a mixture of astonishment and amusement. "And all this time I thought you were one of the nice ones."

"I am a nice one."

"Maybe." Her reluctant smile was the sexiest thing he'd seen since the last time he saw her smile. A familiar heat flared to life again, warming the blood that pulsed through his veins. The intensity grew stronger with every minute he spent in her presence.

"If I'd known it was an option, that massage would have been yours." He reached for her hand, but pulled back before touching her. He arched his brow, seeking her permission.

She unfolded her arms and held out her hand. Her demure grin broadened as she gave him a slight nod.

After securing her consent, Daniel gently kneaded her soft palm, parroting the motions the massage therapist had made earlier, working his thumbs along the fleshy pad of her hand then moving up to her fingers. The satiny feel of her skin drugged his senses. Had he ever felt anything this soft?

He had to mentally pull himself back when he noticed his breaths growing shallow. He was treading on dangerous ground here. Over these past two weeks his attraction to her had intensified to an outrageous level. He could feel her nearness on his skin.

He'd told himself this was nothing more than a harmless workplace crush. He'd had a few of those since his breakup with Joelle. One of those crushes had even led to a couple of dates with a coworker in the Liaison Division back at FinCEN.

But this felt different. It felt...charged. And as he relished the softness of Samiah's palm against his fingertips, his ability to call his feelings inconsequential was dwindling. He should have dropped her hand and walked away. Instead he asked, "Are you still upset I didn't give you my massage?"

"Yes," she said. She tipped her head to the side, her grin turning devilish. "You're good and all, but I'm sure the professionals were better."

"You're right. They were amazing."

She snatched her hand back and stuck her tongue out at him. Daniel laughed, and recaptured her hand.

"What if I perfected my technique? Would that be enough to make up for my mistake?"

Awareness saturated the air around them. It was dense and electric and not something he had ever experienced while working a normal operation.

Samiah's eyes dropped to their hands. He could feel her fingers tremble as she cautiously slid them from his grasp.

"I...uh...I need to get back to my office."

It had shaken her too. He could hear it in her voice. Daniel sucked in a breath, then slowly released it.

"Yeah. Yeah, me too." He hooked his thumb toward his desk. "Well, I don't have an office, but you know, back to my cubicle. Desk," he corrected. "It's just a desk. No cubicles here, which is a little weird, but whatever."

Fuck. He was stammering like a scared teenage boy asking his dream girl out on a date.

"Privacy isn't high on Trendsetters' list of priorities." Her smile was a touch more subtle this time, as if she was afraid to show too much emotion. She wiggled her fingers in a friendly wave. "Thanks for the massage."

He watched her walk away, mentally lambasting himself for allowing that to go as far as it had. He could barely keep his head about him just being near her. What did he think would happen when he actually *touched* her?

He couldn't let himself touch her again. No matter how damn soft her hands were.

* * *

Scrutinizing the handwritten notes from one of the half-dozen steno pads and mountain of Post-its strewn about her living room sofa, Samiah took a swig from the bottle of elderberry kombucha she'd picked up on her last grocery store run. She still wasn't sold on it, but the fermented tea was starting to grow on her.

She referenced a sketch of the interface she'd drawn up years ago, noting that she would now have to rework most of it because of the changes in tech design that had been made in just the few years since she'd first come up with the idea for Just Friends. Everything these days was much more streamlined, not clunky and crowded.

She tossed the notebook aside and pitched her head back against the sofa.

"What am I doing?"

She must be out of her mind to think she could develop this app to the point where someone would be willing to invest enough money in it to bring it to market. It needed too much work. She'd never be able to get it all done.

Stop it!

That pesky inner voice had been wiggling its way into her psyche all evening long, trying its best to discourage her. She wasn't falling for it. Yes, she had some hard work ahead of her, but how was that different from every single thing she'd ever attempted? The projects she worked on day in and day out at Trendsetters weren't a cakewalk, but she did them. She put everything she had into *their* work. Why in the hell would she not do the same for herself?

Samiah glanced at the sketches, notes, and research scattered around her. Hell, she was already doing the work. The throng of documents represented months of dedication.

She could do this. She owed it to herself to do this.

She had just under three months before the deadline to submit her idea to the organizers of the Future in Innovation Tech Conference, which meant she had ten weeks to get it all done so that she could devote at least a couple of weeks to testing.

"All right. Let's do this."

She grabbed hold of the checklists she'd created this morning. She had a master list comprising the six big items she needed to tackle, followed by six additional checklists breaking down the various tasks needed to accomplish everything on her master list. Just staring at them brought her a sense of peace. Her brain worked better when she compartmentalized her task into easily digestible chunks.

First up on her list: user retention. She'd spent countless hours studying the market, and one of the biggest downfalls Samiah had noticed with most developers was that they'd designed something that users would use only sparingly.

Incorporating some type of social network was key. Engagement drew people in and made them want to press the in-app purchases button once they'd downloaded the free app. But it had to be different than what was currently out there. She wanted to design something where once people matched, they could set up their own cozy chat rooms that would allow them to communicate outside of the public spectacle of the larger social networks, but those rooms needed to be more versatile than the typical private message.

Common areas.

She sat up straight. "Wait. I like that."

Samiah jotted the words down and circled them. The moment she put pen to paper, the ideas started popping in her head at lightning speed. She hadn't felt like this in way too long, but the tingling of remembrance vibrated along her skin.

She jumped up from the couch and ran to the junk drawer in her kitchen. She knew she had some of those wall-friendly adhesive strips in there somewhere.

She found the strips and raced back to the living room. Using a Sharpie marker, she wrote *Common Areas* in big, bold print and tacked the sheet of paper to the wall, then she picked up a block of Post-it Notes and went to work.

After an hour her wall was covered with bright blue sticky notes, each containing ideas on how to tackle user retention. Samiah grinned despite her mental exhaustion. Wasn't it just an hour ago that she'd stood here contemplating whether she could do this?

"Girl, you got this."

But not before a brain break. She swore there was smoke coming out of her ears.

She raised her arms over her head and leaned back into a long stretch, working out kinks she didn't even know she had. She grabbed her right wrist and wriggled it back and forth, loosening the joint. As her fingers moved down to her palm, it summoned the memory of strong, lean fingers massaging her flesh with firm, yet gentle, strokes.

A low groan unfurled from deep in her throat as images that had no basis in reality impinged upon her fatigued brain. She'd never seen Daniel Collins naked. Had no plans to see Daniel Collins naked. But, holy shit, could she imagine Daniel Collins naked.

And she had. She'd done so way too often over these past couple of weeks.

He wasn't the first coworker she'd fantasized about. She'd spent her first six months on the job visualizing her old supervisor, Carter Green, butt naked and laid out like the centerfold in an old *Playgirl* magazine. But never had she wanted those fantasies to become real. And never once had she gotten the impression that if she signaled her interest, it would be reciprocated. She had no doubts that Daniel would be fully on board.

It wasn't as if he'd been subtle in his attempts at flirting. Oh, he probably *thought* he was being subtle, but after an entire week of the two of them just so happening to meet up at the coffee bar, it became obvious that her newest coworker was interested in more than just macchiatos.

The timing sucked so hard. She could only imagine how different things would be if he'd started working at Trendsetters just a few months earlier. Maybe she would never have met Craig and wouldn't be racking up the views on YouTube right now.

But it also meant she wouldn't have met Taylor and London either. She wouldn't trade that chance meeting for anything. Those two had lit a spark in her. They were the reason she'd lifted the lid on that box in her closet.

Yet another reason why she should keep these naughty little fantasies about Daniel and his magnificent massaging abilities locked away: She'd made a pact with Taylor and London. She'd promised to focus on herself and not on dating.

Besides, she was still treating the burn marks from her last relationship Dumpster fire. She wasn't about to jump into anything else this soon. And with a coworker? She *definitely* didn't need that kind of drama. The few office romances she'd witnessed in her three years at Trendsetters had all ended badly.

She would be content with admiring those ridiculously beautiful cheekbones and engaging in a little lighthearted flirting at the coffee bar, but that was as far as she was willing to go.

CHAPTER NINE

The bell rang out, signaling the end of the three-way flash competition between R&D's Implementation team and the Engineering and Marketing departments. The head of each sector had set the parameters for what they deemed would count as a win for their teams. Implementation met their benchmark; the other two did not.

"Okay R&D, conference room," Barrington Jacobs called.

He was her senior by only two years, but Samiah willingly gave Trendsetters' CEO his due. The man was a genius, and one of her inspirations. He readily admitted that he'd played the kid-stuck-in-the-middle-of-a-nasty-divorce card to get the seed money he needed from his parents, but he'd used that money to grow this company by leaps and bounds.

What she admired most was that, despite the hard work he'd put in to building Trendsetters, Barrington was the first to acknowledge that his privileged background had given him a leg up and eagerly sought to help those less privileged.

Her thought reminded her, she needed to talk to him about donating old computer equipment to the senior center on Lamar. Barrington championed any philanthropic project Samiah brought to his attention. It was mutually beneficial:

Trendsetters received great press and deserving local organizations received much-needed help.

He stood before the conference room, a goofy smile on his face. "Who's ready to spoil their lunch?" Barrington asked before stepping out of the way and leading them inside.

Samiah stopped short. Had she missed the word *heaven* etched across the glass door? Because that's where she was right now. Hands down, this was her vision of heaven on earth.

The table that stretched across the length of the room was laden with all the makings of the perfect ice cream sundae. The line started at the left side, with an array of glass sundae and banana split bowls waiting to be filled. Next were square platters that held bananas, mixed berries, brownies, and blondies, followed by six large cylinders of various ice cream flavors, including a nondairy vegan vanilla. She whisked past that one and heaped two scoops of buttered pecan ice cream into her sundae glass.

She sprinkled on candied pecans and butterscotch chips from the two dozen toppings offered, then drizzled on warm caramel. She'd skipped her half-hour gym appointment for the past three days, but there was no way she could justify missing it today. She added another drizzle of caramel and some whipped cream. Better make it worth her while.

"How amazing is this, huh?" Keighleigh asked as she approached Samiah with a cup of plain vanilla ice cream, no doubt the vegan one. She probably wasn't even vegan. Just wanted to be seen as different. "Better than the massage the team from Software won, if you asked me."

I don't know about that.

She'd trade this sundae in a heartbeat for another hand massage from Daniel.

"Implementation is finally starting to get the recognition it deserves," Keighleigh continued. "You think Barrington is taking notice? He has to, right? This is the second flash competition we've won since the summer."

It was on the tip of Samiah's tongue to point out that *she'd* done the lion's share of the work for both the flash competitions they'd won. But she wanted to be a team player, so she nodded and stuffed another spoonful of ice cream into her mouth. She'd decided that when it came to Keighleigh Miller, keeping her mouth shut was her best tactic. If she didn't share anything with her, she wouldn't be able to glom onto Samiah's work and claim it as her own.

She now recognized that she'd only empowered Keighleigh when she didn't call her out after the Pflugerville Independent School District incident earlier this year. She'd shared her thoughts on the school system's software issue with a couple of team members at lunch. The next day, Keighleigh presented those same ideas to their supervisor. It was brazen, given that two other team members could vouch for the idea being Samiah's. And it was the first time she'd had solid proof that Keighleigh had usurped one of her ideas and passed it off as her own.

But she'd kept quiet because she knew how it would go down if she'd caused a fuss. Tears would be shed. Fingers would be pointed. And whispers would start floating around the office about how Samiah attacked a coworker. And if she tried to defend herself, they'd ask why she was so angry. It was the same shit over and over again.

Team player, she reminded herself. She would be a damn team player.

After finishing her ice cream, she joined in a discussion

about an upcoming implementation project for one of their long-standing clients, but when they asked for her opinion, Samiah pivoted to another topic. She would test just how well they did without her input.

Her coworkers had come to expect her to run point, even when she wasn't the official team leader. Of course, she shouldered much of the blame for that. She tended to take over a project, because if her name was on it, she wanted to make sure it was done right.

Not anymore. She would do her part and *only* her part; the rest of her energy belonged to the creation of her Just Friends app.

When she noticed that they were starting to clear the sundae fixings, she went over to the table and heaped a scoop of both chocolate and vanilla into a bowl. She topped it with chopped walnuts and bite-size chocolate chip cookies, and covered it all in hot fudge sauce, whipped cream, and two maraschino cherries. She thanked the HR team for arranging today's prize, then carried the sundae down the corridor to Research and Development's software wing.

She found Daniel hunched over his computer with headphones covering his ears, his fingers flying across the keyboard. She remembered a time when all she did was make cool things happen on her computer. She missed those days. She missed actually *creating* stuff. Working on her app would bring back some of that excitement.

Samiah tapped Daniel on the shoulder and cleared her throat.

His body jerked as he whirled his chair around and pulled the headphones off. She felt the smile that lit up his face in her very bones.

Seriously? It's just a smile.

God, but it was such a great smile. He killed her with those dimples.

"Hey. What's up?" he asked.

She ignored what was happening to her nipples as she held the sundae out to him. "Unlike *some* people I know, I am happy to share the bounty when my team wins in a flash competition."

His eyes went wide as his mouth dropped open. "No way! You all got sundaes?" He grabbed the glass bowl from her hands.

"An entire sundae bar, to be exact. It was glorious."

He scooped up a spoonful of hot fudge and moaned as he ate it. Her reaction to the sight of him slowly wrapping his tongue around the spoon was so wholly inappropriate for the workplace she had a mind to report *herself* to Human Resources.

"This is ridiculous," Daniel said. "It's the hot fudge that puts it over the top."

"Better than that massage?"

He nodded, but then shook his head. "Nah. But close."

A shocked laugh escaped. "You are impossible. You could have at least lied to me."

"I don't lie. Sooner or later, you'll get caught."

"Say it again for the people in the back," she drawled. "Especially those named Craig who don't realize that their lies will catch up with them."

"Has he been bothering you?" he asked, abandoning the humor from moments ago.

Samiah shook her head. "He's a coward. I haven't heard from him since that night at the restaurant. Neither have Taylor or London, the other two women in the video."

"Good. That guy doesn't deserve a moment more of your time. Do me a favor; don't waste any more of it on him."

A peculiar sensation pressed against the walls of her chest. It took her a second to recognize it as gratitude.

Over these past couple of weeks, as their lighthearted banter and occasional flirting escalated, Samiah had cautioned herself not to take it too seriously. She would never admit it publicly, but her pride was still raw from the wounds the episode with Craig had inflicted. That vulnerability had the potential to color her perception, causing her to put too much stock into the slightest gesture.

But Daniel's concern seemed genuine. Every morning, during their coffee bar encounters, he never once skipped the chance to inquire about how she was holding up under the weight of the viral video.

Interest in it had finally begun to wane, thank goodness. But it would still be a while before her life was back to normal. No one here had shown more interest in her mental well-being than Daniel. He cared. She didn't realize just how much that would mean to her.

"Thank you for that," Samiah said.

He gave a slight nod, his eyes filled with understanding. "It's nothing you don't already know, but I figured it wouldn't hurt to remind you. We tend to forget how special we really are after something like this happens."

Did he have a guidebook to prep him with the exact words she needed to hear?

Samiah knew better than to play the *if only* game. Engaging in hypotheticals was the equivalent of buying a first-class ticket to Disappointmentville. But she couldn't help thinking how different things would be if only she'd met him a few weeks earlier.

She'd heard the terms bandied about before—work spouse,

office hubby, wusband. But she'd never found anyone at Trendsetters who fit the bill.

Until Daniel.

Although she wasn't sure that label still applied. A typical work spouse shouldn't trigger the chemical reaction she experienced whenever she was around him.

She'd all but given up on there being any guys like Daniel still out there—genuinely sweet, empathetic, and the kind of sexy that made you want to apologize to his mama for thinking such naughty thoughts about her son. Guys like that were all happily married and living lives that seemed to come directly out of a Subaru commercial. What were the chances she'd actually stumbled upon her ideal man just as she'd promised to give up men for a while?

Her timing was for shit.

Daniel returned to his ice cream. "So, how did you know exactly what I like on my ice cream sundaes?" he asked, breaking off a chunk of chocolate chip cookie and popping it in his mouth. "You haven't been stalking me online, have you?"

"Do you make a habit of discussing your sundae preferences on social media?" she asked, giving his shoulder a playful nudge. "It wasn't hard to figure it out. You make yourself at least one mocha a day, and if there's a granola bar with chocolate chips in the bowl, that's what you go for."

The brow with a faint scar marring it arched. "So you *have* been paying attention to what I like, huh?"

Her face instantly grew hot. *Oh, God.* If he mentioned something about her blushing, she'd never be able to face him again.

"Don't flatter yourself," Samiah retorted in an attempt to shift the focus back to him. "I only pay attention because I want to make sure I get my granola bar before you raid the kitchen."

He shook his head. "Nope. That's not the reason."

"How do you know?"

"Because you're not a chocolate fan. At least not when it comes to the granola bars. You like the ones with peanut butter." He glanced up at her, his brown eyes glittering with irrepressible mischief. "Why do you think there's always at least one waiting for you?"

Samiah's heart clutched. "You put a granola bar in the bowl for me?"

He caught her gaze and held it, earnestness supplanting his amusement. "I don't like seeing you disappointed. You've had enough of that in the past couple of weeks."

The breath seeped from her lungs in a measured exhale, replaced with an emotion she would have to think long and hard about before she was willing to put a label on it. A heady, charged energy pulsed between them, pure and intense and unnerving.

Could she even trust this feeling, or was this her bruised ego searching for a salve to soothe the burn Craig's cheating had wrought?

Snapping the connection before it sucked her in even deeper, Samiah deployed one of her most reliable tactics, sassiness. "Well, it's the least you can do for not gifting me that massage," she said.

He too must have been shaken by the potency of what passed between them. With feigned aggrievement, he slapped a hand over his heart. "Will I ever live that down?" His amusement slowly receded. Raw sincerity appeared in its place. "Why don't you let me make it up to you by taking you to lunch?"

Samiah's head reared back, a thrilling panic slamming against the walls of her chest.

Say yes!

No. Don't say yes.

"I...uh...I just ate all that ice cream," she sputtered.

Lamest. Response. Ever.

Daniel leaned forward, the sinful gleam in his eyes the kind of look fathers warned their daughters about.

"The ice cream was okay, but it isn't enough to fill you up." He gestured over his shoulder, toward his computer. "I need to give this code refactoring another hour or so. Once I'm done, why don't you let me treat you to a late lunch?"

Okay, so maybe she was reading too much into it. Maybe the guy was just really hungry. She'd had lunch with coworkers before. It had never been a big deal. Why did it have to be one this time?

Because none of your other coworkers compelled you to fling your panties off.

Stop!

She could have lunch without losing her damn panties. In fact, this lunch was the *perfect* opportunity to show herself that she absolutely could handle an office friendship without expecting it to grow into anything serious. For the next six months, a serious relationship was no longer her goal.

Daniel had been a bright spot in what could have been two extremely dark weeks. If she allowed herself to get in her own way, she would be depriving herself of what could become a genuine friendship.

Leaning in to retrieve his empty ice cream bowl, she smiled. "Meet you in an hour."

CHAPTER TEN

What in the fuck are you doing?

The question ping-ponged around Daniel's head as he strode down the open corridor toward Samiah's office. He didn't have to go through with this. He could plead temporary insanity; say he'd asked as a joke after the ribbing she'd given him over the massage.

No, he couldn't do that. That would make him look like an asshole.

He could just admit that he hadn't been thinking. That he knew it was inappropriate to ask her out, even to lunch. Except Trendsetters didn't have any rules against coworkers getting together for lunch. They did it all the time.

That didn't mean *he* could do it. *He* wasn't a typical Trendsetters employee. And FinCEN sure as hell frowned upon agents becoming romantically involved with potential subjects while on an op.

But Samiah wasn't a subject or a target, so did it even matter?

Of course it mattered! He could play around with semantics all he wanted to, but when it came right down to it, Lowell Dwyer would have his ass if he caught wind of any of this.

Decision made, Daniel continued to Samiah's office, only to find it empty.

Well, hell, maybe he wouldn't have to make up any excuses. Looks as if she'd come to her senses.

"I'll be there in a minute."

He turned at the sound of her voice. She waved to him from Aparna Bajwa's desk, where the two were both pointing at something on a computer monitor. A second later, she left Aparna's station and started for him, her smile gaining vibrancy as she approached.

God, but that smile was gorgeous.

"I was thinking—" she started.

"Samiah . . . I don't—" he said at the same time.

They both stopped. Her forehead dipped into a slight V with her frown. "You don't what?"

I don't think we should have lunch. It was one simple sentence. *Just say it.*

"I don't know if you like poke, but there's a place that just opened around the corner that I thought we could go to."

Dude, what the fuck? That was *not* what he was supposed to say.

She regarded him with a hint of uncertainty before her features relaxed into another of those breath-stealing smiles. How could he say no to that smile? He wanted to live in that smile.

"I've been eyeing that place," she said. "Let me grab my purse."

"You don't need it. It's my treat, remember?"

"Oh, I know it is," she threw over her shoulder, her eyes twinkling with amusement. "But I can't leave my access card."

The delay gave him yet another opportunity. He could

pretend he'd forgotten about a special project Morgan asked for help on. He could fake a stomachache. Anything.

But he didn't say a damn word as he stood there waiting for her to lock up her computer and grab her purse from the desk drawer. As he held the door open for her and then followed her out of the office. As he waited for her as she stopped to speak to Jamie at the front desk. So many chances to back out, yet he didn't. Couldn't.

And even as he told himself they were just two coworkers grabbing a bite to eat, he knew what he *wanted* it to be. He wanted this to be a date.

After arriving at the restaurant, Daniel asked Samiah what she wanted from the menu, then went up to the counter and ordered two salmon and avocado poke bowls. He brought the bowls to the table Samiah had chosen and took the seat across from her. As he added an extra dash of soy sauce to his bowl, he asked, "How long have you been at Trendsetters?"

He already knew this, of course, but they'd never discussed it.

"I had my three-year anniversary this past August."

"Only three years? And you're already a team leader?"

His reaction wasn't totally feigned. He'd been genuinely bowled over when he'd read it on her dossier. The speed at which she'd risen among the ranks was impressive.

"Wait." Samiah's brow furrowed with confusion. "Didn't they tell you? I'm a total badass when it comes to that company. I rule that shit."

Daniel wiped his lips to hide his smile, then sat back and crossed his arms over his chest. "Is that so? Does this mean you can demand anything you want and the powers that be at Trendsetters will provide it?"

"Damn right. Except, of course, if it's a back rub that my team didn't earn."

"Hmm..." He concealed his laugh with a cough. Straightening in his chair, he said, "That seems only fair. And because I *did* earn that back rub, I guess that means I'm actually the one who rules that shit, right?"

"No sir," she said, her musical laugh wrapping itself around him. "You've got a few more years to put in before you even get close to ruling anything."

Except he would only be here a few more weeks. A few more days if he was able to catch a lucky break with this case. Daniel sobered. *Lucky* no longer seemed like the appropriate word, not when it meant he'd never get the chance to explore what could become of the attraction that pulsed like a heartbeat between himself and Samiah.

This lunch date—whether she considered it a date or not—was likely the only one they would ever have. And if this was the extent of the personal time they would get to spend with each other, he wouldn't waste any more of it thinking about how little time he had left with her.

"I've been meaning to thank you," Samiah said after swallowing a bite of fish.

He sucked soy sauce off his thumb. "For what?"

"For being such a decent guy when it came to that stupid video. I appreciate that."

"That was a hard thing for you to go through. Seems rude to continue to harp on it."

"Tell that to your coworkers."

There wasn't much hostility behind her indelicate snort, but Daniel could tell it still bothered her.

"Now that you've mentioned it, how *are* you holding up

post going viral?" He put his hands up. "I'm only asking because I really am concerned."

"I know you are," she said. "I appreciate that too." She swirled the chopsticks around the bowl, mixing up the vegetables. "Things are starting to die down a bit. At least the friend requests on Facebook aren't in the hundreds anymore."

"The views on the video have slowed a bit too," he said.

"You've been checking?"

Daniel shrugged. "Just wanted to see how long your celebrity status would last. Gotta decide if I should move on to someone else."

Amusement gleamed in her deep brown eyes. "I think there's one of a dog riding a vacuum cleaner that's getting all the attention now."

"Told you dogs were better than cats. I bet he handles the fame better too."

"The dog can have the fame," she said, some of that spark leaving her eyes. "I never asked for it." Her shoulders dropped with the sigh she released. "But at least I found out Craig was a dog before things got too serious with him. I consider myself lucky, despite the unwanted notoriety."

Daniel stared at her bent head for several moments. He should let it go. It was obvious she was uncomfortable talking about this.

He stabbed at a pink square, but then set the chopsticks on the rim of his bowl.

"There's something about how all of that went down on that video that I can't figure out." *So much for letting it go.* But then she encouraged his question with a nod. "You learned about the other date on Twitter, right?"

"Actually, it was my sister, Denise. She's the Twitter fanatic.

I was at home getting ready for a date I was supposed to have with Craig later that night. Of course, Denise had no way of knowing I was connected to the guy when she started reading those tweets. Craig and I hadn't been seeing each other for very long. I hadn't introduced him to family or anything."

"So how did you get to the restaurant so quickly? Wait, how did you even know which restaurant to go to? It wasn't mentioned in any of the other woman's tweets."

"Taylor."

"Come again?"

"The woman he was out on the date with? Her name is Taylor. The tall one with the gorgeous hair is London. And I knew which restaurant because it's the same one he'd taken me to for our first date. It just so happens to be in my neighborhood. The moment she mentioned the volcano sushi roll in her tweet, I knew where to find him."

"Ah." He nodded. "Guess that makes sense. I know that restaurant. I haven't been there, but I've seen it while out running."

"Oh, do you live nearby?"

Daniel realized he'd just outed himself.

No, he hadn't outed himself; he'd just given himself a credible reason for being in her neighborhood. Not that he planned to run into her. He'd decided to never put himself in that predicament again.

But it didn't hurt to establish the story. Just in case.

"No, I live near the Triangle," he said. "It's nice up there, but I like running along the river and sometimes through downtown."

"It's gorgeous, isn't it?" Her eyes lit up. "The moment I moved to Austin I knew this area was where I wanted to live."

"You're not from here?"

She shook her head. "Houston. The Third Ward. Or, as the rest of the world knows it, the place where Beyoncé grew up."

He tipped his head in acknowledgment. "Living among royalty, huh?"

"She is the Queen Bee." Samiah laughed. "And she still does a ton for her community. Much more than you see in the news."

"Does your family still live there?"

"Mom and Dad do. My older sister moved here last year. She and her husband both teach middle school math with the Austin ISD. Independent School District," she tacked on.

He took a sip from his bottle of ramune. "Must be nice to have family here with you. I haven't lived near mine for a while. My mom said she'll disown me if I'm not home for Thanksgiving."

"You'd better buy that plane ticket now." Her sly grin was so lovely it hurt. "Angry mamas are to be avoided at all cost. Especially around the holidays."

"Speaking from experience, huh?" Daniel chuckled.

"Oh, yeah. I've gotten 'the look' on more than one occasion."

"If it's anything like the look from a Korean grandma, you have my sympathies."

"Oh, your grandma is in Philadelphia too?"

"Philadelphia?" His brow rose. "How did you know that? You've been checking me out?" Her cheeks immediately darkened with her blush. It was the most beautiful thing he'd seen in years. Everything about her was the most. The most enchanting smile, the most engaging laugh, the most captivating eyes, the most intriguing mind. With every additional moment he spent with her, he became more entranced by her.

He was within an inch of falling over the edge. He needed to take a step back. Shit, make that *several* steps back. He had to walk a fine line between playing a role in a casual, lighthearted office flirtation that he could possibly convince his supervisor back at FinCEN was necessary for pulling off this undercover job, and plunging head first into lust with this woman.

The first would get him a reprimand, but it was survivable. The second would be career self-sabotage.

"Well, the fact that you seem to own sports gear from every single Philly sports team was my first clue," she finally answered. "But, yeah, I asked about you," she added with a rueful smile, as if she knew she'd been caught and didn't care. She pulled her bottom lip between her teeth and Daniel's breath arrested in his lungs. He'd give anything to have just one taste of those lips.

Fuck.

He shifted in his seat, trying to stave off the images that usually came to him in his dreams. Annoyed by the route his brain had taken yet again, he settled his elbows on the table and tried to recapture the relaxed, lighthearted mood of a few minutes ago.

"It's not as if I'm trying to hide anything," he said. "I'm proud to be Philly born and raised."

"So what brought you all the way to Austin? Was it the job?"

He nodded, returning to his poke. "I'd been hearing a lot about Trendsetters, so I kept my eyes open. Job openings are like unicorns at that place."

"We have an extremely low turnover rate. We even have a few people who left Silicon Valley to come here."

"Cost of living alone would do that, but I understand the appeal." Going with the story they'd set up back at FinCEN, he said, "I'd never visited Austin; the Thursday before I started at Trendsetters was the first time I'd ever stepped foot in the city. It's great here. And you can't beat the weather."

"That's because it's unusually mild as we head into the fall this year. Just wait until summer rolls around," Samiah warned. "You'll see how you like those jogs along the river when the thermometer is nearing three digits."

"Aw, don't tell me that." Daniel groaned. "Just the other day I had to stop in the middle of my run and peel my shirt off."

Her gaze dropped to his chest. "That must have been nice." Her horrified eyes shot back up to his face, wide with dismay. "I said that out loud, didn't I?"

He coughed, a feeble attempt to dislodge the desire clogging his throat. Daniel could feel the heat on his face rising. "Yeah, you did," he said.

A potent, electric charge sizzled in the air between them, a sensation so strong he felt it on his skin. It put to rest any hope that this could remain something between friendly coworkers. He wanted to be more than just a friend, and he didn't give two fucks about being her coworker.

But that's all he could be to her. Anything else would jeopardize everything he'd worked for.

His fingers clenched the napkin he'd picked up. Daniel had never resented his job more than he did at this very moment.

"Umm...wow," Samiah said with a nervous laugh. "Well,

okay. Umm...we should probably head back. I've got a ton of work on my desk."

"Samiah—"

She snapped her fingers. "I totally forgot that Keighleigh wanted to talk about some...something." She started to push back from the table, but Daniel stopped her, capturing her wrist.

"Samiah, wait." She looked down at his hand, then back to his face. He let go. "Look, do you want to maybe do something one day?" *What in the hell was he doing?* "Something other than lunch?" he clarified.

Shit, he was asking her out. On a *real* date.

"I've read about how great the scenery is around here and how there are all these great trails to explore, but I haven't had a chance to venture out. I just thought maybe...I don't know. Maybe you could join me."

"Trails? Do you hike?"

"Yeah." He nodded. "I haven't been able to do much lately. Do you hike?" he asked. That hadn't been in her dossier.

"I do." A soft smile replaced the panic that had been in her eyes a moment ago. "I know it doesn't sound like something a girl from inside the Loop in Houston would be into, but I love it."

"Do you want to go hiking one of these days?" *Don't say it.* "Maybe this weekend?"

Shit.

He'd pushed too hard. He could tell by the caution that entered her eyes, as if just realizing that, apart from their coffee bar encounters, they didn't know each other all that well.

"Not this weekend," Daniel corrected before she totally shut him down, which she would have every right to do. "Why don't we grab lunch a few more times. I can tell you about my Philly upbringing, and you can tell me what it was like growing up in Beyoncé's backyard. Then, maybe, by next weekend you'd feel more comfortable hiking through the woods with someone who you've known all of three weeks."

"Was it that obvious?"

"You're smart to be cautious, Samiah. And I'm not here to make you feel uncomfortable. I just thought... maybe," he said with another shrug.

"I'll think about it," she said.

Daniel couldn't curb the smile that spread across his face if his life depended on it. "That's a start."

He pushed away from the table and gathered the remnants of their lunch, depositing the food in the compost bin and the recyclable containers in their proper place. Then he held the door for her to exit the restaurant.

As he walked alongside Samiah on the way back to their building, alarm bells continued to ring out through his brain. He chose to ignore them.

He liked her. He wanted to get to know her better. If there was a rule against it at Trendsetters, he hadn't come across it. As for FinCEN? As long as it didn't get in the way of him doing the job he came here to do, why should it matter who he became involved with?

Yeah, tell that to the boss.

CHAPTER ELEVEN

You're not ready?"

Samiah looked up from her computer and experienced a sudden flush of warmth throughout her body. Daniel leaned against the wall just inside her door, looking like a midday snack. The least he could do was try not to be so damn gorgeous all the time.

It was the cheekbones. She was supremely jealous of those high, angular, pronounced-without-being-too-pronounced cheekbones. And don't get her started on his deep brown eyes or that flawless warm, golden skin. His African American and Asian makeup forged a medley of the most scrumptious features.

So. Un. Freaking. Fair.

"Am I ready for what?" she asked.

He made a point of looking at his watch as he pushed away from the wall and strode into her office. "I do believe we're supposed to have lunch."

"Oh, really?" She propped her elbows on her desk, folded her fingers, and rested her chin on them. "I don't remember agreeing to lunch today."

"Didn't we establish this already? Me and you. Lunch.

Until you're comfortable enough with me to explore some of the hiking trails around town?"

"But we had lunch yesterday."

"Hey." He held his hands up. "I don't know how they do it in Houston, but up in Philly we tend to eat lunch every day." He shrugged. "Maybe it's a regional thing."

Samiah clamped her lips together, taking a moment to collect herself. If she laughed she would only encourage him.

"You think you're cute, don't you?" she said. The moment she did, she wished she could snatch the words back.

That delectable dip in his cheek appeared with the emergence of his smile. He advanced several steps and perched his hands on the edge of her desk. His eyes glittering with amusement, he said, "The question is, do *you* think I'm cute?"

His unrepentant grin was evidence that he was enjoying this way too much. So was she.

And *that* was the problem.

She couldn't do this. She'd decided last night that resisting—no matter how irresistible the dimple and the man who possessed it was—was her only option. She'd made a pact with London and Taylor to focus on her personal goals. Getting involved with anyone, even on a casual basis, would blur that focus.

"I really can't," Samiah said. The light in his eyes dimmed and his smile faded by several degrees. "I'm so bogged down right now, and then I have a meeting out in Wells Branch in less than—" She glanced at the time on her computer. "Shit, in less than an hour."

"Wells Branch? That's even further up than where I live. What's going on all the way out there?"

"I'm meeting with the directors of a foster care center.

Trendsetters offers technical support to nonprofits that can't afford IT staffs. It's one of the projects I spearhead."

He nodded. "Owen mentioned something about that during my orientation. I guess it's not just lip service like most of the companies I've worked for. They really take giving back to the community seriously around here."

"I make sure they do, even if I have to do it myself," Samiah said. "And that's, unfortunately, why I can't have lunch with you today," she lied. "Sorry."

"You will have something to eat, right? Even if you have to eat it at your desk?"

"I was planning to grab a granola bar. Just an FYI. You know, in case you want to make sure there's a peanut butter one in there."

That slow, easy smile reappeared. She wasn't 100 percent sure, but there was a pretty good chance the sensation she felt below was her panties melting.

"Will you pencil me in for lunch tomorrow?" Daniel asked. "I'm not sure how you're ever supposed to get comfortable with me if we don't do this lunch thing."

He wasn't even trying to be adorable right now and it still took everything she had not to give in to his irresistibleness.

"I'll try to make myself available." She would have to come up with a list of excuses she could use if she planned to stick to this pact she'd made. Her phone rang. "It's the foster care center's director," Samiah said. "I need to take this. Hello?"

Sorry, Samiah mouthed.

He lifted his shoulders in an *it is what it is* shrug before shoving his hands in his pockets and backing out of her office, resignation evident in the rueful slant of his lips.

She stared at his retreating back as he walked down the hallway, not tearing her eyes away until he turned the corner.

It took a second to remember there was someone on the other end of the phone call. She returned her attention to the center's director, who asked if their meeting could be postponed by an hour. The moment Samiah ended the call, she clicked into her messaging app to tell Daniel that she was free for lunch. But then she stopped herself. She could have made lunch work even if the director hadn't pushed the meeting back. That wasn't the reason she'd turned down his invitation.

She was doing the right thing. It didn't matter how perfect Daniel seemed. Craig had seemed perfect in the beginning too.

No. That wasn't true. Craig had never seemed perfect. It was unfair to even compare the two men. With her relationship with Craig—if it could even be called that—she'd shouldered the lion's share of the work, not only starting the conversations but keeping them going. With Daniel, it was effortless. When they met for their morning coffee they never had a problem finding topics to discuss. She knew his favorite music artists—a bunch of rappers from the eighties and nineties who were probably grandparents by now—and that he could recite verbatim entire scenes from *The Hunt for Red October*.

If her life depended on her knowing Craig's favorite movie, her family would be picking out funeral clothes.

But just because you know a person's favorite movie or that they prefer mochas to regular coffee doesn't mean you *know* them. Who's to say Daniel wasn't a serial dater, just like Craig. He could have hookup partners all over this country.

You know that's not true.

No, she didn't know. And whether it was true or not didn't matter. Her priorities had shifted. Finding a man was no longer on the list. It was time she focused on *her*.

Her stomach retaliated against her with an angry growl, but just as she was about to head to the kitchen, John came into her office with his laptop open and one of their newest clients, the owner of a string of pet boutiques that was on the verge of franchising her successful business, on a video conference call. Samiah spent the next hour talking the client down from the proverbial ledge. She didn't even get the chance to grab that granola bar for lunch before it was time to leave for her meeting in Wells Branch.

She packed her laptop into her bag and locked up her desk. She wouldn't worry about coming back to the office once she was done with her meeting.

She'd made it just past the Water Wall in Trendsetters' lobby when she heard someone call her name. "Hey, Samiah."

She turned to find Justin Vail striding toward her, with Daniel trailing a few steps behind. He stood alongside Justin, his hands shoved into his pockets.

"I'm glad I caught you before you left," Justin said. "I realized that Daniel hasn't seen any of our nonprofit work in action. I thought he could join you at the Right Path today, get a firsthand look at what you do."

"Gotta love this immersive training," Daniel said.

The effort to suppress her laugh nearly did her in. Samiah cleared her throat and nodded. "I'll be happy to show Daniel the ropes." She turned to him. "Are you ready?"

"Absolutely."

After they boarded the elevator, Samiah turned, prepared

to tell him that he wasn't fooling anyone with his little end-around move. But before she could speak, the elevator doors opened on the twenty-first floor and several people joined them. It wasn't until they entered the parking garage that she finally got the chance to call him out on his sly maneuvering.

"You think you're slick, don't you?" Samiah asked as they walked to her car.

"What? You think I orchestrated this?"

"Yes."

"Wrong. This was all Justin."

"Sure," she said with an eye roll.

"It's the truth." He held his hands up. "Justin asked if I knew anything about Trendsetters' charitable work. When I said that I didn't, he asked if I was interested in seeing it play out firsthand."

"Oh, so an hour after I turn you down for lunch, I'm supposed to believe you're now here because you want to learn about the company's 'charitable work'?" She made air quotes.

"I happen to be *very* interested in my new employer's philanthropic deeds. To insinuate that I have an ulterior motive for joining you is just wrong, Ms. Brooks."

She choked on a laugh. "You are so full of shit."

"Not the first time I've had those words directed at me," he said as they arrived at her car. He held the driver's side door open for her and draped an arm over the top of it. "But I should warn you, I've also heard that I tend to grow on people." He winked. "Be prepared."

Was she really expected to resist him? In what universe was it possible to meet someone as genuinely sweet, charming,

and incorrigible—but in the very best way—and not reciprocate their obvious interest?

Once in her car, they headed up I-35. Staring out the
passenger-side window, Daniel remarked, "I've been here
nearly a month and haven't been north of Highway 183. I
need to take some time to explore this city."

"Have you been to Lake Travis yet?"

"No, but I heard it's beautiful out there."

"It is. It should definitely be on the list of places for us to
hike. Once I'm more comfortable being alone with you." She
held up a finger. "This doesn't count."

"It totally counts."

"It does not. We're alone, but it's work-related."

"Are you making up these rules as we go along?"

"Maybe." She tipped her chin in the air. "It doesn't matter
when the rules were made, you still have to abide by them if
you want me to be your hiking trails tour guide."

"Well, I guess I'll need to follow your rules, because I
definitely want that." The rich, deep timbre of his voice set
off a faint tremor low in her belly.

Samiah sped up by an extra five miles per hour. The
quicker she arrived at the center, the quicker she could escape
the confines of this car, which seemed to have contracted
since she left the office. Or maybe it was the sudden, potent
dose of pheromones whirling around that had taken up all
the space.

The directors of the Right Path foster care center were
waiting for them when they pulled up to the nondescript
building located in a strip mall just off the highway exit.
Samiah made introductions and then followed the couple into
a cramped, windowless office.

During their nearly two-hour-long meeting, where they were shown the center's woefully inadequate and antiquated computers, along with the hundreds of files that needed to be digitized, Samiah paid attention to Daniel's attentiveness. He provided thoughtful suggestions and offered to support the center's efforts in any way he could.

He is not perfect.

She had to occasionally remind herself that, despite all evidence to the contrary, there had to be something wrong with Daniel Collins. There were no perfect people. There had to be a flaw lurking somewhere. She wished he'd go ahead and reveal it already. Maybe then her mind would stop with this insane tendency it had to paint him as the most genuine, giving, exemplary human being she'd encountered in ages.

He turned to her as they exited the center.

"Do you know how much the work Trendsetters is doing is going to help them?" he asked.

"That's the point," Samiah said, charmed by his enthusiasm. "The funds they save can be better put to use by helping place more kids."

"I can get behind a company like this," he said with a nod. Once settled in her car again, he continued. "But here's what I don't get. Why are *you* the one doing this? Isn't this the kind of thing HR handles? It doesn't seem like it would be in Implementation's wheelhouse."

"I know," she said. "But it's my baby."

"This particular project?"

"No, Trendsetters' work with nonprofits. Barrington established a program for charitable giving from the beginning, but there's a big difference between throwing money at an organization and doing actual hands-on work. I thought Trendsetters could do more, so I started doing more."

"Most people don't think this way. You do know that, don't you?"

She flipped on her blinker. "I know, but it's important to me." Several beats passed before Samiah continued. "I've worked hard to get where I am, but I didn't do this by myself. When I was a freshman in high school, a bunch of people at my church back in Houston collected money to send me to a computer summer camp. Many of them didn't even know things like that existed. They'd raised money to send some of the boys to football and basketball camp, and they'd help to fund cheerleading camp, but computer camp?

"I have no doubts that I would still accomplish everything I've set out to accomplish without any help—as my mom is so quick to point out, I'm too damn stubborn not to." Samiah laughed. "But having people who believed in me enough to offer their support gave me a leg up. I want to do that for others. I think this world would be a better place if more people reached out to help others."

He was quiet for so long that Samiah glanced over at him to make sure he was still paying attention. He was. He stared at her with a hint of wonder in his eyes.

"What?" she asked.

He shook his head. "You're just... you're really different from this other person I know."

It didn't take a degree in computer science to figure this one out. "I assume you're talking about an ex."

He nodded and shrugged. "Joelle wasn't big into doing for others," he said. "As in, she *never* did anything for anyone else. Hearing how important it is to you to give back, it just reminds me that not everyone is out for themselves all the time." The corner of his mouth tipped up in a sad yet adorable grin. "Like you said, the world would be a better place if more people thought that way."

"What are you doing tomorrow?" she asked before she could stop herself or consider the question's implications.

His forehead furrowed. "Just hanging out at my crib."

She should end the conversation right here. Just play the question off as mild curiosity or making small talk.

"Why don't you get yourself some hiking boots after work today. There's a nice trail in Bastrop I think you'd enjoy."

Or just ask him out.

"You sure about that?" His eyebrows nearly touched his hairline. "You don't want to do a few more lunches together? Maybe get to know me better before sneaking off to the woods with me?"

She glanced over and fought to curb her body's reaction to the devilish smile tracing across his lips. "I think I can trust you."

Whether or not she could trust herself around him was an entirely different matter.

CHAPTER TWELVE

Y ou're not getting tired on me already, are you?"

If there was a way to capture the pure delight radiating from Samiah without seeming like a creep, Daniel would have taken the picture with his phone already. She'd been tossing those teasing grins his way all morning, along with the jabs about him lagging behind.

Why would he want to catch up with her? This vantage point afforded him a magnificent view of her tan shorts stretching deliciously over an ass that, up until now, he hadn't given himself permission to fully appreciate. He was all too happy to stay a couple of steps behind.

"I can handle whatever you throw my way," Daniel returned.

"Oh really?" She winked. "We'll see about that."

She picked up speed, charging up the winding, well-trodden path that cut through the dense cluster of towering bald cypress and sycamore trees. He'd been amused by her attempts to test him, suggesting they take the more demanding walking trail and setting an aggressive pace from the very outset. As far as Samiah knew, he was a lifelong computer geek who spent most of his time behind a monitor. He'd own up to being a computer geek, but he'd also spent months trekking across the shrubland of Djibouti with fifty pounds of gear strapped to his back and a Marine Corps–issued M16A4 rifle nestled against his chest.

Still, a vigorous hike was a vigorous hike. They were both puffing for air by the time they broke free of the thick trees and came upon an outcropping of limestone that jutted out over a rushing stream.

"Holy shit, this is beautiful," Daniel said.

"Onion Creek," Samiah said. "Worth the hike?"

He glanced over and had to catch his breath at the portrait she created. The sun filtering through the wispy clouds cast a warm glow over her profile, making her sumptuous brown skin even more alluring. The urge to reach over and run the backs of his fingers along her cheeks—still flush from their hike—overwhelmed him.

"Absolutely," he said.

She turned to him, and all the fantasies he'd tried his hardest to suppress slammed to the forefront of his mind. Curbing the impulse to lean into her and taste those lips he'd dreamed about for weeks took a strength he hadn't realized he possessed.

Just ask her. That's all it would take. One simple question.

He already had the answer. It was staring right back at him. The lambent arousal flickering in her eyes, the way her lips parted slightly; she gave off the kind of vibe that couldn't be mistaken. Three weeks of steadily escalating flirtation had to lead to something. Maybe this was it. This moment when they were finally alone, away from all distractions, from every hindrance that could get in the way of exploring where the undeniable attraction between them could lead.

All he had to do was ask.

But then, in the pulse of a heartbeat, Samiah seemed to come to her senses. Her eyes widened and she took several steps to the left, increasing the distance between them.

Daniel ran a hand down his face and sucked in a shallow breath in an attempt to gain back some of the control he'd lost.

What in the hell was he doing? Was he *trying* to earn the top spot on Lowell Dwyer's shit list? Or worse, get himself pulled from this case? If his supervisor knew about what he was up to this morning, Daniel had no doubt he'd have him on a plane to Virginia by this afternoon.

Peering out over the creek, Samiah cleared her throat and asked, "So, um...how are you adjusting to Trendsetters?"

"It's been...surprising," he said, giving her an honest answer for once.

She regarded him with a curious quirk to her brow. "Really? How so?"

"It's just not what I'm used to." Daniel shrugged, picking up a quarter-size chunk of limestone and pitching it into the water. "The atmosphere is so different from all the companies I've worked for in the past. Most sit you in a plain gray cubicle and expect you to spend the day slaving behind a computer screen. It's all about what you can produce. Trendsetters puts a lot of effort into building a sense of cohesiveness among their employees. I like it. You don't see that everywhere."

"How many places have you worked?" she asked, an incredulous tinge to her laugh. "You make it sound as if you've been with a dozen companies already."

"No, no. Not a dozen." More like *two* dozen.

Dammit, he knew better than to allow that kind of slipup. The average twenty-eight-year-old software engineer with his academic background would have had approximately two-point-five employers at this stage of his career, not counting a couple of internships. It was the opposite of typical to have completed four years in the Marines and another two infiltrating companies engaged in white-collar crimes.

He should never have put himself in the position of having to discuss his employment background. The less details he shared, the better.

"Hey, I don't know about you," Daniel said, needing to change the subject, "but I could use a little sustenance before we get back on the hiking trail." He slipped a hand in the side pocket of his cargo shorts and pulled out his secret weapon. "Can I interest you in a snack?"

Samiah burst out laughing at the sight of the granola bar.

"How could I say no to that?" she said, her grin a reminder of why it was so hard to say no to this... this thing that had blossomed between them.

They settled down on the massive gnarled roots of an old cypress. Daniel held her hand as she found purchase before taking a seat next to her.

"So, where did you work before Trendsetters?" he asked, handing her a granola bar. Because she wasn't a subject, the dossier on Samiah had been pretty high level, covering her academic background and the various roles she'd held at the company, but he didn't have anything on her career prior to Trendsetters.

"I worked for one of the other tech companies in the city right after grad school, but that lasted less than a year. I started at Trendsetters three years ago." She held her hands up. "And I know what you're thinking. 'It took you *that* long to finish grad school?'"

"Hey, I understand. Grad school is no joke."

"Actually, I went to summer school and carried a full workload so that I could finish a semester early, but that's only because I got a late start. I earned a degree in education before I found the courage to tell my family that I didn't want to follow in my parents' footsteps."

He stopped in the middle of tearing the wrapper from his bar. "You were going to be a teacher?"

She shook her head, but took a sip from the plastic water bottle that had been strapped to her hiking belt before answering. "No, I was never going to be a teacher," she said.

After it became obvious that she had no plans to elaborate, Daniel asked, "So why . . . ?"

She lifted a long, spindly branch from the ground and began drawing curlicues in the soft earth.

"Even as I sat in all those early childhood education classes, I knew I wasn't going to teach. I've known that I wanted to work in the tech industry—and not just as a computer science teacher—since high school." She released a sigh. "But I didn't want to disappoint my mom and dad. They were both teachers. My sister is a teacher who went ahead and married a teacher. Education is a big deal in my family."

"I get that," he said. Pursuing higher education and military service were a given in his family.

"Anyway, I stuck with it so that I'd have the degree. My dad has this saying: The world will always need teachers and nurses, so as long as you have a degree in either of those fields, you'll always have a job."

"Nursing?"

"Hard pass. The sight of blood makes me queasy." She

tilted her head. "Come to think of it, I have the same reaction at the thought of teaching a bunch of fourth graders."

Daniel shook in an exaggerated shudder, drawing a laugh from her.

"So, you went through four years of undergrad, got your degree in education, and then did it all over again to earn the software engineering degree?"

"At least I already had the prerequisites out of the way," she said with a shrug. "And because I absolutely *loved* what I was learning, it was way more interesting the second time around."

His gaze fixed on her profile, he wondered how many layers there were to her that he had yet to uncover.

"I think you would have been an amazing teacher," Daniel said. "But it would have been a waste. You kick ass at your job."

"Thank you."

"Seriously, you're amazing. I've watched the other lead engineers, and not a single one has the kind of command over their team that you do. I hope Trendsetters realizes how lucky they are to have you."

"Oh, believe me, they do. I know *exactly* how valuable I am, and I make it a point to remind them on a regular basis. I am the rarest of rarities: a diversity unicorn."

"A what?"

She ticked items off on her fingers. "I'm young, black, female, and I know my shit. I check off nearly all of the diversity boxes. I'm worth more than gold to companies that want to show how incredibly 'inclusive' they are."

The sarcasm dripping from her words gave an indication of just how she felt about that.

"But there's more to it than just checking off boxes," he said. "They wouldn't have hired you just to fill some quota."

"I did say that I know my shit," Samiah said, her grin the very definition of cheeky. But the earlier lightness in her eyes had dimmed. "I've earned every single bonus and promotion I've ever received. But, still, it can be exhausting."

"How so?" he asked.

She stared contemplatively at the surrounding foliage. After several weighty moments drifted by, she pointed the branch she held to a spot on the ground. "Do you see those ants?"

Daniel looked to where she pointed. It took a second for his eyes to adjust to the monotonous color palette, but he finally made out the ants walking in a single-file line through the terrain of fallen leaves, slippery rocks, and disturbed earth.

"Yeah, I see them," he said.

"You see the ones carrying the pieces of leaves? Their burden has to be ten times their body weight, yet they're faithfully carrying it, because that's just what has to be done." She pushed at a rock impeding the ants' path. "That's my existence. The pressure to be perfect is overwhelming."

"No one expects you to be perfect."

She looked over at him, her expression indulgent, as if pandering to a naive child. "How long have you been in this industry?"

"Long enough." Daniel nodded, feeling a touch foolish now that he realized where she was going with this.

"I'm sure you've suffered through a few uncomfortable moments as a person of color in the tech industry," Samiah said. "What you've experienced? Multiply that by ten and it'll give you a taste of what I face on a daily basis. Women in general have a hard time being taken seriously in this industry, but a black woman?" She huffed out a humorless laugh. "We're not expected to be good at math and science. We're not expected to understand lexical analysis, or method overloading or any of the concepts that we all work with every single day. It feels as if I'm living under a microscope, Daniel. As if I'm expected to fail at any moment." She pointed to the ground. "And like that ant, I'm carrying the weight of so many others on my shoulders."

"But why would you put that kind of pressure on yourself?"

"It's not as if I *asked* for the pressure, but I can't pretend it's not there. If I mess up that gives Owen Caldwell the excuse he needs to ignore the résumé of every black woman that comes across his desk. He can simply say that they tried it, but the last one they hired didn't work out. Why should they take a chance on another?" She put a hand up. "And I am not overreacting. I've seen it happen before."

He wanted to refute her words, but how did he know if what she was saying wasn't the absolute truth? Like every other industry, the tech world could be a shitty place. He'd had a few thinly veiled remarks hurled his way while under-cover at various software companies. He'd brushed it off, knowing he wouldn't be around long enough to make calling it out worth his time.

But he'd never had to consider how his performance on the job could affect the chances of those coming up behind him. He couldn't imagine having to shoulder that kind of pressure day in and day out.

"I'm sorry to unload on you like that," Samiah said. "My sister is the one who usually suffers through my venting. It's just...it's a lot."

"You don't have to apologize to me, Samiah."

He was the one who should be apologizing. He was the one lying to her face. Confiding something so intimate required a level of trust he didn't deserve from her.

"If you ever need to vent, I'm here," Daniel said. "That goes for more than just venting. Whatever you need, just ask."

"Thanks for the offer." The grateful look in her eyes made him want to offer her the world. "You can start by throwing the next flash competition."

He pitched his head back and laughed, grateful for the levity after their heavy conversation.

"I don't know about that," Daniel said. "What if the next prize is cupcakes from that place that sells out within the first hour every day?"

"Oh, if that's the case I'm willing to fight you for it."

He bumped her shoulder with his. "How about we share?"

Her eyes dropped to his mouth, the corners of hers curving up in the most enchanting of smiles.

"Deal."

* * *

Samiah thought she'd be on time for once, but true to form, she was the last one to arrive for the weekly meet-up with Taylor and London. At least she had a good excuse this time. Because London had only a couple of hours between shifts, they'd decided to meet near the hospital where she worked. Dealing with Austin rush-hour traffic—something Samiah normally avoided at all cost—would make anyone late. And in need of a drink.

"I swear I tried to get here on time," Samiah said, placing

her purse with the others on the lone empty chair. "Did you all order already?"

"I had to," London said. "I need to be back at the hospital by seven."

"I thought you had two hours before your next shift started. Did a surgery get moved up or something?" Taylor asked.

She shook her head. "The only time I perform surgeries at night is if they come through the emergency room. I need to head back early because I'm meeting with a couple of the other doctors before my shift starts. We're having a powwow about some bullshit going on at the hospital."

The bite in London's tone was so unlike her. "So, that sounds serious," Samiah said. "Is it?"

"It has the potential to be." She dipped a fried eggplant into marinara sauce and swirled it around, but then set it back on the plate uneaten. "It has taken me longer than it should have to recognize that bureaucracy and red tape can literally kill people. And there are some who just don't care. The bottom line means more, regardless of how much it adversely affects patients. I just..." She shook her head. "This is not what I signed up for. I became a doctor to *help* people. To help *children*."

In the short time she'd known her, Samiah had already become accustomed to London's mordant, sometimes dark sense of humor. Case in point, last week, when she shared that she'd lost a patient. Despite her obvious pain, she'd managed to smile through it, and by the time dessert rolled around she'd had them all laughing to the point that they drew stares.

But *this* London? This was the first time she'd seen *this* London.

It was a striking reminder that they all bore crosses when it came to their respective careers, some heavier than others. London's was no doubt the heaviest of all. Not only did her work have life-and-death consequences; she was under more professional scrutiny than Samiah could imagine.

She'd run across articles of people accomplishing extraordinary things in their respective fields, but unless it had something to do with tech, Samiah usually scrolled past it. It wasn't until she'd looked into London's background that she discovered her new sister-in-catfishing-notoriety was a legitimate rock star in the world of pediatric surgery.

She'd lost count of the number of Ones to Watch lists bearing the name London Kelley, MD. Not only was she featured on just about every medical website Samiah found having to deal with pediatrics, but there had been over two dozen articles in medical journals that London had authored.

The fact that she'd given Craig Walters the time of day was a testament to just how slim the pickings were when it came to Austin's dating scene. Craig wasn't worthy enough to check London's coat at the door, let alone date her.

It also made London's current demeanor that much more jarring. Her normally imperturbable calm was absent.

"I don't know anything about dealing with hospital bureaucracy, but if you need a shoulder to cry on or someone to just listen while you rage a bit, I'm here," Samiah told her.

"Me too," Taylor added. "And if you need to work out some frustration, I suggest kickboxing. I'll even be your sparring partner."

"Thanks," London said with a strained smile. "Although sex would be a much better strategy for relieving my frustration."

"Sorry, can't help you with that one," Taylor said. "Tried it with a girl once and it just wasn't for me."

She'd only known her a couple of weeks, but Samiah already knew not to be surprised by anything Taylor said.

"Well, that's enough about the bullshit I'm dealing with at the hospital," London said. "What about you two?" She gestured to Samiah with the eggplant she'd just picked up again. "Anything interesting happen with you this week?"

I wanted to make out with my coworker in McKinney Falls State Park.

"Same old, same old," Samiah answered.

She was not going to feel guilty about keeping Daniel a secret. Honestly, what was there to tell? That they'd had lunch together? That she'd made him an ice cream sundae? That she'd spent every night this week dreaming about them screwing like bunny rabbits along the trails they'd hiked last weekend?

Nope. Not gonna share that.

But after much internal debate, there was something Samiah had decided to share with her two new friends.

"Actually, I do have some news," Samiah said, dabbing her lips with a napkin. "Remember when I said I was going to find a hobby during this six-month dating hiatus? Well, I've decided to use my time to work on something else. It's something I've been toying with off and on for a few years now." She turned to Taylor. "And I have you to thank for bringing it back to my attention."

"You are very welcome," Taylor said. "Now what am I taking credit for?"

Samiah surreptitiously sucked in a breath before saying, "I'm developing a phone app to help facilitate platonic friendships for people moving to new cities."

There. It was done. After years of keeping it to herself, she'd spoken the words out loud to other humans. There was no turning back.

"Well, not just for people moving to new cities," she further clarified. "It's for anyone really, but the concept first popped into my head after I moved to Austin. You mentioned how hard it has been for you to make friends since moving here, and it reminded me about this idea I'd had. I think it's time I see it through."

"I'd use it," London said before popping a fried gnocchi into her mouth.

"Umm..." Taylor held up her phone, a grimace twisting her lips. "Sorry to burst your bubble, babe, but there are a bunch of apps like that already."

Samiah shook her head. "Not like mine."

She expounded on the commercial element her idea would bring to the friend finder app market, using Taylor's personal fitness venture as an example.

"Holy crap, that's phenomenal!" Taylor said. "I am *so* in! I want to be your first vendor!"

"Give me a minute to actually create the app first," Samiah said. She was damn near giddy at their enthusiasm.

Her hesitancy at sharing her idea with anyone, even her sister, was twofold. Samiah knew once she broadcasted her plans, she would feel compelled to follow through with them. Not only to follow through, but to succeed at the highest level. She would not tolerate anything less than world domination. But there was so much more to it than that.

Divulging the premise for the Just Friends app made it susceptible to being poached by anyone with a working knowledge of software design—or with enough money to hire someone with the knowledge. She'd built up a healthy measure of mistrust over the years, due in part to having her ideas usurped by coworkers like Keighleigh Miller. She counted every painful stab in the back as a hard lesson learned and had vowed never to let it happen again.

She thought about Daniel, and how she'd been so close to telling him about her app during their time at McKinney Falls. Yet, even with this budding, several-steps-past-friendship thing slowly building between them, Samiah couldn't risk sharing her idea with him. If she gave a detailed explanation about the technology behind Just Friends at this table, Samiah would bet her beloved Mustang that Taylor and London's eyes would start to gloss over before she even got to wireframes and back-end structure. But a software engineer with Daniel's level of expertise? He could have the app on the market before she had a chance to present it to a single potential investor. She couldn't take the chance.

And that's why she needed to honor the pact she'd made with these two and put dating on the back burner. Getting involved with Daniel—with anyone—right now would only result in her not putting all her heart and soul into her app. If she was going to prove that she could do this, she couldn't allow anything to distract her.

And daydreaming about Daniel Collins had become one helluva distraction.

CHAPTER THIRTEEN

Daniel finished off the final number string, pressed ENTER, then sat back in his chair as he watched the coding he'd worked on all morning materialize into a flawlessly designed personnel management portal for one of Trendsetters' smaller clients. Who would have thought accounting software could be so damn sexy?

The rush he experienced had become familiar in the time since he'd started this job. This was his twenty-second undercover operation with FinCEN, but it was the first that had allowed him to do the kind of work he would have been doing if he'd chosen another career path. It wasn't too late. If he stepped away from his job with the Treasury Department, Daniel had no doubt he would have his pick of positions at some of the top firms in the country. That wasn't cockiness, that was knowing what he brought to the table. With the experience he'd gained working for FinCEN, along with his military background, he could command a quarter million a year and potential employers would consider it a bargain.

But it just wasn't in his heart. He appreciated the opportunity to sit at this computer every day and indulge in his first love, but duty to country had been instilled in him at an early age. He could never be truly happy if he ignored that call to serve.

"Hey, Daniel, did you hear what happened to Mike?"

He looked up from his monitor to find Jerry Johnson standing before his desk with the wide-eyed excitement of someone who'd had too much coffee and not enough sleep.

"Umm, no. Who's Mike again?"

"Mike Epsen. Tall guy with the glasses."

He'd just described one-third of Trendsetters' workforce, but okay.

"I think I know who you're talking about," Daniel lied. "What happened to him?"

"Got hit by a bus."

He blinked. Hadn't been expecting that. "Excuse me, he what?"

"I guess I should say his bike got hit by a bus. It clipped the rear tire and sent him tumbling onto the side of Barton Springs Road."

"Is he okay?"

"Six broken ribs, broken collarbone, and more bruises than they can count, according to his wife."

Damn. Must have been a hell of a fall. "With all the bike lanes here, you'd think a bike rider would be safe," Daniel commented.

"I know right?"

The crazed, wired look in old Jerry's eyes was starting to freak him out.

"Well, thanks for letting me know, man," Daniel said. "I appreciate it." He pointed at his computer screen when Jerry didn't make a move to leave. "I need to get back to this."

"Yeah, yeah. I hear ya. I've gotta get back to work too."

Daniel had just donned his headphones in hopes of dissuading the Jerry Johnsons of the office from bothering him further when his cell phone rang. The ringing abruptly stopped, then was immediately followed by a text message:

Sorry, right number. HQ

It was the code he and his counterpart back at FinCEN, Preston August, had devised to alert the other when there was an urgent need to connect. The HQ meant that he was to call FinCEN's headquarters in Virginia.

Daniel grabbed his jacket and told Jamie at the front desk that he needed to make a quick run to the convenience store across the street. He'd come up with a list of excuses to leave the office in case of emergencies such as this one. It wasn't easy. Trendsetters provided so much for their employees that his usual excuses—latte runs, a need for over-the-counter meds, even trips to the post office—weren't applicable.

Once outside, Daniel used his encrypted cell to call into headquarters. He asked to be patched into Preston's phone, pacing back and forth between two parking meters as he waited.

"August," Preston answered after several intermittent beeps.

"It's Collins. What's up?"

"Vegas is going to happen."

Daniel stopped walking. His heart began to pump at twice the normal rhythm. "How do you know?"

"How do you think I know?" came Preston's sarcastic reply. Guess it paid to be married to the daughter of the head of the org's enforcement division.

"Don't hold me to this," Preston continued. "But I'm pretty

sure it's between you and Bryce when it comes to the lead. If you want this job—and you *want* this job, Daniel—you need to get Austin wrapped up ASAP. I gotta go," he finished, ending the call without giving Daniel a chance to respond.

Waving away exhaust from a passing souped-up dual cab pickup truck, Daniel perched on one of the steel bollards that lined the sidewalk in front of the building and stared down at his phone.

Vegas was the one he'd been waiting for since he'd started at FinCEN two years ago. Rumors of money laundering between an intricate network of off-the-strip casinos, bail bondsmen, and check-cashing outfits had been floating around since before he joined the bureau. It was the kind of job that made an ordinary agent a legend.

He wanted it. *God* did he want it.

And he didn't want Bryce to get it.

"That asshole," Daniel snorted.

He couldn't even hear the man's name without getting pissed. Bryce Stewart had been his nemesis since the day Daniel started at FinCEN, which had been only three months after Bryce signed on. Top of his class at Annapolis, then on to Pitt where he'd finished with a perfect record, Bryce strutted around FinCEN with his chest out, like the rest of them should be grateful that he'd deigned them worthy enough to work with.

The man had become damn near apoplectic when Daniel strolled in with his Phi Beta Kappa key and Stanford degree, and just as much praise—if not more—than Bryce had garnered. Daniel had never been overly competitive. He didn't care if the Marine next to him was able to run a more impressive four hundred, or if he wasn't the fastest at writing code. He'd always been content to just put his head down and focus on his work.

Bryce was the one who'd made this into a competition, and now Daniel was borderline obsessed with getting the best of him.

Vegas was the prize. Everyone knew it, and everyone knew what it would mean to whomever was tasked to run it.

"I have to get it," he whispered.

But he wasn't going to get anything if he didn't solve his current case.

He went back inside and caught the elevator up to the twenty-second floor. He cut through the Sales Department, dodging a Texas-shaped stress ball being tossed back and forth by a couple of guys he still didn't know by name. When he turned the corner, he caught sight of Justin Vail standing at his desk.

Why was his supervisor waiting at his desk?

"Hey, Justin," Daniel said. "Sorry I wasn't here. I had to run out for a minute—"

Justin waved him off. "Don't worry about it. Can you come into my office? I need to ask you something."

A weight as heavy as a solid brick of gold settled in Daniel's stomach.

Oh shit oh shit oh shit.

Had he been made?

He'd been extra diligent about covering his tracks this past week. Yesterday, when he'd had his best opportunity yet to breach the Cybersecurity Department, after he'd found the room's coded doorlock hadn't latched completely after the last person entered the room, he'd decided against it. The risk of getting caught had been too high. It turned out to be the right decision. The head of security had walked out just a few seconds later. Daniel had managed to play it off, but maybe he hadn't been as convincing as he'd thought. Had someone become suspicious?

By the time they reached Justin's office, Daniel had chosen the story he would use out of the five he and his team back at FinCEN had devised were someone to make him while on a job.

"I—" he started.

"Did you hear about Mike?" Justin cut him off.

Mike?

"Yeah, I did," Daniel said. "Jerry Johnson just told me. Sounds as if Mike's lucky to be alive."

He really needed to figure out who this Mike guy was.

"I went to the hospital to see him yesterday," Justin said. "He's in good spirits, but in a lot of pain."

Daniel nodded in sympathy. It would be nice to know what any of this had to do with him. Did Trendsetters have some program for helping injured employees that they wanted him to get some training on like everything else?

"I'd like you to take Mike's place on a new project that's starting up," Justin said, putting to rest his speculation. "I know the two of you aren't in the same department, but given the work you did at Four Corners Technologies, I think you'd be a good fit."

Daniel did a mental rundown of the various jobs on his résumé. Four Corners Technologies. India. Quality control analyst.

"What's the project about?" he asked.

Justin gestured for him to follow. "Come with me. The new team is getting together for their initial kickoff meeting."

Daniel followed him out of the office and into the larger, more traditional conference room. About a dozen people from various departments sat around the table. Justin nodded to John Kim. "He's agreed to join," his supervisor said. Then he turned to the others.

"With Mike out for the duration of this project, I've asked Daniel to come on as his replacement. Daniel did Quality Control on a previous project for a defense contract with the DOD. To be honest, even if Mike was available I would still bring Daniel in. He's a good match for this team.

"As you all know, this project sprung up quickly, and has a very short, four-week turnaround, so things will move at a pretty good clip. John will serve as co-captain." Justin paused as the door opened. "And here's our other co-captain."

Daniel's stomach bottomed out. At the same time his heart skipped a beat.

Samiah walked into the conference room looking like his favorite daytime fantasy come to life. Her strawberry-red jacket cinched at her waist, and she didn't have to turn around for him to know that the fabric of her skirt stretched perfectly over her equally perfect ass.

"Now that Samiah is here, we can get started," John said. He turned to her. "Good news. Daniel is going to take Mike's spot. One of us can catch him up to speed once we're done here, but I'm sure he'll be able to step right in."

"Undoubtedly," Samiah said. She inclined her head toward Daniel. "Welcome to the team."

His heart did that triple-time beating thing again. So much for trying to keep his distance from her while on the job.

Yet that wasn't the biggest hiccup when it came to his current situation. Last night, while discussing the near disaster that happened outside of Trendsetters' Security Department with Quentin, they'd both agreed that instead of breaching security, the smarter move was for Daniel to get placed on the Cybersecurity team. He'd intended to start implementing the plan he'd come up with today by planting a security glitch into a small vulnerability he'd discovered in one of the projects he'd been working on, then bringing the solution to his supervisor. Being put on this new team was an unexpected curveball.

But what recourse did he have? Because he was new to the company, being placed on a special project team so soon into his new job would be seen as a huge leg up to the average employee. If he wanted to look suspicious, all he had to do was turn down such a prestigious honor.

He would have to find a workaround. Maybe he could stay late. He could simply say that he didn't want to leave his other team members in the lurch, so he was putting in some extra hours to cover his work on his other projects.

"We all know how this works," John was saying. "It's full immersion time. Whatever you were working on prior to coming to this meeting, put it out of your head. Other team members on those projects will tackle the workload."

Fuck. Was the guy reading his mind?

"We have a finite number of days to develop, test, and implement this software, and it will require one hundred percent of your time and effort," Samiah added.

The sound of her voice alerted Daniel to his most immediate issue, figuring out how he would work so closely with Samiah Brooks without losing his ever-loving mind.

CHAPTER FOURTEEN

Booyah!"

Samiah looked up from her laptop and had to clamp her lips together to stifle her laugh.

If sexy and adorable had a baby together, the result would be Daniel Collins. He sat huddled at the table they'd commandeered in the break room/kitchen area, that zippered Phillies hoodie he loved so much shielding his eyes.

"Does anyone even use that saying anymore?" she asked.

"What saying?" His eyes remained on his computer screen.

She shook her head. "Never mind. I forgot who I was speaking to." Going by his music taste, his head was probably filled with stale phrases from the nineties.

Her eyes narrowed as she regarded the excitement dancing in his eyes. "Are you even working over there?" She leaned forward, stretching toward his end of the table. "Will I see a video game on that screen if I come over to your side?"

"Why would I need to play a video game when working in Kotlin is so much more fun?" He stopped typing and removed the hood. "That has to be the coolest shit ever. What other programming language is this seamless?"

"You do realize if you say that to anyone outside of this

office they'll look at you as if you've grown a second head, right?"

"People do that already." A thousand Adderall-addicted butterflies began to dance in her belly at the sight of his teasing grin.

Daniel shoved his hand in the brown paper bag filled with house-made potato chips that came with the sandwiches they'd had delivered and popped one in his mouth. Leaning back in his chair, he said, "So, tell me something. When a company comes to Trendsetters with a project like this, that it needs completed in a short amount of time, is there an extra fee for the rush job?"

"Definitely," she answered. "A big one."

His brow arched. "How big?"

"Stupid big, to use phrasing you'd understand."

His intoxicating grin broadened and Samiah immediately started thinking of other slang she'd heard when binge-watching old episodes of *The Fresh Prince of Bel-Air*. If that's what it took to elicit that smile, she was game.

"You can get an idea of how big the fee is based on the manpower that's required. The Leyland Group is paying an obscene amount of money if they have both John and me working as co-captains." She closed her laptop to preserve the battery as she assumed his pose, leaning back in the chair and crossing her arms over her chest. "And I'm not sure if you were told this, but there will be a bonus for being a part of the team. Trendsetters doesn't keep all those extra earnings. They spread the wealth to the employees who helped to make it happen."

"Just when I think this company can't impress me more." He shook his head. "Now I understand why the turnover rate is so low. Once you land a job here, why would you ever want to leave?"

As they sat there chatting, the pact she'd made with Taylor and London gnawed at her conscience. This was so unfair. How could she have known just one day after that impassioned, hungover speech she'd made in her living room that Daniel Collins would walk through the doors at Trendsetters and become her scrumptious new obsession?

After the shit she'd been through when it came to dating, how could anyone expect her to turn a blind eye to the undeniable attraction brewing between them?

It had been hard enough to resist him after their near kiss on the hiking trail. Now that they were working on the same team? Forget it. Resistance was for exercise bands and political activists. Not for a single woman who had to work with this delicious human being day in and day out.

But, dammit, the fact that she didn't *want* to resist him was exactly why she *should*!

Her pact with Taylor and London was only the tip of a giant iceberg of reasons why she should absolutely fight this attraction to Daniel. She'd just had a mental debate over whether she had the time to devote to new friends. How much more of her energy would a brand-new relationship cannibalize? And that didn't take into account the overtime she would have to put in over these next few weeks while working on this new project.

No. She couldn't do it. She could *not* allow herself to get caught up in anything beyond the lighthearted flirting they'd engaged in so far. Anything else would take way too much time away from working on Just Friends. Now that she was done with her feasibility assessment and had moved solidly into the prototype development, every spare moment was precious.

Of course, when it came to reasons she should absolutely, without a doubt, not even consider dating Daniel Collins, the boyfriend project pact she'd made with Taylor and London, and the time she needed to work on her app, paled in comparison to the big, fat elephant in the room.

In this *actual* room. This room where they *worked* together. As *coworkers*!

There was no formal policy prohibiting interoffice relationships, but Samiah got the sense it was frowned upon, especially between supervisors and subordinates. She could recall the gossip floating around Trendsetters not long after she arrived, about a former supervisor who'd started a relationship with a programmer. There was never an official reprimand, but that gossip had lasted for months.

She wasn't *technically* Daniel's boss, but as team co-captain on the Leyland Group project, it placed her in a position of authority. She could not ignore the potential hit her reputation would take if word got out that she was getting extra friendly with the hot new guy at the office.

Then again, fuck it. She spent these past few weeks at the center of the juiciest gossip to hit the Trendsetters offices in months. What was a little more?

Daniel turned his attention back to his computer, but she continued to study him from her side of the table. After several minutes passed, he lifted his head, a wary look in his eyes.

"What?" Daniel asked.

She wanted to bring up the near kiss but knew better than to do that while they were both in this big, empty office all alone. Instead, she thought about something else from their time at McKinney Falls.

"The other day, while we were hiking, you mentioned how quickly I've advanced in my career, but the same can be said for you. Based on the office grapevine—"

"I'm part of the office grapevine?"

"You're practically the vineyard. At least among a certain population. The female population," she clarified. "And according to that grapevine, you were in the military before going to college and graduating at the top of your class from Stanford. Are you some kind of whiz kid or something?"

"Or something," he said.

She tapped her fingers against her lips. "I don't think so. I think you *were* the whiz kid. I'll bet you were one of those brainiacs who graduated from high school at fourteen."

"Sixteen."

Her eyes widened. "Sixteen?"

"I never said I wasn't smart." He shrugged. "But I don't think I qualify as a whiz kid. I finished high school a year early and enrolled in Carnegie Mellon. I got a few semesters under my belt before I enlisted, and then transferred to Stanford once I put in my four years with the Marines."

"Why the Marines?" She held up a hand. "And please, please, *please* tell me it's because you love their uniforms."

He grinned. "Those are some sharp threads, aren't they?"

"Did you just say sharp threads?" She laughed. "You listen to nineties rap music and talk like someone out of a seventies sitcom."

"Hey!" His injured look was cuteness personified.

"I'm sorry," she said. "I think it's adorable."

"Now *that's* interesting," he replied, his voice dipping an octave. "I take it adorable is a good thing in your book?"

Her gaze dropped to his mouth and the way it curved up ever so slightly at the edge. She pulled her bottom lip between her teeth and nodded. "Adorable is a very good thing."

Slow down, girl.

It may be impossible, but she should at least *try* to resist him just a little bit longer. Maybe.

She took a sip of her watered-down iced latte. "So, how does a semi–whiz kid end up in the Marines?"

"Same way a software engineering genius earns a degree in early childhood education. Family tradition."

"Touché," Samiah said. "How many years were you a Marine?"

"Once a Marine always a Marine," he said, sounding like a commercial for the armed forces. "But I officially served for four years, which is certainly *not* the tradition in my family. Everyone else is career military, from my great-great-grandfather all the way down to my mom and dad."

"Your mom?" Samiah slammed both her palms on the table and gasped. "I can't believe I just asked that. See how deep this patriarchal bullshit runs? *Of course* your mom was military. Why the hell wouldn't she be?"

"Not only is she military, but she has a higher rank than my dad. They met when they were both stationed at a base in South Korea, which is exactly where her grandparents met when my great-grandfather was there fighting in the Korean War."

"They met at the same place your mom's grandparents met? That is too amazing not to be made into a Netflix movie."

"That's nothing. The *really* crazy part is that my mom

grew up two towns away from my dad, but they didn't start dating until years later, when they were halfway around the world. Even crazier? For three years in a row, while they were both in high school, they competed against each other in the statewide science fair."

"Stop it. I can't stand the cuteness of this story." She put her hands up. "The important question is, who won in the science fair?"

"My mom. All three times they competed."

"Yes," she said with a fist pump.

His dimple reappeared, and just like that, she was toast. She shouldn't even try fighting this attraction. What was the point?

"When they met again at the base in Korea, my mom had no idea who Dad was, but he remembered her the moment he heard her name. She'd been his nemesis throughout high school, but he'd also had the biggest crush on her."

"Oh, my God." Samiah flattened her palm against her chest. "I love this story so much. The only thing that can make it more perfect is if she still has her science fair trophies and makes him polish them once a month."

"No." He chuckled, shaking his head. "The trophies are long gone, but she loves to tell that story." He sobered, his amusement mellowing into a reflective wistfulness. "It's been a while since I saw them. I'm way overdue for a trip back home."

"Or maybe you should invite them to come down to Austin?"

"That's not a bad idea. It would be a great escape from those Philly winters."

She drew curlicues in the condensation that had collected on her cup. "Were they upset when you left the Marines?"

"Not necessarily because I left." He looked over at her, a hint of embarrassment in his tone. "My mom didn't approve of *why* I left."

"Let me guess." Samiah rolled her eyes. "A girl."

He nodded, but didn't elaborate. She tried to convince herself for a half second that she wouldn't pry, but who was she kidding?

"Will you force me to ask the obvious question, or will you just spit it out already?"

His laugh echoed around the empty office space. "I'm not sure which question is most obvious."

"Throw some answers my way and I'll tell you if you're hot or cold."

"Okay." He nodded. "We were together for about six years, off and on, but that's not all that unusual when one half of the couple is enlisted and then goes off to California to finish school. That answer enough for you?"

"You're warm."

"We broke up about eight months ago."

Eight months wasn't very long considering they were together for six years, but it was long enough for him to have gone through a few rebound women.

And just why are you worried about his rebound ratio?

Because being a rebound girl sucked. That's why.

Samiah still wasn't sure she wanted to be his anything, but if being his rebound chick was a part of the scenario, she knew she didn't want any part of it.

"Am I still just warm," Daniel asked. "Or am I hot yet?"

Soooo fucking hot. But that's not what he meant.

"You're a quick wash off in the tub kind of hot. I'm looking for a nice, long soak with a really good book kind of hot."

"The hot that scalds a normal human being. I don't know how you women can sit in a tub of boiling water."

"Because we're not babies," she said. "And since you apparently can't figure out the obvious question, I'll just come out and ask it. Why did you and your ex-girlfriend break up?"

He set his elbows on the table and rubbed his hands together. After a lengthy pause, he finally said, "She didn't agree with my career choice."

Samiah frowned. "But you left the military for her. Or did I interpret that wrong?"

"Nope, you got it exactly right. She asked me not to reenlist. Said she wanted me to do something safer."

"So what was her problem? What could she possibly find unsafe about you being a software engineer?"

"She didn't have a problem with that part. She had a problem with me choosing to return to Philly instead of staying out west to make the big bucks in Silicon Valley. My well-being wasn't nearly as important to her as the well-being of my future stock portfolio."

"Ouch." It couldn't be easy to discover that someone you'd given six years of your life to was only in it for the money. "Did you consider doing what she asked? I know Silicon Valley isn't for everyone, but it's a pretty common dream in our industry."

"It wasn't for me." His shoulders lifted in a dismissive shrug. "As I think back on our relationship, I've come to the realization that Joelle and I weren't as compatible as I thought we were. I'm now convinced that the only reason we lasted as long as we did is because I was gone most of the time."

Samiah tried to read between the lines, but this was a hard one. On the surface he seemed at peace with how things had turned out. Would that still be the case if she looked deeper? She wasn't sure she wanted to.

"I guess it's better that you figured out it wasn't meant to be before you did something that would be harder to walk away from," she said. "Like marriage."

"In six years we never came remotely close to discussing marriage. We never really moved in together. I spent most of my time with her when I was home, but I still had my place and she refused to give hers up." He snorted. "That was probably the biggest indication that things would eventually end. And once our relationship was over, I felt freer than I had in years. She's a huge part of the reason I'm here in Austin now. This is all a part of my clean break."

"It seems as if your ex-girlfriend's loss is Trendsetters' gain," Samiah said. "I think we owe her a debt of gratitude."

His brow lifted in a casual arch. "Is that the only good thing about me being here? That it's a benefit for Trendsetters?"

His voice held a silken challenge that coasted along her nerve endings, sending ripples of pleasurable awareness scampering across her skin.

Samiah shook her head. "No. That's not all."

Her eyes dropped to his lips. He pulled the bottom one between his teeth and her nipples grew tighter than fine-tuned piano strings. With his eyes still locked on hers, he released the catch on his chair and rolled it to her side of the table.

Was this really about to happen?

The better question was, should she *let* this happen? She'd already cataloged the myriad reasons she should pull away. Forget crossing the invisible line on inappropriate sexual behavior in the workplace; the moment her lips touched Daniel's, all of the *rah-rah, I am woman, hear me roar, I don't need a man to make me happy* bullshit she'd fed Taylor and London wouldn't be worth a damn thing.

She didn't care. Her tingling nipples told her this kiss would be worth it.

Leaning forward, Samiah wrapped her fingers around the back of his neck and brought him in close. The moment their lips touched, her expectations were confirmed.

So. Totally. Worth. It.

The first few moments were as chaste as a couple of seventh graders stealing a kiss at their first junior high dance, but within seconds they'd reached horny-high-schoolers-going-at-it-underneath-the-bleachers status. His tongue pushed past her lips, advancing on her like she imagined he advanced on enemy lines back when he was a soldier. She was no match for him.

Samiah concentrated on the feel of his soft yet firm, extremely kissable lips. And that tongue; the way it flicked and teased and moved in ways that awakened parts of her that had gone dormant. Her body's awareness heightened with every succulent stroke of it.

It had been way too long since she'd been kissed like this, like the other participant actually gave a damn about her enjoyment of the act. His tongue ebbed against hers, pushing inside once again, sending wave upon wave of sensation crashing through her. It seemed instinctive the way their mouths moved together, her lips demanding more just as he became more urgent.

His enticing chest beckoned, so she pressed herself against him, frenzied excitement shooting through her as her sensitive nipples met his lean, toned muscles. Even as she mentally warned herself to slow down, Samiah abandoned her chair and straddled his lap, her skirt riding up her thighs. His worn denim jeans felt like heaven against her skin, gently abrading her inner thighs as she positioned herself on top of him.

Pleasure surged through her, an intense knot that started deep within her belly, then fanned out like a wildfire throughout her body. She braced her hands on either side of his frame, flattening them on the table. Then she deepened their kiss, plunging her tongue in a rhythm that matched the rocking of her hips.

He palmed her ass, squeezed and caressed it, his deft fingers kneading her with just the right amount of pressure to elicit a strangled moan from deep in her throat.

Stop this, a warning voice rang out in her head. *Not here. Not now.*

"We have to stop," Samiah said against his open mouth.

"I know," he replied.

Yet neither of them made an attempt to break apart. Daniel shoved one hand in the hair at the base of her head while he used the other to pull her even tighter to him.

It would be so easy to take this to the next level. To pull her skirt up to her waist, draw her panties to the side, and invite him inside her aching body.

And that's when she finally pulled away. She could not, *would* not, go there.

Ragged breaths struggled to escape her lungs, which burned with the need for oxygen. Samiah knew she looked like she'd been hit with a boulder.

It was only fair. That's exactly the way she felt.

CHAPTER FIFTEEN

Daniel pulled a pair of sweatpants over his basketball shorts and zipped up his fleece hoodie. He walked out of the bathroom, into the living room, and just shook his head. Quentin sat on the sofa in a short-sleeved T-shirt.

"Are you sure you're not going through some kind of male menopause or something?" Daniel asked.

"I've always been warm-blooded." Quentin looked over his shoulder and chuckled. "Dramatic much?"

"Nope." Daniel forced the zipper all the way up and pulled the hood over his head, cinching the drawstring underneath his chin. "I freeze my balls off whenever you're here."

"Everyone knows I like it on the chilly side. They should have warned you before FinCEN agreed to this joint taskforce." He held up several sheets of paper. "Did you notice how the Wi-Fi activity in most of the Uruguay properties escalated in July?"

"Yeah, but I didn't find it unusual," Daniel said, lifting the sheets from Quentin's grasp. "That's the heat of soccer season. Die-hard fans are willing to spend money to stream their favorite teams." He grabbed his iPad. "But it's worth making a note. The bad guys could be thinking that same thing. It would be smart to use a time when Wi-Fi activity is up to funnel more logins."

"And we've already established that the people behind this scheme are smart," Quentin said.

"Too damn smart," Daniel grunted. The iPad dinged with a notification that the department meeting with FinCEN would be starting in another five minutes. "I've got my weekly conference with headquarters. How long you plan on staying?"

"I'll be here a while." Quentin gestured toward the kitchen. "I brewed a fresh pot of coffee while you were in the shower. Grab yourself a cup. Stay warm."

He snorted a laugh. "Thanks."

He could use a cup of coffee for both the warmth and the caffeine boost. Too many late nights of trying to find a way into Trendsetters' security had him dog-ass tired. But a cup of coffee was no longer just a cup of coffee for him. There was an irrevocable association with a certain coworker tied to it. He doubted he'd ever be able to drink coffee again without thinking of his morning ritual with Samiah.

Not reaching for her again last night had been the hardest fucking thing ever. In retrospect, Daniel recognized that he should be grateful she'd had the presence of mind to slow things down. But another part of him—the part that had tortured him throughout the night by mentally continuing past the point when Samiah had stopped them—*that* part resented the hell out of the way his night had ended.

Moments after they'd pulled apart, Samiah had packed up her computer and hauled it out of the office. And he'd come back to this empty apartment. Alone.

Forgoing the coffee, he went into the computer room

and fell into the rolling desk chair. He shut his eyes tight, trying his best to quell the barrage of images barreling to the forefront of his mind at the very thought of her. He couldn't do this now. He had a video conference call in two minutes. He needed to funnel all his energy into delivering a credible explanation of why things weren't moving fast enough on this job.

Not that anyone at FinCEN had expectations that weren't being met. It was his own internal timeline that was pushing him to work harder and stress over the fact that he hadn't been able to breach Trendsetters' security.

The lack of movement on this job—on finding even one solid lead—was driving him crazy.

Yeah, that's not the only thing about the job that's driving you crazy.

He needed to focus. Until he was able to get out of his own head and do his damn job, he wouldn't be good for shit. He logged into the video conferencing software. Lowell Dwyer's melon-shaped head took up the entire screen.

"Collins," Daniel said, letting everyone know he was there.

"Hey, Daniel." It was Thaddeus Mitchum. "My ex-sister-in-law said you've got to go to a restaurant called County Line. She said they have the best barbecue in Texas."

"Bold claim for such a big state," Daniel replied.

"Bring some back with you when you wrap up this job," Thad tacked on.

Dwyer cleared his throat. "Now that Collins is here, that's everyone. Why don't we start with you, Daniel. What do you have for us on the Austin job?"

He fed them a short overview about the various Trendsetters employees he'd been looking into and how being put on the special project for the Leyland Group was both a help and a hindrance.

"The plus side is that several of those we had on the initial subject list are also on this special project team, so it gives me an opportunity to get a better read on them. There are a couple who have stuck out to me by virtue of their personalities. One guy, Jake Gorge, keeps talking about his fantasy football team and how he's hoping to win the big prize at the end of the season. I've heard a bit of gossip that he may have a gambling problem."

"One big enough that he needs to launder money to fund it?" his supervisor asked.

Daniel shrugged. "I haven't gone deep enough to ferret that out, but I've flagged him." He adjusted his monitor so that he could be more centered in the screen shot. "Of course, the drawback to being put on this new team is that I won't be able to make a case to join the Cybersecurity Department."

"That was a long shot anyway. You've got other mechanisms in place. Utilize those to infiltrate their system, even if it takes a little longer than you'd like. Remember, Collins, you don't take down an operation of this size overnight. You millennials need to learn patience."

If his supervisor caught wind of what Daniel had been doing, he would be singing a different tune. The litany of things he should be working on could fill this entire room. He had a list of potential targets to investigate. Gigabytes of files his FinCEN colleagues had managed to access awaited his review. That's what he should have been doing instead of seeing how far he could get his tongue down Samiah's throat.

He'd gotten it pretty damn far.

Fuck. Stay focused!

As the others gave a rundown of their current investi-gations, Daniel used the time to gain some control over his thoughts. He needed to get his head back in the game and stop allowing himself to get derailed from his overall goal.

"I'm sure everyone has noticed that Stewart isn't here." Dwyer's deep voice corralled his attention away from his musing. "He's gone under. He got one of the suspects in the Kolinsky case to flip. The cooperator gave him key informa-tion on how the oligarch was able to gain access to those millions of credit reports. It may be the thing that cracks this case wide open."

Daniel's muscles froze as a deep chill spread from his core throughout his entire body. While he was here in Austin doing his best imitation of the nerdy love interest in a rom-com, Bryce Stewart was kicking ass and taking names on his undercover investigation. Why not just hand the Vegas job over to him right now?

There was more at stake than simply one-upping his office adversary. This job was his opportunity to prove that he'd chosen the right career path. If he closed his eyes, he could hear Joelle's voice in his head, telling him that he was wast-ing his skills working in the public sector. Those words had affected him more than he was willing to admit. His need to show her—to show himself—that he'd made the right choice when he joined FinCEN was as important to him as getting the best of Bryce.

And just like that, Daniel knew what he had to do.

When he arrived at Trendsetters the next day, he was refocused and ready to tackle the tasks Lowell Dwyer had entrusted him to complete. His original game plan had been to devote 40 percent of his time to doing Trendsetters' work and the other 60 percent to ferreting out whoever was behind this money-laundering scheme.

Somewhere along the way, he'd lost sight of his goal. The allure of playing around in all these cool coding languages, falling into the routine of a normal tech-world job, had distracted him from his plan.

That all stopped today.

For the next three hours, Daniel switched between the five windows opened on his monitor, all the while surreptitiously scanning the iPad that lay flat on his desk, partially obscured by several folders and printouts. On the iPad was one of the databases he'd managed to infiltrate. It showed him the login data for every Trendsetters employee, which allowed him to track how long they were accessing the system both at work and remotely.

With this information he could record the IP addresses and have the guys back at FinCEN run them. If anyone sought entry into their work files from a remote address while abroad, it would give him an idea of who was possibly allowing someone else to get into their system. It wouldn't be the smoking gun they were looking for, but it was a valuable data point.

Daniel was so focused on work that he didn't hear Samiah's approach. She tapped him on the shoulder, causing him to jerk to attention.

His body's reaction to her touch was instantaneous, his skin growing hot and tight. He looked up and was catapulted back to last night and the exquisite feel of palming her curvy ass.

Holy. Fuck.

Daniel cleared the lust from his throat before answering, "Hey." He removed his headphones and let them hang around his neck.

"Are you actually doing the impossible?" Samiah asked. He frowned, not following. "Working without coffee," she clarified with a laugh. "You didn't get any this morning."

"Um, yeah." His chuckle held a lot less amusement than hers had. "I came in extra early. Got my cup before you even got here."

"Oh." Her head reared back slightly. "Okay. Well, what do you feel like eating for lunch? I'm in the mood for a burger. Maybe we can grab sliders at that pub around the corner?"

Daniel removed the headphones from around his neck and set them on the desk. He'd rather strut down the hallway in nothing but combat boots than do what he was about to do, but it was necessary. He'd succumbed to too many distractions already, this preoccupation with Samiah being the most intrusive.

"I know it was my idea to have the standing lunch date, but I'm not sure that's the best thing anymore," he said. "This new project is going to have all of us busy. I think it's better if I just grab a quick bite here at my desk and work through lunch these next few days."

He immediately felt like a steaming pile of elephant shit.

Her brows shot up before dipping into a deep V with her frown.

"Okay," she finally said. "I guess that makes sense." There was a crispness to her voice that hadn't been there before. "Although, I don't see why bouncing ideas off each other over a couple of burgers wouldn't be considered working."

God, he hated this.

"It's just . . . it's not a good idea," Daniel said.

The seconds that ticked by were some of the most uncomfortable of his life. Her shoulders straightened, her chin lifting as she stared down at him. If not for the nerve jumping in her stiff cheek, Daniel would have thought his words were no big deal.

"Fine," she said. The word was clipped. Final.

With that she turned and started back toward her office.

"Samiah—" Daniel called in a voice that was barely a whisper.

Letting her walk away was the smart move here. The *only* move. Hell, he could subvert Trendsetters' security tomorrow and see this job come to an end. What would he say to her then? Sorry about lying to you? We'll probably never see each other again, but thanks for lighting my world on fire with that kiss, and for paying my salary with your tax dollars?

Yeah, that would go over well.

He put the headphones back on and returned his attention to his computer screen. He needed to finish up this Austin job so that he could move on to the next. It would be better for everyone.

* * *

Samiah pitched her head back and gloried in the rays of sunshine streaming through the trees overhead, welcoming the warmth on her face. She'd happened upon the rarest of rare finds, an empty bench in what was possibly her favorite spot in the city, the Japanese garden in the botanical gardens at

Zilker Park. An oasis in the middle of the city, teeming with brightly colored flowers, willowy trees, and ponds filled with lily pads, this was the place she came to when she needed to get outside of her own head and just exist.

She definitely needed it today.

She balanced the pen and steno pad on her knee, and read over the impressive list of ideas she'd brainstormed in the short time she'd been out here. She'd debated whether she wanted to bring anything work-related to her favorite sanctuary, especially while on her lunch break, but decided that when it came to her app, this was the perfect spot to work. She didn't want Just Friends to feel like a job. It should bring joy.

She was due a little joy after the sour taste left in her mouth yesterday following Daniel's rebuff. It had hurt, but she was no longer angry.

Okay, so she was a little angry, and maybe just a bit confused.

She'd prepared herself, knowing things would now feel different between them. You didn't spend several minutes with a guy's tongue down your throat without expecting a shift in how you interacted with each other. But that complete one-eighty? No, she hadn't expected that.

His brush-off had bruised her already tender ego, but it had also been the wake-up call she'd needed. After ending her relationship with Craig, the last thing she should have done was walk into this thing with Daniel.

She had yet to define exactly what it was that had blossomed between them over these last couple of weeks. A few lunches and a single weekend of hiking—something she'd wanted to do anyway, but could never find someone to do it with—did not a relationship make. That kiss, however, had placed them well past the friendly coworker mark.

That kiss.

When she looked back on this period years from now, she would be able to pinpoint the moment they'd taken a wrong turn. If it weren't for that kiss, this thing with Daniel wouldn't be anything more than a really nice friendship with a dose of lighthearted flirting thrown in.

In a perfect world, they could forget about that kiss and go back to being friends. But the world wasn't perfect. Although that kiss had been close.

She closed her eyes and sucked in a slow, calming breath, seeking the peace she'd found when she'd first happened upon this bench.

Maybe if she gave it some time, gave herself a little space, she could approach Daniel with an offer of friendship and nothing more. It was something to consider.

But not yet. She was still too deep in her feelings to entertain thoughts of being his friend.

Her phone vibrated with a text. She slipped her phone from her jacket pocket and her heart jumped into her throat at the sight of Denise's number. Samiah immediately calmed herself down. If there was an emergency with the baby, her sister or Bradley would call instead of texting. Goodness, she was going to give herself a heart attack if she didn't stop jumping into worst-case scenario mode every time she heard from her sister.

You free to talk? Denise's text read.

Instead of texting back, Samiah called. "Hey, what's up?"

"Hey," came her sister's surprised greeting. "I didn't call because I didn't want to disturb you if you were in a meeting."

"Nope, we're good. I'm taking an extended lunch break. What's up?" she asked again.

"I need a favor."

"It's too early to ask me to babysit."

"Har har," Denise said with a snort. "Although, now that I think about it, this is another form of babysitting."

"What is it?"

"Bradley is teaching eighth graders this year, and part of the curriculum is job shadowing. One of his students, a little girl named Tomeka, is really great at math—nearly genius level, according to Bradley—and she wants to be a software engineer when she grows up."

"Yes," Samiah said.

"I haven't asked you yet."

"You're going to ask if she can shadow me at work, and the answer is absolutely yes."

Samiah could practically hear her sister's relieved smile through the phone.

"Thank you so much, honey. I just know it would be so powerful for her to see someone who looks like her working in technology. Not just working in it, but killing it."

The pride blossoming in her heart was so overwhelming Samiah feared it might burst. To hear her big sister, the woman she'd looked up to her entire life, describe her in that way had a greater impact on her than any praise from the powers that be at Trendsetters could ever have.

"However, there is a slight issue," Denise tacked on, the hesitancy in her voice causing Samiah's *oh, shit* antennae to perk up.

"Job Shadow Day is tomorrow, and Tomeka's parents share a car, and her dad works all the way in Kyle. So she needs someone to pick her up and bring her back to school. I would do it, but you know what the doctor said about me driving."

"No," Samiah said. "You're not driving."

The million and one things cluttering her desk demanded that she make an excuse for why she couldn't do this, but she ignored it. She would get it done, even if she had to stay at the office until midnight. This was too important.

"I'll handle it," Samiah said.

"Awesome. Bradley will make sure you're placed on the authorized pick-up list," Denise said. "Tomeka will be so excited. Do you have any idea how much this will mean to that little girl?"

As a matter of fact, she did. She'd been that little girl. She'd been an eighth grader who'd excelled at math and science and loved learning how things worked. But instead of encouragement, many of her teachers had sought to impede her dreams of entering the tech field. How often had she been berated for thinking too highly of herself, of not being realistic in her aspirations? What a difference it would have made if she'd had a peek into what life could be like for her as a young black woman working with computers day in and day out.

No one should have their dreams discouraged the way hers had been. If not for her stubbornness, and an overpowering desire to prove wrong anyone who'd tried to discount her abilities, she likely would have allowed them to sway her. How many other young women of color saw their dreams succumb to a similar fate?

Not on her watch. Not anymore.

"Just give me the details on when and where to pick her up and I'll be there," Samiah said. "I'll make sure Trendsetters lays out the red carpet for her."

"Thank you again, hon. Love you," her sister said.

"Love you too." She ended the call with Denise and saw a text had come through from Taylor. She'd written one word in all caps: EMERGENCY.

Samiah's stomach dropped as she immediately hit the call button.

"Hey," Taylor answered in a hushed voice.

"What's going on?" Samiah whispered. "Where are you? Are you okay? Have you been kidnapped?"

"Kidnapped?" Taylor asked, her voice now at a normal level.

Samiah sat up straight. "Hold on. Why were you whispering a second ago?"

"Because the lady next to me in line is all in my business," Taylor said. "I know you were listening to my last phone call," Samiah heard her say somewhat distantly, as if she'd pulled the phone away from her mouth. A second later, she said, "So, what's up?"

"You tell me what's up," Samiah said. "You just texted emergency in all caps."

"Oh, yeah, that. So, I have a meeting with this woman in Bee Cave today," she said, referring to a suburb just west of Austin. "She's in charge of some kind of homeschooling consortium type thing. I think it's just a bunch of rich parents who pooled their money to start their own school because they don't want their kids attending public school. Anyway, she wants to hire me to teach phys ed three days a week."

Samiah brought a hand up to her head and rubbed her temple. "Is that what you call an emergency?"

"Well, she needs to know by this afternoon," Taylor said. "The problem is, I'm not sure I want to commit to something like that. But if I don't take the job, she has someone else she's going to offer it to." Her dramatic sigh had Samiah rolling her eyes.

"I don't know what to do," Taylor continued. "What if I accept her offer and I don't like it? And it will definitely eat into the time I've set aside for my boyfriend project. I have less than six months to get my shit together before I find Mr. Perfect."

Was this what it was like to have a little sister? Had she put Denise through this over the years?

"So, do you have any advice?" Taylor asked. "I didn't want to bother London, but I really needed to talk this through with someone I can trust."

"Oh, so it was okay to bother *me* at work, but not London?"

"Well, you're not literally saving the lives of sick children." She had a point.

Retrieving the steno pad from where she'd set it on the bench, Samiah flipped to a fresh page. "Let's come up with a pros and cons list. It's always the first place I start. Think about what you would be giving up if you took this job, then list the pros and cons and decide if it's worth it."

"Is it really that simple?"

"Sometimes," Samiah answered. "Don't make it any harder than it has to be."

"You're right," she said, her relief evident in her voice. "And to think I almost emailed my older brother to ask his advice on this. That would have been a disaster."

"How so?"

"You don't want to know the details. Just trust me, it would have ended in me smashing my phone on the ground. Thank goodness I now have actual friends I can bounce ideas off of," she said. "Okay, I'll talk to you later. I've got a pros and cons list to write up."

"Good luck," Samiah said before ending the call.

Considering how close she'd come to ghosting them, Samiah couldn't get over just how much she'd come to appreciate her new sisters-in-arms. It begged a question she hadn't thought to ask, but one she couldn't help but contemplate based on what happened yesterday. With Taylor and London in her life, did she even need Daniel Collins's friendship?

Their morning coffee ritual had come at a time when her ego and heart needed a boost, but what had once been a pleasant diversion had become a distraction she couldn't afford. Case in point, the twenty minutes of her lunch break she'd spent thinking about him instead of working on her app. She was falling into the same trap she'd gotten caught in before.

His rejection yesterday hurt, but she was slowly coming to realize that it was for the best. Her focus should be on her goals. She would make sure it was from here on out.

CHAPTER SIXTEEN

Securing his headphones over his head and pulling the drawstring of his hoodie tight, Daniel tried to block out everything and everyone around him. The atmosphere in the office today was too damn cheerful; it clashed with his shitty mood. There were office-wide high fives going around for the Sales team, who'd just landed a contract with a national coffeehouse chain, one Trendsetters had apparently been courting for months. Then there was the cake and coffee celebration for those with birthdays in September, which he should have been happy about—who in the hell didn't like cake?—but all that did was remind him that he wouldn't be here to share in the monthly celebration when his birthday rolled around.

But what had caused the most excitement around the office today was a certain munchkin-size visitor who seemed to be charming the pants off every Trendsetter employee she came in contact with. Samiah had arrived with the young girl just before lunchtime—what was once *his* time. Everyone had lost their minds, as if they'd never encountered a cute kid with a beaming smile and bubbly personality before.

Daniel had watched as surreptitiously as possible as Samiah took her on a tour of the office. She'd played around on the computers and even sat behind Barrington's desk so she could have her picture taken.

They now stood just two desks down from him, at Amy Dodd's station. He hadn't seen their approach; he'd felt it. The sensation that rushed along his skin whenever Samiah was near had alerted him.

The middle schooler—Tomeka—enthusiastically nodded at whatever Amy had just said. She raced to the other side of the desk and sat in front of the computer. Samiah looked on like a proud auntie.

She'd ignored him all day. Although Daniel wasn't sure what he would say if she actually *had* talked to him. What about his situation had changed between the moment before he'd kissed her and now? Nothing.

He was still here to do a job that required him to lie to her. A job he shouldn't allow himself to get distracted from. A job that would possibly be in jeopardy if his superiors found out that he'd kissed her the other night.

The difference, of course, was the DEFCON levels of agony he'd experienced since he'd turned down her invitation to lunch. How had he not realized just how much he would crave her? He'd become as addicted to seeing her smile in the morning as he was to the coffee he no longer allowed himself to have for fear of running into her at the coffee bar.

This is why he needed to concentrate on the job at hand. The sooner he solved this case, the sooner he'd be out of here. And out of this misery. At least that's what he'd been telling himself. He knew it was naive as hell to think he would just forget about Samiah the moment he left Austin, but he was going with it.

Daniel felt a tap on his shoulder. He lifted his headphones

from one ear and looked up at Morgan, who thankfully had halted her pursuit of him.

"What's up?" he asked her.

She hooked a thumb over her shoulder. "Amy's calling you."

He removed the hoodie and swiveled his chair around toward Amy's desk. Samiah stood there with an expression he couldn't quite name. Disinterest, maybe?

"What do you need?" he directed at Amy.

"Tomeka is learning JavaScript. Why don't you come over and show her the trick you showed me?"

Daniel noticed Samiah visibly stiffen at the suggestion. *Shit.* Had he really messed things up so badly that she didn't even want him around her?

He considered coming up with an excuse so that he wouldn't ruin her day by invading her space, but they couldn't avoid each other forever. Their team was set to meet in an hour to discuss progress on the Leyland Group project.

"Sure," Daniel said. "Give me a sec." He saved his work then went over to Amy's, trepidation traveling along his spine as he approached. Samiah remained stoic, her expression unreadable.

"Daniel, this is Tomeka Sanderson," Amy said. "She's shadowing Samiah for the day and wants to create video games when she graduates from college."

"That's a pretty cool job," he said. "Which games are your favorites?"

As the girl rattled off an extensive list of popular video games, Daniel tried to get a read on Samiah. She didn't seem angry, which was a relief. Neither did he sense any acrimonious vibes from her. She seemed . . . indifferent.

That wasn't good. Not at all. He'd rather her curse him out or slap him in the face, anything but apathy.

It was no less than he deserved. He'd spent these past few weeks shamelessly flirting with her because she was so fucking smart and beautiful and funny, all the while knowing that nothing could ever come of it. He'd strung her along. Which made him a class-A piece of shit.

He quickly guided Tomeka through JavaScript, then returned to his desk, not wanting to subject Samiah to his presence any longer than necessary.

Their avoidance dance was prolonged yet again after the status update with the Leyland Group project was postponed to Monday. Daniel had remained at his desk all afternoon, his head bent over the keyboard as he counted down the minutes until he could leave. Computer monitors throughout the office systematically went dim as, one by one, his coworkers closed up for the night. Some would be back bright and early tomorrow morning, despite it being the weekend. He would do the same. Maybe tomorrow would be the day he breached Trendsetters' security and found the break he needed in this case.

He got up for a bottle of water and noticed a glow coming from Samiah's office. She'd switched the glass-paneled walls to frosted, but he could see her outlined behind the desk.

Should he go to her? Did he even have the right? Why would she entertain anything he had to say after the way he'd blown her off? And why should he try when he knew he could be gone at any minute? It was selfish, bordered on cruel.

Yet, none of that mattered.

Call him selfish, but right now his singular mission was easing the ache that had gripped him and wouldn't let go. Whether she told him to piss off or found a way to forgive him, he had to at least try to make things right with her.

He went back to his station and locked his computer.

Pulling in a deep breath, he started for her office, rapping his knuckles on the door twice when he arrived.

"Come in," she called.

Daniel entered, but her attention remained focused on the papers strewn about her desk.

"Hey," he softly called.

Her shoulders stiffened, but she didn't look up. "Yes?"

He shifted his feet, shoving his hands into his pockets. He hadn't felt this nervous since the time his old master sergeant caught him and a bunch of his fellow Marines at a strip club near Pendleton.

"I...umm...I'm sorry to disturb you, but can we talk?"

She finally lifted her gaze to his. Her face remained a mask of indifference. "What do you need?"

He closed the door behind him before moving toward her desk. Once there, he found himself at a loss for words. Should he just admit he'd fucked up, fall to his knees, and beg for forgiveness?

"I wanted to apologize," he said. He waited for her to speak. She didn't. The atmosphere in the office grew a thousand times more uncomfortable.

Daniel swallowed and tried again. "I'm trying to come up with the right words here, but I'm worse at this than I thought."

Samiah brought her elbows up on the desk, clasped her fingers, and rested her chin on them.

"Let me give it a try," she said. "Now, the last thing I want to do is speak for you, however, if *I* was the one apologizing, it would go something like this. 'Dear Samiah, I am *so* sorry for acting like a jerk after spending the last three weeks openly flirting with you.'"

He started to speak, but she held up a hand and continued.

"'And, yes, I know that *I'm* the one who went in for that kiss, but things got a little too real, so I pulled away like a coward. It must suck to have someone treat you that way, and I feel like a complete dick.' How was that? Does that apology work for you?"

Daniel shoved his hands deeper into his pockets and swallowed hard. "Couldn't have said it better myself."

The last two minutes would have been easier to endure if her declamation had held even a hint of humor. It hadn't. She was pissed.

This was hard. And awkward. And exactly what he deserved.

"Did that apology work for *you*?" he asked, turning the question back on her.

She dropped her hands and pushed away from her desk. "You don't owe me any apologies, Daniel."

"Yes, I do." He walked up to her desk. "And you're right, I do feel like a dick."

"So what happened?" She threw her hands up in the air. "Why did you all of a sudden decide I wasn't good enough to have lunch with?"

Shit. He shut his eyes and pitched his head back.

"That's not what I think, Samiah." He hated that he had to continue this lie, but what choice did he have? He couldn't tell her about the reprimand he would face if his real boss discovered what he was doing.

He settled for a partial truth.

"Look, I know this is no excuse, but I'm still a bit gun-shy after everything that happened with my ex." He held his hands out in a plea. "Yours is the only real friendship I've made since moving to Austin and it would kill me if I've ruined it." Regret lodged in his throat, but he swallowed past it, desperate to make this right. "Is there any way possible that we can still be friends after this?"

She continued to stare at him with that blank, impassive air about her. After several excruciatingly painful moments passed, she leaned back in her chair, folded her hands over her stomach, and said, "You have all the nerve in the world, do you know that?" She huffed out a breath and shook her head, but then shocked the hell out of him when she said, "I guess we can try."

Daniel was afraid to trust what he thought he'd just heard.

"Is that everything?" she asked.

"Umm...yeah." He nodded, the tension in his body slowly ebbing as the strain in the room began to recede. "Thank you."

Her smile was pleasant enough, but it didn't reach her eyes. She shut down her desktop and retrieved her purse from the bottom desk drawer.

"Are you calling it a night?" Daniel asked.

"Yes." She stood, pulling the purse strap over her shoulder. "I have a standing date on Friday evenings."

The lump of unpleasantness that lodged in his throat nearly cut off his air supply, but he swallowed it down like nasty medicine. If there was one thing he didn't have the right to feel, it was jealousy.

"Have a good time," Daniel said. At least he didn't choke on the words.

"Thank you." She looked at her reflection in the now blank monitor and smoothed a hand over her flawless hair. "I always do."

The effort it took to stand there and watch her ready herself for a date with someone else nearly killed him. He accepted it as his penance for being an asshole toward her.

She walked past him, leading the way out of her office, but instead of following, he called, "Samiah, wait!"

She turned. Daniel's heart thumped against the walls of his chest as he approached her. He expelled a deep breath, then admitted, "What I said a few minutes ago? That was a load of bullshit. I don't want to be just a friend to you. That's not even close to what I want.

"This." He gestured between them. "This wasn't supposed to happen. I came to Austin to start fresh. I was supposed to lose myself in my work and not allow anything to get in the way of that." He huffed out a laugh. "But then I saw you making coffee, and everything I *thought* I wanted went out the window."

He swallowed hard and decided to go for broke.

"I want more than friendship. I shouldn't. It goes against all the ground rules I set for myself when I moved here. But I can't help but want more of you."

She was silent for so long he wasn't sure if she was ever going to answer. Pregnant, nerve-racking moments ticked by, the air covered in a thick layer of unease.

"You're not the only one who wasn't looking for this to happen," she finally said, both her tone and gaze tinged with accusation. "You know the shit I've been through recently. *Everybody* knows the shit I've been through." She shook her head. "I didn't want this either. This was supposed to be *me* time. I made a promise that I would focus on myself and not bother with society's bullshit expectations about having a man in my life."

His throat tightened with the realization of just how badly he'd messed things up. These past couple of days had apparently given her the chance to put things into perspective and recognize that she didn't need *him* distracting *her*. If that wasn't the most ironic bite in the ass.

"But, dammit, I like you."

Daniel's head popped up at her declaration. "What?"

"I like you too damn much for my own good," Samiah said. "I would love to tell you to go to hell, but instead all I want to talk about is how I couldn't help but think about you when I heard someone in my building playing the Beastie Boys yesterday."

His lungs expanded to the point of pain as gratitude overwhelmed him. Daniel had to stop himself from leaning forward and tasting her lips.

"I don't want to like you this much," Samiah said.

"I promise not to make you regret it," he replied.

This time, her smile reached her eyes. "Maybe we can take things a bit slower? You have to admit that sucking face while at work was pretty unprofessional."

Laughing, he reached for her hand, his heart swelling with unexpected emotion when she allowed him to take it.

"I want whatever you want," he said. "You set the pace and I'll follow."

"I think I can handle that," she said, her eyes softening. "But I still need to go." She released his hand. "Taylor and London will be waiting for me. We have a standing date on Fridays. I don't want to be late."

Taylor and London?

He had no right to the bone-melting relief that rushed through him, but damn if it didn't nearly bring him to his knees.

"See you back here on Monday? I'll be at the coffee bar," she said.

"Unless you want to meet sooner," he countered before he could stop himself.

Fuck! Didn't she just say she wanted to go slow?

"What did you have in mind?" she asked, her eyes narrowing slightly.

He lifted his shoulders. "I'd planned to come in tomorrow and do some work on the Leyland Group project."

"I'm working on it this weekend too," she said. "But I was going to work from home." She pulled her bottom lip between her teeth. "You can come by. Just to work," she quickly added.

Breaking out into the MC Hammer dance would be the corniest thing ever. But, then again, she seemed to find his fascination with old-school-rap cute.

"I'll bring lunch," Daniel said instead.

"Deal," she replied with a firm nod. "Oh, there's an Asian fusion place up near the Triangle that makes the best Korean short ribs. I've been craving them for ages."

"You're joking, right?" Daniel said with a frown. "The only way we eat Korean is if I cook it."

"You cook?"

Daniel nodded. "Just tell me when and where."

"I'll text you my address." Her subtle grin left him breathless as he watched her walk away.

Once back at his desk, Daniel sat for a long moment, running all the different ways this could go wrong through his head. Getting even more involved with Samiah was the last thing he should be doing. He knew this.

But he'd be damned if he cared.

* * *

Samiah spotted Taylor sitting alone at their favorite high table and gave herself a mental high five for not being the last one to arrive for once. She would never be first. She'd learned that Taylor was one of those *you're on time if you're five minutes early, you're late if you're on time* kind of people. It had to be that military upbringing. That's probably why Daniel always made it to the office before she did, even on the mornings when she did clock in on time.

The corners of her mouth drew up, and she realized just the thought of him brought a smile to her face.

Oh, God. She *so* hated herself right now. When had she become this girl?

For one thing, she shouldn't have forgiven him so quickly. He deserved to sweat a while longer. At the very least she should have let him go on thinking that she had a real date tonight.

She'd caught his reaction when she mentioned that she had plans. That beautiful, well-pronounced jawline betrayed him, stiffening in response to her announcement. As if he had any right whatsoever to be jealous when *he* was the one who'd gone all "we should just be friends" on her.

Her nails bit into her palms as the anger of the last few days crept back in, yet, in an instant, her heart grew all melty at his charmingly awkward apology.

Samiah rolled her eyes. She'd totally become *that* girl.

But she kinda liked it.

"Over here!" Taylor waved her over. "London had to take a phone call," she said, pointing toward the door that led to the bar's outside patio.

Well, damn. Guess she'd have to take away that mental high five.

"Have you all ordered yet?"

"Ceviche, a cheese plate, and those fried Brussels sprouts that are to freaking die for. Oh, and margaritas, of course. Watermelon's okay, right?"

"It's my jam," Samiah said.

"Are you ready for this?" Taylor asked. She flattened her palms on the table and released a deep breath. "I decided to take the homeschooling job."

"Wow. Really?" Samiah's eyes widened. "Tay, are you sure—"

"Hey! About time you made it," London said, cutting her off. She rounded the table, giving Samiah a hug before climbing onto her chair just as the waiter arrived with their tapas and margaritas. "So, did she tell you about her new job as a schoolteacher?" London asked, popping a crispy Brussels sprout in her mouth.

"Not a schoolteacher," Taylor argued. "It's basically what I'm doing now, just with clients all under four feet. And they're paying me two hundred bucks a class! That's six hundred a week! Twenty-four hundred a month."

"Yeah, not to brag, but I got all As in math," London said.

Taylor stuck her tongue out at her. "Well, I didn't, so let me flex my quick addition skills for a minute." She took a sip of her margarita before continuing. "Seriously, guys, do you know what I can do with an extra twenty-four hundred dollars a month? And for only three hours of work per week? I couldn't pass that up."

"But it's not only three hours. You have to take time to plan out the classes, then do the evaluations on the back end," Samiah said. "And drive all the way out to Bee Cave."

"Yeah, I know. I can handle it."

"So what does this mean for your plans to grow your fitness consulting business?" London asked.

"That's my question," Samiah said. "You're the one who came up with this idea to dedicate six months to working toward our goals. As I recall, teaching phys ed to a bunch of kids wasn't on that list."

Taylor glanced down at the table. When she looked back up, Samiah detected a hint of disappointment in her eyes. She wasn't sold on this homeschooling thing either.

Samiah reached over and covered her hand. "You know, hon, money isn't everything."

Taylor pulled her hand away. "Says the one with the fancy-ass downtown condo and high-paying tech job."

Point made.

"Okay, yes, money is nice. It's great. But so is enjoying your work. How long will you continue to push your dreams to the side, Taylor? How happy do you think you'll be if you put your consulting business on the back burner for months—maybe even years?"

Taylor picked up her glass and drained it before setting it on the table with a thump.

"If it means I can make my rent, then it really doesn't matter." She lifted her shoulders in a defeated shrug. "Dreams are good and all, but a sistah got bills to pay."

"Amen," London said, holding her hand up for a high five.

Taylor reached over to slap her palm, but then pulled back. "Wait! You're a rich doctor, what do you know about bills?"

"Want me to show you what I pay in malpractice insurance and student loans?"

"Ah, okay." They high-fived each other across the table.

Samiah considered pointing out that she hadn't always lived in her fancy-ass condo. She knew what it was like to dodge phone calls from bill collectors. At one time, her parents had a script next to the telephone with the various excuses they were to give if anyone called asking about a late payment.

But that wasn't her life anymore, and she would not apologize for no longer having to fret over how she would keep the lights on.

Still, Taylor's struggle was a stark reminder of just how lucky she was. Now that she'd completed the prototype and moved into the design phase of her app, it was costing more time, money, and brainpower than she'd anticipated, but Samiah couldn't imagine how much harder it would be to do this work while also worrying about how her mortgage would get paid.

She had zero excuses when it came to realizing *her* dream. She'd better not squander it.

After getting refills on their margaritas, the conversation turned to the phone call London had been on when Samiah arrived.

"You should have seen the transformation," Taylor said. "She went from my homegirl London to Dr. Kelley in two seconds flat. And from what I can tell, Dr. Kelley does not play."

"No, she does not," London said. "I'm ready to start kicking asses and taking names all over that hospital. They're driving me crazy." She took a healthy sip of her drink, before continuing. "Although, I do have something I need to confess, ladies."

"What?" they both asked.

"I almost gave my goodies to this cute locum tenens anesthesiologist who worked at the hospital this week."

"*What?*" Samiah screeched.

"Details," Taylor said.

"First, tell us what a locum whatever is?" Samiah asked. "Is that some kind of special pediatric anesthesiologist or something?"

"No, it just means he came to the hospital through a

staffing service, and thank God his was a short-term contract. If I had to endure another week of staring at those scrubs stretching across his perfect little ass I don't think I would have been able to stop myself from tackling him. Last thing I need is to get written up by HR for harassing a cute doctor who's five years my junior," she said. "I have enough problems with hospital management as it is."

"I can relate," Samiah muttered.

London and Taylor both stared expectantly at her.

"You can?" London set her elbow on the table and cradled her chin in her palm. "How so?"

Great. This should teach her to keep her side comments to herself.

"Okay, I guess it's my turn to step into the confessional," Samiah said. "I've kinda been seeing someone at work." She put her hands up before either could speak. "Okay, let me clarify. We haven't actually gone on an official date or anything. We've grabbed lunch a few times, and I took him hiking out at McKinney Falls State Park." Samiah sucked in a deep breath and then confessed in a rush, "And we kissed while working late at the office. And, oh my God, it was so good. And I'm *so* sorry!"

"Sorry?" London asked. "Sorry about what?"

"Yeah, what are you sorry for? You better get it where you can, girl! Gimme some!" Taylor held her hand up for a high five.

"Wait, wait, wait. What's going on here? What about the boyfriend project?" She pointed to Taylor. "You laid the ground rules. No dating for six months while we all work on ourselves so that when we are ready to find a man, we really are ready. I feel like I'm breaking the sisterhood pact or something."

Taylor waved that off. "Let me find someone who's worth

my time. I'm leaving both you bitches in the dust. Just kidding," Taylor tacked on the end. "So, this kiss? Was it the 'oh, that was nice, now let me get back to watching *Friends* reruns' kind, or the 'oh, shit, this dude wrecked me. Let me fix my hair and makeup' kind?"

"It was the 'let me run to the drugstore and buy a pregnancy test' kind."

"Hell yes!" Taylor whooped.

"It's been too damn long since I had one of those," London said. "All right, tell us about him. And when did this even start? We all just gave Craig the boot a few weeks ago."

"His name is Daniel and he started at my job the Monday after the video went viral." She nervously tucked her hair behind her ears. "I had absolutely no intentions of dating, I promise. It kinda just happened." She smiled. "I like him. He's sweet."

"And he can get you pregnant with a simple kiss. I'm jealous," Taylor said.

"So, you guys aren't upset that I've already broken the rules?"

"The whole point of this thing is finding joy," Taylor said. "And when I look at your face right now all I see is joy." With a teasing grin, she asked, "My only question is, does he have friends?"

Her lungs expanded with gratitude.

"So what does this mean for the boyfriend project?" she asked.

"It means that you're way ahead of us." London looked at Taylor. "I'm not sure we can call ourselves Hashtag Squad Goals if there's only one person in the squad reaching her goals. We'd better get our asses in gear."

CHAPTER SEVENTEEN

Samiah's heart started breakdancing like the people in those eighties hip hop videos she'd caught herself watching on VH1 as she approached the nondescript gray door. The excited flutter in her chest had become a common occurrence. She'd texted Daniel a couple of minutes ago to let him know that she'd arrived. Before she could knock, the door opened and he greeted her with the kind of smile one reserved for opening presents on Christmas morning, his eyes crinkling at the corners.

She held up a pink-and-brown paper sack. "I brought cupcakes. I figured if we use them as incentive, we'll get more work done."

His brow arched as he leaned forward and placed a chaste kiss on her lips. "I can think of a better incentive, but I guess cupcakes will work."

She couldn't decide if it was his voice or his words that had her panties on the verge of evaporating. Probably both.

He relieved her of her laptop case and the bag of cupcakes and moved to the side so she could enter. "Come in. I was just fixing us lunch."

She entered the apartment, more curious than she dared to admit. It was the first time he'd invited her to his place since they began seeing each other in earnest, a fact that had started to bug her. Samiah understood his explanation of not wanting to expose her to his mercurial roommate, but after either hanging out at her place or going out to restaurants, it was nice to finally get this tiny peek into his world.

It wasn't much.

The apartment, with its gray walls and drab carpet, was as sterile as a dentist's office. Actually, there were framed cross-stitched Bible verses hanging on the walls at her dentist's office, courtesy of his wife. This place didn't have a single thing, not even a picture of his family, displayed. Was it the roommate? Did the guy have something against clutter or sentiment or basic human emotion?

"No TV?" Samiah asked.

"I stream on my laptop," Daniel said from the kitchen. It was separated from the sparse living room by a counter that held a single fruit bowl and nothing else.

She caught a whiff of the aroma flowing from the kitchen and her mouth started to water.

"What are you doing in there?" She made her way to the kitchen.

"I wanted to treat you to a taste of home," he said, glancing up from the cheese he'd been grating into a bowl.

Next to the stove sat a plate with julienned onions and green bell peppers. Red meat, sliced so thin it was nearly see-through, rested on a cutting board, with a long loaf of bread wrapped in cellophane just to the right of it.

"I couldn't find proper hoagie rolls, but this will do in a pinch," Daniel said, gesturing to the bread.

"You're making me cheesesteak?" Samiah clasped a hand to her chest. "I feel honored."

"As you should. I'll cook Korean food for anyone who asks, but when it comes to my beloved cheesesteak? You have to be extra special to earn one of those." He leaned over and treated her to another of those sweet, delicate kisses. "And, yes, you are extra special."

She was floored by how quickly she'd come to expect those kisses. Whether quick pecks like the one he'd just given her or those that left her breathless and searching for her words, his kisses had become one of the most enjoyable parts of her day.

This was never supposed to happen.

She'd removed everything about finding a man from her checklist. It wasn't a priority, at least not for the next five or so months. Over these past couple of weeks, she'd debated back and forth with herself, coming up with all the reasons she should tell Daniel that it was better if they go back to being just friends. But she could never bring herself to follow through with it.

It was just so damn easy to be with him. Prior to him, she'd always felt a compulsion to perform. The men she'd dated all seemed to have certain expectations of her. Or maybe she was the one who'd set those expectations for herself. Either way, it felt like work. She was constantly on.

Not with Daniel. For the first time in forever, Samiah felt as if she could relax and just...be. There was no pressure, no pretense. She could just exist in this undemanding, enjoyable place they'd discovered with each other.

They ate their cheesesteaks, which she had to admit were family reunion cookout–worthy, then settled in to work. She kicked her shoes off and brought her feet up next to her on the sofa. Daniel immediately captured both feet, set them in his lap, and began to massage her soles as he continued reading through the white papers he'd been reviewing on his laptop.

She nearly orgasmed then and there, despite there being nothing sexual about his leisured kneading. It was the fact that he so unselfishly thought to attend to her needs that did it for her. It was more than any other man she'd been with had ever done. It made her wonder, had she been too lax in the standards to which she'd held her previous boyfriends, or was Daniel just that far above them?

She nestled her head against the throw pillow and allowed his magical fingers to lull her into a relaxed state as she worked on the proposal for the Leyland Group. Fifteen minutes later, she cursed her bladder for interrupting her peace.

"I hate to end this," she said, leveling herself up on her elbows. "But I need to go to the bathroom."

He gave her foot a squeeze then removed it from his lap.

"It's down the hallway, on the left." He rose from the sofa when she did, and for a moment she thought he was going to offer to show her, but then he said, "I'll get the cupcakes ready."

"Okay now," she said, holding up a hand. "I don't know how you do it in your family, but in mine we divide them up so that everyone gets to sample each flavor."

"Such a fair, diplomatic approach," he said, that adorable dimple making an appearance. "I'm used to the Marines, where it's every man for himself. And if you happen to get the cupcake another person wanted really bad, you mercilessly tease them about it."

"If I don't get a taste of that salted caramel, I may just have to hurt you."

One brow arched. "You promise?"

She was downright appalled at her body's reaction to the deep, resonant timbre of his voice.

His fingers brushed her wrist before gently capturing it and tugging. Instinctively, she wrapped her arm around his neck and pulled him closer, crushing her lips to his. He made her feel bold and playful and so many other delicious things. When was the last time she'd felt so carefree, so content? Samiah was falling in love with the person she was when she was with him.

Swallowing a mournful groan, she ended the kiss before things got out of hand. Much more of that and her favorite Rice University T-shirt would be on the floor, along with the rest of her clothes.

"Bathroom," Samiah said against his lips. She gave his firm ass a squeeze and pat. "Get the cupcakes."

She went down the hallway and opened the first door on the left.

And stopped short.

It looked like the cockpit of a spaceship. Four huge monitors and equally huge computer towers occupied two L-shaped desks that stood flush against each other. There were enough peripherals to stock a discount computer store.

"Not that one," Daniel called as he rushed to her. The excitable edge to his voice was…new. He reached around her and pulled the door closed. "Sorry," he said. "That's my roommate's. He works from home."

"As what, Captain Kirk's right-hand man? And where does he sleep? It's only a two-bedroom apartment, right?" She hooked a thumb at the closed door. "I didn't see a bed in there."

"He sleeps on the sofa. The freelance work he does requires a lot of equipment, so much that it doesn't leave room for a bed."

"That's…umm…weird. But okay."

He shrugged. "He is weird, but he's a nice guy."

Her Spidey senses went on red alert. "You didn't find him on Craigslist or something like that, did you? I know you're still fairly new to Austin. Finding a roommate on short notice couldn't have been easy."

"I didn't find him on Craigslist." His laugh was more relaxed. "He's the brother of a buddy of mine from the Marines."

Well, that explained it. It was his nature to do for others, even if it meant living with his friend's weird brother who'd rather sleep on a couch than reduce his computer usage by a monitor or two.

He directed her to the bathroom. Once done, Samiah returned to the living room to find a plate with several quartered cupcakes and two glasses of milk.

"You really do think of everything, don't you?" she said, pointing to the dessert spread. "And they all look evenly divvied up."

He raised his hands. "Hey, I'm not risking getting cut over cupcakes. We each have equal portions."

She burst out laughing as she reclaimed her spot on the sofa. She unfolded two paper napkins and gently placed one in each of their laps.

"Okay, so how are we going to do this? Do we try the same flavors at the same time, or alternate and give our opinions?"

"Alternate," he said. "You can be the guinea pig for the peppered bacon and chocolate one."

"What? You don't think that sounds good?"

"Not even a little bit."

She rolled her eyes, picked up the aforementioned sweet and spicy cupcake, and took a huge bite. Samiah did her best to school her features, but when a bit of pepper caught at the back of her throat, she couldn't help but cough.

"Okay, okay. You win," she said, gulping down milk. "This is awful. I don't know what I was thinking."

"Admit it, you were going for the shock factor."

"Maybe," she said with a laugh.

He held up one with light green frosting. "Now, this white chocolate and honeyed pistachio is more my speed."

Samiah looked on as his teeth sank into the moist cake. She suddenly found herself breathless, awareness blossoming within her chest, vibrant and wild and uncontainable.

"You have frosting right here," she said, pointing to the side of his mouth. He started to reach for it, but she caught his wrist. "Let me."

She leaned over and closed her mouth over his, scooping up the speck of sugary icing with her tongue before slipping it between his lips. A groan climbed from somewhere deep in his throat as his palm immediately wrapped around the back of her head and brought him to her. Samiah straddled his lap, clutching his face between her hands and holding him steady as their tongues teased and tarried, playfully vying for dominance in their sensual game.

His hands slid up her stomach and then over her breasts. He cradled them, gently squeezing and releasing before capturing her nipples between his thumb and forefingers and tweaking them through the fabric of her T-shirt. She felt him growing hard between her legs and it took every single drop of willpower within her not to grind against him. If she did that her clothes would melt and she'd have her naked thighs around his waist in a matter of seconds.

Wait? Was that a bad thing?

Yes, yes it's a bad thing.

At least it was for now. Sex would take this to a level she wasn't quite sure she was ready to reach.

With one last swipe of her tongue inside his insanely delicious mouth, she braced her hands against his chest and pushed away.

"Slow," Samiah said. "We're supposed to take this slow, remember?"

He let his head fall back against the sofa cushion and released a pained groan. "I remember." He lifted his head, his eyes narrowed. "We never actually defined slow. You drive a Mustang GTE. Your definition of slow has to be pretty close to mine."

"What's your definition?" she said.

"One more kiss like that and the clothes come off."

And now she needed an ice pack for her underwear.

"I can work with that definition," Samiah said.

She climbed off his lap while she still had the strength to do so and resumed her spot on the sofa. She picked up the document she'd been reviewing, resentment building with each word she read. She'd been working on this project for Trendsetters all day. It was the weekend. *Her* time. She should have been working on her app.

She'd decided to forgo any work on Just Friends when she'd agreed to work at Daniel's, still reticent when it came to divulging her concept to someone with the knowledge to take the idea and make it their own. But she no longer had that fear. She trusted him.

"Can I talk to you for a minute?" Samiah asked.

He set the glass of milk on the coffee table, slight alarm in his eyes. "About?" he said, wiping the back of his hand across his lips.

"It's nothing bad," she said. "It's actually pretty cool. At least I think it is."

Sensing his confusion, Samiah reached into her bag and took out her personal iPad. She clicked onto the app design and handed it to him.

"What's this?"

"A project I've been toying with off and on for a few years. About a month ago I decided to finally do something about it."

He studied the screen for a moment, his forehead creasing in confusion. "Is this a dating app?"

"Not exactly. It's an app for finding platonic relationships instead of romantic ones. I call it Just Friends."

Fighting off the niggle of trepidation skirting along her spine, she gave him a more detailed explanation of the app's features than she'd given to Taylor and London, knowing he would understand the technology behind the design.

"It also has its own social network," Samiah added.

"And the vendors? This isn't like the normal advertising you see on most platforms. Users will know about this up-front, right?"

She nodded. "It's one of the reasons I'm hoping users will sign up for it, because they want those curated experiences."

"This is genius, Samiah." He continued staring at the iPad with unabashed awe. "Honestly, I'm blown away."

She tried not to preen *too* much, but damn, it was hard. Humility had never been her strong suit. "Surprised no one has come up with something like this before, aren't you?"

He studied her face for a moment then slowly shook his head. "Actually, I'm not. I'm not surprised at all that you were able to conceive something no one else has thought to do." His eyes roamed her face, the brown orbs round with wonder. "I've witnessed how that brilliant brain of yours works. It's an amazing tool, one that continues to enthrall me more and more every second I'm around you."

Samiah would argue to the death that she didn't need his validation. Owning her abilities, believing in herself when others didn't—it was her thing. It was at the very heart of her identity.

But she couldn't ignore the effect his words had on her. She just didn't know what to do with it. Or how to respond without admitting that, deep down, his acknowledgment of her skills fed a part of her that was hungry for that kind of affirmation.

Instead, Samiah called upon a reliable standby. Humor.

With a sly grin, she said, "You're trying to sweet-talk your way into my pants, aren't you?"

His dimples became even more pronounced. "I'm forever trying to sweet-talk my way into your pants." He kissed her on the nose. "But I meant every word. And if you need any help with the designs or figuring out the specs, I'm here."

The trepidation she'd been fighting off meandered along her nerve endings, but before she could voice any objection, he added, "Although I understand if you want to do this on your own. You've taken it this far, you deserve to have all the glory when this app hits big."

Gratitude engulfed her, amassing like a thick cloud within her chest and causing her throat to ache.

"Thank you," Samiah said. "I appreciate the offer, but you're right, I want to do this myself. It's my baby. I want to be the one to bring it into the world."

"And when you do, it will be amazing."

He leaned forward again, this time kissing her on the lips.

CHAPTER EIGHTEEN

Samiah angled her head back against the sofa's sloped arm and inhaled a satisfying breath, filling her lungs with HEPA-filtered air, redolent with the pine-scented solution the cleaning service had used to polish her hardwood floors this morning. The moment she and Daniel returned from indulging in croissants and coffee at the café a couple of blocks over, she'd kicked her shoes off and immediately placed her feet in his lap, the move automatic.

At odd moments a reminder would pop into her head that this was not her normal. She'd become so comfortable with the routine they'd established these last few weeks, it took effort to remember a time when dating wasn't this easy. Daniel had a way about him that made everything feel relaxed and uncomplicated. And natural. Something about this felt *so* natural.

It also made her anxious to move beyond foot rubs. Their decision to take things slowly had been supplanted by her need to have those strong fingers massaging something other than her feet.

Eventually.

There were still too many factors to consider before they

took that next step. For one thing, she and Daniel had started going out only a couple of weeks ago. When it came to pleasure, she fully endorsed the idea that a woman should choose when, with whom, and which way she wanted to receive it. But as for her personal dating life, Samiah preferred to take things slow. She didn't have a standard timetable—at least not anymore—but she had to be sure about a person before she allowed things to get physical.

At the very least she and Daniel should wait until after they were done with the Leyland Group project, just in case Owen Caldwell decided to sneak a no-fraternizing rule in the employee handbook while she wasn't looking.

Yes, she should wait. Waiting was the proper thing to do—the smart thing.

Samiah still wasn't entirely convinced her reasoning held much water, but it was the only rationalization she'd managed to come up with that explained why they were on this sofa instead of in her bed, burning off the calories from breakfast in the most naked, sweatiest way possible.

She tore her focus away from the sight of the subtly defined muscles undulating underneath his T-shirt as he kneaded her soles, bringing her attention back to the laptop resting on her thighs. She'd spent an hour collaborating with Daniel on the best solution to address the Leyland Group's security vulnerabilities, but then Samiah had switched to working on Just Friends. She'd made a commitment to herself to get this app done, and she was no longer willing to compromise.

She'd been struggling with this latest design issue for days now. For some reason, whenever she tried to toggle between users, it would lock up on her.

Samiah growled.

"Hey, what's wrong?" he asked, his forehead furrowing beneath the rim of his eyeglass frames. She'd learned about the glasses only when he'd lost a contact during their hike in Bastrop last weekend. She'd asked him to keep wearing them because Daniel Collins in glasses was the sexiest fucking thing she'd ever seen in her life. He rubbed her foot. "You hit a roadblock?"

"Just a speed bump." At least when she compared it to the other headaches waiting for her. "It's driving me crazy because this was supposed to be the easy part."

She picked up the sticky-note pad and began to jot down thoughts.

"Uh-oh," Daniel said. "I know things are getting serious when you break out the Post-its."

"Ha ha." This wasn't the first time he'd teased her about her obsessive use of sticky notes. "I told you, using the different color Post-its helps to organize my thoughts when I brainstorm. I've been trying to make the transition from one user to another smoother, but it's just not happening. I can't figure out why it keeps timing out."

He glided his hand higher up her leg and looped it around to cup her calf. Giving the muscle a gentle squeeze, he said, "You do realize that no investor will expect this to be perfect straight out of the gate, don't you? It's a prototype. You're allowed to have glitches."

"No, I'm not." She shook her head. "I can't half-ass this. It *has* to be perfect."

"No it—"

"Yes, it does!" The words came out sharper than she'd intended. "Shit."

She took a moment to regain her composure, then reached

over and cupped his jaw, bearing the familiar burden of having to offer comfort when she was the one who wanted to be comforted right now.

"Look, I know it's hard for you to understand, but you haven't been in my shoes, Daniel. Do you have any idea how steep the hill I have to climb is just to get people in this industry to take me seriously? So many write me off the minute I walk into a room, or when they learn that the S in SBrooks at Trendsetters dot-com stands for Samiah and not Samantha or Sarah or some other 'nonethnic' name. I'm not a perfectionist because I want to be one, it's because I *have* to be one."

He studied her face for several long moments before softly whispering, "I get it."

It suddenly occurred to her how insensitive it was to think that he, as a biracial man, couldn't understand where she was coming from.

"I'm sorry," Samiah said. "Of course you get it. I'm sure you've had your share of similar experiences."

"No, don't apologize. I have had my own experiences, but I won't even try to compare them to what you've endured." He shook his head. "They're not the same. People don't doubt my abilities. If anything, they expect me to be better than I really am—as if the half-Asian dude *must* be a genius when it comes to computers—which I guess is the flip side of the same coin." He took her hand and placed a gentle kiss in the center of her palm. "It's different for you. You have to be twice as good to get half as far."

Her eyes fell shut, her throat thickening with a swift wave of emotion. Relief overwhelmed her; having her feelings validated brought unexpected solace to her battered soul.

"Yes," she choked out on a whisper. "That's exactly it." She opened her eyes to find Daniel's beautiful face filled with understanding. "Thank you for acknowledging it."

Samiah sucked in a deep breath, then released it. It was difficult to grasp just how freeing it felt to tell her truth without fear of being branded a complainer or excuse-maker or any of the other labels people slapped on her when she tried to explain the pressure she'd been under to perform.

"Back when I was in high school, I tested out of all my regular classes and was placed in AP ones," she started, her voice raspy. She took a moment to swallow down the emotion that still overwhelmed her. "No matter how hard I worked, it was never good enough. While my other classmates were praised, teachers asked me why I didn't do this, or how could I miss that, or wouldn't it have been better if I'd done it this way instead of that way?

"I've had to deal with those questions my entire life, Daniel. But I discovered that if I don't give them the chance to ask them—if I do whatever I can to make it perfect on the first try—then I've taken away their power. They can't doubt my abilities if I don't give them that chance."

His eyes roamed her face. "I wish I knew how to fix it."

Desperate to lighten the mood, she pinched his cheek. "Well, you are a genius and all . . ."

"There's a genius in this room, but it's the one who's creating a kick-ass app from scratch." He caressed her cheek. "I just hate that you're under so much pressure to get it right. It's so fucked up. Everyone gets the chance to make mistakes."

"Not me." She shook her head. "I'm not afforded the luxury of making a mistake. When I mess up, it just makes it that much harder for the next bright young black girl who has so much to contribute to this field. I refuse to get in her way."

"Why are you so amazing?"

"Because I have to be," Samiah said with an overly bright smile as she willed herself into a better mood. "But thank you for noticing." She picked up the tablet, determined to get this right. "And thank you for listening to my bitch-and-moan fest. Now that I've gotten that off my chest, maybe I can get through the rest of the night without pitching this thing out the window."

She woke up her laptop, but before she could click into the software, Daniel took hold of it and set it on the end table opposite of where she could reach it.

"What are you doing?"

He lifted her feet from his lap and placed them on the floor. "Come on," he said. "You need a break."

"I don't have time for a break."

"So we'll make time."

"Daniel—"

He captured her cheeks between his palms. "Samiah, you're driving yourself crazy. You've been so focused on this app that you've probably worked yourself into programmer's block."

"Programmer's block?" she deadpanned. "Really?"

"It's a thing. I swear it is. It's like writer's block, but for geek heads. Give this a rest for a few hours. Once you get out of your own head, you'll be able to focus." He nudged her. "Why don't we check out a club? I've been here nearly two months and haven't stepped foot on Sixth Street. You can give me the local's view of Austin's night life."

"I'm not local, remember?"

"You're more local than I am."

She narrowed her gaze, but when it came to curbing her laugh, she couldn't do it.

"You know I'm only agreeing to this because of those dimples, right? They're pretty hard to resist."

"My best weapons, by far." That already irresistible grin had the nerve to get even sexier. "Make that my second best."

Her stomach quivered, a shudder rushing through her as his bold assertion triggered an earth-shattering reaction throughout her bloodstream. Maybe they shouldn't leave her condo after all.

Don't go there.

But, goodness, she was ready to go there. So damn ready.

"Go on." Daniel nudged his chin toward her bedroom. "I keep a change of clothes in my car in case I go for a run. I'll go get it while you change."

"Fine. I'll go clubbing with you." She stood. Starting for her room, she threw over her shoulder, "But you have to promise to dance."

"Wait." Samiah felt herself being pulled by the hem of her shirt. She turned to him. "I don't dance," he said.

"You do now." She stuck her tongue out, then took off for her bedroom, more excited than she'd felt about anything in a long time.

Neither of them were feeling the first two clubs they tried. She hadn't realized just how dramatically her taste in both music and atmosphere had changed until faced with the prospect of listening to that head-thumping beat for more than ten minutes. It was a good thing Daniel had an old soul when it came to music; he didn't launch a single complaint when she asked to leave.

She was surprised when he agreed to join her at a salsa

club, and even more surprised when she dragged him on the floor and he salsaed better than she did.

Strobe lights illuminated the dance floor with streaks of magenta, amber, and violet, the rich hues whirring to the rhythm of the high-energy Latin music pulsing like a heartbeat throughout the club. Samiah hadn't had a particular purpose in mind when she'd pulled on her favorite Betsey Johnson midi dress with the ruffled hem, but it turned out to be the perfect choice for tonight. The flouncy fabric caressed her thighs with every twist and twirl. She felt sexy. Alive.

Free.

She had never felt so fucking free. Her makeup had long since melted off, and her hair was no doubt a mess from their nonstop dancing in the sweltering nightclub. But she *did not care*. Not even a little bit. The only thing she cared about right now was soaking in as much fun as possible.

"You owe me an explanation, mister," she said when she twisted toward Daniel.

"What for?"

She made a turn and spoke over her shoulder. "I thought you said you couldn't dance?"

He caught her wrist and pulled her in close. "I never said I *couldn't* dance. I said I don't." He released her, then hauled her back with a reverse cross-body move that set her panties on fire. "Back when I was deployed, we had to find ways to keep ourselves occupied. One of the guys from my squadron was from Miami. He gave free lessons."

She swayed her hips back, then came forward, bracing her chest against his. "You're just full of surprises, aren't you?"

His gaze dropped to her lips. "More than you know."

Her heart rate skyrocketed, her shallow breaths causing her

breasts to pulse against his solid chest. An ache she'd tried her best to ignore throbbed low in her belly, an indicator of the pleasure that awaited her. All she had to do was ask for it.

Instead she stepped back and pressed her hand to her throat. "If I don't get something to drink I'm going to die in the middle of this club."

He took her by the hand and led her off the dance floor. They made their way toward the large semicircular chrome bar that encompassed the far left side of the club, but as they drew closer she felt the muscles of Daniel's forearm stiffen. His steps faltered.

"Hey, what's wrong?" Samiah asked.

"What?" He looked at her and then just beyond her to a couple sitting at one of the pub tables in the area surrounding the bar. "It's nothing," he said. "I just noticed a friend."

His stride was measured as they approached the table. The guy, whose haircut—shaved on the sides and long on the top—made him look younger than the crow's feet etched into the corners of his eyes betrayed, stared at Daniel, a curious lift to his brow.

"Uh, hey," Daniel said. "Didn't expect to see you here."

"What are the chances?" the man returned. He extended a hand to her. "I'm Quentin. And this is my wife, Angelle."

"Quentin? Your roommate?" It was only after the words left her mouth that Samiah realized how rude they sounded. "I'm sorry," she said. "I'm Samiah."

She shook both their hands with a polite smile, but inside questions were ping-ponging like a rubber ball in her head.

This was his Marine friend's little brother? Who was sleeping on the couch? And had a wife? Why was his roommate married? None of this made sense.

"I thought you said you'd be working at Trendsetters well into the night," Quentin said. "Decided to take a break?"

"Yeah, we needed a breather," Daniel replied.

There was a tense, awkward vibe humming in the air, and she wasn't sure what to make of the forced smiles between the two men. Now she understood why Daniel had never invited her over while his roommate was there. If these last few minutes were any indication, life in that apartment must be hell.

They left Quentin and Angelle after a few more minutes of unbearably uncomfortable conversation, ordered their drinks from the bar, and brought them to a table that had just been vacated on the opposite side of the club from Daniel's roommate.

Samiah took a sip of the blood orange margarita the bartender had recommended, then set it on the table. Holding up a hand, she said, "Okay, I have to know." She hooked her thumb back at the table. "What in the heck was that about?"

"What?"

"Um, your roommate? First, why does it look as if he graduated from high school in the nineties, and why is he married?"

Daniel took a long swallow of his club soda. "He and his wife are separated," he finally said. "He mentioned they were trying to work things out." He hunched a shoulder. "I guess that's what tonight is about."

Based on the way they were holding hands and staring at each other like a couple of teenagers in love, she would say they had more than worked things out. But why would someone who was temporarily separated from his wife expend the amount of time and effort it must have taken to achieve that computer setup back at their apartment?

"And I guess he did graduate in the nineties," Daniel continued. "He's forty."

"When you said he was the younger brother of a fellow Marine, I just assumed he was, you know, young."

"I probably should have explained this in the beginning. That fellow Marine was my old gunnery sergeant," he said. "That's why Quentin is there. You don't say no to your old gunnery sergeant, even if you're no longer active duty."

"Ah." Samiah nodded. She guessed that made sense.

Of course, if one of *her* old bosses had asked her to share an apartment with his or her forty-year-old sibling, that *hell no* would have shot out of her mouth quicker than a bullet. But she wasn't here to analyze the psychology behind military relationships; she was here to enjoy herself.

She finished off her drink in a single swallow, grabbed Daniel by the wrist, and dragged him back to the dance floor.

Maybe, later on, she would enjoy *him*.

CHAPTER NINETEEN

A mélange of bright pinks and blazing oranges streaked across the mirrored windows of the high-rise next door as the setting sun continued its leisurely plummet below the horizon. The nightly ballad of file drawers sliding shut, desk lamps clicking off, and computer monitors drifting into sleep mode played throughout the office as, one by one, his coworkers wrapped up their workday. By his count they were down to less than ten people in the entire office. He could work with that number.

Daniel maintained the appearance of being swamped at his desk, all while discreetly monitoring the stairs that led to Trendsetters' second floor.

"Are you trying to make the rest of us look like slackers?"

He jerked around. "Hey, John!" Daniel tried to cover his surprised flinch by reaching for his water bottle. "Didn't realize you were still here."

"I have to pick the oldest kid up from football practice. Makes more sense to hang around the office instead of driving up to Round Rock then driving back down."

"Ah, yes. I've heard stories about how seriously Texans take their high school football."

"Almost as seriously as we take our barbecue," John said. "My fourteen-year-old freshman made the junior varsity team. My wife doesn't like it, though, which is why I'm tasked with all football practice duties."

"Ouch." Daniel searched for his best good-natured laugh.

John peered at his Apple Watch. "I need to get going. Hey, I'm sorry about this new twist with the Leyland project. That's how these things go sometimes. It'll make for late nights for all of us."

"Whatever the customer wants." Daniel hunched his shoulders in a *what are you gonna do* shrug. "That deadline is looming. I figured I'd stay late tonight and make as much headway as possible."

"Man, am I happy Justin put you on this team." John clamped him on the shoulder. "I'll see you tomorrow. Take it easy."

"You too. And good luck to your son's team this year."

"Not my son," John said with a proud smile. "It's my daughter. She's the placekicker." He pointed at Daniel. "Don't stay here all night."

Playing the part of the dedicated night owl willing to sacrifice his evening for the sake of the job might score him a few brownie points, but this wasn't about impressing Trendsetters' upper management. There was only one reason he remained in this near-empty office. It was time he make a true attempt to enter the security division's inner sanctum.

Today marked eight weeks since he'd started at Trendsetters. Call him cocky, but he'd figured by now he would be back in Virginia getting briefed on his next assignment. The fact that he hadn't gotten past the damn door of the Security Department was in-fucking-conceivable.

There were only two people in Trendsetters' Cybersecurity division tonight, but they hadn't left the room unmanned for a second. Earlier in the evening, Daniel had downloaded malware to his desktop in an attempt to draw them out. He'd waited until one of them went to the restroom, then quickly deployed the malware and put a call in to security.

He had no way of knowing that, at the time, the remaining guy happened to be helping a Trendsetter employee who was working remotely. Daniel's malware problem wasn't considered a big enough issue to elevate it, so he'd had to wait for the employee who'd gone to the restroom. It was a completely wasted effort. Worse, it eliminated that option from his toolkit. If he employed the malware again security would most likely flag him for being careless.

Realistically, he knew his chances at breaching security tonight were nil, but Daniel still wasn't ready to go home. Quentin was there. He'd done his best to avoid his "roommate" since running into him at the Latin dance club on Saturday. He knew the censure he'd get—the censure he deserved—and he wasn't in the mood for it.

Earlier, before he'd decided to take a run at breaching the Security Department, he'd asked Samiah to dinner, even though he knew her Monday nights were earmarked for binge-watching the few television shows she allowed herself to watch. But she wasn't watching *Grey's Anatomy* tonight. She was having dinner with her parents who'd driven in from Houston. When she told him about her plans, he'd immediately started to mentally thumb through his closet, trying to figure out what he was going to wear. And then he realized that she hadn't invited him to join her.

For a large swath of his afternoon, Daniel hadn't been able

to focus on anything other than what it meant that Samiah didn't want her family to know about him. Apparently, she didn't want her friends to know about him either. Not that he wanted to intrude on her girls' night out Friday rituals—he would decline if she ever asked him to tag along—but she had yet to suggest he stop by to meet Taylor and London. Was he mistaken in thinking that a woman would want to introduce her new boyfriend to her friends?

Unless she didn't consider him to be her boyfriend.

They hadn't discussed official labels or anything like that. And just because Joelle had paraded him around like a live-action G.I. Joe doll to her friends didn't mean Samiah would do the same. Maybe he was reading too much into this.

No matter what, the fact that he wasn't meeting her parents, or her sister and brother-in-law, or even her friends, was a stark reminder of where things actually were between them. Fuck, it was a reminder that there shouldn't even be anything between them at all. What excuse could he give if anyone back at FinCEN discovered what he'd been up to with Samiah? It was in only the rarest circumstances that any kind of romantic involvement with a subject was allowed—those cases where an agent's cover had the possibility of being blown.

Samiah's tangential affiliation with Hughes Hospitality didn't come close to justifying what he was doing. Allowing himself to get in too deep with her could lead to detrimental consequences.

"You're already in too deep," he said with a groan.

He needed to break this case open and get the hell out of Austin. It was the only way he could see himself giving up the drug that was Samiah Brooks.

Daniel forced himself to put her out of his head. He wouldn't make any more attempts to access the database tonight, but he still had legitimate work he could be doing right now, both for Trendsetters and for FinCEN. The final specs for the Leyland Group's new customer management system were due within the next week. And, back at FinCEN, Preston had asked for help on a case that was tied to one Daniel had worked on last year.

He forwarded the old emails and voicemails to Preston, then returned to working on the back-end architecture for the Leyland Group's WLAN design. Their team had been told just this morning that Leyland's upper management decided to go with this configuration, which, coincidentally, was the same one Hughes Hospitality had used for their wireless local area network. Suddenly, being placed on this team worked in his favor. He now had access to information that had been previously out of his reach.

As he read over the details of the initial design, a name on the original team popped out at him.

"What the—?"

Daniel switched between screens, his heart suddenly thumping with enough bass to rival every track on Dr. Dre's *The Chronic* album.

"No way," he whispered.

He looked over each shoulder to make sure he was alone, then pulled out his tablet and clicked on the folder that contained the dossiers he'd been briefed with before starting at Trendsetters. He scanned the file names and, once he found the one he was looking for, tapped to open it. The work history section went back only two and a half years. FinCEN had gathered as much information on Trendsetters' employees as possible, but he'd been told before leaving Virginia that some files were incomplete.

"I'll be a son of a bitch," Daniel whispered. Why hadn't he made this connection?

He shut down his computer, quickly packed up his gear, and left the office, all thoughts of avoiding Quentin forgotten. If the man still wanted to rail at him over his relationship with Samiah, he could do it once he and Daniel talked through this newest revelation.

When he opened the door to the apartment, he found Quentin in his usual spot, on the sofa surrounded by files and reports.

"Well, well, well," Quentin sang, his eyes still on his case files. "Look who decided to make an appearance."

"Mike Epsen worked on the Hughes Hospitality account when it first came to Trendsetters."

Quentin set the file folder on the sofa and turned. "Isn't that the guy who got hit while riding his bicycle? The one whose place you took on that new project?"

Daniel nodded as he walked over to him and handed him the iPad with Mike's dossier.

"Hughes Hospitality had been on FinCEN's radar for months, but it was an anonymous tip that drew our attention to the Trendsetters connection. Dwyer said the tipster kept in regular contact, never revealing himself or a name, just making sure they knew the laundering was still going on. About two weeks ago the tips stopped coming. Just went completely dark."

"Around the same time Mike Epsen's bicycle had an unfortunate meeting with the front fender of that bus," Quentin said. "But, seriously, do you think a city bus driver is somehow connected to this?"

"No, the bus driver wasn't at fault." Daniel shook his head. "Didn't I tell you? I got the whole story a couple of days after the accident. A car encroached on the bike lane, which caused Mike to swerve into the bus. But the driver of the car never stopped. Everyone has been going on the assumption that the person driving the car was texting or distracted in some way and just didn't see what happened. But now?"

"My old boss had a saying, coincidences are just connections that haven't been made yet," Quentin said. "I think this is a piece of that connection."

"That accident was no accident. It was meant to scare him into silence."

"Mission accomplished." Quentin looked up at him. "Do you think your girlfriend can shed some light on it?"

Daniel dropped his head back. Staring up at the kidney-shaped water stain on the ceiling, he released a deep sigh. "You couldn't wait to go there, could you?"

"I'm just saying." Quentin held his hands up. "If you're going to violate rules, at least make it work in your favor. Find a way to bring Mike's name up in conversation. Ask her how his department is handling his absence, if coworkers have had to step in for Mike in the past. Maybe she can give you some clues that can help you figure out if he's your tipster."

"Or maybe I can go and see Mike for myself," Daniel said.

"I'd clear it with FinCEN before taking that step." He gestured at Daniel's iPad. "Let them know about that ASAP. It may be all the evidence you need to convince Dwyer that you need to take this investigation to the next level. Who knows, you may be on your way back to Virginia sooner rather than later."

Daniel nodded, but the sudden onset of nausea in his belly was telling.

He was here for one reason only, to uncover who had been using Hughes Hospitality as a front to launder money. He should be euphoric at the thought of catching a break in this case. That Vegas job—the prize—was waiting for him, like a golden ticket sitting behind protective glass, just out of his reach. This possible connection between Mike Epsen's accident and the money laundering could be the key to unlocking that glass box.

So why did the thought of bringing this case to a close leave such a horrible taste in his mouth?

CHAPTER TWENTY

Squinting, Samiah leaned forward until the laptop was only a few inches from her face. She could hear her mother's voice in her head, yelling at her not to put her eyes too close to the screen or else she'd burn her eyeballs. Too late. Between her phone, laptop, tablet, and two computer monitors at work, she spent at least 80 percent of her day staring at a retina screen. The damage was already done.

An anxious flutter rolled through her stomach as she examined the API she'd spent much of the past few weeks building and tweaking, then tweaking and rebuilding. This was it. The deciding factor when it came to making the deadline for the Future in Innovation Tech Conference. She'd already accepted that if she wasn't able to validate the JSON API schema, she wouldn't bother signing up for one of the coveted spots at FITC when it came to Austin in the spring.

The closest she'd ever come to experiencing something akin to a panic attack swept through her as her finger hovered over the keyboard. The countless hours she'd pumped into creating this app, the dreams she'd attached to it; it all came down to this single component.

She crossed her fingers, then pressed ENTER and watched

as the colorful pinwheel turned and turned and turned on the screen.

The screen blinked and when it came back, her schema had been validated.

"Ohmigod, ohmigod, ohmigod!" Samiah jumped up from the sofa and slid across her living room floor in her socks, underwear, and shirt, à la Tom Cruise in *Risky Business*. It felt as if a balloon filled with glitter had just exploded inside her chest.

Her immediate thought was to share her news with Daniel. Her fingers fumbled as she typed out the text message and sent him a snapshot of her laptop screen.

He replied with a GIF of a man break-dancing, his track-suit, thick gold chain, and Kangol cap straight out of 1985. Samiah burst out laughing. The reply was so on brand.

A few minutes later, her phone vibrated with another text from Daniel: BUZZ ME UP.

She called him. "Are you downstairs?"

"Yeah. I was on my way to surprise you with dinner when you texted. I know you've been swamped trying to build this API and figured you hadn't taken the time to eat."

It felt as if her heart had swelled to three times its normal size. After the years she'd spent settling for so far less than what she deserved, it was acts like this one that showed her how truly special Daniel was. It meant more than any expensive, grand gesture ever would.

She called down to the building's concierge and gave the doorman permission to let him up. She considered remaining in her T-shirt and underwear, but decided to throw on a pair of shorts. As much as she wanted to hang an OPEN FOR BUSINESS sign on the rim of her panties, social conventions drilled into her by her very proper mother demanded she be a bit more refined.

She answered the door and refinement went out the window.

There was nothing particularly exceptional about a simple black T-shirt and jeans, but on Daniel Collins the harmless combination looked lethal. The soft jersey fabric contoured over his sculpted chest and subtly muscular biceps. His well-worn jeans clung deliciously to his hips, accentuating his slender yet powerful build. All she could think about was peeling them off.

"Congratulations," Daniel said. "It seems to me we have a reason to celebrate."

"I would say so," Samiah replied. She caught her bottom lip between her teeth, then grabbed the hem of his T-shirt and pulled him into the condo.

She relieved him of the bag from her favorite Mexican restaurant, set it on the table in her small foyer, closed the door behind him, and pressed him against it.

"Okay, Collins, this can go one of two ways: If you're not ready to take this next step, you can sit here and eat dinner while I go to my room and get myself off. Or, *you* can get me off—no, we can get each other off. Then we can eat tacos naked—there's really no better way to eat them. But that's only after we've both come at least twice. So, which works for you?"

"Coming twice," he said. "Definitely coming twice. And then naked tacos."

"I was hoping you'd say that," Samiah said.

She captured his face in her hands and crushed her mouth to his. His tongue quickly delved past her lips, probing with hurried, insistent strokes. She had been anticipating this for weeks. Daydreaming about it. Craving it. If ever there was a reason to finally give in to this insane pull between them, celebrating this breakthrough with her app was as good as any.

Daniel's hands went to her waist, then down to her ass, his caress wild and fervent. He clutched her tight, pulling her flush against him. Samiah's nipples instantly hardened while everything else went soft and hot. She felt herself melting under the heat of his passionate response.

Her lips still connected with his, she started moving, dragging him toward her bedroom, stepping out of her shorts and flinging them toward the sofa as they made their way past the living room.

"This feels like rom-com movie sex," she said against his lips.

He chuckled. "Is that a good thing?"

"As long as we don't break any bones and end up in the emergency room."

"What about the headboard?" he asked.

She pulled back slightly and stared at him. "Did I hear that correctly? Did you just promise me headboard-breaking sex?"

His brow lifted in the sexiest way imaginable. "You got a problem with that?"

Samiah flattened her palm against his chest and pushed him into her room.

"Get in the bed."

He grabbed her by the waist and traveled with her down onto the bed, climbing up her body and planting kisses along her neck and shoulder. Samiah pulled his T-shirt over his head, then went to work on his jeans, unbuttoning them and ripping the zipper with such zeal she nearly broke it.

They shoved the rest of their clothes off, then worked as a team to roll on the condom he'd taken from his wallet.

"Stupid question time," Daniel said as he braced his hands on either side of her head. "Are you sure about this?"

"That *is* a stupid question. The stupidest question *ever*."

"I know, but I still have to hear you say it," he said.

"Yes!" Samiah shouted. "Yes, please, give me the headboard-breaking sex you promised!"

He grinned. "I hope these walls are well insulated. I guess you'll know by the way your neighbors look at you from now on."

He dipped his head to capture her mouth. At the same time, he hooked his arm in the cradle behind her knee and brought her leg up as he plunged into her. Samiah bowed, her back lifting from the mattress, reaching for him.

Each stroke sent her careering closer to the edge, the intensity of the sensations spiraling through her so fierce they stole her breath away. She wrapped her other leg around his and began to move, pumping her hips in rhythm to his thrusts, closing her eyes and concentrating on the sharp beams of pleasure shooting across her skin like fireworks.

"This is...so good," Samiah moaned. "So...good."

She felt Daniel's lips at her ear. "It's about to get better," he whispered.

He slipped out of her and traveled down her torso, peppering her stomach with kisses before hooking her legs over his shoulders and bathing the spot between her legs with his tongue. Her response was pure reflex, her muscles moving of their own volition. She clamped her thighs against his head and squeezed.

"Samiah—"

She released his head. "Oh, shit, I'm sorry," she said. "I don't want to kill you."

His eyes glittered with amusement, his grin so sexy she nearly climaxed at the sight of it.

"There are worse ways to go, but it'd be a damn shame if I died in the middle of this." His brow quirked. "Now, can I finish down here?"

"Please," she breathed.

His tongue was like magic, casting an exquisite spell on her with each delicious stroke. Every cell in her body tensed, her skin growing taut as her pleasure built just below the surface. Two strokes more and she blew apart, her orgasm so intense she shook with it.

"God, you're beautiful when you do that," Daniel said.

She felt beautiful. And sated.

But that didn't mean she was ready to stop.

She reached for him and captured his mouth, wicked pleasure assaulting her as she tasted the difference between this kiss and the last. Was there anything hotter than experiencing the taste of herself in his mouth?

He changed out the condom, quickly rolling on another, then he charged back up her body, seizing her by the waist and twisting so that she was on top. Samiah straddled his hips, her eyes once again falling closed as she sank onto the length of his erection. She rolled her hips, undulating in a slow back and forth motion, relishing every slide of his body. But when he clasped his hands on her hips and started to guide her, she began to pump like the fate of all humanity rested on how vigorously she rode his dick.

It was fast and furious, this second journey to orgasm.

The wave crashed into her with a force so strong her limbs went weak.

Samiah fell face forward, collapsing onto Daniel's chest, her entire being replete with satisfaction. She felt his heart beating against her cheek and decided this was how she wanted to spend the next three hours. Forget naked tacos. The only thing she was hungry for was this feeling of total and complete contentment.

He shifted slightly so he could remove the condom, discarding it in a wad of tissues from the box on her bedside table. Then he settled back down, clasping a hand over her hip and tugging her toward him.

She propped her elbow up and cradled her cheek in her palm. "If this is what I have to look forward to every time I have a breakthrough with the app, expect quite a few breakthroughs, Mr. Collins."

His deep, sexy chuckle traveled across her skin, a sinfully delicious sensation that teased her sensitive nerve endings.

"I'm not sure I like the thought of us sleeping together being tied to your app. What happens when you're done with it?"

She laughed. "I'm not even in the neighborhood of done. Trust me, there are many more breakthroughs to be had before I get there."

He peered at her, a skeptical arch to his brow. "I'm not sure I believe that."

"Believe it," Samiah said. "I hate admitting this, but I'm still so nervous about this entire thing."

Nervous and scared. But confessing that would kill the mood for her.

"But why?" Daniel asked, clearly oblivious to the threat his questions had to her postsex buzz. His fingers drifted along her arm, moving in a languid caress. "You're so damn good at your job. Why don't you think you wouldn't be just as good at the app?"

"Simple. I can't control what happens with the app," Samiah answered. "With the job—not just the job at Trendsetters, but *any* job I ever take—I know that I can succeed as long as I do what's expected of me. And, because I *am* me, I'm not going to stop at just what's expected. I'm going to go above and beyond."

"Of course," Daniel said.

"That's just how I roll," she said with a laugh. "But it's different with the app. I can create the most amazing thing ever, but what if I can't find an investor? What if I put in all this work, am lucky enough to find an investor, and then the app tanks?"

"You wouldn't be the first person to experience that," Daniel said.

"I know, but it...it scares me," she said.

She swallowed hard, a thick lump of emotion catching in her throat as one of the most profound memories from her childhood came crashing to the surface.

"Back when I was in the third grade, just before my eighth birthday, I woke up one night and went into the kitchen for a Capri Sun." She smiled. "They were supposed to be school snacks only, but I would sneak one from the refrigerator and blame it on my sister." She blew out a deep breath. "I remember walking in the kitchen and hearing this strange sound I'd never heard before coming from the breakfast table. I walked just beyond the kitchen island and noticed my dad bent over, his arms folded atop the table, his head resting on them.

"He was crying."

Silence stole across the room, the only sounds those of the light traffic on the city streets below.

"I asked him what was wrong, even though I knew I'd get scolded for being up past my bedtime. But instead of telling me to go back to bed, he brought me onto his lap and apologized to me. He said we wouldn't be able to go to the zoo for my birthday because they needed to save money. He'd lost his job earlier that week." She nestled against Daniel's chest, resting her cheek on his smooth skin. "This all happened before he became a teacher," she continued. "My dad went back to school in his thirties, got his degree, and started teaching just as I entered high school. Thankfully, it wasn't at *my* high school," she said with another laugh.

"But that night, when I saw my daddy crying like his heart had broken in two, it did something to me. He was Superman in my eyes. He was the person who put a Band-Aid on my cuts and kissed them when I cried. Seeing him in that state is something I will never, ever forget.

"That night, he told me to make sure I controlled every part of my life, because when you're not in control awful things can happen and you can't do anything about it. That's why I need to control as much as possible."

She'd worked enough of this out in her head some time ago, and knew that her rigid adherence to her checklist had something to do with this intense need she always had to be in control, but she'd never put voice to the words.

It was only recently that Samiah began to wonder if this was why she'd never pursued a real relationship before either. Because she couldn't control the way someone felt about her.

Just the prospect of finding herself in such a vulnerable state caused her breath to hitch.

"You may think you can't control what happens with this app, Samiah, but you do. You control how it looks, how it operates, everything. And when you're done with it, it's going to be so brilliant that you won't be able to field all the offers you're going to get. You have nothing to be afraid of."

He dipped his head and captured her mouth in a kiss that stole the breath from her lungs, and the fear that suddenly came over her had nothing to do with her app or her job or anything else.

The thing she feared for the most right now was her heart.

CHAPTER TWENTY-ONE

A crisp wind, scented with an amalgam of freshly cut grass, earthy wet soil, and burning hickory from a nearby smoke-house restaurant, hit his face the moment he opened his car door. Per Samiah's instructions, he'd parked near the baseball diamond on the south bank of Barton Creek in Zilker Park. Despite the early hour, nearly half the parking spots were already filled with Austinites eager to enjoy what promised to be a beautiful Sunday.

Daniel still couldn't describe the sheer euphoria that swept through him when Samiah asked if he wanted to join them. Her friend Taylor wanted to test out a boot camp–style fitness class and needed feedback before adding it to her repertoire. He didn't care that he was here to play guinea pig. She was opening up another part of her world to him; that's what counted.

Leaving her, naked and twisted up in those silken silver sheets this morning, was, without a doubt, the hardest thing he'd done since returning from his final deployment. He would carry the memories from last night with him long after he returned to Virginia. The sounds she'd made, the sensation of her damp skin sliding against his, the way it felt to sink into her warm, welcoming body. Memories of the way she'd responded would stay with him forever, a mental storage bin of erotic keepsakes he could open whenever he wanted to replay one of the most amazing nights he'd ever experienced.

It scared the hell out of him. Because those same memories would no doubt torture him once she was no longer in his life.

Instead of turning left and driving toward the freeway when he pulled out of her building's parking garage in the early hours before dawn, he'd headed in the opposite direction, grabbed a cup of weak coffee from an all-night diner, and meandered around downtown Austin for a full hour. Concerns over what these past few weeks meant to his future dominated his thoughts. This wasn't a random hookup that he could walk away from. Last night had left an indelible mark on him. There *was* no walking away.

Extricating himself from the web he'd allowed himself to become enmeshed in would require skills Daniel wasn't sure he possessed. Most frightening, he wasn't sure he wanted to get out of it. He didn't want to even think about how he would get out of this because he knew it would fucking kill him to leave.

Except he had to leave. If there was one given in all of this, it was that his time in Austin was temporary.

The question was, when he *did* leave, would he have the chance to tell Samiah goodbye or would he just disappear? It could go either way. He'd had jobs in the past where he was there one day and gone the next. No forwarding address. No Facebook profile for his coworkers to find him. Nothing. He became a ghost.

That's not how it always went down. Sometimes, he was required to play the clueless coworker. If local authorities were able to execute the capture without his intervention, he would pretend to be as shocked by the arrests as any of the other employees at Trendsetters. And then, out of the blue, one of his grandparents would fall ill, necessitating his immediate return to his family.

It always worked like a charm. Everyone would understand when, a few weeks later, he unfortunately had to turn in his letter of resignation. He began laying the foundation for this excuse his very first week on the job, casually mentioning to a sufficient number of coworkers just how important his family was to him. Not a single person would be surprised when he made the hard choice to pack up and leave. They never were.

When it came to this particular job, it would be Dwyer's call. If his boss decided leaving Trendsetters without a trace was the safest exit strategy, that's how it would play out. A part of him wanted it to happen that way. At least then he wouldn't have to see the hurt in Samiah's eyes. Or, even worse, the hate.

Fucking coward.

Daniel shut his eyes, damn near gasping at the pain that pierced his chest just at the thought of having to explain to Samiah that he'd spent the past two months lying to her. She would despise him. How could she not? She'd become YouTube famous for cursing out a guy who'd lied to her about his true identity. It would be ridiculous to think she would easily forgive him for doing the same.

"You don't deserve her forgiveness," Daniel whispered.

He didn't deserve *her*. Period. If he was a halfway decent

human being, he would turn around right now, drive to that dull, sparsely furnished apartment, pack up his few belongings, and be on a plane to Virginia by tonight.

Any thoughts of doing that vacated his brain the moment he spotted her. She congregated with a group of at least a dozen women underneath the shade of a massive pecan tree. She'd told him to meet her at what was affectionately known as the Monkey Tree, one of the park's landmarks, and a favorite for outdoor exercise enthusiasts because of the natural cover it provided from the blazing Central Texas sun.

The magnitude of this moment wasn't lost on him. Introducing him to people outside of their work life was a significant step. It signified a level of trust he hadn't earned. He was lying to her, dammit. All of this was a fucking lie!

His steps halted. He sucked in a deep breath and closed his eyes again.

Walk away.

He could still do it. He could turn around this very instant, before she spotted him. All he would have to do is tell Dwyer that he'd been compromised. He could be back in his little cubbyhole at FinCEN's headquarters by Tuesday morning. Samiah would be hurt and confused by his sudden, unexplained departure, but how much worse would it be if he allowed this to go on?

He opened his eyes and realized he couldn't do it.

It made him the worst kind of bastard. Dishonest. Selfish. Unrepentant. Because as inexcusable as it was to continue this subterfuge, that's exactly what he would do. The alternative— saying goodbye—was unbearable.

He continued on. He would deal with the silos of regret he'd been collecting later, when Samiah was no longer a part of his life. He had her for now. And he would savor every delicious minute.

She noticed him when he was about twenty feet away. He watched as she said something to the statuesque woman he recognized from the viral video—London—before breaking away from the group and advancing toward him. Her eyes were as bright as her radiant smile. The thought of eventually leaving her, of having to live without that smile, caused an ache to settle deep in Daniel's chest. How could he contemplate giving her up until he absolutely had to? She was like a drug, his own sweet addiction.

"Hey there," she said as she approached. She grabbed him by both hands, leaned forward, and placed a quick kiss on his lips. "Thanks for coming all the way back out here on a Sunday morning," she said.

"Did you really think I would turn down an invitation to be next to you when I knew you'd be wearing skintight clothes?"

She tipped her head to the side, her lips tilting in a flirty grin. "I wouldn't think the thought of seeing me in clothes would be all that exciting after last night."

"Now that I know exactly what's hidden underneath those clothes, it's a thousand times more exciting."

Her warm brown cheeks darkened even more. Making her blush gave him as much pleasure as cracking a case that had been cold for thirty years. Making her call his name out as he plunged deep inside her gave him enough pleasure to kill him.

Leaving her would destroy him. There was no way around it.

"Come on." She tugged him forward. "I'll introduce you to London and Taylor."

He recognized both women from the YouTube video. Taylor had dressed the part of drill sergeant, her camo-colored workout pants and cropped sports top an exact match to the cap she wore. TAYLOR'D CONDITIONING was embroidered in red on the front panel. With those defined arm muscles, she looked as if she could kick ass as thoroughly as any sergeant he'd served under.

London, on the other hand, seemed as if she'd been dragged from bed kicking and screaming. That she was here to support her friend's endeavor was a testament to the bond the three women had formed in the short amount of time they'd known each other.

"London, Taylor, this is Daniel Collins. Daniel, this is London Kelley and Taylor Powell."

"Nice to meet you, ladies." He shook both their hands.

"Same," London said, her gaze assessing and a touch amused. She looked over at Samiah. "A certain project looks to be complete."

"Maybe," Samiah said after clearing her throat. Daniel had no idea what that was about.

She motioned to Taylor. "The two of you have something in common. Daniel here is a military brat. Both his parents served. In fact, he was in the Marines for..." Her forehead furrowed. "How long?"

"Four years," he provided.

"Marines?" Taylor's brow arched. "You guys are scary. Don't think this will be your normal PT." Her mouth curled up in a grin. "I'm a lot harder than your average drill sergeant." She clapped her hands together. "Okay, people. Are we ready to get this started?"

"No," London said.

Samiah burst out laughing as she took London by the arm. "Remember, this is just a test run. She's going to take it easy on us."

Less than five minutes into their workout, it became apparent that Samiah was mistaken and he had been correct. When it came to a kick-ass PT session, Taylor Powell held her own against any of his past drill sergeants.

CHAPTER TWENTY-TWO

No. No. No. That's not going to work."

Samiah massaged her right temple with the blunt end of her electronic pencil and cursed herself for laughing off Taylor's suggestion that she start diffusing essential oils to help relieve work-related stress. She'd trade her favorite pair of Malone Souliers pumps for a few drops of lavender and eucalyptus right now.

She glanced at the time on her computer and realized this impromptu brainstorming session had been going on for an hour already, which meant she would have to tack another hour onto her workday to get the rest of her work done. If someone could guarantee that she could get French roast coffee in prison, she would happily murder each and every one of the people sitting in her office. How could such brilliant minds be so bad at coming up with original ideas?

"Guys, look. I'll admit that Huston-Tillotson University came to us with a unique problem, but it shouldn't be this hard to formulate a workable solution that won't require them to triple their tuition cost." Samiah held up both hands. "You all know how much I hate clichés, but seriously, it's time to start thinking outside the box."

"Well, they did say they were willing to throttle their bandwidth during peak hours," Amy said.

"Yes, which gives us a starting point when it comes to devising a system that will meet all of their needs without breaking the bank." She swiveled to her monitor and logged into the online collaboration software used for strategy discussions.

"I'm setting up an Insight Room," Samiah continued. "I talked it over with Justin and Bianca in the Cybersecurity Department. They've agreed to restore a higher level of security access to those of us who worked on the Anderson project last year. That work is proprietary, but because the university's issues are similar, I think we can use those things that aren't proprietary from Anderson to figure out a solution for Huston-Tillotson. We can do this, gang."

She ended the meeting, and the team filed out of her office. Everyone except for Keighleigh Miller. Samiah had barely tolerated having her in here after the bullshit she'd pulled yesterday, and she had the nerve to stick around?

"Do you need something?" Samiah asked, her tone deliberately unwelcoming.

Keighleigh hunched her shoulders and smiled. "I just wanted to make sure there were no hard feelings after what happened with Grant yesterday."

"You mean the part where you presented my ideas on the Swiss Burger account as if they were your own?"

Samiah had emailed her proposal to her team for feedback. Not twenty minutes later, Grant Meecham came into her office, praising the ingenious plan Keighleigh had sent to him.

Keighleigh's smile wobbled slightly. "I was just so excited after the long hours we've all spent on Swiss Burger. I wanted Grant to know about the idea ASAP."

Samiah leaned back in her chair and steepled her fingers over her stomach.

"So, you were so excited the thought of mentioning that *I* was the one who came up with the solution completely slipped your mind? Is that what happened?"

"You know Grant." Her coworker shrugged dismissively. "He doesn't look at individuals. He's all about the team effort."

Samiah arched a brow. "So why didn't you tell him it was the *team* that proposed the idea? I saw the email you sent to Grant."

Keighleigh's eyes bulged.

"Yes," Samiah continued with a nod. "He was so thrilled with your idea that he forwarded the email so I could read it myself. You presented *my* idea as if it was your own. You didn't mention the team." Samiah pushed up from her chair and marched toward her. Lowering her voice, she said, "I've tolerated this kind of bullshit in the past, but no more. I'll be damned if I just sit here while you take credit for my work."

Her eyes had grown to a cartoonish size. "It...umm...it's not that at all," she said. "You should take it as a compliment."

The fuck?

"A compliment?" She was two seconds from taking off her shoes and earrings and going straight-up Houston Third Ward on this bitch. "You can keep your damn compliments," Samiah said. "I don't need them. If you try that shit you pulled yesterday again, I will literally kick your ass up and down these hallways, you hear me?"

Samiah straightened her shoulders. "I have work to do. You can go back to your desk, or straight to HR. I don't care. But you need to get out of my office. Now."

If she wasn't so pissed, Samiah would have laughed at

the shock on her coworker's face. But this wasn't a laughing matter. Keighleigh Miller was well on her way to making a career out of taking credit for other people's work.

"Not this one," she said as she watched Keighleigh scuttle away from her office.

Having adequately disposed of her nemesis, she returned to her desk and the profusion of projects cluttering her day planner. The minute she sat, Justin Vail's face popped up on her interoffice messaging app. Samiah, do you mind coming into my office? We need to talk to you.

Well, hell. Keighleigh must have run to HR.

No problem, she replied.

Minutes later, Samiah approached her supervisor's office, prepared to defend herself. At the same time, she understood that Keighleigh could have taken her words as a physical threat and reported it that way. With Trendsetters' zero-tolerance policy when it came to office violence and harassment, Samiah may have put her job in jeopardy.

Justin's office walls had been switched from clear to opaque, something he rarely did. She couldn't stanch the instant panic that began to spread to her extremities. She entered the office and the panic escalated to mass internal hysteria.

Justin sat behind his desk. Barrington Jacobs, Trendsetters' CEO, perched against the front of the desk, his arms folded over his chest and feet crossed at the ankles.

She was being fired.

But why would the company's owner be in on her firing? That was a job for Human Resources.

Samiah cleared her throat. "You wanted to see me?" she asked, trying not to jump to the worst-case scenario.

"We do. Please, sit." Justin motioned to the empty chairs

in front of his desk. She sat, and Barrington took the seat opposite hers.

"We won't keep you long," her supervisor started. "I know you're swamped with finishing up the Leyland Group and Swiss Burger projects—although Grant told me about Keighleigh's great idea for that one."

She bit the inside of her cheek.

Deep breaths.

"We have a proposal for you," Barrington started. "How would you like to head up your own department?"

Samiah's head snapped back. She blinked several times. If someone was recording her right now, no doubt she'd be a meme on Twitter by the end of the day.

Oh, wait! Thanks to that viral video she was already a meme on Twitter.

Pay attention.

"I would like that very much," Samiah answered. She looked to Justin. "Are you leaving?"

"No way," he said with a laugh. "You'll have to wrestle me away from here. It's not the R&D Department, although I'm sure you would give me a run for my money if you ever set your sights on my job." He folded his hands on his desk. "The department we want you to run doesn't officially have a name yet. In fact, it's not officially a department just yet. As of right now, we're calling it Trendsetters Outreach."

Samiah repeated the title, unable to mask her confusion. "Can you expound a bit?"

"The work you've been doing, like reaching out to schools and women's shelters and adoption centers, it's elevated Trendsetters' profile in the community and the industry."

"It has also made an impact on the company as a whole,"

Barrington said. "Your coworkers see the positive work you're doing and they want to contribute. Take that middle schooler who shadowed you the other day. What was her name? Tomeka?"

Samiah nodded.

"That made such an impact. I've had several employees approach me about bringing in students interested in STEM. Someone even suggested we devote an entire day to it."

"I like that idea," Samiah said.

"So do I. Look, I want Trendsetters to be here for a long time," Barrington said. "The only way the company survives once I'm living out my retirement years on a private island near St. Barts is if we start grooming future computer engineers and software developers early."

She could totally see the company's young CEO retiring by age forty and enjoying a life of leisure on an island somewhere in the Caribbean.

"What does this mean for my position in R&D?" she asked. If either said that they would offer it to Keighleigh she would pitch a fit.

"Aparna Bajwa would be promoted into your position," Justin said. "She deserves it."

Samiah let out a relieved breath. She could absolutely get behind that.

"And my team in this new Outreach Department?" she asked. "Do you have people in mind?"

"Now, I know we tend to work in teams," Justin said, reaching over to the Newton's cradle on his desk. He pulled back one metal ball and sent it careening into its neighbor. "However, because this is a new position that we're testing—"

"Implementing," Barrington interrupted as he grabbed

the swaying balls, putting a halt to their clacking. "Testing makes it seem as if we won't go through with it if it doesn't work the way we're expecting it to. That's not going to happen. We'll try things out, see how they work, and adjust if necessary, but this is here to stay."

"Yeah, that's what I meant," Justin said. "Because this is a new position we're *implementing*, we'd like you to be the sole architect. You get to mold and shape the new department. As it grows we'll bring people in to join your team."

Now that she knew she wasn't being fired, Samiah regained a bit of the control she thought she'd lost. She sat up in her chair and placed her folded hands in her lap. "Is it too early to discuss salary?" she asked.

"Gotta respect how direct you are." Barrington chuckled. He tapped Justin's desk as he stood. "I'll leave the rest to you."

Samiah continued to study her supervisor as the CEO vacated the office.

"So?" she asked. "Will my pay be comparable to that of other department heads?"

"Not yet," Justin said. "Pay grade–wise, this would be a lateral move, for the time being." He held his hands up again. "It does come with a significant onetime bonus. We can't ask you to take on something like this without monetary enticement," he added with a good-natured grin. "As the new department gets better established and more employees are added to it, you will get a pay raise. Not only that, but Barrington is pledging three percent of the company's annual revenue to outreach programs.

"You do a lot of good already, Samiah. Just think of how much more you can do with that kind of budget."

That's exactly what she was thinking about. In the past few years she'd cajoled management into committing acts of charity here and there—donating gently used computer equipment, sponsoring youth sports teams, purchasing box fans for a local drive that provided seniors with relief during the scorching summer months. With this new position, she wouldn't have to finagle funds for her goodwill pet projects. She would have hundreds of thousands of dollars—possibly millions if Trendsetters had a good year—at her disposal. The possibilities made her skin tingle.

"There's one other thing," Justin said.

She straightened in her seat. "What's that?"

"You'll need to remain in your current position for a few months while concurrently building the Outreach Department. Aparna is leaving for Jaipur next week. She's had this trip scheduled for her father's sixtieth birthday celebration since the spring, and she'll be there for a month. When she returns, it will likely take another two to three months to transition, and that's being conservative."

Samiah surreptitiously sucked in a shallow breath. Four months of essentially working two jobs. Was she expected to sleep and eat? She barely had time for those things now.

"You've given me a lot to consider," Samiah said. "When do you need an answer?"

"That's the other thing."

"You said there was one thing," she said.

"I meant one thing as in *two* things." He held a hand up. "I know. I know," Justin said. "Here's the thing. We need to know as soon as possible."

"Why the rush?"

He had the decency to look sheepish. "Barrington doesn't

want you to think we're only starting this new department to make the company look good, but—"

"But you need to make the company look good," she said.

"Trendsetters will be profiled for *Tech News Watch* magazine next month. I don't have to tell you how impressive that is."

No, he didn't. *Tech News Watch* was one of the largest trade magazines for the tech world.

"We want this Outreach Department up and running before the reporter gets here."

"You want me to build a new department from scratch in a month, while also juggling the rest of my current projects?"

"Did I mention your bonus will be significant?" Justin asked. "Look, Samiah, I know this is a lot, but there's not a single person in this company who could do the job that you would do. However, if you're not up to it, there are a couple of other people on my list."

"Don't go giving away my department before I even get the chance to run it," she said. "Can I have a day or two to think it over?"

He nodded. "Let me know by Monday."

She pushed up from the chair and thanked Justin for the opportunity. Having the chance to mold this new endeavor into her own vision was intoxicating. But as she made her way back to her office, all she could think about was what she would have to give up in order to make it happen.

* * *

The deluge that had sabotaged their plans to hike the Walnut Creek Trail continued to pound against the floor-to-ceiling windows of Samiah's living room. Other than the occasional ding from the elevator or a faint car horn blaring from twenty-one stories below, the steadily intensifying rain provided the only sound throughout the condo.

It had been this way for much of the morning. Long stretches of comfortable silences were interrupted by Samiah's sporadic musings about the new position she'd been offered at Trendsetters. Daniel glided his fingers lazily through her hair, massaging her scalp as she continued to debate whether she should take it.

He felt her stiffen a moment before she sat up.

"Oh, my God, I'm an idiot," Samiah said. "Why didn't I think of this sooner?"

"Have you figured it out?" he asked.

"Yes, of course! Well, I've figured out why I'm having such a hard time figuring it out. It's because I haven't made a checklist! I need to write down all the pros and cons." She started to rise, but he gently stayed her with his palm.

"No list-making," Daniel said. "You said you were going to relax today, remember?"

"I tried. It's not working. How can I relax with this all up in the air?"

Daniel lifted her head from his lap and scooted down to the opposite end of the sofa. He claimed her right foot and started to knead the sole of it with his thumbs. Her eyes fell closed and she released a satisfied groan.

"Okay, run it by me again," he said. "What are all the reasons you want to take the job?"

Her eyes still closed, she started ticking the list off with her fingers. "For starters, I would be a department head. It doesn't even matter that it's only a department of one for the time being. That kind of thing looks great on any résumé."

He squeezed her foot. "You planning to start sending out résumés?"

"No, but I don't take anything for granted. Something can happen tomorrow in the tech world and Trendsetters can tank. I learned a long time ago that the key to being in control of your own destiny is to always be prepared, no matter how safe things may feel now."

"Smart woman."

"Thank my dad for that." She sat up, balancing on her elbows. "Another huge notch in the pro column is the fact that I get to create this department from the ground up. Trendsetters is basically giving me carte blanche to mold it into what *I* want it to be. It's hard to turn down that kind of power."

"I knew that had to be a part of it." He chuckled. "Power is quite the seductress."

"Can you blame me? I'm not in this job for my health; I'm in it to get ahead. But the best part about all of this is that running this Outreach Department will put me in a position to help other people get ahead too."

"So it's not just about you getting ahead."

"It's never just about me," she said. "I always have to consider how I can help those coming up behind me." She folded her arm over her eyes and released a regretful sigh. "That's what makes this such a hard decision."

"I'm not sure I follow," Daniel said. "So far, everything you've laid out has been a pro. Are there any cons at all?"

She nodded. "A big one." With another sigh, she said, "If I accept what Trendsetters is offering, I will have to put my whole heart in it. I'm looking at months of ridiculous hours at the office until Aparna is able to transition full-time into my current job."

And just like that, Daniel recognized where this was leading.

"You would have to put your app on the back burner," he said as understanding dawned.

His throat constricted at the resignation in her brief, dispirited nod.

"Exactly," she said, her voice small. Crushed. "I've been working on this app for years, Daniel. The deadline for submissions for the FITC is just a few weeks away. If I accept this new position, there's no way I'll have enough time to get the app ready before the deadline. I've never had the kind of momentum behind it that I do now. If I don't make that deadline, I'll probably never see it through."

"So, essentially, a yes to Trendsetters is a no to my own dreams."

Daniel hated the defeat in her eyes. He smoothed his palm over her calf. In a quiet voice, he said, "Well that answers the question for you, doesn't it?"

"No, it doesn't. It's just the opposite. I'm left with an impossible decision and I have no idea which path I should choose."

He paused for a moment, searching for his words. Seeing how upset she was, he wanted to make sure they were the right ones.

"Samiah, I'm sure it's occurred to you that you can still work for the Outreach Department, even if you're not the one who gets it off the ground. You said that Barrington seemed to be one hundred percent behind the idea. He won't do away with it if you say no. He'll just put someone else in the position."

"It needs to be me," she said. "I know I sound cocky, but

I'm the best person for this job, Daniel. Barrington has more compassion than ninety-nine percent of the CEOs out there, but he isn't doing this for altruistic reasons. This is to help Trendsetters' image in the tech world. I want to make sure that Trendsetters isn't the only winner here. No one else they put in that job will make an effort to seek out young people of color—specifically young *women* of color—and bring them into STEM, or into Trendsetters. It's not because they don't think it's important. Some don't have a connection to the neighborhoods where the people I believe they should recruit live. Others just don't see it as a priority.

"I've witnessed this time and again. Hiring directors will look at two résumés and hold all things constant. They don't factor in how much harder that young black engineer had to work in order to get into that same position, and how that engineer will bring that same work ethic to the company." She shook her head. "There is so much good that can come from this."

"The same could be said for Just Friends," he pointed out. "Who knows what it could lead to? You may be five years away from building your own Trendsetters, Samiah."

"But can I afford to take that chance when so much is at stake? How selfish would it be of me to turn down the opportunity to do something that would make life better for so many more, simply because I've held this dream for an app that may never make it out of development?"

"It *will* make it out of development," Daniel said.

"But what if that's as far as I can take it? What if I pass on being the department head and my app idea falls flat? Then what? I'm relying on someone like Owen Caldwell or—God forbid—Keighleigh Miller to do the right thing when it comes to outreach?"

She dropped her head back on the arm of the sofa and covered her eyes with her forearm again.

He paused for a beat before offering in a quiet voice, "You can always do both."

She shook her head. "I'd rather choose a path and give one hundred percent. It wouldn't be fair to either if I half-assed this."

"What about if you had help?" She lifted her arm and peered at him from where she lay. He shrugged. "I do know my way around computer software and app development. I can help you get the app finished."

"No," she said with an emphatic shake of her head, then got up from the sofa and walked over to the wall of windows overlooking downtown Austin.

Daniel debated whether to give her some space, but only for a second. He joined her at the window, wrapping his arms around her middle and settling his chin against her shoulder.

"I'm sorry," she whispered. "I didn't mean for that to sound as harsh as it did."

"No need to apologize."

"Stop being so nice." She brought a hand up and ran it along his jaw. "Thank you for the offer," she continued. "But this is something I have to do on my own. As I've said before, this app is my baby. If it ever goes to market, I want to know that I did it on my own."

"*When* it goes to market," he corrected. "And I understand where you're coming from." He pressed a kiss to the indentation between her neck and collarbone. "But it's not as if I'm asking for co-developer status or anything, Samiah. I'm just saying that if you need some extra hands, I'm here."

"I know." She turned and settled her arms against his shoulders, clasping her slim fingers behind his head. "But I want to do this on my own. I *need* to do it on my own. I've held this dream for so long that this app is now a part of me. And at the end of the day, I want to be able to say that it was through my own blood, sweat, and tears that it came to be."

She rested her head against his chest. Daniel enveloped her in his arms, pressing a kiss to her temple as he stared out at the watery scene beyond the double-paned windows.

He'd offered his help out of desperation to erase the sadness from her eyes. But as he thought about it, he couldn't help but face a soul-crushing reality. He would be long gone by the time that tech conference came to Austin.

He didn't have a hard-and-fast end date for this job, but he'd worked under Lowell Dwyer long enough to know that his boss had one. Daniel figured he had another month to uncover the individuals behind the money-laundering scheme before Dwyer either replaced him with someone else or scrapped the entire operation until they could gather more intel and try again.

He didn't like it, but he understood those tough calls were sometimes necessary. Every operation had a cost-benefit analyst attached to it. There were a shitload of financial crimes being committed out there, and there was only so much manpower FinCEN could devote to each case. Trendsetters was a big one, but there were even bigger fish out there.

Like Vegas.

Shit. What was he going to do about Vegas? Was he willing to give that job up? A job that could make his career before he turned thirty?

It didn't matter. By the time Samiah finished developing

the prototype for her app, he would be gone. He'd banished those thoughts to far-off corners of his mind and tried not to think of them. But the reality remained.

She tipped her head back, looking up at him. "You know what's funny about you offering to help me with the app? You shouldn't have even known about it. I wasn't going to tell you."

"Why not?"

"Because you have the skills to steal my idea and develop it for yourself."

"Hey—"

"Not that you would," she quickly acknowledged. "But I'm overly cautious when it comes to stuff like that. I've been burned before."

He frowned. "Is this about Keighleigh?"

"Believe it or not, there was someone worse than Keighleigh." She tipped her head to the side. "Actually, that stunt she pulled this past week has them neck and neck, but this previous incident had a much bigger impact."

Daniel took her by the hand and backed up until he could perch on the arm of the sofa. He tugged her between his open legs and ran his hands along her sides, settling them at her waist.

"Tell me what happened."

The tension he felt radiating from her told him that this still affected her.

"It was at my very first job. I worked for one of the other huge tech companies that will remain nameless, but for a while they basically owned much of Austin. I was fresh out of grad school and soaking wet behind the ears—that's how my old supervisor described me. I developed a fix for an issue they'd been having with their recovery software, and was so excited that I stupidly shared it with a coworker. He immediately passed the idea off as his own. I tried to bring proof that it had been my idea, but I was accused of not being a team player. Since he had so many years at the company, he was given the benefit of the doubt, and I earned the reputation of being a selfish grandstander."

"That's bullshit. It was your idea."

"That's the cutthroat world of the tech industry. That guy is now the senior VP of Product Design at another firm." She shrugged. "I'm not saying he doesn't deserve that position, but I've followed his career. His rise to the top stemmed from my idea." Another shrug. "I've had to deal with similar situations throughout my career. I learned to keep my cards close to my chest, especially around those who have the knowledge to take my ideas and run with them."

"Just to be clear, I would never do that to you. Ever."

No, he just lied to her face about who he really was.

"I know," she said. She leaned forward and pressed a kiss to his lips. "Knowing you wouldn't turn around and stab me in the back is the only reason I was finally able to share it with you. It's nice to have someone in this industry that I can trust." She kissed him again. "Hey, do you like Jamaican food? I'm in the mood for curried goat and plantains."

"Sounds like the perfect rainy day meal," he answered around the lump of self-loathing lodged in his throat.

Once she'd left the room, Daniel threw his head back and shut his eyes tight. She was going to hate him for a long, long time once the truth finally came out. Possibly forever.

And he would deserve it.

CHAPTER TWENTY-THREE

H ow about the Leyland Group Lovelies?"

Groans wafted up to the high ceilings as Sam Hilton shielded himself from the balled-up notebook paper, candy wrappers, and Post-it Notes being hurled his way.

"Don't let them get to you," Daniel said. "They may not appreciate your humor, but I do."

A yellow highlighter sailed toward him.

"Duck and weave, dude," Sam said. "It's the only way to survive this crowd."

Daniel tilted his chair back until he met with resistance, then gently bounced back and forth as he absorbed the scene before him. All the conference rooms were occupied, so the Leyland Group team had commandeered a corner of Trendsetters' huge kitchen and break area. Some had dragged in nearby desk chairs and rearranged existing furniture to make a circle, other sat right on the floor.

As he studied his coworkers, he was taken aback by the realization that he would miss this—he'd miss *them*. He averted his gaze from the faces around him, confused by the sudden tightness in his chest. In the nearly two dozen undercover operations he'd worked since joining FinCEN two years ago, he'd become accustomed to his routine. As the quiet but friendly new guy at the office, he came in, did his job, and then left with no regrets.

Not this time. He'd connected with these people on a . level he'd never encountered with past jobs. No doubt it was due in large part to the collaborative office environment Trendsetters fostered, but it was more than that. The creative energy and hunger for innovation he saw in his coworkers reminded him of his college days, when his imagination and drive wasn't stifled by federal regulations and congressional budget cuts. There was a kinship with his Trendsetters R&D teammates, one that harkened back to the comradeship he'd found in the Marines.

He glanced over at Samiah and the tightness in his chest intensified.

Now that he was no longer ignoring the reality of his eventual departure, he couldn't even think about her without regret clawing at his throat. He knew an end date was imminent. His breath caught every time he received a call from the 703 area code. Every passing hour brought him closer to the moment when Lowell Dwyer would pull the plug on this operation. Daniel still didn't know how he would handle that.

Their team broke into groups of three, each working on a different aspect of the last-minute details before their presentation on the Leyland Group project tomorrow. Daniel had just finished his explanation of the backend safeguard that had been added to the software when his phone vibrated in his pocket. It stopped, then started again. He took it out and looked at the screen.

Sorry, right number. HQ

"Hey, I'll be back in a minute," Daniel said.

"Is everything okay?" Samiah asked, her brow furrowing with concern.

"Yeah, just a friend from my days in the Marines," Daniel said. "I've been trying to get hold of him but it's been hard because he's stationed abroad. Who knows when I'll get the chance to speak with him again?"

God, the lies came so easily.

She shooed him with both hands. "Go on. Hurry."

He bent over to kiss her, but remembered where they were and picked up the empty water bottle next to her instead.

What the hell?

They'd both agreed that they didn't want this thing between them to become fodder for the office rumor mill. Samiah had experienced enough of that after the Craig incident. For Daniel, it was more about mitigating the hurt and embarrassment she would undoubtedly face if he had to disappear from Trendsetters without a trace.

He grimaced at the sour taste that thought left in his mouth.

Daniel went downstairs, but encountering yet another downpour, opted for a corner of the lobby to make his call. He switched to his secured cell phone and called into FinCEN headquarters and asked to be patched to Preston August's desk.

"Hey Preston, what's up?" Daniel said when he heard the click on the other end of the line.

"It's not Preston." His spine went rigid at the sound of Lowell Dwyer's gruff voice.

"Sir?" Daniel replied.

"Do you have five minutes to talk, Collins?"

"Yes, sir," was his immediate answer.

"I have a proposal for you," his supervisor began, and Daniel's heart started to thump like a bass drum within his chest. "All intel shows that the outfit in Vegas is preparing to go dark and move their base of operation to Seattle. I want us to move in before they have the chance to do that, and I want you to run lead."

A tidal wave of euphoria surged within his chest and spread to his extremities. This was it. The gold prize.

"You know what I think about you as an agent, Collins," Dwyer continued in what passed for gentle when it came to his brusque tone. "This is the kind of opportunity that can catapult your career. Much more so than what you're doing down there in Austin."

The exhilaration still shuttling through his bloodstream began to wane as the full implication of his boss's offer began to crystalize. If he answered in the affirmative, Dwyer would have him sitting at a gate at Austin-Bergstrom Airport tonight. There was probably a team of people working on the formal explanation email that would be sent to Trendsetters' HR director.

The dread tingling at the base of his neck spidered out to the rest of his body.

He couldn't do it. He couldn't leave. Not this soon. He needed more time.

Seriously, man, what the fuck?

He had a career to think about. The stakes were so high he could barely wrap his head around the enormity of this moment. He'd spent the past two years striving to prove to himself that he'd made the right choice when he turned down all those high-paying tech job offers in exchange for joining FinCEN. To prove he not only belonged, but that he was an asset. As the lead agent on the most monumental case to hit the Financial Crimes Enforcement Network in years, everything he'd been working toward would be within his reach.

But how was he supposed to just pack up and leave? Even if Dwyer gave him time to tie up loose ends, the idea that in a couple of days he would be forced to say goodbye to Samiah forever sent a shock of panic rioting through him.

He couldn't do it. Not yet.

"I...uh...I appreciate this vote of confidence, sir, but—" He stopped. Swallowed. "But, it wouldn't feel right to leave things unfinished here." Wrenching anguish twisted in his gut. "It may not have the panache of Vegas, but I've put too much time and effort into solving this case to just let it go."

A daunting silence stretched out for several moments before Dwyer said, "You never cease to surprise me, Collins. Or to impress me."

Daniel huffed out a humorless laugh. "You're impressed that I turned down a career-changing opportunity?"

"I am. Don't think I haven't paid attention to the friendly competition between you and Stewart."

He wouldn't describe the pissing contest between himself and Bryce as "friendly," but cool, cool.

"There's a healthy rivalry," Daniel said.

"And you know I'll likely offer this job to Stewart now that you've turned it down, right?"

He bit the inside of his cheek to squelch the litany of profanities on the verge of spilling from his mouth.

"I understand that, sir. Stewart's a sharp agent. No doubt he'll thrive in Vegas."

"The case Stewart's working right now is as critical as what you're doing in Austin. The difference between the two of you is that he won't think twice about jumping ship. A half-dozen commendations look impressive on a résumé, Collins, but you know what also matters? Being able to sleep soundly at night, knowing you did the right thing for the right reasons."

Daniel slumped against the cool glass window, his eyes falling shut.

He wasn't doing this for the right reasons. He was doing this because he'd gotten in so deep with Samiah that he had no idea how to get out.

He turned to look out the window; the earlier downpour had dwindled to a light drizzle. A CapMetro bus shrink-wrapped with an advertisement for the Waterloo Music Festival pulled up to the stoplight, a light gray exhaust plume billowing from its tailpipe.

"Thank you for that," he said.

"Get back to work," Dwyer said. "Just because you're passing on Vegas, it doesn't mean I'm letting you hang out in Texas indefinitely. You need to wrap up this case."

"I hear you, sir," he said.

He disconnected the call but remained at the window, his pulse matching the methodic beep of the delivery truck backing into a loading dock across the street.

He'd been cognizant of the fact that the plug would eventually get pulled on this job. Which begged the question, why choose to stay here, knowing his time in Austin was coming to an end, instead of taking Dwyer up on his offer to lead the Vegas job?

Daniel shook his head. It wasn't as if he had to ask that question. He already knew the answer.

He didn't know what to do with the emotions suddenly swirling around in his head. He was with Joelle for six years, and when she gave him an ultimatum between their relationship and his career, he'd chosen the latter. He'd hardly taken time to contemplate it. He'd set out a path for himself once he left the Marine Corps, and his focus had remained on that trajectory ever since.

Where in the hell was that focus now?

He'd lost it his very first day on the job. From the minute he encountered Samiah at that coffee machine and began to see everything through a different lens. From that day he'd started to veer off his well-laid path, deviating to one that he and Samiah could possibly travel together.

But they weren't together. All of this was based on a lie. And when that lie finally came to the surface, the likelihood that she wouldn't want anything to do with him was so great it hurt him just to think about it.

He had to remember what mattered most, his duty to his family and to his career. He'd sacrificed too much. He couldn't jeopardize this thing he'd worked so hard for. Not for anyone, including Samiah.

* * *

With the press of two buttons, Samiah simultaneously dimmed the lights in the conference room and brought the eighty-four-inch Microsoft Surface Hub on the far wall to life, the Trendsetters logo in the center of its touchscreen display. Moving to stand beside the digital whiteboard, she tapped the screen, bringing up the presentation she'd spent much of last night revising after deciding that what they'd collaborated on yesterday just wasn't good enough.

"Our team was tasked with coming up with a workable solution for the Leyland Group's failing customer management software and networking system, including an overhaul of their WLAN design," Samiah opened. "It was a complicated endeavor based on the size and scope, but also due to the sensitive nature of the medical files the company handles. The popularity of DNA tests has turned this into a booming business, and those companies are starting to understand just how important and difficult it is to keep their customers' personal data safe. The number of nefarious things that could be done if their systems are breached is endless."

She tapped the screen again, then used the electronic pen to draw a circle around the design scheme displayed on the smart board.

"We took a multipronged approach, developing a solution that is scalable as the company grows, but also not so involved that it will confine them to only one way of securing data." She handed the stylus to her coworker. "Sam will take us through some detection techniques and expand on how the new vulnerability scanner will work."

After handing the presentation off to Sam, Samiah traversed the length of the conference room, opting to prop her elbow up on one of two standing-height tables that butted against the opposite wall. From this vantage point she could observe the entire room and gauge how the guys in charge were assessing what was being laid out for them.

The reins of the presentation were passed on from team member to team member. None of them had been tripped up by the slight changes she'd made, which once again proved that she and John had put together one of the best teams ever.

She could bring them all with her if she took the Outreach Department head position.

Samiah wasn't even sure where she stood yet regarding Justin and Barrington's offer, but that hadn't stopped her from arranging and rearranging the structure of the department a thousand times in her head. She wanted to bring in people from all aspects of the company, not just Human Resources or the Public Relations departments. Every division had a stake in this. This current project was the perfect example of the magical outcomes in store when creative minds from all areas of the company came together for a common goal.

She could be directing all that magic. All she had to do was say yes.

Samiah tucked those thoughts back into her mental lockbox and returned her attention to the presentation. This wasn't the time or place to let her mind wander.

It was Keighleigh's turn to present. She began by pointing out the various flaws in the Leyland Group's previous applications. After a few minutes, she started to discuss potential patches for unforeseen security risks that might develop in the future. Samiah stood upright, her spine going ramrod straight.

This bitch.

Why hadn't she anticipated this? Of course Keighleigh would pull this kind of bullshit move, despite every single person on their team knowing that she was once again usurping Samiah's idea. This is what she got for scheduling her conniving, spotlight-stealing coworker's portion of the presentation to go right before what should have been *her* big finish.

"This is ingenuity at its finest," Barrington said once the other woman was done. "How do you suppose we implement these potential fixes, Keighleigh?"

Samiah caught the flash of panic behind Keighleigh's strained smile before her coworker pointed to the back of the room and said, "I'll leave that to our fearless team leader to explain."

Seething, Samiah started for the other end of the conference room before Daniel's words stopped her.

"Why don't you go ahead and do it, Keighleigh?"

Every head in the conference room turned to him, but his eyes remained on a stunned Keighleigh Miller. The smile on his face belied the tension emanating from him. He was pissed. For her.

Samiah's heart melted.

"Daniel's right," Barrington said. "Bring this home for us. I'm sure Samiah doesn't mind."

If there was a dictionary entry for *scared shitless*, Keighleigh Miller's face would be in the little square box right next to it. Her wide, panicked gaze flew from Daniel's to Barrington's to the smart board, and finally to Samiah's.

A small part of her—the tiniest, most infinitesimal part that was still capable of empathizing with a fellow human being, even if said human being was straight-up trash—felt sorry for Keighleigh. But then Samiah mentally gut-punched that tiny part of her and sat it in a corner, facing the wall.

Keighleigh deserved every second of the excruciating misery she was no doubt feeling right now. She'd manipulated her way into this job, riding coattails and passing off the ideas of her fellow coworkers as her own, with no thought about the consequences of her actions. Well, it was time baby girl faced the music.

The atmosphere in the room quickly reached nails-down-a-chalkboard levels of discomfort as they all sat there waiting for Keighleigh to continue. In what she could only describe as an attempt to bank a few brownie points to get into heaven, Samiah finally decided to have mercy on her coworker.

Her phone began vibrating in her dress pocket, but she ignored it as she continued onward, plucking the stylus from Keighleigh's hand and tapping the smart board's screen.

"Thanks for setting that up for me, Keighleigh, but I'll take it from here."

Samiah dismissed her with a brief tilt of her head, then went on to succinctly explain the implementation plan. She answered every single question her superiors lobbed at her, showing them just why Trendsetters was lucky to have her. She was impressive as fuck, and everyone in this room knew it.

Once the presentation was done, the Leyland Group team members received the accolades they deserved for a job well done. After a significant amount of backslapping and congratulatory fist bumps, everyone began to file out of the conference room. Samiah lingered behind. So did Daniel.

Once they were alone, she walked up to him and held her hand out. "Brilliant move there, Mr. Collins."

He huffed out a laugh as he shook her hand.

"She had it coming," he said. "How is she going to stand up there and present your part, knowing that we all know she didn't have anything to do with devising that implementation plan?"

"Because she's gotten away with doing things like that from the moment she started here," Samiah said. "Keighleigh has ridden that 'everyone is on the same team' horse into the ground, and no one has called her on it."

"Why not?"

"Because you'll be accused of not being a team player, or of being a show-off."

"Yet that's exactly what *she* did." He hooked his thumb toward the smart board. "That was all about showing off. Someone needed to call her out."

Samiah shrugged. She couldn't argue with him. She was just as culpable when it came to allowing Keighleigh to get away with the shenanigans she'd been pulling since she first started at Trendsetters. They'd all allowed it. But not Daniel. He'd spoken up on her behalf.

Samiah glanced over both shoulders, making sure they were alone and that the windows of the conference room were still opaque. Then she tilted her face up and placed a quick kiss on his lips.

"Thank you for having my back," she said. "It's not easy to find people I can trust around here. It means a lot."

The muscles in his jaw flinched and he averted his eyes.

Samiah frowned. "Is something wrong?"

He blinked hard then shook his head. "No. Not at all." His smile returned. "Congratulations on that presentation. You think we'll get a pizza party out of this?"

"A pizza party? I won't settle for anything less than steak and lobster," Samiah said. "And considering the money the Leyland Group paid for this rush job, I may demand that steak and lobster be served on the deck of a cruise ship in the middle of the Caribbean."

His eyes bugged. "Would they actually do that?"

Samiah burst out laughing. "Don't get too excited. They

don't treat us *that* well here. But you should expect a nice dinner, at the very least. And maybe some premium Trendsetters' swag."

"That works for me."

"Oh, shoot!" Samiah snapped her fingers. "I meant to talk to Justin before he left. We need to discuss my security access."

"What about it?"

"A new team was just formed to help Huston-Tillotson University—a small historically black university here in Austin—with networking issues. It's similar to a project I worked on last year, so they're restoring some of the security clearances I previously had. It'll give me access to all the databases I'll need for research purposes."

"Oh." He nodded. "That's...um...cool. You, uh, want to grab lunch?"

"Sure." Samiah regarded him with a slight frown. He seemed...off. "Just give me a few minutes to check email."

She returned to her desk to find an email from Barrington waiting in her inbox, thanking the entire team for their hard work on the Leyland Group project. As a token of the entire Trendsetters family's appreciation, the team was invited to dinner at the Driskill Grill in the famed Driskill Hotel. On top of that, they were all being treated to a day of adventure at Schlitterbahn Waterpark in New Braunfels.

After weeks of working so closely with them, Samiah wasn't sure she wanted to spend time at an amusement park with her teammates, but whatever. It was a nice gesture.

Her cell phone vibrated again and Samiah remembered the text she'd missed while in the middle of the presentation. She took out the phone and saw a text from London with a link to a gossip site.

She groaned as a still shot of her pointing a menacing finger at Craig Walter's face anchored a headline that caused her eyes to bulge.

"Oh. My. God."

There were two knocks on her door before it opened.

"Hey, are you ready?" Daniel asked, poking his head in her office.

Samiah held up her phone, a grin spreading across her face. "Craig is being sought by the police. He's been scamming seniors out of their social security checks."

"What?" Daniel sprinted to her desk, taking the phone from her. "Takes a special kind of asshole to steal money from elderly folks."

"The same kind of asshole who dates multiple women at the same time and makes a living out of lying," Samiah said. She ejected her access card from her computer, slipped it in her purse, and locked up her desk. "But the authorities are on his tail now, so Craig's cheating and scamming days are numbered. Let's go to lunch. Today calls for celebratory tres leches from that cute cantina on Brazos."

Daniel swept his hand out. "After you."

CHAPTER TWENTY-FOUR

Daniel burrowed his chin deeper into his jacket collar, bracing himself against the brisk wind blowing in from the northwest. The atypically strong, early-season cold front that crawled across the area overnight was the talk at the gas station, Laundromat, and coffee shop he'd visited this morning. Still-green leaves and thick acorns that had been ripped away from nearby bur oaks tumbled along the cracked asphalt.

Daniel shoved his hands in his pockets as he walked around the front fender of the bright green Kia Soul Quentin had just led him to.

"What do you think of this one?" Quentin asked.

"Umm...I don't know. It seems a bit...loud."

"You've never met my Ava." Quentin laughed. "This car is the embodiment of her. Now that Corolla." He pointed to a tan hatchback three spots down. "That's more my Emma's speed. I'm just not sure about buying one an SUV while the other only gets a small sedan. I can already hear the arguments."

He hunched his shoulders. "I don't know what to tell you, man. This is uncharted territory for me."

Daniel had asked Quentin to come over to the apartment

so that he could get his thoughts on a few irregularities he'd come across while looking into the background of a Trendsetters employee who'd left the company under suspicious circumstances last year. When Quentin asked if he could wait until he was done shopping for presents for his twin daughters for their upcoming fifteenth birthdays, Daniel had offered to meet up with him.

When he arrived at this used car dealership in Kyle, just south of Austin, Daniel thought he'd punched the wrong address into his phone's GPS. But Quentin had greeted him and told him this wouldn't take long.

That was two hours ago. He was certain they'd looked at every single car on this lot.

"Do your girls know how lucky they are?" Daniel asked as he peered into the Kia's passenger-side window. "I had to buy my own first car, which is why I rode the bus or subway until I was almost twenty."

"Hey, I'm the one getting off lucky," Quentin said. "Do you have any idea how much a quinceañera costs these days? More than my wedding and my first car combined. Just the damn party favors they wanted to give out would have cost me a couple of grand. At least they'll have the cars throughout college."

"What about this one?" Daniel asked, pointing to another Kia Soul in a nice, sedate cream.

Quentin shook his head. "I know my girls. They won't want to drive the same model. I need to find something that's different but comparable. And it has to be perfect. I don't want to get this wrong and disappoint them."

The guy was in knots. Granted, he'd known Quentin only a couple of months, but Daniel could have never imagined he'd see the formidable, no-nonsense DHS agent in such a state. Was this the kind of thing he was in store for, twisting himself into a tangle of nerves trying to please his future children?

Future children?

Where in the hell had *that* come from? The last time he even thought about children was the day he brought up the subject with Joelle. She'd railed against the thought of having kids. As an only child, he'd considered it, but he'd never had a burning desire either way. He just figured if it happened, great. If not, that was good too.

When had his feelings changed? And why was he suddenly daydreaming about what life could be in the distant future, with him and Samiah celebrating their impending newborn at a joint baby shower, complete with gender-neutral cupcakes and party favors that cost a thousand dollars? He didn't even know if Samiah was open to having a pet goldfish, and here he was thinking about kids.

What was the point when he would be gone in a matter of days? Weeks, if he was lucky. He sucked in a painful breath and tried to quell the overwhelming dread primed to overtake him.

It was time for the knot that formed in the pit of his stomach to start paying rent. It seemed as though it had taken up permanent residence ever since his call with Dwyer earlier this week. His supervisor hadn't given him a definitive end date, but Daniel sensed that time was closing in. He figured he had about a week at the most before Dwyer would insist he wrap up this case.

The idea that he would lose Samiah wrought the kind of agony that would bring most men to their knees, but that wasn't the only thing keeping him up at night. Nor was it his future at FinCEN, or getting the better of Bryce Stewart's showboating ass. The thought of leaving Austin before apprehending the bastards involved in this particular scheme galled him.

And that was *before* receiving that link from Preston last night.

It had taken Daniel to an underground message board on the dark web that indicated the money-laundering ring coming out of the area in Latin America where the Trendsetters case was centered was possibly expanding to new territory. Territory that those who peddled in much darker things than a little washed money operated in. Just thinking about what they could face if the drug cartels and human trafficking outfits learned how easy it was to launder their ill-gotten gains through something like Trendsetters' software caused fear to clog Daniel's throat.

Dwyer wouldn't put as much stock into what they'd read on the message board, seeing as a lot of what came across those were full of conjecture and baseless rumors, but Daniel wasn't willing to take a chance on this being unfounded speculation. It was imperative he solve this case before he was pulled out of Austin.

One week. He would give himself one week to get it done. It wasn't a lot of time, but maybe if he directed more of his focus to doing the work he'd actually been sent here to do, instead of falling in love with a coworker—

Daniel tripped over an orange traffic cone used to delineate the car lot's walkway.

"You okay?" Quentin asked.

"Yeah. Yeah, I'm good," he replied.

Falling in love?

What in the hell was he talking about? He couldn't be there yet. No way would he own up to something that over the top. Shit, he'd been with Joelle for six years, and it took at least half that long before he'd considered himself in love with her.

"Hey, you mind if I ask you something?" Quentin asked.

"Sure, what's up?"

"Why'd you turn down the offer Dwyer made to you?"

Daniel's head reared back. "How do you know about that?"

Quentin just stared at him, one thick brow cocked.

Dammit, he should have known the two men talked. He'd suspected Dwyer was the one who'd requested the Department of Homeland Security place Quentin in the apartment with Daniel, and not the other way around.

"He couldn't share much about what's happening in Vegas, but from what he did share this seems like the kind of case that would spring you over quite a few rungs of that career ladder."

"I told him that I want to see this job through," Daniel finally answered.

"He could always send someone else to take over the Trendsetters case."

"It's not that easy. We had to put this case off for months because Trendsetters' hiring process is so selective," he pointed out.

"If Lowell Dwyer needs to make it happen, he'll make it happen," Quentin said. He folded his arms across his chest and leaned against the driver's side door of a Dodge Ram pickup. "Try again."

Daniel squared his shoulders and assumed a matching pose. "What do you want me to say?"

"That you got in too deep with Samiah Brooks and now you're not sure if you can get out. Or if you even *want* out."

Fuck. He was obviously as transparent as the windshields on these used cars.

Daniel dropped his head to his chest and sucked in a breath. His head popped up at the sound of Quentin's laughter.

"You find this funny?"

"Yes," he replied. "Hilarious, in fact. Do you think you're the first one this has happened to, young buck? How do you think I met my wife?"

Daniel couldn't help his grin. "You're shitting me."

"Nope." Quentin shook his head. "I was still at DEA. She was an informant. Her baby brother got caught up in some rough shit and, being the bold, fearless woman that she is, she volunteered to be used as bait."

"Were you the one who took down her brother?" He nodded. "Damn." Daniel blew out a low whistle. "Thanksgiving must be loads of fun at your place."

Quentin's head shot back with his laugh. "My brother-in-law turned his life around. And he has his big sister to thank for that." He shrugged one broad shoulder. "My supervisor wasn't happy, but he eventually got over it. If you tell him, he'll eventually get over it happening with another one of his agents."

"I knew it." Daniel huffed out a mirthless chuckle. "Hard to believe Dwyer was your supervisor. He doesn't look more than a couple of years older than you."

"He isn't. But he was a hotshot like you. Always has been. Worked his ass off and worked his way up the ranks faster than the rest of us." Quentin's expression became earnest. "He's a good guy. One of the best. And the fact that he thinks you're up to the challenge of this Vegas job says a lot about what he thinks of you."

Daniel rubbed the back of his neck, trying to relieve some of the tension. He squinted, almost afraid to see the other man's reaction to his forthcoming question.

"You think I made a mistake in turning it down, don't you?" Daniel asked.

The scar at the edge of Quentin's mouth inched up. "I'm freezing my ass off while I car shop for two princesses who wouldn't be here if I'd listened to my head instead of my heart when I found myself in your situation almost twenty years ago. I think you did what you think is right for you."

How in the hell was he supposed to know if this was the right move or not? He'd passed on a career-making opportunity for a woman who had yet to introduce him to her family.

Daniel felt his phone vibrate in his pocket. A second later, Quentin's rang. They looked at each other before looking at their phones.

"Shit," Daniel said. "*Shit.*"

"Closing accounts for you too?" Quentin asked.

"This makes three since this morning," Daniel said. "Shit."

He took a breath to stop himself from panicking. This activity could mean any number of things. He doubted he'd been found out, but it could mean that someone had been tipped that law enforcement might be on their tail. No matter what, the fact that three of the eight bank accounts they'd been monitoring had been closed in a matter of hours meant that something was definitely up.

If the money launderers went dark, it could be weeks, even months before they surfaced again. It would be hell to find them. All the work they'd done, the man-hours he'd put in, the money that had been spent to facilitate this job; it would all be wasted.

Shit.

He had to get into that database. It was the quickest way to ferret out who was behind this. If there was such a thing as mission critical, they'd just reached it.

* * *

Samiah tucked the bottle of sparkling water under her arm and carried it, along with three glasses, into the living room, stepping out of London's way as her friend swayed to the smooth, neo-soul sound of Maxwell's "Ascension" strumming from the Sonos speaker system.

"Anyone else feeling a full-circle moment vibe right now?" London asked.

"Not exactly." Samiah held up her wineglass. "Last time we met at my place it was Moscow Mules and leftover sushi. This very nice red wine and gourmet popcorn is tres chic, my friend. Good choice."

"You are very welcome," London said, still doing what Samiah and her cousins used to call "the old folks' dance," rocking from side to side to the rhythm of the classic song. She sauntered over and grabbed a fistful of the rosemary and white truffle popcorn she'd brought with her. "The wine is from a solo trip I took to Italy last year. I've been holding on to it for a special occasion. Hanging out with you two seemed special enough to me."

"You went to Italy? Fun," Taylor said. "I went back when we lived on the base in Germany, but only for a couple of days. I tried leaning over like the Tower of Pisa but fell and broke my elbow."

Samiah did her best to hold it together, but after a few seconds she burst out laughing. "I'm sorry," she said. "That's just so...you."

"Yes, it is so me," Taylor said.

Samiah frowned at Taylor's toneless response.

"Hey." She reached over and gave her a playful tap on the arm. "I was just joking."

"I know." Taylor smiled, but it didn't reach her eyes.

Samiah looked over at London, who held both palms up and hunched her shoulders in confusion.

They'd made plans to meet up at her place before going out for sushi at the place that started it all two months ago. But because Austin was once again in the throes of a raging thunderstorm—seriously, this was more rain than they usually saw the entire fall season—no one wanted to leave the condo. Instead, Samiah took out a lasagna Denise had sent over a few days ago and slipped it in the oven. Now that her sister was nearing the end of her pregnancy, she was in full nesting mode. According to Bradley, their freezer was filled with enough casseroles to feed them for the next six months.

Samiah was more than happy to take a few of those meals off their hands. Sharing a home-cooked meal with London and Taylor beat going out to a restaurant. Samiah had discovered that, when it came to these two, the place wasn't important; it was the company. She'd found something she hadn't known she'd been missing in her life: true girlfriends.

Earlier, when she told them about the position she'd been offered at Trendsetters, Taylor and London both helped her see that no matter how fulfilling heading up the new Outreach

Department might be, giving up on the dreams she had for her app would leave her dissatisfied in the end. She had reached that conclusion days ago, but hearing it from these two—women who *got* her, who understood her—reaffirmed what she already knew to be the only possible choice for her.

Over the course of these last couple of months, the boyfriend project had morphed into something more powerful than any of them had expected. This undertaking moved far beyond getting themselves in a position to find significant others. This was about finding their life's truth.

As she sat here, enjoying good wine and even better company, Samiah recognized that she was solidly on that path.

She looked over to Taylor to find her downing the remaining wine in her glass with one huge gulp, then reaching for the wine bottle.

"Whoa there," Samiah said, plucking the bottle from her hand. "You want to take it easy? Keep that up and you'll be passed out drunk before we slice into the lasagna."

"Good. I'm trying to get drunk," she said.

"No shit. You look like you're halfway there already." Samiah poured San Pellegrino into a glass and switched Taylor's wine stem with the mineral water. "You need to drink some of this before you have more wine," she said. "Now, do you mind sharing why our resident health nut is trying to get drunk?"

Taylor shook her head.

"Nope, you don't get to say no," London said. She perched on the arm of the sofa. "These Friday night get-togethers are supposed to be about having a safe space to air our grievances. From what I've seen tonight, you sure as shit have some grievances you need to air out. Let us hear it."

"Please." Taylor covered her face with both hands and released a groan. "I honestly don't want to talk about it. It's just family crap that I've been dealing with my whole life. I'm over it."

"Over it as in you want to drink yourself into a stupor and then punch the wall, or over it as in we should remove all sharp objects and pills from your apartment before allowing you to be there by yourself tonight?" London asked.

Taylor rolled her eyes. "I'm not suicidal."

"I'm just trying to figure out what we're dealing with here," London said.

"It's the same damn story—no, make that the same damn *nightmare*. My life is a fucking nightmare!"

Samiah's head snapped back at the sheer vehemence in Taylor's agonized outburst. Where was this even coming from? The person sitting before her hardly resembled the happy-go-lucky woman she'd come to know over these past two months.

"Honey, what's going on?" she asked, concern tightening her chest.

"I'm sorry," Taylor said somewhat sheepishly. "That may have been a tiny bit dramatic. It's not as serious as you're probably thinking."

London bounded up from the arm of the sofa, her hands flailing. "Are you for real right now? I was going through the steps for an intervention in my head."

"I'm *sorry*," she stressed. "It's just . . . I come from a family of overachievers," she said. "And I'm tired of being the one who's always asked when I'm going to get my shit together."

"You're only twenty-eight years old," London pointed out.

"You're not expected to have your shit together until you're at least thirty."

"Well, hell, I guess I need to play catchup." Samiah laughed.

Taylor didn't. She turned to London. "How old were you when you finished medical school? Hmm?" She prompted when London remained quiet. "Bet you were younger than twenty-eight."

"I started undergrad early, and went to summer school to finish ahead of schedule," London replied.

"But you were still younger than I am, weren't you?" She turned to Samiah. "And how about you? At twenty-eight you already had a master's degree and were working in your career, right?"

"It's not fair to compare yourself to others," Samiah said. "You can't—"

"No? Really?" Taylor said, cutting her off. "Because my family *always* compares. They live to compare." She started ticking items off on her fingers. "My dad, Mr. Bronze Star himself, was already climbing the ranks of the Army by the time he was my age. Mom had finished law school while raising two children and moving from one Army base to another by my age. My older brother, Darwin? Lawyer. My older sister, Jesamyn? Architect. Even my niece is showing me up. She won the Top Young Scientist award last year.

"And what is Taylor doing? Sitting here without a college degree and keeping her fingers crossed that she can get the chance to teach freaking phys ed to a bunch of homeschooled kids just to make ends meet. I'm tired of being the one everybody in my family looks down on."

She covered her face with her hands and growled. "Argh, I'm sorry. It's just...it's a lot."

Samiah reached over and peeled Taylor's fingers from her face. "Come on, stop this," she said. "I thought we all decided we were no longer living our lives based on what other people think we should be doing. Or because it's what society says we should do."

"That's so easy for you to say," Taylor said. "You're not a failure."

"Okay, that's enough of *that* bullshit." London set her wineglass on the end table. She walked over to Taylor, grabbed her hands, and pulled her up from the sofa. "Look at me," London said, lifting Taylor's chin. "Do you enjoy what you're doing?"

She nodded.

"No. Say it. Answer the question. Do you enjoy being a fitness consultant?"

"Yes."

"Does it make you happy? Happier than anything else you could be doing with your life?"

"Yes," she said.

"Then that's all that matters. Everything else is negative bullshit and you don't need that in your life."

"But I *do* need my family," Taylor said. "As much as they drive me crazy, I love them. I just wish I could have something exciting to share with them when I go home for Thanksgiving, instead of the same old stuff."

"Tell them that you're supporting yourself by doing what you love," London said.

"She's right," Samiah said, rising from the sofa and walking over to join them. "It may not be easy going right now, and you may not be satisfied at the pace that your business is growing, but it *is* growing. And you said it yourself, teaching phys ed to a bunch of homeschooled kids is nothing to turn your nose up at. It will pay the bills while you continue to grow your business."

"Exactly," London said. She pointed at the coffee table. "Now you can drink this wine to celebrate the gains you've made, but I'll be damned if I let you waste another drop of this fantastic Chianti on wallowing. Hell no. This wine comes from happy grapes. It is to be used for celebration purposes only."

The infectious grin Samiah had come to associate with her appeared on Taylor's face. "Well, I do want more wine, so I guess we're celebrating."

"Now *that's* what I want to hear," London said, grabbing the bottle of wine and topping off their empty glasses. She handed them their drinks and lifted hers in the air. "To the only woman I know who can kick your ass with a smile. Your time is coming, Taylor Powell. You just make sure you're ready to make the most of it when it does."

CHAPTER TWENTY-FIVE

Samiah wrapped her lips around the straw and drew in a deep swallow of the pineapple passion fruit kombucha. She guessed some would consider her a convert, if the top shelf of her refrigerator was anything to go on. The yogurts and cottage cheese had been demoted to the second shelf. She set the bottle on her bedside table, picked up her electronic pencil, and made a note in the corner of the screen, just above the proposed spot for the settings button.

She'd switched it from one side to the other, piddled with the thought of going rogue and placing it at the bottom of the app, then settled for the traditional upper right-hand corner. The last thing she wanted to do was frustrate people by changing things up too much.

She used the blunt end of the pencil to move icons around, but wasn't happy with any of the ideas she came up with.

"Just put it away," she blew out on an exasperated breath, setting the tablet next to her on the bed.

Her purpose for picking up the thing in the first place was to help London find a *knock 'em dead* outfit for her upcoming class reunion. They'd messaged each other links to various online stores, but then London was called into an emergency patient consultation and Samiah had switched from her browser to her developer software without even thinking about it.

She would have to break this habit; her brain needed time to recoup. She'd been working on Just Friends almost non-stop since finishing the Leyland Group project and could feel burnout creeping up on her like those extra five pounds that always made it to her hips during the holidays.

She'd experienced burnout at the ripe old age of twenty-seven, only months after she started at Trendsetters. She would not put herself in that position again.

She scooted off the bed and went to her closet, looking for the wide-leg silk jumpsuit she'd bought last year. The red one she'd found for London online had a plunging neckline and attached cape, and it was much better suited for turning heads than the blue pinstripe, but she figured London could try this one on first to make sure she wanted the jumpsuit look before shelling out four hundred dollars.

After locating the jumpsuit, she searched for other looks she could offer London as she bided her time until Daniel could get there. He'd texted earlier, apologizing for running late. His roommate, Quentin, had some big issue with his wife that he was trying to work out and needed Daniel there for emotional support. Samiah did her best to quell her agitation. She couldn't fault him for wanting to be a good friend. If her sister, or Taylor or London, needed her, she wouldn't think twice about running to their aid. She just hoped to God none of her friends called on her when she was feeling this horny.

Her intercom buzzed.

"Thank goodness." She tossed aside the off-the-shoulder sweater she'd just pulled from a hanger and raced to the keypad on her bedroom wall, becoming absurdly happy to see Daniel's smiling face staring back at her from the display screen.

Samiah keyed him in, then moved the tablet from her bed to her dresser and slipped on a pair of shorts before rushing to her front door. She opened it and leaned against the door-jamb, waiting for him. The elevator chimed its arrival. The stainless-steel panels separated and he walked out, turning left and striding toward her condo with purpose.

He stopped two feet in front of her.

"Hey," he said.

"Hey," she answered. She tilted her head toward the open door, inviting him inside. The second she closed the door behind her, she went in for a kiss, wrapping her arms around his head and slamming her body flush against his. It was a chaotic mingling of lips, teeth, and tongue, all vying for position as they tried to inhale each other on their way to the living room.

Without ever relinquishing her mouth, Daniel peeled his jacket off and tossed it on the armless accent chair next to her couch. His hands caught the hem of her T-shirt and pulled it up and over her head, then he peeled down the cups of the bra that should have been off already—*dammit*—and licked first one, then the other nipple with his strong, wet tongue.

Samiah fell back onto the couch and urged him to follow, cradling his head between her hands as he laved her breast with sure, toe-curling strokes. A desperate moan slipped from her lips. As much as she loved foreplay, her body demanded they skip the appetizer and get straight to the main course.

Just as she was about to tell Daniel her wishes, he left her breasts and began pressing light kisses down her torso. He dropped to his knees, hooked his thumbs underneath the rim of her shorts and panties, and tugged them over her hips and down her legs. The ambient air hit her heated center, causing her to shiver. Or maybe it was the man hunched over her. He wedged his shoulders between her thighs and Samiah decided she wanted to remain in this position until the end of time.

"Holy fuck, you look amazing," Daniel said, his warm breath wisping across her sensitive skin.

He ran both palms up and down her thighs before dipping his head and stroking the tip of his tongue between her legs. Samiah braced her hands on either side of her and lifted her lower half up, feeding herself to him. His decadent licks grew more insistent with each sweep of his tongue, spreading her open and delving inside, driving her out of her mind.

Pressure started to build low in her belly, the sensation blossoming from her core and spreading throughout her limbs, until it felt as if her entire body was on the verge of erupting. He wrapped his lips around her clit and sucked hard, and she went off like a cannon, her body's response so powerful she felt it across every single inch of her skin.

Daniel rode out her orgasm on his knees, his mouth still intent on giving her more pleasure than she knew what to do with. He continued his relentless pursuit, sending another heart-stopping orgasm spiraling through her before wrapping her legs around his waist and carrying her to her bedroom. Once there, he did with his powerful erection what he'd done with his mouth, bringing on climax after sweet, fiery climax, until Samiah was ready to surrender every single piece of herself to him.

She gripped his shoulders and levered herself up on her elbows, then with a strong push, flipped their positions.

"Can't a girl get a piece of this action?"

A stunned smile lit up his face. He held his hands up. "Have at it."

Steadying herself with one hand against his tight abdomen, Samiah used the other to guide him inside of her. She tilted her head back, bringing her hands behind her and bracing them on his strong thighs. She rolled her hips back and forth, riding him like her life depended on it.

They found an addicting rhythm; quick, shallow dips followed by slow, deep plunges. That intoxicating tremor fluttered to life in her belly once again. She tried to stave it off, fought to make this time last a bit longer, but when Daniel clasped her waist and held her down just as he tilted his hips upward and thrust into her, her world once again exploded in a blinding burst of sensations that ricocheted throughout her body.

She screamed her release toward the ceiling, then collapsed onto his chest.

"My God," Samiah breathed. "Do the Marines give out medals for this kind of stuff? Is that why you're so good at it?"

She felt his laugh rumbling beneath her cheek.

She snuggled more securely against him, relishing the feel of his warm skin against her body. She could get used to feeling this replete every night.

Goodness, where had that come from? It was insane to even begin thinking in terms of lying beside him on a nightly basis.

But, then again, maybe it wasn't.

She knew couples who'd moved in after dating just a few weeks. Hell, look at the people who met on those crazy reality TV shows. Some of them were making it work despite not knowing anything about their significant other beforehand. At least she and Daniel had been together longer than the people on *Married at First Sight* or *90 Day Fiancé*.

Okay, they hadn't known each other ninety days yet, but what was another thirty days?

"Stop it."

"What was that?" Daniel asked.

"Huh? Nothing," she said. "I need to use the bathroom."

She levered herself up, hoping her legs had the strength to carry her the fifteen or so feet. She could picture herself getting out of bed on wobbly legs and collapsing like a newborn colt just learning to walk.

She made it to the bathroom without injury. When she returned to the bedroom, she found Daniel sitting with his back against the headboard, a deep frown marring his brow as he stared at his phone.

Samiah stopped short. "Is everything okay?"

His head jerked up. "What? Uh, yeah," he said. He set the phone on the bedside table and pulled the cover back, inviting her to join him. Her eyes went straight to the erection that was already growing thick again.

Her pulse started to pound as excitement skidded across her skin.

She was going to be *so* sore in the morning. But she would be satisfied.

* * *

The faint scent of the sweet almond body cream Samiah had rubbed into her skin after their shower wafted up from where she rested, snuggled up next to him, her head nestled against his chest. Daniel stared straight ahead, his eyes set on the dove-gray clay pots that looked as if they were floating on air with the way they were lined along the glass display shelf above her chest of drawers.

His sated body should feel relaxed after a solid hour of starring in *American Ninja Warrior: Bedroom Edition* with Samiah, but rest continued to elude him. His muscles felt at ease, but his brain was hard at work, conjuring boundless nefarious scenarios ever since he'd read that text from Preston. Another two bank accounts had gone dark, and the subject they'd targeted in Belize had gone missing.

The window was rapidly closing. If whoever was behind this closed up all the bank accounts they'd been monitoring, tracking them would be almost impossible.

He had to infiltrate that database. In it lay everything they would need for a capture and conviction. Someone on the Trendsetters side was inflating the number of customers logging into Hughes Hospitality's free Wi-Fi every month. Even if he wasn't able to discover who was behind it, getting into their system would give him the raw data on the actual number of logins. Once they were able to show the discrepancy, that would be enough for a court order.

But none of that would happen if he couldn't bypass their security and access the damn database.

Except now he could.

Daniel sucked in a swift breath, fighting against the wave of nausea that pummeled him. The thought had lingered at the periphery of his conscience since the moment he learned that Samiah's security access had been changed. He'd quickly banished any notion of using her. This job was important, but it could not come at the expense of hers.

As he peered down at her face right now, the tension in his shoulders eased by a tiny degree. She was peace and fire and satisfaction and love all rolled into one. He could *not* do this to her.

But would he ever have a better chance of getting into that system?

Weighing the costs of betraying Samiah versus not betraying her was a game he never wanted to play, but he didn't have the luxury of not playing it. Not anymore. He'd wanted to give himself one more week to infiltrate the Trendsetters licensing database, but now Daniel wasn't sure he had a week to spare. At the rate those bank accounts were closing, he might not have another twenty-four hours before the money-laundering outfit went completely dark.

The implications of that happening sent the tension shooting right back into his muscles. At last count, a little over eighteen million dollars had been laundered through the Trendsetters Wi-Fi payment system software. The money had been used to fund a chain of payday loan businesses, but the DHS had put Quentin on the case because they suspected those were just a front for other criminal enterprises. They had to put a stop to it now. Before more money could be funneled. Before more people met with "accidents" like the one Daniel suspected Mike Epsen had.

There was no question that Mike's accident was related to this case, not after discovering the man had been on the initial rollout team. The fact that the anonymous tipster had been uncommunicative since the accident only proved that those behind the money-laundering scheme who wanted to silence Epsen had accomplished the mission they'd set out to achieve when they ran him into that city bus.

But what if their mission had been something more sinister than a broken leg and a few cracked ribs? What if their target who'd gone missing in Belize had met with a more lethal fate? Could Daniel live with himself if, months from now, it was revealed that what they first thought was a simple white-collar case had a much darker side? That the money laundered through Trendsetters' WiMax software had somehow made it into the hands of a hardened criminal and led to even more crimes?

And because he hadn't been able to complete his mission, even more people were harmed? The answer was simple: He wouldn't be able to live with himself.

This case would haunt him no matter what; the choice before him was one he would give anything not to make. Sacrifice the woman he could very likely see himself falling in love with, or sacrifice the principles that drove every aspect of his career, of his life. Losing either one would send him into his own personal hell. He just had to decide which hell would be worse.

Daniel closed his eyes. His throat felt raw as he tried to swallow past the anguish clogging it.

There was no going back from this. If he went through with his plan, it would obliterate any chance he could possibly have with Samiah. She would hate him forever. And he wouldn't blame her.

But he had no choice. The stakes were too high.

Daniel pulled in a deep breath and opened his eyes. He knew what he had to do.

As gingerly as possible, he slipped his hand underneath Samiah's head and gently shifted her from his chest to a pillow. She stirred and mumbled something unintelligible, but then she turned her head and, moments later, her soft snore started up again. Daniel slowly eased out of the bed and pulled on the sweats he'd left here the last time he'd come over. He padded out of the bedroom and into the kitchen, heading straight for the counter where Samiah had left her purse.

He didn't touch it. For several moments he just stood there staring, and hating himself.

It didn't have to go down like this.

He should come clean to her. Right here, right now. He could reveal the real reason he'd come to Austin, stress the importance of keeping his undercover work under wraps until he could figure out who was behind the money-laundering scheme. He could underscore the potential danger Samiah could face if word ever got out that he wasn't who everyone at Trendsetters believed him to be.

And that danger was exactly why Daniel couldn't say anything. He couldn't risk her unwittingly divulging classified information. Not only would it put this case in peril; it could possibly put Samiah in danger as well. He didn't care how tenuous the link between Mike Epsen and that bicycle accident was; the possibility of Samiah suffering the same fate was enough to solidify Daniel's decision to keep her in the dark. It was better this way.

He closed his eyes again. Sucked in a breath.

He reached for the purse and slowly released the teeth on the zipper one by one, pausing several times to listen for any sounds coming from the bedroom. His heart thumped like a drumbeat within his chest as he angled the purse toward the moonlight streaming in from the large windows. The soft glow glinted off the gold chip that ran along the left edge of the green-and-white access card. He slipped the card out and went over to his jacket. He pulled the scanner from the jacket's inside pocket and inserted Samiah's keycard. A green light blinked methodically as the device accessed the information on the card.

In less than two minutes, it was done. The scanner beeped and the green light went from blinking to solid.

Daniel held his breath, waiting to see if she'd heard the beep. There was no stirring coming from the bedroom. Not a sound.

He shoved the scanner back into his jacket pocket and slid Samiah's access card back into her purse. Then he returned to her bedroom and removed the sweatpants, climbing back under the covers naked and wrapping his arms around Samiah's waist.

But Daniel knew he wasn't falling asleep anytime soon.

Even if she never discovered his betrayal, he knew he would never be able to get past it. With that one move, he'd shattered the trust between them forever.

He closed his eyes.

What good would regret and recriminations do him now? He'd had a choice to make and he'd made it. He would just have to learn to live with it, and hope there was some way that Samiah could eventually forgive him. Some way he could learn to eventually forgive himself.

CHAPTER TWENTY-SIX

Samiah paused on the sidewalk across the street from the Austin History Center and watched as a team of three carried an enormous framed portrait of lavender fields through the building's side entrance. It was reminiscent of the sights she'd encountered on a drive through Fredericksburg in the Texas Hill Country last year, the colors so vibrant she could practically smell the fragrant blooms.

She closed her eyes and inhaled a deep breath. Her nostrils met with the aroma of grilling meat from a food cart fighting with the Drakkar Noir one of her fellow Austinites had apparently bathed in before leaving the house. Instead of standing in a field of lavender, she felt as if she were back at her sixth-grade dance, holding her breath as Terrance Johnson sprayed on more of the cologne he'd snuck from his dad's bathroom cabinet.

She continued up Guadalupe, the brisk wind blowing off Lady Bird Lake and the warm rays from the early-morning sun making for an invigorating contrast. Normally, on a chilly morning like this one, she would drive the five minutes to work, but when she caught sight of the brilliant blue sky outside her bedroom windows, the thought of confining herself to a car was untenable.

The gorgeous day matched her gorgeous mood, and she wanted to soak up as much of it as possible. Which was why, despite the fact that she was already a half hour late for work, she'd decided to take a long detour and visit the Italian bakery on Congress Avenue near the golden-domed state capitol. All was forgiven at the job when you brought pastries.

Samiah turned onto Ninth Street, walking past one of the famed moonlight towers. Listed on the National Register of Historic Places, it was one of only fourteen antique towers that remained in the world, all of which were located in Austin. She stopped at the corner of Ninth and Lavaca Streets, and waved at a chubby-faced toddler strapped in the back seat of a mini-van waiting at the light, laughing when he waved back.

It's when she found herself smiling long after the car with the adorable kid had driven away that Samiah recognized that there was something different about today. Something special. There was a giddiness in the air. A lighthearted exuberance that caused the leaves on the evergreens to appear greener, the brilliant morning sun to seem brighter. Everything she encountered amplified her blissful mood.

She dipped into the Italian bakery and, after waiting in line for ten minutes, emerged with two dozen zeppole, a dozen biscotti, and a loaf of their signature panettone. Armed with enough food to feed the entire R&D Department, Samiah started down Congress back toward the river and Trendsetters' offices.

After six blocks, she turned the corner and stopped short at the sight of all the activity swirling around her building. A crush of bystanders loitered on the sidewalks, their clamorous rumblings accounting for the discordant din she'd heard as she'd approached. She continued toward the building, but her steps faltered when she saw two of Trendsetters' cybersecurity analysts, Bianca Moody and Doug Spade, being led away in handcuffs. They were followed by Owen Caldwell, the HR director, showcasing his own set of cuffs.

"What in the hell?" Samiah nearly dropped the pastries.

She spotted Jamie standing near the receptionist for the law practice on the floor just below theirs. She walked up to the two women.

"Jamie, what's going on?" Samiah asked.

Trendsetters' receptionist, who looked as stunned as Samiah felt, shook her head. "It's crazy. I came down to sign for a couple of packages that had been left at the security desk, and the next thing I know, a bunch of men in blue windbreakers stormed into the building. That was a half hour ago."

"Are they not letting anyone up to the office?"

"They are, but everything feels weird up there right now, so I'm hiding out down here."

Samiah spotted Daniel, but before she could take a step toward him, one of the men wearing a blue jacket with DHS in thick white block letters on the back walked up to him. Her heart stopped beating. For a second, terror, true and gut-wrenching, rushed through her as she waited for the man to make him turn around so they could cuff him. Instead, the man in the windbreaker began conversing with Daniel as if he knew him.

A second later, Quentin Romero joined in.

Samiah took a stunned step back. An uncomfortable chill raced along her skin as she tried to process exactly what was going on.

Why was his roommate here? And why was Quentin wearing one of those dark blue jackets? And why did Daniel look as if he was running the show instead of being questioned by the law enforcement officer? The sense of authority emanating from him seemed both out of place and weirdly appropriate.

Confusion intermingled with the panoply of emotions scattering through her brain. Unsure what to make of any of this, Samiah turned in the opposite direction and entered the lobby. As she approached the elevators, she switched both bakery bags to one hand and flashed her green-and-white Trendsetters' badge with the other, explaining to another set of jacketed DHS personnel where she worked. They allowed her to board the waiting elevator.

Samiah sensed the tension suffusing the office the moment the doors opened on the twenty-second floor. Absent was the laid-back, casual atmosphere and general levity one usually found upon entering Trendsetters. The air crackled with barely contained angst, her coworkers' collective discontent pulsing just below the surface.

She went straight for the kitchen, setting the bakery items she no longer had any interest in indulging in on the long counter next to the coffee station. On the way to her office, she could practically feel the furtive glances following her movements. Her earlier confusion intensified, her body heat rising with every step she took.

By the time she made it to her office, Samiah could feel sweat collecting at the small of her back. She took off her light wool peacoat and hung it on the single brushed-steel peg on the wall behind her desk. She then dropped her purse in the bottom desk drawer, kicked the drawer shut, and set out in pursuit of answers.

Before she made it past the front edge of her desk, Amy

Dodd rushed into her office and closed the door behind her. She slapped the button underneath the light switch that turned the glass walls from clear to opaque and charged toward Samiah.

"Tell me *everything*!" Amy said.

"What are you talking about?"

"You cannot hold out on me! Come on, I want to know what's going on."

"That's *my* question!" Samiah slapped a hand to her chest. "*I* want to know what's going on."

The crease that ran across Amy's forehead became even more pronounced. "Wait a minute," her coworker said. "You mean you weren't a part of it?"

"A part of *what*?" Samiah screeched.

"The sting! Or whatever the heck went down."

She stepped back until her butt met the edge of her desk and then sat. "Start over," Samiah said. "From the beginning. What sting?"

"Apparently there's been some kind of undercover operation going on this whole time. The Fed—like the freaking *Fed*—has been tracking this crazy money-laundering scheme."

"Money laundering?"

"Yes! This is what I've heard so far. Some employees here at Trendsetters were approached by a small group of people from Hughes Hospitality—including some of their *executives*—with an idea to launder money. They were inflating the number of users logging into the Wi-Fi at all of the company's Central American properties. So, if only a thousand people logged on in a week, they manipulated the numbers so that it would look as if twice that many logged on. Then, a couple of months go by, they audit the numbers, find that they overpaid and were refunded." She dusted her hands. "All that dirty money gets washed clean. Genius, right?"

"Goodness," Samiah whispered. It truly was genius.

"They arrested both Doug and Bianca. They were manually inflating the unique logins."

"I saw Owen in handcuffs," Samiah said.

"He's the one who set the whole damn thing up! Mike Epsen was in on it too. He was the mastermind behind all the tech work."

"Mike?"

"Yes! From what I've heard, Mike tried to shut it down, and they sent goons after him. They're the ones who ran into his bike."

Samiah covered her forehead with a shaky palm. This was way more than she could handle before coffee. "It's like something from a movie."

"I just don't understand," Amy said, her eyes wide with confusion.

"People do crazy things for money," Samiah said.

"No, I mean, I don't understand how you don't know about it. Word around the office is that it was *your* access card that was used to breach the system."

Her body went cold. Samiah relinquished her perch on the desk, rising slowly as she mentally fended off the escalating trepidation brought on by Amy's pronouncement.

"What?" she whispered in a voice so thready she barely heard it herself.

Just then, there was an uptick in the muddled chatter that had been humming throughout the office. Samiah reached over to the keypad on her desk and turned the walls back to clear. At least a dozen of the men in the imposing windbreakers charged down the hallway, filing into the large conference room a few doors past her office. Quentin and Daniel brought up the delegation's rear.

Daniel stopped just past her door and looked back at her through the glass wall, his soulful brown eyes teeming with remorse.

And just like that, she knew. He had lied to her.

Her shoulders curled forward as an acute sense of grief struck her dead in the chest. She had no idea when or where it happened, but the guilt she'd observed on his face was unmistakable. He'd taken her access card and used it to breach Trendsetters' security.

He'd *used* her. All this time, he had been using her.

Pain—stark, vivid, and soul-crushing—speared her chest, searing through her like a fiery lance, and the foundation of trust she'd slowly begun to rebuild all but crumbled.

* * *

Samiah tilted her head from side to side, stretching her neck as she read the same paragraph on her monitor for the fourth time without comprehending a damn thing. Her shoulders ached with the need to relax, but the ability to do so continued to elude her.

Her breath caught in her throat as a silhouette appeared on the other side of her office's frosted-glass door. There were three sharp knocks, followed by a soft "Trash collection."

Air whooshed from her lungs as the wave of alarm retreated.

"Not today," Samiah called.

Dammit! She had to get a handle on this. She dove straight

into a fit of edgy panic the moment she heard footsteps clomping down the hallway.

She abhorred this feeling. Absolutely *hated* it!

The memory of the last time she'd felt anything even remotely close to this stole over her. She could still smell the pine-scented cleaner the janitor had just used on the floor outside Principal Parker's office as she sat in that hard plastic chair, waiting for her fifth-grade math teacher, Mrs. Shoals, to arrive. Samiah had been summoned to the principal's office after leaving her own desk and walking over to Damarias Lewis to offer aid. The girl had asked Mrs. Shoals for help with a math problem, but the teacher continued to explain the issue in the exact same way. Samiah had grown tired of their back-and-forth and decided to take matters into her own hands.

She'd learned two things that day: Teachers don't like it when students show them up in class, unwittingly or otherwise. And her old grade school principal had a soft spot for those very same students.

Actually, she'd learned a third thing that day. She discovered that she didn't like being called to the principal's office. And that's exactly how she felt right now.

Justin had given her a heads-up twenty minutes ago. He and Barrington wanted to meet with her to discuss what occurred this morning. The entire office was still stunned that a group of criminals had been working right under their noses. Longtime coworkers or not, there was a consensus that it was a good thing they were now behind bars.

But that was all beside the point as far as Samiah was concerned. What mattered is that she'd allowed her access card to be compromised. She had to answer for that.

Except she *couldn't* answer for that. She had no idea when Daniel had taken her card. She was diligent when it came to securing it, the one who constantly reminded her fellow coworkers that their access card was more valuable than anything else they carried. How was she supposed to explain to her bosses that she'd been so careless with something so important?

The only reasonable explanation was that Daniel had taken it after they'd slept together, either while she showered or as she lay naked and vulnerable in her own bed. She hoped she was wrong, but the nausea in her gut told her she was spot on.

How could you?

She wanted to scream the words in his face. She'd been hurt by men in the past, but Daniel's betrayal surpassed anything she'd ever experienced. And that was before she considered the detriment he'd likely caused to her career.

For a few moments after receiving Justin's summons, Samiah had considered giving it all up. Just pack up her office and quit. Thanks to life lessons courtesy of her dear father, she had enough money in the bank to cover a year's worth of mortgage payments and living expenses. She could walk away from this job and not worry about addressing these questions for which she had no answer.

She thought about all the work she could get done on her app if she didn't have to spend the majority of her waking hours here at Trendsetters, and had to stop herself from grabbing a cardboard box from the storeroom and dumping everything from her desk drawers in it.

But what if potential investors caught wind of what happened today?

Cold dread rushed through her veins. It felt as if she was going to lose the few bites of the granola bar she'd had for lunch.

She was often amazed by just how small this vast tech world could seem at times. It wasn't out of the realm of possibility to think that investors could discover her part in the breach and question her ability to keep customer information secure.

God, the repercussions of Daniel's betrayal reached so much further than she first imagined. The fallout from this could very well sink her dream.

A message popped onto her screen. It was from Justin.

Can you please come to Barrington's office?

The knot that had been slowly tightening in her stomach over the past few hours pulled taut. She could practically feel the deluge of adrenaline flooding her bloodstream, sense it in the uptick of her pulse beat, the sweat that instantly pebbled her hairline, the restive twitch in her muscles.

Samiah flattened her palms on her desk, sucked in a deep breath, and slowly blew it out, reminding herself that no matter what happened in these next few minutes, she still controlled her own destiny. She'd put herself in a position to survive whatever came her way. That realization smothered her apprehension, replacing it with a calmness she wouldn't have thought possible just five minutes ago.

"You're going to be fine," she whispered. Straightening her shoulders, she pushed her chair back, stood, and confidently strolled out of her office.

She could feel the eyes of her coworkers on her as she passed their cubicles, their stares reminiscent of her experience a couple of months ago, after that video with Craig went viral. She'd made it through that episode with barely a scratch. Why should this be any different?

Samiah pressed the touchpad just to the right of Barrington's office door. Once receiving permission through the speaker, she entered the office and took the seat opposite Justin Vail's before it was even offered. If she was to be fired today, she would damn well be comfortable while it happened.

"Well, it's been an interesting day," Barrington started, running a hand through his shaggy blond hair.

"It has," Samiah answered. Cutting to the chase, she said, "I'm not sure I can explain the inexplicable, but if you give me the opportunity to do so, I'll try."

"And what do you consider to be the inexplicable?" he asked.

"How my access card was used to breach the system." She hunched her shoulders. "Frankly, I don't know how it happened. I have my card with me 99.9 percent of the time."

Justin held up a hand. "Daniel already explained to us how he was able to get his hands on your access card."

Samiah's stomach dropped. "Would you mind sharing what he said?"

"He said he lifted it from your purse when you weren't looking, copied it onto a reader, then slipped it back before you even knew anything had happened," Justin said.

She'd suspected as much, but to have it confirmed crushed her spirit. Had he pegged her as an easy mark from the very beginning? Had that been his goal from day one?

He'd arrived at Trendsetters just after that video went viral. Had he calculated that she would be vulnerable because of her breakup with Craig, and, thus, an easy target?

"Daniel also assured us that you had nothing to do with it, that you had no idea he was working undercover."

"No, I did not," Samiah said. She swallowed past her heartache. "No idea at all."

"I'm relieved to hear that," Barrington said. "However, this was still an extremely serious breach of company security. It cannot be ignored."

This was it. Samiah braced herself.

"You will be placed on probation, which comes in the form of your access to any sensitive or proprietary information being revoked for the next six months," Justin said. "That means we will need to pull you off several teams for the time being."

"I understand," Samiah said. She'd put a ridiculous amount of work into the various projects she'd been working on. It was painful to think of the teams moving forward without her.

Samiah waited for the next shoe to drop. Except . . . it didn't.

Wait.

"Is that it?" she asked.

Justin nodded.

Relief whooshed through her. Considering that she firmly believed she would be fired, this was nothing. In fact, she could use the time. She already had way too much on her plate.

Actually, it might work in her favor . . .

"I know I already turned it down, but did the security breach affect your belief in my ability to lead the new Outreach Department?" she asked.

They spoke at once.

"Absolutely not—"

"No—"

"No one is doubting your ability to do your job, or any job, for that matter," Barrington said. "We're not going to sit here and pretend that Trendsetters can afford to lose you, Samiah. Your value far outweighs what this may cost the company in the long run."

Justin ran his palms down his face. "Shit, he had to convince me to revoke your security access at all." He pointed to Barrington. "He doesn't understand the bind this puts us in on the Huston-Tillotson project."

Guilt over what this would cost her team was something she would have to process at a later time. Then again, it wouldn't hurt to remind her team just how much she brought to the table. She'd carried so much of the burden for so very long; some of them weren't going to survive her absence. She gave Keighleigh a week at the most before she came running to her for help.

"I understand that you have to make an example of me, and I'm okay with that," Samiah said. "If this is what it takes to show the rest of the company how important security is, let's do it."

"And this is why it wouldn't have mattered if you *had* been working with the federal government behind our backs," Barrington said. "I'd forgive you just about anything, Samiah. Your attitude and work ethic are far too important to this company."

"We still have some things to work out with investigators, but after this is all taken care of and things are back to normal, I want to revisit our discussion regarding the Outreach Department," Justin said. "You declined the position because you didn't think you could devote time to building the new department while working on your current projects, but now that you won't be working on those projects..." He waved his hand. "We'll talk about all of this later. For now, unfortunately, we have to make an example of you."

Samiah nodded and tried her hardest not to smile. "I understand," she said again.

Could this really be happening? Not only was she *not* going to lose her job, but she was going to gain the time she needed to work on Just Friends and would still be allowed to head the Outreach Department? What she thought would be the most dire moment in her career had turned into an embarrassment of riches.

"Is that it?" she asked.

"That's it," Barrington said. "Thanks for being one of the good ones, Samiah."

This time she did smile.

* * *

The metronomic click of the external hard drive droned on within its slim black casing, the steady cadence thumping in rhythm to his own pulse. Daniel unsheathed a fourth hard drive and connected it to the final computer tower. With a few strokes of the keyboard, it joined the muted percussion of the other electronic equipment. In a matter of minutes, all the computers would be wiped clean.

The machines they'd seized from Trendsetters sat in a secured building at the DHS field office in San Antonio, preparing to be shipped to Virginia, but the computers he'd used in this generic apartment in the Triangle would remain here for use by the next set of undercover agents tasked with locking up the Southeast region's bad guys and saving the day.

He'd spent much of the morning blocking out the racket from the movers as they carried in boxes and stacked them against the walls in the living room. The new tenants, two DHS agents out of Miami-Dade, would be arriving at the end of the week, which meant Daniel still had a few days before he'd have to close up shop and turn the apartment over to them.

He didn't need a few days. His clothes were already packed. Ninety-nine percent of his loose ends tied up. All that was left for him to do was to board a plane and fly back to his bland cubbyhole at FinCEN.

That's not all that's left.

Dread. Heavy, sickening, and profound. It rested in his gut, lodged in his throat; consumed his entire being.

The one final thing he had left to do tormented him, but he knew he couldn't leave Austin without talking to Samiah. The knot in his stomach tightened at the thought of facing her. He refused to take the coward's way out. He would weather her wrath and do his best to explain why he'd taken her trust in him and smashed it with a sledgehammer.

For now, he brooded in silence, watching the faces of his coworkers populate the computer monitor as they prepared for their weekly check-in—the last he'd have in this place he'd called home for the past two months. Despite the ever-present chill in the dark room, Daniel couldn't bring himself to pull on his Phillies hoodie. He didn't want to associate his favorite garment with the revulsion he'd been experiencing from the moment he'd made the call to bring in the DHS and FBI to make the arrests at Trendsetters yesterday.

As his comrades back at FinCEN gathered for their video conference, the accolades began to pour in.

"I didn't think you had it in you, Collins, but you proved me wrong. Good job'."

"Same here."

"I'm still not convinced he had it in him. I think this was just dumb luck," Thaddeus Mitchum said with a good-natured laugh. He pointed at the computer screen. "And don't forget to bring back my barbecue."

Daniel made an effort to smile, but it was half-assed at best. He should be ecstatic. Doubts that this job would come to a successful conclusion had amplified as each week passed. Being able to prove the naysayers wrong was the kind of shit he lived for. Yet he couldn't bring himself to enjoy any of it. Whenever he tried, all he saw was that look of betrayal on Samiah's face yesterday. How could he celebrate anything, knowing that she hated him?

He should have gone to her the moment she'd arrived at Trendsetters, even if it was only to apologize.

But when? *When* could he have gone to her? He hadn't had a chance to eat, to take a piss, to take a damn breath yesterday. And why did he think a simple apology would make any difference if it wasn't followed by a clear explanation of exactly what happened?

Once they were done rounding up all the evidence needed and arresting those involved, they'd spent three hours huddled in the largest conference room at Trendsetters, discussing the details of the operation with Barrington—who, to Daniel's utter relief, had no knowledge of the money-laundering scheme. After answering as many of the CEO's questions as they could, they'd all headed to the local FBI field office for a joint debriefing between DHS, FBI, and the FinCEN personnel involved in the takedown. Where would he have found the time to give Samiah the explanation she deserved?

It was futile to think that she didn't know yet that it was her secured access card that had been used to breach Trendsetters' security system. It was even more useless to hope that she hadn't figured out just how her access card had been obtained, especially after she learned he wasn't who he'd claimed to be these past few months.

Shame burned in his throat.

If he wrote a list of his regrets, it would stretch from here to the Colorado River. Yet the one thing he *should* regret— the one thing that should never have happened at all— was the one thing he wouldn't trade. He'd known from the moment she nearly crashed into him at the coffee station his first day on the job that he should have stayed as far away from her as possible. The attraction had been there from the beginning.

Attraction wasn't the right word. It had always been more than just attraction. The potent, all-consuming pull between them was unlike anything he'd ever experienced before. Pretending he could have ignored it all these weeks was pointless.

It was inevitable that he would end up exactly where he now found himself, trying to figure out how to convince Samiah that everything between them had not been a lie.

"Collins? *Collins!*"

Startled by his boss's uncharacteristic bellow, Daniel snapped to attention. *Shit.* He hadn't even noticed that Dwyer had joined the meeting.

"Sorry, sir," Daniel said. "What was that?"

"How quickly can you be back here for the in-person

debrief? I want you here by tomorrow afternoon, at the latest," he tacked on, not giving Daniel a chance to respond to his initial question.

"Well, I guess that means I'll be there tomorrow," he replied.

Dwyer's curt nod signaled that the matter was settled. Daniel slouched in his chair and listened as the rest of the crew gave a quick rundown of where things stood with their current operations. He knew he was deep in uncharted territory when he couldn't scrounge up an ounce of pleasure over news that Bryce Stewart's job had suffered a setback. There was no room for gloating here. They were all on the same team; they all had the same goal. Putting the bad guys away.

And they all had to make sacrifices in order to get the job done. Daniel just never thought his sacrifice would be so fucking painful.

Once the meeting wrapped up, he logged off the computer for the last time and packed up the four external hard drives, securing them in the laptop case he would carry with him on the plane. He checked his email and saw that a flight had already been booked for him for ten a.m. tomorrow morning.

His eyes fell shut.

Daniel felt raw. It took several tries before he was able to swallow past the knot of thick emotion lodged in his throat. He doubted he'd ever get past the hollowed-out feeling in his chest. The hole there couldn't possibly be filled.

He shut the lamp off on the desk and made his way out of the darkened room. He found Quentin in the kitchen sipping on a bottle of chocolate milk, his butt perched against the counter.

"How'd it go?" Quentin asked. "You the star of FinCEN?"

Daniel shrugged. "I did my job. That shouldn't make me a star."

"Bullshit. This wasn't an easy win. You deserve to celebrate it."

"Yeah, well, I'm not really in the mood for celebrating."

Quentin took a sip from the bottle, then said, "I know you're feeling like shit right now, but you did the right thing."

"Of course I did the right thing," Daniel said. "And we have four people in custody to show for it."

"I'm talking about that *other* thing. The thing you had to do in order to get the job done. She's going to be pissed at you, but if what you had was real, she'll eventually forgive you."

Daniel leaned against the counter, his limbs suddenly lacking the strength to support him.

"Go to her," Quentin said.

His head popped up. "Are you crazy? She would probably run me through with a knife."

"I'm sure she would feel justified in doing so," Quentin said with a nod. "Just take the stab and keep going. Explain as much as you can without jeopardizing the case. Like I said, if it's real, you'll get past this. Remember the story I told you about how my wife and I met? You think it started out all sunshine and roses?"

"I'm guessing that's a no?"

"That's a hell no." Quentin glanced down at his chest. "There are a few cuts under these clothes."

Daniel managed to crack the first hint of a smile he had been able to muster in the last twenty-four hours. "This is probably a bad idea," he said.

"What would be worse? Her slamming the door in your

face—after spitting in your face," Quentin said. "Or you leaving Austin without ever speaking to her? Are you prepared for how shitty that will feel when the numbness wears off in a few days? If you think you hate yourself now, you have no idea what you're in store for. Go to her," he repeated.

He was right. Daniel knew he couldn't leave without making at least one attempt to talk to Samiah. But, if he did, he would have to give up this twisted sense of comfort he'd found in speculating whether she hated him. Wouldn't it be easier to always wonder rather than go to her and have it confirmed?

Fucking coward.

Exhaling a weary breath, he pushed away from the counter. Quentin did the same.

"I'll more than likely be out of here by the time you get back," he said. He set his drink down and held out a hand.

Daniel took it and pulled him in for a one-armed hug. "Thanks for the hospitality."

"Thanks for introducing me to the Wu-Tang Clan."

"It's a tragedy that you're just discovering them, but better late than never."

Quentin tapped him on the back. "Good luck. You've got my number if you're ever in the San Antonio office."

Daniel left him in the same place he usually found him, on the sofa surrounded by documents. He hopped onto the MoPac Expressway to avoid the traffic lights of Lamar Boulevard, but got off at the next exit after crawling for a full twenty minutes in bumper-to-bumper traffic. By the time he made it to Samiah's, the sun had started to set, reflecting streaks of saffron and magenta off her building's sleek glass windows.

He pulled into a nearby spot that had just been vacated, but instead of getting out of the car, he sat behind the wheel for several minutes. An unease he hadn't felt since those nights he'd spent trekking through the archipelagos of Indonesia washed over him.

Why was he even debating this? The chances that she would even allow the concierge to let him up were practically nil. He turned off the ignition, got out of the car, and headed for the lobby.

Apprehension and dread mingled in his gut as he waited for her to answer the concierge's call.

"Hello?"

Daniel's chest clenched at the sound of her voice coming through the speaker.

"Ms. Brooks, Daniel Collins is here to see you," the concierge announced.

A significant pause stretched over the line. Disbelief charged through him when he next heard, "You can let him up."

The concierge nodded toward the elevator bank. The tension flooding his veins intensified as the car climbed upward. Daniel was certain he'd find her waiting for him when he got off on her floor, but the hallway was empty. He walked up to her door and rapped on it twice. It opened.

He swallowed hard, regret residing in his throat like a living thing. He waited for her to invite him in, but after a few exceedingly uncomfortable moments, realized she wouldn't.

"I just want a minute to explain myself," he opened.

Samiah stood in the middle of the doorway. One brow arched as she stared at him, waiting.

Daniel coughed, suddenly unsure where to begin.

"I'm not sure how much you know," he said.

"I know you used my credentials to access Trendsetters' client database, and that you've been lying to me about who you really are. That's really all I need to know," she said.

He nodded. She was right. The ancillary details were worthless. What mattered is that he'd lied to her.

"I didn't set out to steal your access card from the very beginning," he said. "The lies...that's...that's part of my job. I was lying to everybody."

A muscle jumped in her cheek.

"Not that you're like everybody else," he quickly added.

Shit. Could he fuck this up any more than he already had?

"Samiah, please," Daniel pleaded. "Please believe me when I tell you that I never meant to hurt you."

He started to reach for her, but pulled back when she flinched. He shoved his hands in his pockets, but continued to plead.

"Copying your keycard was a last resort. Even after you were given access to exactly what I needed, I refused to use it. It was only after I got word that the money-laundering ring was preparing to go underground that I realized I had to do something. I hate that it had to come at the expense of your trust."

Silence yawned between them, filling the space with an unbearable discomfort as he waited for her to speak. When she did, her voice held not a single drop of emotion.

"I get it," she said. "You were just doing your job."

"I'm sorry," Daniel said again.

"I'm sure you are," she said. "I'd like you to leave now."

Then she shut the door.

CHAPTER TWENTY-SEVEN

Samiah switched the balloon bouquet to her other hand so that she could hit the elevator button to take her up to postpartum recovery at St. David's Women's Center. When the doors opened, she stopped in at the nurses' station and showed them the name tag that had been printed out for her at the hospital's security desk, then continued down the sterile hallway, gently knocking on the door when she came to room 228.

"Come in," came Bradley's voice in a loud whisper.

Samiah walked into the room and instant tears sprang to her eyes. She gasped at the sight of the tiny baby nestled in her brother-in-law's arms. He put a finger to his lips and gestured his head toward Denise, who was asleep in the bed.

Ouch. Her big sister was in dire need of a hairbrush and edge cream. Then again, after spending the past nine hours pushing out an eight-pound baby, Denise no doubt cared little about her edges.

Samiah set the balloons on a nearby credenza and made a beeline for her new niece.

"Oh, my God," she whispered, scooping the delicate bundle from her brother-in-law's arms. "Could she be any more precious?"

Little Aislinn, who was named after Bradley's late mother, had her father's green eyes and pert nose, but everything else screamed Brooks.

If there was anything that could lift her spirits after the abominable mood she'd been in, Samiah had found it in this precious new life that would fill their family with joy for years to come. As she looked upon her niece's beautiful face, Samiah immediately understood why her sister had endured so much. She'd never said it aloud, but she'd thought Denise and Bradley were crazy for spending the thousands of dollars they'd shelled out for fertility treatments. She'd watched her sister take countless shots and suffer through over a dozen painful procedures to become pregnant, and wondered why.

She got it now. This baby, this perfect little human she now held, was worth it all.

"She's so gorgeous," Samiah said to her brother-in-law, who looked almost as ragged as her sister. His red hair stuck up in various spots, and it looked as if he hadn't slept in at least twenty-four hours.

The baby stirred, and then, a second later, started bellowing.

"Oh, shit. What's wrong?" Samiah asked.

"That's the call of the hungry."

She turned to find Denise pushing herself up on her elbows, her fatigue still evident from the deep shadows under her eyes. She held her arms out.

"Bring my love to me," she said.

Samiah carried the baby to her sister's waiting arms and felt her tears returning as she watched her cradle the nursing baby against her breast. The love on Denise's face was unlike anything Samiah had ever seen.

Bradley came up behind Samiah, clamping a hand on her

shoulder. "I'm going to go downstairs and get something to eat," he said. "Either of you want anything?" After they both declined, he gave out kisses, first to Samiah, then Denise, then to the top of his newborn's head.

Once alone, Samiah turned her attention back to her sister and niece.

"She really is the most gorgeous baby I've ever seen in all my life," Samiah said.

"I wholeheartedly agree." Denise smiled down at the baby.

Perching on the edge of the bed, Samiah patted her knee. "How are you feeling?"

"Sore. But it's that good kind of sore. The kind of sore you don't mind." She looked up at her. "How about you?"

"Sore sorta fits," Samiah said with a laugh. "But not the good kind."

"I'm sorry, honey," Denise said.

Samiah waved off her concern. "I'll be fine." She started to rise, but her sister grabbed her wrist.

"No, no, no," Denise said. "You still owe me the whole story about what happened. And I don't want to hear any of that 'I can't talk about it' crap."

"I thought you learned everything you needed to know from Twitter?"

Her sister gave her the stink eye. "You know Twitter doesn't tell the whole story."

It had been a week since federal agents stormed the offices of Trendsetters. Samiah had gone upstairs by the time the local reporters from several news stations arrived, but there had been ample activity for them to capture and upload to their Twitter feeds.

She'd managed to fend off Denise's incessant questions by

telling her that employees had been asked not to discuss it, but Samiah knew that excuse would eventually crumble under the pressure of her nosy sister's badgering.

"Fine." She rolled her eyes. "What do you want to know?"

"Everything. I want to know all the dirt."

"No, you don't."

Dammit, she'd come here to escape thoughts of what happened last week.

"Everything," Denise reiterated. "And I'll know if you're leaving anything out."

Samiah dropped her head back and released an exaggerated sigh. Yet once she began her narrative, she found herself sharing everything, including the romance she'd started with Daniel.

"Are you shitting me?"

"Hey, watch that language in front of my niece."

Denise covered the baby's ear. "I can't believe you were dating a hot federal agent and you didn't tell me!" she hissed. "How could you keep that from me?"

"I didn't tell anyone," Samiah said with a shrug. "Well, except for Taylor and London, but only because I felt guilty about reneging on the boyfriend project thing we have going on."

Denise flapped her fingers toward the credenza that held the flowers and balloon bouquets. "Grab my phone."

Samiah retrieved the phone and settled back on the side of the bed. Still cradling the baby, Denise one-handedly scrolled. After a minute she turned the screen to face Samiah.

"Which one is he?"

Samiah stared at the cadre of men and women gathered together, all with determined looks on their faces. She winced at the stab of pain that pierced her chest at the sight of Daniel.

"The one not wearing a blue jacket," she said.

"I was hoping you would say that. He is *sooo* damn fine. What is he? Black and what?"

"Korean," Samiah said.

"I seriously cannot believe you didn't tell me about him, especially after how worried I've been about you after that mess with that Craig character."

"I'm sorry," she said. "It's probably because of what happened with Craig that kept me quiet when it came to Daniel." She shrugged. "Doesn't matter anymore. He's no longer in Austin. I guess he's off saving the world."

She was about to add "like he did when he was a Marine," but she had no idea if Daniel had even been in the military or if it was part of the persona that had been created for him. Was the adorable story about how his parents met true, or had he made that up? She found herself questioning every single thing he'd ever told her. Not knowing if it had all been a lie was the most difficult part in all of this.

And yet she no longer blamed him.

Did his betrayal still hurt? Of course it did.

Was she still angry? Hell yes, she was still angry.

But this past week had given her time to work through all that had happened, and after considering things from his perspective, she found she could no longer fault him for simply doing his job. She argued with herself that he never should have allowed their relationship to flourish, but he *had* tried to put the brakes on it.

She remembered how he'd pulled away after that very first kiss. But then he'd come back to her, almost apologetically, as if it pained him to do so, as if he knew they shouldn't be together, but he couldn't help himself. Hadn't she felt the same way? Hadn't she tried to fight her feelings for him because she didn't want anything—not even a relationship—to get in the way of her finally achieving her goals when it came to her app? And hadn't she failed miserably?

How could she fault Daniel for not being able to pull away when she hadn't been able to do so either?

No, she no longer blamed him for the sore heart she'd been tending to this week. Eventually, once she had a bit more distance from the raw pain that thoughts of his betrayal continued to heap upon her, she might find a way to even forgive him.

And, just maybe, once the hurt subsided and she could fix herself a cup of coffee at the office without her soul wincing, maybe then she would be able to look back on these last two months and actually smile.

She wasn't there yet.

For now, she would continue her steadfast effort to put Daniel and everything about him out of her head. She was content to find her joy in this new, precious baby girl that had entered their lives.

* * *

Daniel sensed the moment she spotted him. Her steps halted midstride, and her shoulders stiffened.

He had been standing in her condo building's lobby for over two hours. The afternoon security guard, whom he'd never met before, recognized him from the news coverage of the Trendsetters bust. He'd spent over an hour asking Daniel about everything under the sun when it came to his under-cover work. Thanks to easily uploadable cell phone pictures and searchable hashtags, it would be a while before he could go out in the field again. The takedown had happened so quickly that he forgot to assume the guise of the clueless coworker. Now his face was everywhere.

His relief had been immediate when the evening security guard took over. This one, who had been on duty several times when he'd previously visited, kept his eyes on his paperback novel and allowed Daniel to wait in peace for Samiah to get home.

Now, he wondered if he should have come here at all. Now that she stood only a few yards away, it felt as if he was forcing this meeting. She didn't owe him anything, not even her time.

But he had to see her. He needed at least one more chance to explain himself.

The past week had been the hardest of his life. He no longer questioned whether she hated him. How could she *not* hate him after the way he'd betrayed her trust? But maybe if he knew the extent to which she hated him, he could gauge whether he had any chance whatsoever of earning her forgiveness. Not that he deserved it.

He'd spent the past week toiling over what he would have done differently if given the chance. The hard truth was that there was little he would change. Except for one crucial thing.

If wishes were being granted, he wished he had never left her bed the night he stole her access card. If he could rewrite the past, he would have come clean to her as he held her in his arms. He would have told her the real reason he'd taken the job at Trendsetters and would have tried his hardest to impart just how important it was to access that database.

And he would have *asked* her permission to use her credentials to infiltrate the security system.

There was a possibility she would have turned him down. Maybe she would have even gone to the powers that be at Trendsetters and clued them in to what he was doing, but it would have been better than him going behind her back. With that one decision, he'd shattered her trust in him. He wouldn't get it back. He didn't have a right to it.

Still, he hoped for the chance to tell her how sorry he was. If that's all she granted him, that would be enough.

Daniel stood with his hands in his pockets, waiting for her to make her next move. She'd entered the building from the side door near the garage, and had been on her way to the alcove that held the mailboxes when she'd spotted him. Her steps had immediately halted. Puzzlement shrouded her expression, as if he was the last person she'd ever expect to find here.

And why should she expect to see him? He hadn't contacted her since she'd asked him to leave last week. He'd wanted to—had erased no less than a hundred text messages before he could send them. It hadn't felt right to contact her via text. Even a phone call seemed too impersonal. He had no idea what state she was in, and the last thing he wanted to do was cause more pain.

Instead, he'd waited until he could get a day off and booked a flight to Austin. He was scheduled to fly out on a six a.m. flight back to Virginia in the morning. Even if the only thing this trip accomplished was giving him these few moments with her, it would have been worth it. Just seeing her face again, breathing the same air she breathed, made him whole.

Daniel walked to where she still stood, just to the right of a round glass table that held a large vase filled with fresh flowers.

"Uh, hi," he said.

Silence followed his ungraceful greeting. It was awkward and tense and so incredibly uncomfortable it made his skin itch, but his comfort wasn't important right now.

Finally, she responded. "What are you doing here? I thought you'd gone back to DC."

"Virginia," he said. "Vienna, just outside of DC. That's where I've been since…well, since the day after I last saw you. The debrief after months-long operations takes some time."

"Are you back in Austin?"

"Just for today," he answered. "Just for right now. I have to fly back tomorrow."

"Tying up loose ends, I assume? Like the apartment you share with your 'friend's brother'?"

Damn, even her air quotes seemed angry. Daniel swallowed hard. There had been so many lies.

"I moved out of the apartment last week. And my roommate, well, I guess you figured out that Quentin isn't exactly what I presented him to be."

"Is he your partner at whatever place you work up there in Virginia?"

He shook his head. "Quentin is with DHS, Department of Homeland Security. I'm an agent at FinCEN."

"Fin what?"

He looked over both shoulders and stuffed his hands

farther into his pockets. "The Financial Crimes Enforcement Network," he said in a slightly lower voice. "It's a division of the Treasury Department."

She nodded again, but didn't speak. Tension-filled seconds continued to tick away as they maintained this awkward tableau. What should he do? Should he move toward her? Should he offer to relieve her of the shopping bag she held? Should he accept that this is how things would end and say goodbye?

No, he couldn't do that. He couldn't leave without clarifying any misconceptions she might have about the operation he'd conducted here. At the very least, he had to make sure she understood that he hadn't set out to use her.

"Samiah, can we...can we go up to your place?" He raised his hands. "I just want twenty minutes to explain to you what happened."

"I don't need you to explain anything. I already know what happened," she said. She clasped both hands around the shopping bag's handle and sent it on a gentle sway. The crinkle of the plastic hitting her thighs was the only sound in the lobby.

"Not all of it. It wasn't all a lie," he whispered past the emotion clogging his throat. "I need you to know that, Samiah. Please," he pleaded. "Give me twenty minutes."

She pressed her lips together, her expression evolving from pensive to conflicted to, thankfully, one of acquiescence.

"No," she answered.

Daniel's head jerked back. "No?"

"No," she repeated. Then she turned on her heel and left him standing in the middle of the lobby.

CHAPTER TWENTY-EIGHT

Samiah gathered the collection of blue Post-its outlining the procedure for data integration for the Android version of her app—one of the last steps before beta testing—and placed them in order on her kitchen island. She'd glimpsed only the tiniest pinprick of light at the end of the tunnel, but when she considered how long she'd been on this journey, it felt as if achieving her dream of building Just Friends was finally within her reach.

Her decision to use one of the many vacation days she'd accumulated was the best thing she could have done. Apart from a quick visit to Denise's early this morning to welcome Baby Aislinn home, Samiah had sequestered herself in her condo and disconnected herself from all social media.

She'd made a concerted effort to expunge thoughts of everything but her app from her mind. It had worked for the most part.

If only her brain would refrain from its constant, annoying attempts to continue the conversation in the lobby downstairs last night, that would be great. But her brain was having none of that. It insisted on asking questions she didn't have the mental bandwidth to properly examine right now.

What if she'd allowed Daniel to continue with his explanation last night? Would he have revealed that he'd been under duress and had no choice but to lie to her? Would he have apologized?

Does it even matter?

"You know it does," Samiah acknowledged.

After giving herself a few hours to wrestle with her thoughts, she'd finally reached a place where she could accept that things were possibly not as they seemed. Until she granted Daniel the opportunity to explain his actions, she would never get answers to the questions that plagued her. Maybe she would give him that chance the next time she saw him.

If she ever saw him again.

A sharp ache pierced her chest at the possibility that his shocked, wounded expression just before she left him in the lobby might be the last image she saw of him. He couldn't disappear forever, could he? In this day and age of zero privacy, she would eventually be able to track him down. But not until she was ready.

Just as Samiah returned to the sticky notes lined along her kitchen island, her phone chimed with a text. She'd set it to Do Not Disturb, which meant only texts from the few people saved to her favorites list could get through.

It was from Taylor.

> Emergency! Need you at botanical gardens at Zilker Park.

> What's wrong? Are you hurt? Samiah texted back.
> Just get here. Please. came Taylor's reply.

"What in the world..."

What kind of emergency could she have gotten herself into at the botanical gardens of all places?

Samiah's stomach pitched as she recalled a conversation she'd had with Taylor a couple of weeks ago. She'd suggested that the serenity of the rose garden would be the perfect spot for Taylor to hold a tai chi class. Had she gone there and hurt herself doing tai chi?

"Shit," Samiah said.

She changed out of her shorts and into a pair of jeans, but didn't bother to change out of her ratty Rice University T-shirt. If Taylor was spread out on the ground with a sprained back, she wouldn't care about Samiah's clothes.

She grabbed her keys and locked the door behind her, pulling up London's number as she made her way to the elevator. She pressed her name, but ended the call before it could ring. Taylor would have tried contacting London first, especially if she was hurt. London must be in surgery.

Samiah rushed to the parking garage and got into her car, thankful she was only a few minutes from the park. It was just after three p.m., so traffic on Barton Springs Road should still be relatively light. She considered dialing 911 but thought better of it. She wasn't sure what type of emergency situation she was facing.

She turned into the entrance and wound her way up the drive, paying the two-dollar entrance fee and ducking into the first parking space. There were only three other cars parked. That's probably why Taylor had contacted her; there was no one around to hear her yelling for help.

"Shit, shit, shit," Samiah mumbled as she walked past the welcome center.

I'm here, she texted. Where are you?

Japanese Gardens. Look for the Post-its.

Samiah stopped short.

Post-its?

She stared at the message for a heartbeat before swiping her finger across the touchscreen and calling Taylor's number.

She answered on the first ring.

"Go to the first post at the start of the trail, just behind the welcome center. Follow the Post-its," Taylor said. Then she hung up.

What in the hell was going on? If Taylor had pulled her away from her app for some kind of game, she just might have to fight her in the middle of this damn park.

Okay, so that was a lie. Taylor was in much better shape than her. Samiah knew her friend would kick her ass if they went head to head. Still, she would cuss her out over this.

She walked up to the first post. It contained a small plaque with an arrow pointing to the Isamu Taniguchi Japanese Garden. There was a yellow Post-it Note just below the plaque.

I tried to explain.

Samiah immediately recognized that handwriting, and her heart began to thump harder within her chest. She walked another few yards until she came to the next Post-it stuck to the stone gate at the entrance of the Japanese gardens.

I never meant to lie.

She continued walking, snatching another sticky note from the smooth trunk of a slender tree that stood just to the left of the trail and then from another tree on her right.

If I could do it all again.
I would do things differently.

She reached the entryway of the Ten Wa Jin Teahouse. The stone-and-bamboo structure stood as the centerpiece of the serene gardens, the view of the Austin skyline from its rear window one of the best in the city. London and Taylor stood side by side just inside the tiny building.

London handed her one note:

I'm sorry.

Taylor handed her another:

Please forgive me.

"You?" Samiah said, after taking the Post-it from her. She turned to London. "And you?"

"Before you start, let me explain my role in this little exercise that could get us all arrested for vandalism," London said.

Taylor rolled her eyes. "I told you a few sticky notes do not count as vandalism—"

"Zip it," London said, making a cutting motion across her neck. She returned her attention to Samiah. "You should know me well enough by now to know that I was ready to kick Mr. Cute Dimples over there to the curb on your behalf."

Samiah looked to where London pointed. That's when she noticed Daniel standing in the far corner of the teahouse. Her pulse quickened at the sight of him.

"But then I listened to what he had to say," London continued. "And, well, I'm out here in the wilderness putting damn sticky notes on trees and shit. That should tell you something."

Taylor gestured between herself and London. "Samesies." She lifted her palms in the air. "I understand why you banished him to the doghouse, and if that's where you want him to stay, just say the word. But..."

"But what?" Samiah asked, folding her arms over her chest.

"But maybe you should listen to his side of things. Really listen," London said. "Never has the saying 'stuck between a rock and a hard place' described a situation so well. He didn't have a choice."

"He *did* have a choice," Samiah said. "He could have told me the truth."

"Yes, I could have," Daniel said. He took a step forward. "I *should* have." He took another. And another. He walked toward them, his hands in his pockets. He stopped a few feet away. "Can I please have those twenty minutes, Samiah? That's all I'm asking for."

"Give him the twenty minutes," London said.

"Yes, give him the twenty minutes. We'll be right over there." Taylor nudged her chin toward a bench a few steps away.

"No, we won't. We'll go look at the roses or the koi pond or something. But we *will* be *close*," London stressed.

"Thanks, ladies," Daniel said. "I appreciate your help."

London arched a brow. "You better not make me regret

this, Dimples." She pointed two fingers at her eyes and then at Daniel's, as if to say *I'm watching you*. "Remember what I told you." Then she and Taylor left, taking the trail Samiah had just descended.

Once they were alone, Samiah turned to face him and gave him three slow claps.

"I'm not sure what you said to get those two to agree to help you, but you deserve applause."

"Desperate measures," he said.

She nodded, and then walked over to the rear of the teahouse and sat on its stone ledge. She crossed her legs and folded her hands on her knee.

"You asked for twenty minutes," she said. "So start explaining."

* * *

Daniel wiped his sweating palms on the sides of his jeans, the lump in his throat increasing by several degrees. He walked over to where Samiah sat and gestured to the empty space next to her.

"Can I?"

She scooted over a few inches. More inches than necessary.

He settled in next to her and leaned forward, propping his elbows on his thighs and clamping his hands together. "By now you know that I wasn't your regular Trendsetters hire," he started.

"Understatement, but go on," she said. She held a hand up. "No, actually, instead of going through this long, drawn-out explanation, why don't I just ask you some questions about what I don't understand? I don't want this to take up too much of your time. I'm sure you have other things you need to take care of before you leave."

"We can take as much time as necessary, Samiah. I was supposed to fly back this morning, but I canceled my flight."

"Why?"

"Why?" he repeated. "Because I couldn't go back without at least trying to explain things to you. This is the reason I'm here."

Her forehead furrowed. "Wait a minute. You mean you flew all the way from DC just for this? Just to talk to me?"

"I couldn't do it over the phone," Daniel said. He took another deep breath. "We don't have to go through it all step-by-step if you're not up for it. You've probably learned the basics over this past week, that I'm a government agent who came to Austin as part of a joint mission to break up a money-laundering ring."

"That's pretty much all I need to know," she said.

"No." He shook his head. "What you need to know— what *I* need you to know—is that it wasn't all a lie. It wasn't some calculated plan that I formulated from the very beginning." He gestured between them. "This—me and you, our relationship—it was never supposed to happen."

She crossed her arms over her chest again.

"So why did it? Why didn't you pull away? You could have politely put the brakes on this thing between us when you realized it was getting out of hand."

"How?" he asked. "How was I supposed to do that, Samiah?" Daniel stood and began to pace the length of the small teahouse. "Do you have any idea how hard I tried to fight what I felt for you? I *knew* better. Getting involved with someone while working undercover, that's how you end a career." He stopped in front of her, his chest aching with the need for her to understand. "But it didn't matter. I fell so fucking hard for you that *none* of it mattered. I couldn't stay away."

"So you lied to me instead." The tinge of hurt in her voice crushed him.

Daniel closed his eyes as shame seeped into his bones.

"Yes," he said. He looked to her again, struggling to find a way to convey the breadth of his regret. "It was wrong to lie to you, and I'm sorry. I should have done things differently. I could have asked my supervisor to pull me from the case. But that meant I would have had to give you up, and I couldn't make myself do that.

"I know how selfish that sounds. It *was* selfish. Fuck, my bringing you here is selfish. Enlisting your friends to help? Making you think something had happened to Taylor?" Daniel dropped his head back and blew out a deep breath. "Look, you don't owe me anything. Not your understanding or forgiveness. Nothing. But I had to make sure you understood that what I felt for you wasn't a lie. It was real. It remains real."

Time stood still as he waited for her response, the air redolent with significance, the weight of the moment like a living thing.

Samiah stood and clasped her hands in front of her. After several more excruciating minutes, she said, "This past week has given me time to work things out in my head. And I've come to understand why you did what you did."

His brow crinkled. "What do you mean?"

"I mean exactly what I just said. I understand why you were compelled to steal my access card. You had several choices you could have made. For one, you could have trusted me enough to tell me what you were really up to."

He started to speak, but she stopped him, holding up her hand.

"But I also understand that you had another, much harder choice to make: You could use my card to access that database or allow a group of shitty criminals to get away with committing their shitty crimes. Honestly, when I think about it, it's actually *not* a hard call to make. You did what had to be done."

"But not at your expense," he said. "You could have lost your job." Daniel's heart dropped. "Wait, *did* you lose your job? Did they fire you over this?"

"No." She shook her head. "Barrington understood as well. He revoked my access to the secured databases, but in the most ironic twist in all of this, that turned out to be a godsend. I've gotten more work done on my app this week than I ever would have if I was still being pulled in eight hundred directions at work. I even took the day off to finish up the data integration testing." She shoved her hands in her back pockets and hunched her shoulders in a shrug that seemed much too casual for such a momentous conversation. "It's taken me a few days to arrive here, but after looking at the situation from your perspective, I've come to the conclusion that you truly had no other choice. You did what you had to do. I'm not going to hold that against you."

"Samiah..." There was no way it would be this easy. She could not be this amazing? There had to be a catch.

"You know," she continued, the corner of her mouth tilting up in a brief smile. "Even if it *had* cost me my job, I think I would have eventually gotten over it. I don't mind being collateral damage if it means some really bad people get caught."

"But it wasn't my place to put you in the position of sacrificing a job that means so much to you."

She shook her head again. "My job at Trendsetters doesn't make me. I can always find a new one." She shrugged again. "Or, I can work full-time on Just Friends. I've put myself in a position where I'm not dependent on any single job."

She crossed her arms over her chest and tilted her head to the side.

"You have cleared up the one question that bothered me the most this week, so thanks for that."

"What question?"

"I was unsure if you'd started out with the plan to steal my access card from the very beginning," she said.

"No." Daniel shook his head so emphatically he nearly hurt his neck. "Please believe me when I say I didn't set out to use you or to hurt you."

Her lips eased into a relaxed smile. "Then that's all that matters."

He was too afraid to hope, but he had to ask. "Samiah, what are you saying?"

"I'm saying that if you had given me just a little more time, I would have eventually called to tell you everything I just said. And you could have saved whatever ridiculous amount of money you spent on airfare."

Relief crashed into him. God, he didn't deserve this. He didn't deserve her at all.

"It was worth every penny just to see you," Daniel said.

She walked up to him and tugged on his shirt's hem, pulling him closer. "You keep that up and you're going to find yourself in an ill-advised relationship again, Daniel Collins." She pulled back, her brow furrowing. "That *is* your real name, isn't it?"

"Yes, that's my real name," he said. He leaned forward and rested his forehead on hers. "And there is nothing stopping us from being in a relationship anymore. We're free and clear."

"Are we?" She wrapped her arms around his neck.

"Yes." He nodded. "Is it too soon to admit that I am completely in love with you, Samiah Brooks?"

"Hmm, I'm not sure," she said. "I'll have to wait until London and Taylor get back and ask them what the boyfriend project handbook says about that."

He arched a brow. "The boyfriend project?"

"I'll explain later. For now, just kiss me."

EPILOGUE

"Are you sure this recipe calls for a fourth cup of chili flakes? That seems like a lot."

"I'm sure. *Buldak* literally means 'fire chicken,'" Daniel said. He gestured to the small jar of deep red paste. "And when it comes to heat level, the chili flakes have nothing on the gochujang over there."

"This dish is going to kill me," Samiah said, experiencing true fear as the delicious-smelling sauce gurgled in the saucepan.

"I thought you said you liked it spicy. Don't wimp out on me now." He leaned over and placed the sweetest kiss on her lips. "You'll love it, I promise."

She would probably end up in the ER, but she'd deal with that disaster if it came to pass. Whatever the outcome of their meal, it would be worth it just for the opportunity to watch Daniel Collins's sexy ass go to work in the kitchen. Having a man who cooked was one thing, having a man who looked like *that* when he cooked? That was #lifegoals. She'd reached an entirely new level of living her best life.

"What time is your flight tomorrow?" Samiah asked, unable to suppress the poutiness in her tone.

"Six."

"*In the morning?* You're not expecting a ride to the airport, are you?"

His head flew back with his crack of laughter. "If I was planning to ask you, I guess I have my answer."

She moved to stand behind him, wrapping her arms around his waist and resting her cheek on his leanly muscled back. "I'm one hundred percent down with being the supportive girlfriend, but I don't do early mornings."

"I'll catch a cab," he said over his shoulder. "My meeting starts promptly at ten, so it was either leave tonight or take the first flight out in the morning." He turned in her arms, settling his clasped hands at the base of her spine. "I don't mind waking up before the crack of dawn if it means I get to spend the night with you."

The naughtiest tingles swept through her, causing her body to rival the heat level of the killer chicken they were about to eat.

She hated that he would be gone for an entire two weeks, but when he came back to Austin at the end of the month, it would be permanent. Well, as permanent as things were in his line of work.

Over these past two weeks, she'd learned that his job took him to all parts of the country, and even sometimes out of the country. He'd been back to the DC area twice already, and would be flying to some country in the Baltics next month. He couldn't even disclose which country. It would take her a minute to get used to the lack of transparency, but she would do what she had to do. If Daniel was willing to pack up his life and move to the San Antonio/Austin field office in order to be with her, she could learn how to deal with his demanding job schedule.

He kissed the tip of her nose. "Will you miss me?"

"No," she said. He pinched her ass. "Fine." She laughed. "Yes, yes, I will miss you terribly. Especially your cooking."

"Maybe by the time I return I'll be able to invite you to *my* place to cook," he said. He'd spent the past couple of weeks in a hotel just south of downtown, which meant any cooking was done at her place.

Samiah had been upfront when it came to her feelings about their living arrangements. They didn't know each other well enough to move in together just yet. It was as simple as that. She still wasn't sure if everything she *thought* she knew about him was fact or just part of the persona that had been created for his undercover job at Trendsetters. They were still feeling their way around the fallout of everything that happened last month.

Even so, when he texted her yesterday to let her know he'd found an apartment not too far from the hotel where he was now staying, she'd told him to sign a six-month lease instead of a full year. She suspected he wouldn't make it through half of that. She wanted him here with her.

His arms still wrapped around her waist, Daniel nudged his chin toward where she'd placed her tablet on the kitchen counter. "Is it done?" he asked.

Samiah could barely contain the smile that broke out over her face.

"It's done," she said. She'd taken three additional vacation days and used them to put the finishing touches on her app and the application for the Future in Innovation Tech Conference.

His eyes narrowed. "Is it ready to send, or did you find even more things you want to tweak?"

"No more tweaking! I promise. Everything is complete and ready to upload. I just have to press the submit butt—" Her phone trilled. She looked to where she'd set it on the kitchen island. The selfie Taylor had saved under her name stared back at her.

"It's Taylor," Samiah said. "I'll call her back later." The phone stopped ringing, but then immediately started again.

"Just answer it," Daniel said.

"Well, I guess this *is* technically later." She reluctantly extricated herself from his hold and answered the phone. "Hello—Taylor, slow down!"

Samiah listened as Taylor—in the most Taylor way— started ranting about ruining her career before it could even get started.

"Oh, my God, would you please slow down," Samiah said. She paused, then yelled, "Wait, you *what?*"

"I cursed out a bunch of kids!" Taylor screeched. "In front of their parents! I was fired! My life is over! How am I supposed to go home for Thanksgiving at the end of the month and explain to my family yet again that I am the biggest fuckup on the planet?"

Samiah put a hand to her forehead. "Okay, just calm down. It can't be that bad."

"It kinda is," Taylor said. Something about the switch in her tone of voice caused a prickling sensation to race along Samiah's spine.

"What do you mean?" she asked.

"Um, do you think you can come down to the jail on Eighth Street and bail me out?"

"*What!*"

"So, totally *not* my fault, but after I cursed out the kids, I may have grabbed the chair one of the mothers was sitting in and ran over it with my car. Not may have, I did. I did run the chair over with my car."

"With her in it?"

"No!" Taylor said.

Samiah heard a muffled voice in the background, followed by Taylor's "okay, okay, I'm almost done." She came back on the line. "I have to get off the phone and London is at the hospital, so I kinda need you to do this. Can you?"

"I'm on my way," Samiah said. "Don't damage anyone else's property before I get there!"

"Can't make any promises," Taylor said before ending the call.

She hung up the phone and looked over at Daniel. "Can I get that killer chicken to go?"

"What's going on?"

She shook her head. "It would take too long for me to explain it. I'll give you the full story after I get back from the county jail."

His eyebrows shot up.

"Don't ask," Samiah said. "Seriously, I'm learning that when it comes to Taylor Powell, it's better not to ask." She held up a finger. "However, there is one thing I promised I would do, and I refuse to put it off a minute longer." She picked up her iPad and brought it over to him. Then she slid two wineglasses from the hanging rack, poured elderberry and grape kombucha in both, and handed one to Daniel. "I am not leaving before I do this."

She pressed the submit button on the iPad, sending off her submission.

Clinking her glass against his, she proclaimed, "Here's to the future winner of the standout app of the Future in Innovation Tech Conference Awards."

"Here's to you," Daniel said. Then he took the glass from her hand. "Now let's go bail your friend out of jail."

ACKNOWLEDGMENTS

The list of people I want to thank is so vast it could fill a second novel.

As always, thanks to my family for constantly having my back. Because of your unfailing support, I am able to live out my dreams.

To my agent, Evan Marshall, for championing my work and being there whenever I need advice.

To my editor, Leah Hultenschmidt, and the dedicated team at Forever. Thank you for believing in this book.

To my critique group. I am a better writer because of you four fabulous women. Thanks for eighteen years of encouragement, hard work, and most of all, friendship.

To my Monday night Wordies group. Thank you for inviting me into the fold.

To my Rochonettes! Thank you for being the best fans a writer could ask for!

Thank you to Jasmine Gabrielle and Kia Mona for giving me advice on how the young kids speak these days.

Thank you to my fellow black romance writers who continue to produce amazing books. Your words matter. And to the readers, bloggers, and allies who offer support. Thank you for being there for us.

Lastly, thanks and praise to the "still small voice" that reminds me that there is a higher power waiting to guide me through every struggle and obstacle I face.

> *Then you will call on me and come and pray to me, and I will listen to you.*
> —Jeremiah 29:12